'As always, Rankin proves himself the master of his own milieu. He brings the dark underside of Edinburgh deliciously to life . . . Rankin's skill lies mainly in the confident way he weaves the disparate threads into a cohesive whole' *Daily Mail*

'His novels flow as smoothly as the flooded Forth, and come peppered with three-dimensional characters who actually react to and are changed by events around them . . . This is Rankin at his raw-edged, page-turning best . . . With Rankin, you can practically smell the fag-smoke and whisky fumes'
Time Out

'A first-rate thriller' *Yorkshire Evening Post*

'The internal police politics and corruption in high places are both portrayed with bone-freezing accuracy. This novel should come with a wind-chill factor warning' *Daily Telegraph*

'Real life and fiction blur in this cynical, bleak tale. You'll love every second of it' *Daily Mirror*

'Rankin strips Edinburgh's polite façade to its gritty skeleton' *The Times*

'Rebus is the kind of detective who enjoys a deep dark mystery with a good moral conundrum'
New York Times

'Rankin writes laconic, sophisticated, well-paced thrillers' *Scotsman*

'First-rate plotting, dialogue and characterisations'
Literary Review

Born in the Kingdom of Fife in 1960, Ian Rankin graduated from the University of Edinburgh in 1982, and then spent three years writing novels when he was supposed to be working towards a PhD in Scottish Literature. His first Rebus novel, *Knots and Crosses*, was published in 1987, and the Rebus books are now translated into over thirty languages and are bestsellers worldwide.

Ian Rankin has been elected a Hawthornden Fellow, and is also a past winner of the Chandler-Fulbright Award. He is the recipient of four Crime Writers' Association Dagger Awards including the prestigious Diamond Dagger in 2005 and in 2009 was inducted into the CWA Hall of Fame. In 2004, Ian won America's celebrated Edgar Award for *Resurrection Men*. He has also been shortlisted for the Anthony Awards in the USA, and won Denmark's *Palle Rosenkrantz* Prize, the French *Grand Prix du Roman Noir* and the *Deutscher Krimipreis*. Ian Rankin is also the recipient of honorary degrees from the universities of Abertay, St Andrews, Edinburgh, Hull and the Open University.

A contributor to BBC2's *Newsnight Review*, he also presented his own TV series, *Ian Rankin's Evil Thoughts*. He has received the OBE for services to literature, opting to receive the prize in his home city of Edinburgh. He has also recently been appointed to the rank of Deputy Lieutenant of Edinburgh, where he lives with his partner and two sons. Visit his website at www.ianrankin.net

IAN
RANKIN
LET IT
BLEED

An Orion paperback

First published in Great Britain in 1995
by Orion
This paperback edition published in 1996
by Orion Books Ltd,
Orion House, 5 Upper St Martin's Lane,
London WC2H 9EA

An Hachette UK company

Reissued 2011

A CIP catalogue record for this book
is available from the British Library.

Printed and bound in Great Britain by
Clays Ltd, St Ives plc

The Orion Publishing Group's policy is to use papers
that are natural, renewable and recyclable products and
made from wood grown in sustainable forests. The logging
and manufacturing processes are expected to conform to
the environmental regulations of the country of origin.

www.orionbooks.co.uk

Acknowledgments

Grateful thanks to: Ronnie Mackintosh, for helping me with my inquiries; Councillor Devin Scobie, for steering me through local government; John Mathieson, Staff Training Officer, HM Prison Edinburgh, for his advice; The Scottish Office, especially the Publications Department, New St Andrew's House; staff of Edinburgh City Chambers; staff of LEEL and Scottish Enterprise; staff of Edinburgh Central Lending Library and the Scottish National Library; Jon for the sofa; and the usual nod to everyone at the Oxford Bar.

All inaccuracies are, of course, my own.

The lines quoted by Mrs Kennedy are from *The New Testament in Scots*, translated by W. L. Lorimer (Penguin, 1985).

Avarice, the spur of industry.

<div align="right">(David Hume, 'Of Civil Liberty')</div>

The more sophisticated readers simply repeated the Italian proverb, 'If it isn't true, it's to the point.'

<div align="right">(Muriel Spark, *The Public Image*)</div>

Without women, life is a pub.

<div align="right">(Martin Amis, *Money*)</div>

INTRODUCTION

I first heard the Rolling Stones album *Let It Bleed* when I was only ten or eleven years old. I didn't like the music – at that age I was listening to Marc Bolan and not much else; it was my sister's boyfriend who was the Stones fan. I did find the lyrics intriguing, however. Even though I barely understood the references, I could tell that there was something 'dirty' about them. They hinted at sex, debauchery, violence and drugs. There was even one song ('Midnight Rambler') which seemed to be about a real-life serial killer. I eventually had to buy the album for myself.

By this time, however, I was in my twenties and had already written a couple of books. I was also working as a music journalist and hi-fi equipment reviewer in London. *Let It Bleed*, with its fantastic studio sound, soon became a constant on my Linn Sondek, and when the time came, in 1994, to write the seventh John Rebus novel, I felt emboldened to borrow the album's title.

Though the book is set in the depths of an Edinburgh winter, it was written at my house in south-west France, mostly in blazing summer heat. (I'd long since given up the hi-fi job, but still used the Linn record deck.) I'm not sure now if working on the book provided me with some sort of internal air-conditioning, but one thing I knew was that during any cold snap in Edinburgh you would want your central heating to be working. Hence the pun in the title – what Rebus really needs to bleed in the book is a radiator.

For a little while in the 1990s, I became convinced that in order to make a decent amount of money I would have to transfer my skills to television. I had already made several attempts at scripts for the established cop show *The Bill*. At meetings with the production team, I learned that each *Bill* script had to contain three scenarios, and that none of the action could involve the cops' private lives or show them off-duty. Somehow I couldn't stick to this formula. At around the same time, television had shown some interest in Rebus. I attended more meetings, this time with the BBC, and tried writing a few scripts (both adaptations and original stories), but seemed to hit a series of walls. Eventually, I started pitching non-Rebus ideas at my TV contacts, but still to no avail. All of which, however, may go some way towards explaining the slam-bang action opening of *Let It Bleed*. It's still something I'd love to see on the big screen, done Hollywood-style: a night-time car chase in a blizzard, with the Forth Road Bridge beckoning. Fantastic.

Let It Bleed was a political novel, in that it used local and national politics for much of its plotting. By this time I had a real-life detective on my side, a fan of the books who had pointed out various procedural errors in previous stories. And with a few published novels under my belt, I was a known commodity in Edinburgh, so could approach complete strangers (council officials, for example) with a view to aiding my research. On my trips back to Edinburgh for *Let It Bleed*, I slept on a friend's sofa, asked a lot of questions at the reception desks of various government agencies, and bought a few lunches and rounds of drinks. In some ways, the new book would be a return to the Edinburgh of my second novel, *Hide & Seek*. Both stories are concerned with the changing face of Edinburgh, its

attempts to embrace new employment opportunities (meaning new technologies) while still retaining a sense of identity. Structural change to Scotland's capital was already under way: there was a plan for one of the breweries to open a theme park near the Palace of Holyrood. Eventually, the site would house Our Dynamic Earth and the Scottish Parliament instead, but at the time I was filled with a sense of glee: a theme park built on booze! Well, why not? Several city landmarks, including the Usher Hall, had been built with cash from brewing dynasties. The least we could do in the late twentieth century was celebrate our national relationship with alcohol: hence the use of a favourite Martin Amis line at the very start of the book: 'Without women, life is a pub.'

While there is an abundance of action in *Let It Bleed*, it is also, to my mind, rather a soulful book. We are allowed access to Rebus's thoughts as never before. We learn why he likes music, and why he turns so frequently to the bottle. Memories from his childhood are revealed, adding to our sense of him as a three-dimensional human being. The book contains some of my favourite scenes and images (for example, Rebus's visit to a dry-stane dyker, or his invitation to a Perthshire shooting party), and ends with a few loose ends left straggling. Those loose ends seemed realistic to me, but irritated my American publishers to such an extent that they asked me to consider contributing an extra final chapter for US publication. This I eventually did, though I didn't feel it added anything to the sum of the book (which is why it's not being reprinted here). Between times, some old friends return to the series (Rebus's daughter Sammy; his ex-lover Gill; the reporter Mairie Henderson). This, plus the fact that Rebus is back in his old flat, having jettisoned

the students he'd been renting the place to, gives the book a solid, comfortable feel. By now I was confident in my ability to write a decent crime story, and to recreate Rebus's world . . . which probably explains why I would be at pains to make my next book so different, providing me with a fresh set of challenges.

But for now, I was happy. I knew the inside of Rebus's head. And he was happy, too, happy with his booze, cigarettes and music:

'After a drink he liked to listen to the Stones. Women, relationships and colleagues had come and gone, but the Stones had always been there. He put the album on and poured himself a last drink. The guitar riff, one of easily half a dozen in Keith's tireless repertoire, kicked the album off. I don't have much, Rebus thought, but I have this . . .'

On the album *Let It Bleed* there's a song about the Boston Strangler. Mick Jagger had written about a real-life crime. And what was good enough for Mick was surely good enough for me, as my next novel would demonstrate.

May 2005

xiv

One

BRIDGES

1

A winter night, screaming out of Edinburgh.

The front car was being chased by three others. In the chasing cars were police officers. Sleet was falling through the darkness, blowing horizontally. In the second of the police cars, Inspector John Rebus had his teeth bared. He gripped the doorhandle with one hand, and the front edge of his passenger seat with the other. In the driver's seat, Chief Inspector Frank Lauderdale seemed to have shed about thirty years. He was a youth again, enjoying the feeling of power which came from driving fast, driving a wee bit crazy. He sat well forward, peering through the windscreen.

'We'll get them!' he yelled for the umpteenth time. 'We'll get the bastards!'

Rebus couldn't unlock his jaw long enough to form a reply. It wasn't that Lauderdale was a bad driver ... Well OK, it wasn't *just* that Lauderdale was a bad driver; the weather bothered Rebus too. When they'd taken the second roundabout at the Barnton Interchange, Rebus had felt the car's back wheels losing all grip on the slick road surface. The tyres weren't brand new to start with; probably retreads at that. The air temperature was near zero, the sleet lying treacherously in wait. They were out of the city now, leaving traffic lights and junctions behind. A car chase here should be safer. But Rebus didn't feel safe.

In the car in front were two young, keen uniforms, with a DS and a DC in the car behind. Rebus looked into the

wing mirror and saw headlights. He looked out of the passenger-side window and saw nothing. Christ, it was dark out there.

Rebus thought: I don't want to die in the dark.

A telephone conversation the previous day.

'Ten grand and we let your daughter go.'

The father licked his lips. 'Ten? That's a lot of money.'

'Not to you.'

'Wait, let me think.' The father looked at the pad, where John Rebus had just scribbled something. 'It's short notice,' he told the caller. Rebus was listening on an earpiece, staring at the tape recorder's silently turning spools.

'That attitude could get her hurt.'

'No ... please.'

'Then you'd better get the money.'

'You'll bring her with you?'

'We're not cheats, mister. She'll be there if the money is.'

'Where?'

'We'll phone tonight with details. One last thing, no police, understand? Any sign, even a distant siren, and next time you see her'll be the Co-op funeral parlour.'

'We'll get them!' Lauderdale shouted.

Rebus felt his jaw unlock. 'All right, we'll get them. So why not ease off?'

Lauderdale glanced at him and grinned. 'Lost your bottle, John?' Then he jerked the wheel and pulled out to overtake a transit van.

The phone caller had sounded young, working-class. In his mouth, 'understand' had become *unnerstaun*. He'd spoken of the Co-op. He'd used the word 'mister'. Young working class, maybe a bit naïve. Rebus just wasn't sure.

4

'Fife Police are waiting the other side of the bridge, right?' he persisted, shouting above the engine whine. Lauderdale had the poor gearbox pounding away in third.

'Right,' Lauderdale agreed.

'Then what's our hurry?'

'Don't be soft, John. They're *ours*.'

Rebus knew what his superior meant. If the front car made it over the Forth Road Bridge, then it was in Fife, and Fife Constabulary were waiting, a roadblock erected. It would be a Fife collar.

Lauderdale was on the radio, talking to the car ahead. His one-handed driving was only a little worse than his two-handed, shaking Rebus from side to side. Lauderdale put the radio down again.

'What do you reckon?' he said. 'Will they come off at Queensferry?'

'I don't know,' Rebus said.

'Well, those two L-plates in front think we'll catch them at the toll booths if they decide to go all the way.'

They probably would go all the way, too, driven by fear and adrenaline. The combination tended to put blinkers on your survival mechanism. You ran straight ahead, without thought or deviation. All you knew was flight.

'You could at least put on your seatbelt,' Rebus said.

'I could,' said Lauderdale. But he didn't. Boy racers didn't wear seatbelts.

The final slip-road was coming up. The front car sped past it. There was nowhere to go now but the bridge. The roadlighting high overhead grew thick again as they neared the toll booths. Rebus had a crazy notion of the fugitives stopping to pay their toll, just like everyone else. Winding down the window, fumbling for the coins ...

'They're slowing.'

The road was spreading out, suddenly half a dozen lanes wide. Ahead of them stood the row of toll booths, and

beyond that the bridge itself, curving up towards its mid-point as the steel coils held its carriageway in suspension, so that even on a clear, bright day you couldn't see the far end when you drove on to it.

'They're definitely slowing.'

Only yards separated the four cars now, and Rebus could see, for the first time in a while, the back of the car they were chasing. It was a Y-registration Ford Cortina. The overhead lighting allowed him to make out two heads, driver and passenger, both male.

'Maybe she's in the boot,' he said dubiously.

'Maybe,' Lauderdale agreed.

'If she's not in the car with them, they can't harm her.'

Lauderdale nodded, not really listening, then reached for the radio again. There was a lot of interference. 'If they go on to the bridge,' he said, 'that's it, dead end. There's no way off for them, unless the Fifers fuck up.'

'So we stay here?' Rebus suggested. Lauderdale just laughed. 'Thought not,' said Rebus.

But now something was happening. The suspects' car ... red tail-lights. Were they braking? No, reversing, and at speed. They hit the front police car with force, sending it shunting into Lauderdale's.

'Bastards!'

Then the front car was off again, veering crazily. It headed for one of the closed booths, hitting the barrier, not snapping it off but bending it enough to squeeze through. The sound of metal sparking against metal, and then they were gone. Rebus couldn't believe it.

'They're on the wrong carriageway!'

And so they were, whether by accident or design. Picking up speed, the car was racing north along the southbound lanes, its headlights switched to full beam. The front police car hesitated, then followed. Lauderdale looked ready to do the same thing, but Rebus reached out a hand

6

and tugged with all his might on the steering-wheel, bringing them back into the northbound lane.

'Stupid bastard!' Lauderdale spat, slamming the accelerator hard.

It was late night, not much traffic about. Even so, the driver of the front car was taking some risk.

'They'll only have this carriageway blocked, won't they?' Rebus pointed out. 'If those lunatics make it to the other side, they could get away.'

Lauderdale didn't say anything. He was looking across the central reservation, keeping the other two cars in sight. When he reached out for the radio, he all but lost control. The car jolted right, then harder to the left, slamming the metal side-rails. Rebus didn't want to think about the Firth of Forth, hundreds of feet below. But he thought of it anyway. He'd walked across the bridge a couple of times, using the footpaths either side of the roadways. That had been scary enough, the ever-present wind threatening to gust you over the side. He felt a charge in his toes: a fear of heights.

On the other carriageway, the inevitable was happening, the incredible just about to begin. An articulated lorry, up to speed after a crawl to the top of the rise, saw headlights ahead of it where no headlights should be. The suspects' car had already squeezed past two oncoming cars, and would have slipped into the outside lane to pass the artic, but the artic's driver panicked. He pulled into the outside lane and his hands froze, foot still hard on the accelerator. The truck hit metal and started to rise. It went up into the air, hanging over the central reservation, which was itself a network of steel lines. The trailer snagged and the cab snapped forward, breaking free of its container and sailing into the northbound lanes, sliding on sparks and a spray of water, directly into the path of the car in which Lauderdale and Rebus were travelling.

Lauderdale did his best to hit the brakes, but there was nowhere to go. The cab was sliding diagonally, taking up both lanes. Nowhere to go. Rebus had a couple of seconds to take it in. He felt his whole being contract, everything trying to be where his scrotum was. He pulled his knees up, feet and hands against the dashboard, tucking his head against his legs ...

Whump.

With his eyes screwed shut, all Rebus had to go on were noises and feeling. Something punched him in the cheek-bone, then was gone. There was a shattering of glass, like ice cracking, and the sound of metal being tortured. His gut told him the car was travelling backwards. There were other sounds too, further away. More metal, more glass.

The artic cab had lost a lot of its momentum, and contact with the car stopped it dead. Rebus thought his spine would crack. Whiplash, did they call it? More like brick-lash, slab-lash. The car stopped, and the first thing he realised was that his jaw hurt. He looked over to the driver's seat, reckoning Lauderdale had landed one on him for some unspecified reason, and saw that his superior wasn't there any more.

Well, his arse was there, staring Rebus in the face from its unpromising position where the windscreen used to be. Lauderdale's feet were tucked beneath the steering-wheel. One of his shoes had come off. His legs were draped over the steering-wheel itself. As for the rest of him, that was lying on what was left of the bonnet.

'Frank!' Rebus cried. 'Frank!' He knew better than to pull Lauderdale back into the car; knew better than to touch him at all. He tried opening his door, but it wasn't a door any more. So he undid his seatbelt and squeezed out through the windscreen. His hand touched metal, and he felt a sizzling sensation. Cursing and drawing his hand

8

away, he saw he'd placed it on a section of uncovered engine-block.

Cars were pulling to a stop behind him. The DS and DC were running forwards.

'Frank,' Rebus said quietly. He looked at Lauderdale's face, bloody but still alive. Yes, he was sure Lauderdale was alive. There was just something ... He wasn't moving, you couldn't even be sure he was breathing. But there was *some*thing, some unseen energy which hadn't departed. Not yet at any rate.

'You all right?' someone asked.

'Help him,' Rebus ordered. 'Get an ambulance. And check the lorry-cab, see how the driver is.'

Then he looked across to the other carriageway, and what he saw froze him. He couldn't be sure at first, not totally. So he climbed up on to the metal spars separating the two carriageways. And then he was sure.

The suspects' car had left the carriageway. Left it altogether. They'd somehow vaulted the crash-barrier, slid across the pedestrian walkway, and had enough velocity left to send them through the final set of railings, the ones separating the walkway from that drop to the Firth of Forth. A wind was whipping around Rebus, blowing the sleet into his eyes. He narrowed them and looked again. The Cortina was still there, hanging out into space, its front wheels through the rails but its back wheels and boot still on the walkway. He thought of what might be in the boot.

'Oh my God,' he said. Then he started to clamber over the thick metal tines.

'What are you doing?' someone yelled. 'Come back!'

But Rebus kept moving, only barely aware of the drop beneath him, the amounts of space between each metal bar and its neighbour. More space than metal. The cold metal felt good against his stinging palm. He passed the back of the lorry. It had come to rest on its side, half on the

roadway, half resting on the central gap. There was a sign on its side: Byars Haulage. Jesus, it was cold. That wind, that damned eternal wind. Yet he could feel he was sweating. I should be wearing a coat, he thought. I'll catch my death.

Then he was on the carriageway, where a line of cars had come to an untidy stop. There was a proper gap between carriageway and walkway; a short distance, but all of it fresh air. Where the Cortina had made contact it had buckled the rails. Rebus stepped on to them, then made the short leap on to the walkway.

The two teenagers had stumbled from their car.

They'd had to climb over their seats and into the back in order to get out. The front doors led only to a fall. They were looking to left and right, seized by fright. There were sirens to the north. Fife Police were on their way.

Rebus held up his hands. The two uniformed officers were behind him. The youths weren't looking at Rebus; all they could see were uniforms. They understood simple things. They understood what uniforms meant. They looked around again, looking for an escape that wasn't there, then one of them – fair-haired, tall, slightly older-looking – gripped the younger one's hand and started leading him backwards.

'Don't do anything daft, sons,' said one of the uniforms. But they were just words. Nobody was listening. The two teenagers were against the rails now, only ten feet or so from the crashed car. Rebus walked slowly forwards, pointing with his finger, making it clear to them that he was going to the car. The impact had caused the boot to spring open an inch. Rebus carefully lifted it and looked in.

There was nobody inside.

As he closed the boot, the car rocked on its fulcrum then came to rest again. He looked towards the older of the boys.

'It's freezing out here,' he said. 'Let's get you into a car.'

10

Then things happened in slow motion. The fair-haired boy shook his head, almost smiling, and placed his arms around his friend in what looked like nothing less than an embrace. Then he leaned back against the rail and just kept leaning, taking his friend with him. There was no resistance. Their cheap trainers held against the road surface for a second, then slipped, legs flicking up and over as they fell into the darkness.

Maybe it was suicide, maybe flight, Rebus thought later. Whatever it was meant to be, it was death for sure. When you hit water from that height, it was like hitting concrete. A fall like that, through the dark, and they didn't scream, didn't utter a sound, and couldn't see the water rising to meet them.

Only they didn't hit water.

A Royal Navy frigate had just left Rosyth Dockyard and was gliding out towards the sea, and that's what they hit, embedding themselves in the metal deck.

Which, as everyone said back at the station, saved the police frogmen from a thankless sub-zero dip.

2

They took Rebus to the Royal Infirmary.

He travelled in the back of a police car. Frank Lauderdale was being brought by ambulance. Nobody knew yet how bad his injuries were. The frigate had been contacted by radio from Rosyth, but the crew had already found the bodies. Some had heard them hitting the deck. The frigate was returning to base. It would take a while to hammer the deck back into shape.

'I feel like I've been hit with a hammer myself,' Rebus told the nurse at the infirmary. He knew her; she'd treated him for burns a while back, rubbed lotion on and changed the dressings. She smiled as she left the little booth where he lay on an examining table. When she'd gone, Rebus took another account of himself. His jaw hurt where Lauderdale's fist had connected prior to flying through the windscreen. The pain seemed to be burrowing deep, like it was getting into the nerves of his teeth. Otherwise he didn't feel too bad; just shaken. He lifted his hands and held them in front of him. Yes, he could always blame the trembling on the crash, even if he knew he trembled a lot these days, smash or no smash. His palm was blistering nicely. Before putting on a dressing, the nurse had asked how he got the burn.

'Put my hand on a hot engine,' he'd explained.

'Figures.'

Rebus looked and saw what she meant: part of the engine's serial number had been branded on his flesh.

The doctor finally put in an appearance. It was a busy night. Rebus knew the doctor. His name was George Klasser and he was Polish or something, or at least his parents were. Rebus had always assumed Klasser was a bit too senior to do the night shift, yet here he was.

'Bitter outside, isn't it?' Dr Klasser said.

'Is that supposed to be funny?'

'Just making conversation, John. How do you feel?'

'I think I'm getting toothache.'

'Anything else?' Dr Klasser was fussing with the tools of his trade: penlight and stethoscope, a clipboard and non-working Biro. Eventually he was ready to examine the patient. Rebus didn't put up much of a fight. He was thinking of drinking: the creamy, almost gas-free head on a pint of eighty-bob. The warming aroma from a glass of malt.

'How's my chief inspector?' Rebus asked when the nurse returned.

'They're taking X-rays,' she told him.

'Car chases at your age,' Dr Klasser muttered. 'I blame television.'

Rebus took a good look at him, and realised he hadn't ever really looked at the man before, not properly. Klasser was in his early forties, steel-haired with a tanned and prematurely ageing face. If you only had head and shoulders to go on, you'd guess he was taller than was actually the case. He looked quite distinguished, which was why Rebus had pegged him for a senior consultant, something like that.

'I thought only lackeys and L-plates worked nights,' Rebus commented, while Klasser shone a light in his eyes.

Klasser put down the light and started to squeeze Rebus's back, prodding it like he was plumping up a cushion.

'Any pain there?'

13

'No.'

'What about there?'

'No more than usual.'

'Hmm … In answer to your question, John, I notice *you're* working nights. Does that make you lackey or L-plate?'

'That hurts.'

Dr Klasser smiled.

'So,' Rebus said, easing his shirt back on, 'what've I got?'

Klasser found a pen that worked and scribbled something on his clipboard. 'By my estimate, the way you're going, you've got a year, maybe two.'

The two men stared at one another. Rebus knew precisely what the doctor was talking about.

'I'm serious, John. You smoke, you drink like a fish, and you don't exercise. Since Patience stopped feeding you, your diet's gone to hell. Starch and carbohydrate, saturated fat …'

Rebus tried to stop listening. He knew his drinking was a problem these days precisely because he'd learned self-control. As a result, few people noticed that he *had* a problem. He was well dressed at work, alert when the occasion demanded, and even visited the gym some lunchtimes. He ate lazily, and maybe too much, and yes, he was back on the cigs. But then nobody was perfect.

'An uncanny prognosis, Doctor.' He finished buttoning his shirt, started tucking it into his waistband, then thought better of it. He felt more comfortable with the shirt outside his trousers. He knew he'd feel even more comfortable with his trouser button undone. 'And you can tell that just by prodding my back?'

Dr Klasser smiled again. He was folding up his stethoscope. 'You can't hide that sort of thing from a doctor, John.'

Rebus eased into his jacket. 'So,' he said, 'see you in the pub later?'

'I'll be there around six.'

'Fine.'

Rebus walked out of the hospital and took a deep breath.

It was two-thirty in the morning, about as cold and dark as the night could get. He thought about checking on Lauderdale, but knew it could wait till morning. His flat was just across The Meadows, but he didn't fancy the walk. The sleet was still falling, beginning to turn to snow, and there was that stabbing wind, like a thug you meet in a narrow lane, one who won't let you go.

Then a car horn sounded. Rebus saw a cherry-red Renault 5, and inside it DC Siobhan Clarke, waving towards him. He almost danced to the car.

'What are you doing here?'

'I heard,' she said.

'How come?' He opened the passenger-side door.

'I was curious. I wasn't on shift, but I kept in touch with the station, just to find out what happened at the meet. When I heard about the crash, I got dressed and came down here.'

'Well, you're a sight for sore teeth.'

'Teeth?'

Rebus rubbed his jaw. 'Sounds crazy, but I think that dunt has given me toothache.'

She started the car. It was lovely and warm. Rebus could feel himself drifting off.

'Bit of a disaster then?' she said.

'A bit.' They turned out of the gates, heading left towards Tollcross.

'How's the CI?'

'I don't know. They're X-raying him. Where are we going?'

15

'I'm taking you home.'

'I should go back to the station.'

She shook her head. 'I called in. They don't want you till morning.'

Rebus relaxed a little more. Maybe the painkillers were kicking in. 'When's the post-mortem?'

'Nine-thirty.' They were on Lauriston Place.

'There was a shortcut you could have taken back there,' Rebus told her.

'It was a one-way street.'

'Yes, but nobody uses it this time of night.' He realised what he'd said. 'Jesus,' he whispered, rubbing his eyes.

'So what was it?' Siobhan Clarke asked. 'I mean, was it an accident, or were they looking to escape?'

'Neither,' Rebus said quietly. 'If I'd to put money on it, I'd say suicide.'

She looked at him. 'Both of them?'

He shrugged, then shivered.

At the Tollcross lights they waited in silence until red turned to green. A couple of drunks were walking home, bodies tilted into the wind.

'Horrible night,' Clarke said, moving off. Rebus nodded, saying nothing. 'Will you attend the post-mortem?'

'Yes.'

'Can't say I'd fancy it.'

'Do we know who they were yet?'

'Not that I know of.'

'I keep forgetting, you're off-duty.'

'That's right, I'm off-duty.'

'What about the car, have we traced that?'

She turned towards him and laughed. It sounded odd to him, there in that stuffy overheated car, that time of night, with all that had gone before. Sudden laughter, as strange a sound as you'd ever hear. He rubbed his jaw and pushed an

exploratory finger into his mouth. The teeth he touched seemed solid enough.

Then he saw feet suddenly sweeping out from under two young bodies, the bodies leaning back into space and disappearing. They hadn't made a sound. No accident, no escape attempt; something fatalistic, something agreed between them.

'Cold?'

'No,' he said, 'I'm not cold.'

She signalled to turn off Melville Drive. To the left, what he could see of The Meadows was covered in a fresh glaze of slow. To the right was Marchmont, and Rebus's flat.

'She wasn't in the car,' he said flatly.

'There was always that possibility,' Siobhan Clarke said. 'We don't even know she's missing, not for a fact.'

'No,' he agreed, 'we don't.'

'Just two daft laddies.' She'd picked up the expression, but it sounded awkward given her English accent. Rebus smiled in the dark.

And then he was home.

She dropped him outside his tenement door, and refused a half-hearted offer of coffee. Rebus didn't want her to see the dump he called home. The students had moved out in October, leaving the place not quite his. There were things not quite right, not quite the way he remembered. Cutlery was missing, and had been replaced with stuff he hadn't seen before. It was the same with the crockery. When he'd moved back here from Patience's, he'd brought his stuff back in boxes. Most of the boxes were in the hall, still waiting to be unpacked.

Exhausted, he climbed the stairs, opened his door, and walked past the boxes, making straight for the living room and his chair.

His chair was much the same as ever. It had remoulded

17

itself quickly to his shape. He sat down, then got up again and checked the radiator. The thing was barely warm, and there was a racking noise from within. He needed a special key, some tool that would open the valve and let it bleed. The other radiators were the same.

He made himself a hot drink, put a tape into the cassette deck, and got the duvet off his bed. Back at his chair he took off some of his clothes and covered himself with the duvet. He reached down, unscrewed the top from a bottle of Macallan, and poured some into his coffee. He drank the first half of the mug, then added more whisky.

He could hear car engines, and metal twisting, and the wind whistling all around. He could see feet, the soles of cheap trainers, something close to a smile on the lips of a fair-haired teenager. But then the smile became darkness, and everything disappeared.

Slowly, he hugged himself to sleep.

3

Down at the City Mortuary in the Cowgate Dr Curt was nowhere to be seen, but Professor Gates was already at work.

'You know,' he said, 'you can fall from any height you want; it's just that last damned half-inch that's fatal.'

With him around the slab were Inspector John Rebus, Detective Sergeant Brian Holmes, another doctor, and a pathology assistant. The Preliminary Notification of Sudden Death had already been submitted to the Procurator Fiscal, and now the Sudden Death Report was being prepared on two deceased males, probable identities William David Coyle and James Dixon Taylor.

James Taylor – Rebus looked at the mess over which Professor Gates was fussing and remembered that final embrace. Ain't it good to know that you've got a friend.

The force of the impact of the bodies upon the steel deck of Her Majesty's naval frigate *Descant* had turned them from human beings into something more like hairy jam. There was some on the slab – the rest sat in gleaming steel buckets. No next of kin was going to be asked to participate in a formal identification. It was the sort of thing they could just about accomplish by DNA-testing, if such proved necessary.

'Flatpacks, we call them,' Professor Gates said. 'Saw a lot at Lockerbie. Scraped them off the ground and took them to the local ice rink. Handy place, an ice rink, when you

19

suddenly find yourself with two hundred and seventy bodies.'

Brian Holmes had seen bad deaths before, but he was not immune. He kept shuffling his feet and shifting his shoulders, and glaring with hard, judgmental eyes at Rebus, who was humming scraps of 'You're So Vain'.

Establishing time, date and place of death was straight-forward. Certified cause of death was easy too, though Professor Gates wasn't sure of the precise wording.

'Blunt force trauma?'

'How about boating accident?' Rebus offered. There were some smiles at that. Like most pathologists, Professor Alexander Gates MD, FRC Path, DMJ (Path), FRCPE, MRCPG, was possessed of a sense of humour as wide as his letter-heading. A quite necessary sense of humour. He didn't look like a pathologist. He wasn't tall and cadaverously grey like Dr Curt, but was a bossy, shuffling figure, with the physique of a wrestler rather than an undertaker. He was broad-chested, bull-necked, and had pudgy hands, the fingers of which he delighted in cracking, one at a time or all together.

He liked people to call him Sandy.

'I'm the one issuing the death certificate,' he told Brian Holmes, who filled in the relevant box on the rough-up Sudden Death Report. 'My address care of Police Surgeoncy, Cowgate.'

Rebus and the others watched as Gates made his examination. He was able to confirm the existence of two separate corpses. Samples were taken of veinous blood for grouping, DNA, toxicology, and alcohol. Usually urine samples would be taken also, but that just wasn't possible, and Gates was even doubtful about the efficacy of blood testing. Vitreous humour and stomach contents were next, along with bile and liver.

Before their eyes, he started to reconstruct the bodies:

not so they became identifiable as humans, not entirely, but just so he could be satisfied he had everything the bodies had once had. Nothing missing, and nothing extraneous.

'I used to love jigsaws when I was a youngster,' the pathologist said quietly, bent over his task.

Outside it was a dry, freezing day. Rebus remembered liking jigsaws too. He wondered if kids still played with them. The post-mortem over, he stood on the pavement and smoked a cigarette. There were pubs to left and right of him, but none were yet open. His breakfast tot of whisky had all but evaporated.

Brian Holmes came out of the mortuary stuffing a green cardboard file into his briefcase. He saw Rebus rubbing at his jaw.

'You all right?'

'Toothache, that's all.'

It was, too; it was definitely toothache, or at least gum-ache. He couldn't positively identify any one tooth as the culprit: the pain was just there, swelling below the surface.

'Give you a lift?'

'Thanks, Brian, but I've got my car.'

Holmes nodded and tugged up his collar. His chin was tucked into a blue lambswool scarf. 'The bridge is open again,' he said, 'one lane southbound.'

'What about the Cortina?'

'Howdenhall have it. They're fingerprinting, just in case she ever was in the car.'

Rebus nodded, saying nothing. Holmes said nothing back.

'Something I can do for you, Brian?'

'No, not really. I was just wondering ... weren't you supposed to be at the station first thing?'

'So?'

'So why come here instead?'

It was a good question. Rebus looked back at the

21

mortuary doors, remembering the scene all over again. The artic, assuming the crash position, Lauderdale spread across the bonnet, then seeing the other car ... a final embrace ... a fall.

He shrugged non-committally and made for his car.

Chief Inspector Frank Lauderdale was going to be all right.

That was the good news.

The bad news was that DI Alister Flower was looking for temporary promotion to fill Lauderdale's shoes.

'And with the funeral meats not yet cold,' said Chief Superintendent 'Farmer' Watson. He blushed, realising what he'd said. 'Not that there's ... I mean, no funeral or ...' He coughed into his bunched fist.

'Flower's got a point though, sir,' said Rebus, covering his boss's embarrassment. 'It's just that he's got the tact of a tomcat. I mean, somebody'll have to fill in. How long's Frank going to be out of the game?'

'We don't know.' The Farmer picked up a sheet of paper and read from it. 'Both legs broken, two broken ribs, broken wrist, concussion: there's half a page of diagnosis here.'

Rebus rubbed his bruised cheekbone, wondering if it was responsible for the broken wrist.

'We don't even know,' the Farmer went on quietly, 'whether he'll walk again. The breaks were pretty severe. Meantime, the last thing I need is Flower and you vying for any temporary promotion it may or may not be in my power to give.'

'Understood.'

'Good.' The Farmer paused. 'So what can you tell me about last night?'

'It'll be in my report, sir.'

'Of course it will, but I'd prefer the truth. What was Frank playing at?'

22

'How do you mean?'

'I mean driving around like the Dukes of Hazzard. We've got expendables for that sort of escapade.'

'We were just maintaining a pursuit, sir.'

'Of course you were.' Watson studied Rebus. 'Nothing you'd like to add to that?'

'Not much, sir. Except that it was no accident, and they'd no intention of getting away. It was a suicide pact: unspoken, but suicide all the same.'

'And why would they do that?'

'I've no idea, sir.'

The Farmer sighed and sat back in his chair. 'John, I think you should know my feelings on all of this.'

'Yes, sir?'

'It was an utter balls-up from start to finish.'

... And that was putting it mildly.

They were only there because of power, because of influence, because a favour was asked. That was how it had started: with a discreet call from the city's Lord Provost to the deputy chief constable of Lothian and Borders Police, requesting that his daughter's disappearance be investigated.

Not that anything unlawful was hinted at. It wasn't that she'd been abducted, assaulted, murdered, nothing like that. It was just that she'd walked out of the house one morning and not come back. Yes, she'd left a note. It was addressed to her father and the message was simple: 'Arseholes, I'm off.' It was unsigned, but was in the daughter's handwriting.

Had there been a disagreement? An argument? Strong words? Well, it was impossible to have a teenager in the house without the occasional difference of view. And how old was the Lord Provost's daughter, little Kirstie Kennedy? There came the crux: she was seventeen, and a

mature, well-educated seventeen at that, well able to look
after herself and old enough legally to leave home any time
she wished. Which should have taken the matter out of the
police's hands, except ... except that it was the Lord
Provost asking, the Right Honourable Cameron McLeod
Kennedy, JP, Councillor for South Gyle.

So the message filtered down from the DCC: take a look
for Kirstie Kennedy, but keep it quiet.

Which was, everyone agreed, next to impossible. You
didn't ask questions on the street without rumours starting,
people fearing the worst for the subject of your questions.
This was the excuse given when the media got hold of the
story.

There was a photograph of the daughter, a photo police
had been given and which somehow the media got their
paws on. The Lord Provost was furious about that. It
proved to him that he had enemies within the force. As
Rebus could have told him, if you went *demanding* a favour,
someone down the line could come to resent it.

So there she was, on TV and in the papers: little Kirstie
Kennedy. Not a very recent photo, maybe two or three
years out of date; and the difference between fourteen or
fifteen and seventeen was crucial. Rebus, father of a one-
time teenage daughter, knew that. Kirstie was grown up
now, and the photo would be next to useless in helping
trace her.

The Lord Provost quietened the media hubbub by
giving a press conference. His wife was with him – his
second wife, not Kirstie's mother; Kirstie's mother was
dead – and she was asked what she'd like to say to the
runaway.

'I'd just like her to know we're praying for her, that's
all.'

And then came the first phone call.

It wasn't hard to phone the Lord Provost. He was in the

phone book, plus his appointments number was listed alongside every other councillor in a useful pamphlet handed out to tens of thousands of Edinburgh residents.

The caller sounded young, a voice not long broken. He hadn't given a name. All he'd said was that he had Kirstie, and that he wanted money for her return. He'd even put a girl on the phone. She'd squealed a couple of words before being pulled away. The words had been 'Dad' and 'I'.

The Lord Provost couldn't be sure it was Kirstie, but he couldn't not be sure either. He wanted the police's help again, and they told him to set up a drop with the kidnappers; only there wouldn't be money waiting for them, there'd be police officers and plenty of them.

The intention wasn't to confront but to tail. A police helicopter was brought into play, along with four unmarked cars. It should have been easy.

It should have been. But the caller had selected as drop zone a bus stop on the busy Queensferry Road. Lots of fast-moving traffic, and nowhere to stop an unmarked car inconspicuously. The caller had been clever. When it came time for the pick-up, the Cortina had stopped on the other side of the road from the bus stop. The passenger had come hurtling across the road, dodging traffic, picked up the bag full of wads of newspaper, and taken it back to the waiting car.

Three of the police cars were facing the wrong way, and it took a devil of a time to turn them round. But the fourth had radioed back with the suspect car's whereabouts. The helicopter, of course, had been grounded earlier, the weather being impossible. All of which left Lauderdale – officer in charge – furiously gunning his car to catch up with the race, and shedding years in the process.

Rebus hoped it had been worth it. He hoped Lauderdale, lying strapped up in hospital, would get a thrill from

remembering the chase. All it had given Rebus were a sick feeling in the gut, a bad dream, and this damned sore face.

There was a collection going around to buy something for the chief inspector. Pointedly and all too quickly, DI Alister Flower put in a tenner. He was walking around with his chest stuck out and a greasepaint smile on his face. Rebus loathed him more than ever.

Everybody kept looking at Rebus, wondering if he'd be promoted over Flower. Wondering what Rebus would do if Flower suddenly became *his* boss. The rumours piled up faster than the collection money. It wasn't even close.

Rebus was not alone in reckoning the kidnapping for a hoax. They'd know for sure very soon, now that they had traced the car, located its owner, discovered that he'd loaned it to two friends and gone to those friends' shared house only to find nobody home.

The car owner was downstairs in an interview room. They were telling him that if he was straight with them, they'd forget about the car's lack of proper insurance. He was telling them story after story, the life and times of Willie Coyle and Dixie Taylor. Rebus went down to listen for a while. DS Macari and DC Allder were doing the interview.

'Detective Inspector Rebus enters, twelve-fifteen hours,' Macari said for the benefit of the tape recorder. 'So,' he said to the seated youth, 'how did they make out, Willie and Dixie? Both on the broo, but you can always supplement the broo, eh?'

Rebus stood against the wall, trying to appear casual. He even smiled towards the car owner, nodded to let him know everything was all right. The car owner was in his late teens, presentable enough, neatly dressed and groomed. He wore a discreet silver-loop earring in his right ear, but no other jewellery, not even a watch.

'They got along,' he said. 'Like, the dole money's no' bad, even social security, you can live on it if you're careful.'

'And they were careful?' Macari paused. 'Mr Duggan nods his head.' This again for the tape recorder. 'So why would they pull a stunt like this?'

Duggan shook his head. 'I wish I knew. I never got an inkling. Willie'd never asked for a loan of the car before. He said he had something to shift.'

'What sort of thing?'

'He didn't say.'

'But you loaned him the car anyway.'

'Like I say, Willie's the careful sort.'

'And Dixie?'

Duggan gave the hint of a smile. 'Well, Dixie's different. He needed looking after.'

'What? Was he soft in the head like?'

'No, he was just laid back. He didn't ... it was hard to get him interested.' He looked up. 'It's hard to put into words.'

'Just try your best, Mr Duggan.'

'Ever since school, Willie and Dixie had been best pals. They liked the same music, same comics, same games. They understood one another.'

'And they shared digs ever since they left home?'

Rebus liked Macari's style. Around the station they called him 'Toni', after the character in *Oor Wullie*. He'd managed to get Duggan relaxed and talkative; he'd forged a relationship. Rebus wasn't so sure of Allder; Allder was one of Flower's men.

'I think so,' Duggan was saying. 'They were right close. We had a book at school once. It had two characters like them in it, one daft and the other not.'

'*Of Mice and Men*?' Rebus offered.

'I thought that was Burns,' Allder said.

27

Rebus indicated to Macari that he was leaving.

'Inspector Rebus leaves room, twelve-thirty hours. So, Mr Duggan, to get back to the car ...'

As ever, Rebus timed his exit just wrong. Alister Flower was walking along the corridor towards him, whistling 'Dixie'.

'There's a lad in there,' Rebus reminded him, 'has just lost two pals, one of them called Dixie.'

Flower stopped whistling and barked a short, unpleasant laugh. 'Must've been my, you know, subconscious.'

'You've got to be conscious to have one of those,' Rebus said, moving away. 'Which sort of disqualifies you.'

Flower wasn't letting him off so easily. He caught up with Rebus at the double doors. 'Things'll be different when I'm Chief Inspector,' he snarled.

'Yes, they will,' Rebus agreed. 'Because by then they'll have cured cancer and put a man on Mars.'

Then he pushed through the doors and was gone.

4

He drove out to Stenhouse. It was further out of town than he remembered, and nicer too. Quiet, once you came off Gorgie Road. Two-storey semis with tidy front gardens and swept pavements. Some of the doorsteps looked scrubbed; his mother had got down on her knees with all the other women in their cul-de-sac a couple of times a week to scrub the step with hot soapy water or bleach. A dirty front step reflected badly on the home within.

Rebus was more used to central Edinburgh, tenement city. The little suburbia managed to surprise him. Salt had been put down along the pavements and roads. In summer the neighbours would be out gossiping over fences, but this was winter and they were hibernating.

An Edinburgh winter could be a real stayer, starting early in October and lasting into April. The days were not constant: sometimes it was twilight all day; other times, with fresh snow on the ground, the sun's glare scoured your eyes. People walked everywhere squinting, either peering into the gloom or protecting themselves from the fierce light.

Today was a twilight day, the sky a dull maroon, threatening a fall. Rebus stuffed his hands into his pockets and felt the small paper bag. He'd found an ironmonger's on Gorgie Road, and had been directed to a specialist shop where he'd been sold a radiator key. Now he looked around, found the house he was looking for, and walked up to the front door.

'Afternoon sir,' said Siobhan Clarke, answering his knock. 'How are you feeling?'

Rebus pushed his way inside. The house wasn't much warmer than outside. In the living room, Brian Holmes was flipping through a collection of CDs.

'Anything?' Rebus asked.

Holmes stood up. 'There are a few newspapers with items about the Kennedy case. Probably gave them the idea. No sign she's ever been here. Pretty unlikely she'd run about with dossers like those two. She's a Gillespie's girl; Willie and Dixie were strictly comprehensive.'

'Looks like a straightforward hoax, sir,' Clarke agreed.

Rebus was looking around. He turned to Clarke. 'Say you're a well brought-up wee lassie, good school, nice lifestyle. Say you want to run away from home and just disappear for a while, maybe for ever. Would you take up with people your own class, or would you head downmarket, where nobody'd know you and nobody'd care?'

'Down to guys like Willie and Dixie you mean?'

Rebus shrugged. 'I'm only speculating. If you were to ask me, I'd say she's done what every runner from Scotland does – gone to London.'

'God help her,' Holmes said quietly.

'So, have you finished looking around?'

'No, sir.'

'Then don't let me stop you. In fact, plug that electric fire in and I might even lend a hand.'

Brian Holmes searched in his pockets for coins for the electric meter, then they got to work.

There were two bedrooms, one tidy, the bed made, the other a mess. The tidy room belonged to Willie Coyle, as a letter from the DSS lying by the bed confirmed. There were books on a bookshelf, most of them brand new. Rebus wondered which bookshop had been losing stock recently. He pulled out something called *Trainspotting*, and saw that

there were some sheets of paper hidden behind the row of books. The sheets were stapled at one corner, professionally word-processed with charts and graphs. They seemed to comprise a business report, a plan of some kind.

Holmes looked over his superior's shoulder. 'Don't tell me Willie was an entrepreneur?'

Rebus shrugged, but rolled the report up and put it in his pocket.

'In here!' Siobhan Clarke called. By the time they reached her, she was pulling out her haul from beneath Dixie Taylor's bed. Three disposable syringes, still in their wrappers, a candle burnt to a nub, and a dessert spoon blackened on its bottom.

'No sign of any skag,' she said, standing up and straightening her hair.

'I'll check beneath the other bed,' Holmes said.

Rebus was smiling. '"Skag"?' he said. 'What sort of books have *you* been reading?' Then his face turned serious. 'Better call for backup, give this place a thorough going over.'

'Right, sir.'

When Rebus was alone in the room, he examined the syringes. There was a fine layer of dust on the packets, and little balls of fluff lay in the spoon. Dixie obviously hadn't used his works in some time. Rebus went to the bathroom, checking for Methodone or whatever the doctors gave you these days to wean you off. But he found only flu powders, paracetamol, mouthwash. He checked the mail again, but found nothing from any hospital or rehab centre.

Then he phoned Professor Gates and asked about the blood samples.

'I haven't had the results yet. Is there a problem?'

'Possible heroin use,' Rebus said. 'At least by one of them.'

'I could check the bodies again. I wasn't really looking for puncture marks.'

'Would you find them if they were there?'

'Well, as you saw yourself, the bodies aren't exactly pristine, and IV users are good at hiding their wounds. They'll inject into the tongue, the penis –'

'Well, see what you can do, Professor.' Rebus put down the phone. He suddenly didn't feel comfortable indoors, so went to get some air. He lasted thirty seconds outside, then went next door and pushed the bell. A middle-aged woman opened the door, and Rebus started to show her his ID.

'I know who you are,' she said. 'It's a crying shame, those poor wee lads. Come in, come in.'

Her name was Mrs Tweedie, and she kept a warm house. Rebus sat down on the sofa and rubbed his hands, getting some feeling back into them while avoiding the burn on his palm.

'Did you know them well, Mrs Tweedie?'

She watched him take out his notebook and pen. 'You don't mind, do you?' he asked.

'Not at all, but I thought I might make us a cup of tea first. Is that all right?'

That was just fine with John Rebus.

He sat there for over half an hour. The room was so hot he thought he might nod off, but what Mrs Tweedie had to say brought him wide awake.

'Nice lads, the pair of them. Helped me home with my shopping once, and wouldn't stop for a cup of tea.'

'You saw them often?'

'Well, I saw them coming and going.'

'Did they keep regular hours? I mean, were they active at night?'

'I wouldn't know. I'm not late to bed. They sometimes played their music a bit loud, but all I did was turn up the

telly. If they were having a party, they always warned us in advance.'

Rebus brought out the Kirstie photograph. 'Have you seen this girl before, Mrs Tweedie?'

'Gracious, yes!'

'Oh?'

'I saw her in the *Daily Record*.'

Rebus felt his hopes sink. 'But never round here?'

'No, never. I saw their landlord often though.'

Rebus frowned. 'I thought these houses were council-owned?'

Mrs Tweedie nodded. 'So they are.'

Rebus started to get it. 'But it's not Willie's and Dixie's names in the rent book?'

'They explained to me that they were ... er, sub-something.'

'Sub-letting?'

'Aye, that's it. From the lad who had the house before them.'

'And what's his name, Mrs Tweedie?'

'Well, his first name's Paul. I don't know his second. Nice young lad, always smartly dressed. Only thing I didn't like, he wore one of those ...' She tugged her ear and made a face. 'Doesn't look at all right on a man.'

'Paul Duggan?' Rebus suggested.

She tried the name out. 'You know,' she said, 'you could be right.'

As Rebus drove out on to Gorgie Road he had a song in his head. It was an old Neil Young number, 'The Needle and the Damage Done'. He stopped the car in front of the jail to collect his thoughts. An access road ran from Gorgie Road up to the gatehouse, the tall fence, and the solid building behind with its massive door and large clock. Though not yet five o'clock, it was dark, but the prison was well lit.

Officially it was HM Prison Edinburgh; but everyone knew it as Saughton Jail. The main building looked like a Victorian workhouse.

They'd have ended up in jail, he thought to himself. They knew even a hoax kidnapping was a serious offence.

Willie Coyle, the taller, the fair-haired of the two. Rebus was imagining what had gone through Willie's mind in those final seconds before he took the plunge. Dixie and he would go to jail. They'd almost certainly be separated: different wings if not different jails. Dixie would have no one to look after him. Rebus thought of Lenny in *Of Mice and Men*. Dixie had been an injector, maybe he'd been helped off, helped by his friend Willie. But in Scotland's jails, there were plenty of drugs. Of course, you'd have to have something to trade, and a boy Dixie's age always had something to trade.

Had Willie weighed up the options? And had he then hugged his friend, hugged him to death? Rebus was beginning to like Willie Coyle. He was wishing he wasn't dead.

But he was, they both were. Cold and commingled on the slab, leaving not much behind except the fact that Paul Duggan was a very cool customer indeed. Rebus would be talking to Paul Duggan, sooner rather than later. But for now he had other people to see, another appointment. It was the one appointment he'd known all day he would keep, come hell or high water.

5

There was a gas-fire, the kind that gave out actual flames, burning in what looked like the original grate; and smoke too, though the smoke came from cigarettes and pipes. The TV was on, all but drowned out by the live music. As often happened on a winter's evening, Edinburgh's folk musicians managed to find themselves in the same pub at the same time. They were playing in a corner: three fiddles, a squeeze-box, a *bodhran*, and a flute. The flautist was the only woman. The men were bearded and ruddy-cheeked and wore thick-knit jumpers. The pints on their table were three-quarters full. The woman was thin and pale with long brown hair, but her cheeks were bright from firelight.

A few customers were up dancing, arms linked and birling in what space there was. Rebus liked to think they were just keeping warm, but in fact they looked like they were having fun.

'Three more halfs and a couple of nips,' he told the barman.

'And what are your friends drinking?'

'Ha ha,' said Rebus. He was flanked at the bar by his drinking companions, George Klasser and Donny Dougary. While Klasser was known as 'Doc', Dougary was called 'Salty'. Rebus didn't know either of them very well outside the confines of the pub, but most evenings between six and half-seven they were the best of pals. Salty Dougary was trying to be heard above the general confusion.

'So what I'm saying is, you can go anywhere on the

superhighway, *any*where, and in future it'll be even bigger. You'll do your shopping by computer, you'll watch telly on it, play games, listen to music … and everything will be there. I can talk to the White House if I want: I can download stuff from all over the world. I sit there at my desk and I can travel anywhere.'

'Can you travel to the pub by computer, Salty?' a drinker further down the bar asked.

Salty ignored him and held his thumb and forefinger a couple of inches apart. 'Hard disks the size of credit cards, you'll have a whole PC in the palm of your hand.'

'You shouldn't say that to a policeman, Salty,' George Klasser offered, causing laughter. He turned to Rebus.

'How's that tooth?'

'The anaesthetic helps,' Rebus said, tipping the last of his whisky into his mouth.

'I hope you're not mixing alcohol and painkillers.'

'Would I do that? Salty, give the man some money.'

Salty stopped talking to himself. The barman was waiting, so he pulled out a ten-pound note, watching its sad ebbing as it flowed into the till. Salty was called Salty because of salt and sauce, which were what you put on your chip-shop supper. The connection being chips, since Salty worked in an electronics factory in South Gyle. He'd been a late arrival in 'Silicon Glen', and was hoping the industry would continue to prosper. Six factories before this one had closed on him, leaving long periods of jobless space between them. He still remembered the days when money was tight – 'I could have collected Social Security for Scotland' – and watched his money accordingly. He made microchips these days, feeding an assembly plant on Clydeside and another in Gyle Park West.

'Yé dancing?'

Rebus half turned to see a woman grinning toothlessly at

36

him. He thought her name was Morag. She was married to the man with the tartan shoelaces.

'Not tonight,' he said, trying to look flattered. You could never tell with the man with the tartan shoelaces: dance with his wife and you were flirting; turn her down and you were, by implication, snubbing *him*. Rebus rested his foot on the polished brass bar-rail and drank his drinks.

By eight o'clock, both Doc and Salty had left, and an old guy in a shapeless bunnet was standing next to Rebus. The man had forgotten his false teeth, and his cheeks were sunken. He was telling Rebus about American history.

'I like it, ken. Just American, not any other kind.'

'Why's that?'

'Eh?'

'Why just American?'

The man licked his lips. He wasn't focusing on Rebus, or on anything in the bar. You couldn't be sure he was even focusing on the present day.

'Well,' he said at last, 'I suppose it's because of the Westerns. I love Westerns. Hopalong Cassidy, John Wayne ... I used to like Hopalong Cassidy.'

'*Could It Be Forever*,' said Rebus, 'that was one of his.'

Then he finished his drink and went home.

The telephone was ringing. Rebus considered not answering; resistance lasted all of ten seconds.

'Hello?'

'Hello, Dad.'

He flopped into his chair. 'Hello, Sammy. Where are you?' She paused too long. 'Still at Patience's, eh? How are you?'

'Fine.'

'How's work?'

'You really want to know?'

'Just being polite.' Fatherly, he thought suddenly: I

37

should have said fatherly, not polite. Sometimes he wished life had a rewind function.

'Well, I won't bore you with the details then.'

'I take it Patience is out?' It stood to reason: Sammy never called when she was home.

'Yes, she's out with ... I mean *at* something. She's out at something.'

Rebus smiled. 'What you really mean is that she's out *with* someone.'

'I'm not very good at this.'

'Don't blame yourself, blame your genes. Do you want to meet?'

'Not tonight, I'm dog-tired. Patience asked ... she wondered if you'd like to come to tea some day. She thinks we should see more of one another.'

As usual, thought Rebus, Patience was right. 'I'd like that. When?'

'I'll ask Patience and get back to you. Deal?'

'Deal.'

'Well, I'm off for an early night. What about you?'

Rebus looked down at his chair. 'I'm already there. Sleep tight.'

'You too, Dad. Love you.'

'You too, pet,' Rebus said quietly, but only after he'd put down the phone.

He went over to the hi-fi. After a drink, he liked to listen to the Stones. Women, relationships, and colleagues had come and gone, but the Stones had always been there. He put the album on and poured himself a last drink. The guitar riff, one of easily half a dozen in Keith's tireless repertoire, kicked the album off. I don't have much, Rebus thought, but I have this. He thought of Lauderdale in his hospital bed; Patience out enjoying herself; Kirstie Kennedy in a Charing Cross cardboard-box. Then he saw cheap trainers, a final embrace, and Willie Coyle's face.

Rebus just couldn't seem to drink him off his mind.

He remembered the report he'd found hidden in Willie's bedroom. It was on the kitchen worktop, and he went to fetch it. It was a business plan, something to do with a computer software company called LABarum. The text explained that the dictionary definition of 'labarum' was 'moral standard or guide', and the reason the company would use upper case for the first three letters was to emphasise *L*othian *A*nd *B*orders. The business plan discussed future development, costings, projected balance sheet, employment range. It was dry, and it was couched in the conditional. Rebus got out the phone book but found no listing anywhere for LABarum.

Someone had been working on the text, underlining some phrases, circling words, doing jotted calculations beside the graphs and bar charts. Sentences had been deleted in red pen, words changed. Some points had been ticked. Rebus couldn't know if the handwriting was Willie Coyle's. He didn't know if Willie had owned such a thing as a red Biro. But he *did* wonder what such a document was doing hidden in Willie Coyle's bedroom. When he turned to the last sheet, there was a word scrawled diagonally across it and underlined heavily. The word was DAL-GETY. He flipped through the report again but found no other mention of Dalgety. Was it a person, a place, another company? The word was scored into the paper in blue ink. It was impossible to say if it was in the same hand as the amendments and marginalia.

He poured another drink – this would be his last – and flipped the album over. He was annoyed, more with himself than anyone. It was case closed after all: a couple of desperate hoaxers fell off a bridge and died. That was all. He should have cleared it from his mind by now. Yet he couldn't.

'Damn you, Willie,' he said out loud. He sat down again

with his drink and picked up the business plan. There were a couple of letters in the top right-hand corner, written faintly in pencil. CK. He wondered if they were an abbreviation for 'check'.

'Who cares?' he said, trying to concentrate on the music. What a shambles the band were, yet sometimes they could get it so exactly right that it hurt.

'Here's to you, Willie,' Rebus said, raising his glass in the air.

6

It wasn't till he woke up in the morning freezing that he remembered the radiator key in his jacket pocket. The pipes were gurgling, the boiler roaring away, yet the radiators were barely warm.

He got coffee and a bacon roll from a café and had breakfast in his car on the way to work. There was a hard frost on the ground, and the sky was leaden, threatening worse. It had taken him five minutes to scrape the ice off his windscreen, and even so it was like driving a tank, peering through the one clear slit.

A message on his desk warned of a nine-thirty meeting in the Farmer's office. Rebus felt he deserved another coffee, and made for the canteen. A lone woman sat at a table, slowly stirring a beaker of tea.

'Gill?'

She looked up. It was Gill Templer. Rebus's face broke into its first grin of the year. He pulled out a chair and sat down.

'Hello, John.' Her eyes were on her drink.

'I thought you were in Fife.'

'Yes.'

'Sex Offences Unit, isn't it?'

'That's it.'

He nodded, trying to ignore the coolness in her tone. 'You look good.' He meant it too. Her short dark hair was feather-cut, long crescents sweeping over both ears to her cheeks. Her eyes were emerald green. She hadn't changed a

41

bit. Gill Templer smiled an acknowledgment but didn't say anything.

Brian Holmes put a hand on Rebus's shoulder. 'Those pathology tests have come in.'

'Oh?'

Holmes went to fetch himself coffee and a dough-ring, Rebus following. 'So what's the news?' he asked.

Holmes took a bite out of his dough-ring and shrugged. 'Nothing,' he mumbled, swallowing. 'The professor can't confirm the presence of heroin or any other drug in the blood of either deceased. He thinks he may have a couple of jab marks on one corpse, but they're not recent.'

'Which body?'

'The shorter.'

'Dixie.' Rebus lifted his coffee and left Holmes to pay for it. When he turned, Gill Templer wasn't at the table any more. She had left the beaker of tea untouched.

'Who was she?' Holmes asked, tucking change back into his pocket.

'Someone I used to know.'

'Well, that narrows things down.'

Rebus picked a new table for them to sit at.

DI Alister Flower looked like he was on his way to a fashion shoot for one of the stores on Princes Street.

'Run out of dummies, have they?' Rebus asked, entering Farmer Watson's office.

Flower was wearing a light blue suit with blue shirt and a black and white tie with a zig-zag motif. He'd set things off with polished brown loafers and what looked like white tennis socks. Rebus sat down next to him and realised his own shoes could do with a polish. There was a speck of grease from the bacon roll on his shirt.

'I've called this meeting,' the Farmer was saying, 'to put your minds at rest.'

'Inspector Flower's mind's always at rest, sir,' Rebus said.

Flower attempted an unselfconscious laugh, and Rebus realised how desperate the man was.

'See, John,' said the Farmer, 'you always have to make a joke of things.'

'Leave them laughing, sir.' But the Farmer wasn't laughing, and Rebus knew what that silence meant – as long as Rebus maintained 'an attitude', he'd find promotion impossible.

Which left Alister Flower.

'Aly,' the Farmer began. Flower sat to attention; Rebus had never seen the trick before. 'Aly, can I get you a refill?'

Flower looked at his cup, then gulped the contents down. 'Please, sir.'

The Farmer got up from his desk, took Flower's cup, and walked to the coffee machine. He had his back to both men when he spoke.

'The temporary replacement for Frank Lauderdale will start immediately.'

It hit Rebus then. It was like he'd assumed a new, much greater mass.

'Her name,' the Farmer went on, 'is Gill Templer.'

Flower made straight for the toilets, where he could conduct a swearing match with the mirror. Rebus walked thoughtfully back to the CID room. Gill was already there, reading a pathology report.

'Congratulations,' he said.

'Thank you.' She kept on reading. He didn't budge till she stopped and looked up at him. 'John?' she said quietly.

'Yes, boss?'

'My office.'

Lauderdale's name was still on the door; they wouldn't

43

bother with a new plaque, not yet. But Rebus noticed she'd already changed a few things.

'Don't bother sitting,' she said. Rebus brought out a packet of cigarettes. 'Come on, you know the rules: no smoking.'

He put the cigarette in his mouth. 'I'll just suck on it then,' he said.

She closed the door, then went to Lauderdale's desk, resting against it, folding her arms.

'John, there's a lot of history here.' Rebus looked around the office. 'You know what I mean. I hear you and Dr Aitken have split up.'

Rebus took the cigarette out of his mouth. 'So?'

'So you're on the rebound, and I don't want you thinking *I* could be your springboard. Don't go thinking you can jump me a few times before you dive back in the pool.'

Rebus smiled. 'Did I catch you rehearsing in the canteen?'

'All I mean is, let's leave the past well alone, let's keep things professional.'

'Fine.' He put the cigarette back in his mouth.

She went behind the desk and sat down. 'So, what can you tell me about these two imbeciles who shut the Forth Bridge?'

'Hoaxers, maybe with debts or a habit to finance. Desperadoes. No sign that they ever knew the girl. Howdenhall checked the car; there are none of her prints inside.'

'So why were you so interested in the toxicology results?'

'Was I?'

'Someone came looking for you in the canteen to tell you they'd arrived.'

Rebus smiled again. 'I just wonder if maybe they were working for someone else.'

'Do you have a name?'

'Paul Duggan. He loaned the desperadoes his car. Plus they were sub-letting his council house.'

'That's illegal.'

'Yes, it is. We might want to ask him a few follow-up questions.'

She thought this over, then nodded. 'What else are you working on?'

He shrugged. 'Not a lot, it's always quiet this time of year.'

'Let's hope it stays that way. I know your reputation, John. It was bad enough when I knew you, but the story goes that it's even worse these days. I don't want trouble.'

Rebus looked out of the window. It had started snowing. 'Weather like this,' he said, 'there's never much trouble in Edinburgh, trust me.'

7

Hugh McAnally was universally known as Wee Shug. He didn't know why people called Hugh always ended up nicknamed Shug. There were a lot of things he didn't know, and never would know. He wished he'd spent his time in jail bettering himself. He supposed he'd bettered himself in some ways: he could use machine tools, and knew how a sofa was put together. But he knew he wasn't educated, not like his cell-mate. His cell-mate had been really clever, a man of substance. Not like Shug at all; chalk and cheese, if you came down to it. But he'd taught Shug a lot. And he'd been a friend. Surrounded by people, a jail could still be a lonely place without a friend.

Then again, what difference would it have made if he'd been brainier? None at all really, not a jot.

But he was going to make a difference to his life this evening.

It was another grievous night, a wind that was like walking through razor-blades.

Councillor Tom Gillespie wasn't expecting many souls to make the trek to his surgery. He'd get a few complaints from the regulars about frozen and burst pipes, maybe a question about the cold weather allowance, and that would be about it. The constituents in his Warrender ward tended to be self-reliant – or easily cowed, depending on your point of view. Depending on your politics. He smiled

across the room towards the extravagance he called a secretary, then studied the art on the classroom walls.

He always held his surgery in this school, third Thursday of every month during term-time. Between consultations he would catch up on correspondence, dictating letters into a hand-held recorder. The Central Members' Services Division at the City Chambers typed the letters up. For general political matters, matters relating to his party, there was a separate admin assistant.

Which was why, as Gillespie's wife had pointed out on numerous occasions, a private secretary was such an extravagance. But as the councillor had argued (and he was *very* good at argument), if he was going to get ahead of the crowd he needed to be busier than the other councillors, and above all he needed to *seem* to be busier. Short term extravagance, long term gain. You always had to be thinking in the long term.

He used the same rationale when he resigned his job. As he explained to his wife Audrey, half the district councillors had other jobs beside the council, but this meant they could not concentrate all their energies on council or political business. He needed to seem so busy that he had no time for a day job. Council committee meetings took place during the day, and now he was free to attend them.

He had other arguments in his favour, too. By working on council business during the day, his evenings and weekends were relatively free. And besides (and here he would smile and squeeze Audrey's hand), it wasn't as if they needed the money. Which was just as well, since his district councillor's basic allowance was £4,700.

Finally, he would tell her, this was the most important time in local government for twenty years. In seven weeks' time there would be new elections and the change would begin, turning the City of Edinburgh into a single-tier

authority to be called the City of Edinburgh Council. How could he afford not to be at the centre of these changes?

Audrey, though, had won one condition: his secretary should be an older woman, plain and homely. Helena Profitt fitted that bill.

Thinking of it, he never really won an argument with Audrey, not outright. She just snarled and spat and started slamming doors. He didn't mind. He needed her money. Her money bought him time. If only it could save him the purgatory of these Thursday nights in the near-deserted school.

His secretary brought her knitting with her, and he could measure how quiet things had been by how much she got done in the hour. He watched her needles work, then went back to the letter he was writing. It wasn't an easy letter to write; he'd been trying for over a week now. It wasn't the sort of thing he could trust to dictation, and so far all he'd managed were his address at the top and the date beneath.

The school was quiet, the corridors well lit, the radiators burning away. The caretaker was busy somewhere, as were four cleaners. When the cleaners and the councillor had gone home, the caretaker would lock up for the night. One of the cleaners was a lot younger than the others, and had a tidy body on her. He wondered if she lived in his ward. He looked at the clock on the wall again. Twenty minutes to go.

He heard something slam, and looked over to the classroom door. A short man was standing there, looking deathly cold in a thin bomber-style jacket and shabby trousers. He had his hands deep in his jacket pockets and didn't look inclined to remove them.

'You the councillor?' the man asked.

Councillor Gillespie stood up and smiled. Then the man turned to Helena Profitt. 'So who are you?'

'My ward secretary,' Tom Gillespie explained. Helena

Profitt and the man seemed to be studying one another.
'Can I help you?'

'Aye, you can,' the man said. Then he unzipped his
jacket and drew out a sawn-off shotgun.

'You,' he said to Miss Profitt, 'get the fuck out.' He
pointed the weapon at the councillor. 'You stay.'

Helena Profitt ran screaming from the classroom and nearly
knocked over the cleaners. A pail of dirty water clattered to
the wooden floor.

'I've just polished thon!'

'A gun, he's got a gun!'

The cleaners stared at her. A sound like a tyre exploding
came from the classroom. Miss Profitt, who had fallen to
her knees, was joined by the other women.

'What in Christ was that?'

'She said a gun.'

And now there was a figure in the doorway. It was the
councillor, almost in control of his legs. He looked for all
the world like one of the paintings on the classroom wall,
only it wasn't paint that spattered his face and his hair.

Rebus stood in the classroom and looked at the paintings.
Some of them were pretty good. The colours weren't
always right, but the shapes were identifiable. Blue house,
yellow sun, brown horse in a green field, and a red sky
speckled with grey ...

Oh.

The room had been cordoned off by the simple act of
placing two chairs in the doorway. The body was still there,
spreadeagled on the floor in front of the teacher's desk. Dr
Curt was examining it.

'This seems to be your week for messy ones,' he told
Rebus.

It was messy all right. There wasn't much left of the

49

head except for the lower jaw and chin. Stick a shotgun in your gub and heave-ho with both barrels and you couldn't expect to win Mr Glamorous Suicide. You wouldn't even make the last sixteen.

Rebus stood beside the teacher's desk. There was a pad of lined paper on it. Scribbled on the top sheet was the message, 'Mr Hamilton – allotment allocation', alongside an address and telephone number. Blood had soaked through the paper. Rebus peeled off this first sheet. The sheet below was obviously the start of a letter. Gillespie had got as far as the word 'Dear'.

'Well,' Curt got to his feet, 'he's dead, and if you were to ask for my considered opinion, I'd say he used that.' He nodded towards the shotgun, which lay a couple of feet from the body. 'And now he's gone to the other place.'

'It's just a shot away,' said Rebus.

Curt looked at him. 'Is the photographer on his way?'

'Trouble getting his car to start.'

'Well, tell him I want plenty of head shots – pun unavoidable. I gather we've a witness?'

'Councillor Gillespie.'

'I don't know him.'

'He's councillor for my ward.'

Dr Curt was pulling on thin latex gloves. It was time to search the body. Initially, they were looking for ID. 'Cosy as this room is,' Dr Curt said, 'I'd prefer my own hearth.'

In the back pocket of the deceased's trousers, Rebus found an official-looking envelope, folded in two.

'Mr H McAnally,' he read. 'An address in Tollcross.'

'Not five minutes away.'

Rebus eased the letter out of the envelope and read it. 'It's from the Prison Service,' he told Dr Curt. 'Details of assistance open to Mr H McAnally on his release from Saughton Jail.'

* * *

50

Tom Gillespie had a wash in the school toilets. His hair was damp and lay in clumps against his skull. He kept rubbing a hand over his face and then checking the palm for blood. His eyes were red-rimmed from crying.

Rebus sat across from him in the headteacher's office. The office had been locked, but Rebus had commandeered it when the head arrived at the school. The cleaning ladies were being given mugs of tea in the staffroom. Siobhan Clarke was there with them, doing her best to calm down Miss Profitt.

'Did you know the man at all, Mr Gillespie?'

'Never seen him in my life.'

'You're sure of that?'

'Positive.'

Rebus reached into his pocket, then stopped. 'Do you mind if I smoke?' From the odour of stale tobacco in the room, he already knew the head wouldn't mind.

Gillespie shook his head. 'In fact,' he said, 'give me one while you're at it.' Gillespie lit the cigarette and inhaled deeply. 'Gave up three years ago.'

Rebus didn't say anything. He was studying the man. He'd seen his photo before, in election rubbish pushed through the letterbox. Gillespie was in his mid-forties. He wore red-rimmed glasses normally, but had left them on the desk. His hair was very thin and wispy on top, but curled thickly either side of his pate. His eyes had thick dark lashes, not just from the crying, and his chin was weak. Rebus couldn't have called him handsome. There was a simple gold band on his wedding finger.

'How long have you been a councillor, Mr Gillespie?'

'Six years, coming up for seven.'

'I live in your ward.'

Gillespie studied him. 'Have we met before?'

Rebus shook his head. 'So this man walks into the classroom ...?'

51

'Yes.'

'Looking for you in particular?'

'He asked if I was the councillor. Then he asked who Helena was.'

'Helena being Miss Profitt?'

Gillespie nodded. 'He told her to get out ... Then he turned the shotgun around and stuck the end of it in his mouth.' He shivered, ash falling from his cigarette. 'I'll never forget that, never.'

'Did he say anything else?' Gillespie shook his head. 'He didn't say *any*thing?'

'Not a word.'

'Do you have any idea why he did it?'

Gillespie looked at Rebus. 'That's your department, not mine.'

Rebus held the stare until Gillespie broke it by looking for somewhere to stub out the cigarette.

There's something in you, Rebus thought, something below the surface that's a lot cooler, a lot more deliberate.

'Just a few more questions, Mr Gillespie. How are your surgeries publicised?'

'There's a district council leaflet, most homes had one delivered. Plus I put up notices in doctors' surgeries, that sort of place.'

'They're no secret then?'

'What good would a councillor be if he kept his surgeries secret?'

'Mr McAnally lived at an address in Tollcross.'

'Who?'

'The man who killed himself.'

'Tollcross? That's not in my ward.'

'No,' Rebus said, getting to his feet. 'I didn't think it was.'

DC Siobhan Clarke sat in on the interview with Helena

Profitt. Miss Profitt was still bawling, her few utterances barely decipherable. She was older than the councillor, maybe by as much as ten years. She clutched a large shopping-bag on her lap as if it was a lifebuoy keeping her afloat. Maybe it was. She was short, with fair hair which had been permed a while back, most of it lost now. A pair of knitting needles protruded from her bag.

'And then,' she wailed, 'he told me to get out.'

'His exact words?' Rebus asked.

She sniffed, calming a little. 'He swore. He told me to get the f-u-c-k out.'

'Did he say anything else?'

She shook her head.

'And you left the room?'

'I wasn't about to stay!'

'Of course not. What did you think he was going to do?'

She had not yet asked herself this. 'Well,' she said at last, 'I don't know what I thought. Maybe he was going to hold Tom hostage, or shoot him, something like that.'

'But why?'

Her voice rose. 'I don't know. Who knows why these days?' She collapsed into hysterical sobs again.

'Just a couple more questions, Miss Profitt.' She wasn't listening. Rebus looked to Siobhan Clarke, who shrugged. She was suggesting they leave it till morning. But Rebus knew better than that; he knew the tricks the memory could play if you left things too long.

'Just a couple more questions,' he persisted quietly.

She sniffed, blew her nose, wiped her eyes. Then she took a deep breath and nodded.

'Thank you, Miss Profitt. How long was there between you running out of the classroom and hearing the shots?'

'The classroom's at the end of the corridor,' she said. 'I pushed open the doors and bumped into the cleaning

ladies. I fell to my knees and that's when I heard ... that's when ...'

'So we're talking about a matter of seconds?'

'Just a few seconds, yes.'

'And you didn't hear any conversation as you left the room?'

'Just the bang, that's all.'

Rebus rubbed the bridge of his nose. 'Thank you, Miss Profit, we'll get a car to take you home.'

Dr Curt was finished in the classroom. The Scene of Crime Unit had taken over, and the photographer, who had finally arrived, was changing film.

'We need to secure the locus,' Rebus told the head-teacher. 'Can this room be locked?'

'Yes, there are keys in my desk. What about opening the school?'

'I wouldn't if I were you. We'll be in and out tomorrow ... the door might be left open ...'

'Say no more.'

'And you'll want to get the decorators in.'

'Right.'

Rebus turned to Dr Curt. 'Can we move him to the mortuary?'

Dr Curt nodded. 'I'll take a look at him in the morning. Has someone gone to that address?'

'I'll go myself. Like you say, it's only five minutes away.' Rebus looked to Siobhan Clarke. 'See that the Procurator-fiscal gets that Preliminary Notification.'

Curt looked back into the room. 'He'd only just been released from prison, maybe he was depressed.'

'That might explain a suicide, but not one like this: the amount of forethought, the setting ...'

'Our American cousins have a phrase for it,' Curt said.

54

'What's that?' Rebus asked, feeling he was walking into another of the doctor's punchlines.

'In your face,' Dr Curt obliged.

8

Rebus walked to Tollcross.

He had a taste in his lungs and a scent in his nostrils, and he hoped the cold might deaden them. He could walk into a pub and deaden them that way, but he didn't. He remembered a winter years back, much colder than this. Minus twenty, Siberian weather. The pipes on the outside of the tenement had frozen solid, so that nobody's waste water could run away. The smell had been bad, but you could always open a window. Death wasn't like that; it didn't go away just because you opened a window, or took a walk.

There was ice underfoot, and he skited a couple of times. Another good reason for not having a drink: he needed his wits about him. He'd copied McAnally's address into his notebook. He knew the block anyway; it was a couple of streets up from the burnt-out shell of the Crazy Hose Saloon. There was an intercom at the main door. He flipped on his lighter and saw that MCANALLY was the third name up. His toes were going numb as he pressed the button. He'd been rehearsing what to say. No policeman liked to give bad news, certainly not news as bad as this. 'Your husband's lost the heid' just didn't fit the bill.

The intercom clattered to life. 'Don't tell me you've lost the keys, Shug? If you've been drinking and lost them, you can freeze your arse off, see if I care!'

'Mrs McAnally?'

'Who's that?'

56

'Detective Inspector Rebus. Can I come up?'

'Name of God, what's he done?'

'Can I come up, Mrs McAnally?'

'You better had.' The intercom buzzed, and Rebus pushed open the door.

The McAnallys lived one floor up: for once Rebus had been hoping for the top storey. He climbed slowly, trying to prepare his speech. She was waiting at the door for him. It was a nice new-looking door, dark-stained wood with a fan-shaped glass motif. New brass knocker and letterbox too.

'Mrs McAnally?'

'Come in.' She led him down a short hall into the living room. It was a tiny flat, but nicely furnished and carpeted. There was a kitchenette off the living room, both rooms adding up to about twenty feet by twelve. Estate agents would call it 'cosy' and 'compact'. All three bars of the electric fire were on, and the room was stifling. Mrs McAnally had been watching television, a can of Sweetheart stout balanced on one wide arm of her chair, ashtray and cigarettes on the other.

She looked feisty; no other words would do. Cons' wives often got that look. The prison visits hardened their jawlines and turned their eyes into distrustful slits. Her hair was dyed blonde, and though she was spending the night in, she'd still polished her nails and stuck on some eyeliner and mascara.

'What's he done?' she said again. 'Sit down if you like.'

'I'll stand, thanks. The thing is, Mrs McAnally ...' Rebus paused. That's what you did: you lowered your voice respectfully, said a few introductory words, and then you paused, hoping the widow or widower or mother or father or son or daughter would twig.

'The thing is what?' she snapped.

'Well, I'm sorry to have to tell you ...'

57

Her eyes were on the television. It was a film, some noisy Hollywood adventure.

'Could we maybe have the sound down?' he suggested.

She shrugged and pressed the remote. The 'mute' sign came up on the screen. Rebus suddenly noticed how big the TV was; it filled a whole corner of the room. Don't make me say the words, he thought. Then he saw that her eyes were glinting. Tears, he thought. She's holding them back.

'You know, don't you?' he said quietly.

'Know what?' she snapped.

'Mrs McAnally, we think your husband may be dead.' She threw the remote across the room and got to her feet. 'A man committed suicide,' Rebus continued. 'He had a letter in his pocket addressed to your husband.'

She glared at him. 'What does that mean? It means nothing. Might have dropped it, somebody might've picked it up.'

'The deceased ... the man, he was wearing a black nylon bomber jacket and some light-coloured trousers, a green jersey ...'

She turned away from him. 'Where? Where was this?'

'Warrender Park.'

'Well then,' she said defiantly, 'Wee Shug went down Lothian Road, his usual haunts.'

'What time were you expecting him home?'

'Pubs are still open, if that answers your question.'

'Look, Mrs McAnally, I know this isn't easy, but I'd like you to come down to the mortuary and look at some clothing. Would that be all right?'

She had her arms folded and was rocking on the balls of her feet. 'No, it wouldn't be all right. What's the point? It's not Wee Shug. He's only been out a week, one miserable week. He can't be dead.' She paused. 'Was it a car run him over?'

'We think he took his own life.'

'Are you mad? Took his own ...? Get out of my house! Go on, out with you!'

'Mrs McAnally, we need to –'

But now she was swiping at him, catching him with her solid fists, propelling him before her, out of the room and down the hall.

'Keep away from him, do you hear? Keep away from both of us. This is nothing but harassment.'

'I know you're upset, Mrs McAnally, but an identification would clear things up, put your mind at rest.'

Her blows lost some of their power, then stopped altogether. Rebus's burnt palm stung where she'd caught it.

'I'm sorry,' she said, breathing hard.

'It's only natural, you're upset. Do you have a neighbour, a friend, someone who could be with you?'

'There's Maisie next door.'

'Fine. What if I get a car to pick you up? Maybe Maisie can go with you?'

'I'll ask her.' She opened the door and stepped out on to the landing, shuffling along to a door marked FINCH.

'I'll use your phone if that's all right,' Rebus called, retreating back into the flat.

He took a quick look around. Just the one bedroom and bathroom, plus a box room. He'd seen the rest of the place already. Again, the bedroom was very nicely furnished, pink ruched curtains and matching bedspread, a small dressing-table covered in bottles of perfume. He went into the hall and made a couple of calls: one to order a car, the other to make sure someone from CID would be at the mortuary to help with the ID.

The door opened and two women came in. He'd been expecting Mrs Finch to be around Mrs McAnally's age, but she was in her early twenties, leggy with a short, tight skirt. She looked at him as if he might be some warped practical joker. He offered a smile in return which mixed compassion

with interest. She didn't smile back, so he had to content himself with the sight of her long legs as she helped Mrs McAnally down the hall and into the living room.

'A wee Bacardi, Tresa,' Maisie Finch was saying, 'it'll calm your nerves. Before we do anything else, we'll have a wee Bacardi and Coke. Have you any valium about the place? If you haven't, I think I've some in my bathroom cabinet.'

'He can't be dead, Maisie,' Tresa McAnally wailed.

'Let's not talk about him,' Maisie Finch replied.

Strange advice, Rebus thought, making ready to leave.

9

It wasn't much of a walk from Tollcross down to C Division HQ on Torphichen Place, but Rebus knew he was getting further and further away from his own flat. He didn't intend walking back, and hoped Torphichen would have a spare car he could use as a taxi.

There was a tall bald man in a thick shabby coat in reception. The man had his arms folded and was staring at his feet. There was no one behind the desk, so Rebus pressed the buzzer. He knew it would keep buzzing till someone arrived.

'Been here long?' he asked.

The man looked up and smiled. 'Evening, Mr Rebus.'

'Hello, Anthony.' Rebus knew the man. He was one of Edinburgh's homeless, one of the army who sold copies of *The Big Issue* every twenty yards or so along Princes Street. Rebus usually bought a copy from Anthony, whose sacred pitch was outside the St James Centre. 'Here to help us with our enquiries?'

Anthony gave a gap-toothed grin. 'Just keeping warm. I told the desk officer I was waiting for DC Reynolds, only I saw Mr Reynolds go into the Hopscotch Bar on Dalry Road.'

'Which means he's on for a sesh.'

'And I can sit here till somebody tumbles.'

A uniform was emerging into the reception booth. Rebus showed ID and the uniform came and unlocked the door for him.

'You know the way, sir?'

'I know the way. Who's on duty?'

'It's a bit of a graveyard up there.'

Rebus climbed the stairs anyway. Torphichen was an old station, and small, with plain stone walls and a slightly depressing air. Rebus liked it. Certainly he preferred it to the much newer and supposedly ergonomic St Leonard's, his home base. He looked into the CID room. The very man he wanted was sitting at a long, scarred wooden table, reading the evening paper.

'Mr Davidson,' Rebus said.

Davidson looked up, then groaned.

'I want a favour,' Rebus said, walking into the room.

'Now there's a surprise.'

'Have you heard about Warrender?'

'Shotgun suicide?' News got around. Davidson closed his paper.

'The man with the plan was called Hugh McAnally, lived in Tollcross.'

'I know Wee Shug. Wee Bastard's more like it. He'd only just come out of Saughton.'

'Maybe he was pining.'

'Want a drink?'

'Coffee maybe.'

But Davidson was reaching for his coat. 'I said a *drink*.'

'So long as you're not suggesting the Hopscotch. Rat-Arse Reynolds is in there.'

Davidson knotted his tartan scarf. 'All right, let's scotch the Hopscotch. And since you're buying, you get to choose.'

Rebus chose a big public house near Haymarket Station. The public bar was seething, but the saloon was quiet. They ordered doubles.

'Too cold outside to be drinking lager,' Davidson said. 'Your health.'

'And yours.' Rebus sipped and swallowed, feeling the liquid doing its immediate, no-nonsense business. It was almost too good sometimes. 'So,' he said, 'tell me about Wee Shug.'

'Ach, he was a small-timer, used to specialise in hopeless house-breakings.'

'Used to?'

'He moved on to reset, counterfeiting, this and that.'

'So how long had he been inside?'

'This stretch, you mean? Funny that, when I heard he was out I did a quick calculation. He's out early, served a bit under four years.'

'Well, if all we had him on was reset ...'

Davidson was shaking his head. 'Sorry, you misunderstand. My fault. He wasn't sent down for any of his usual tricks.'

'What then?'

'Rape of a minor.'

'What?'

Davidson nodded. 'Thing is, we nailed him for it, but with hand on heart I don't know if it was a clean result.'

'Explain.' Rebus signalled for two more whiskies.

'Well, the lassie was fifteen, but everyone said the same thing – fifteen going on thirty-five. Not a shy lass at all, you should read the interview transcripts. But she was adamant he'd raped her. She was a minor, and the Procurator-fiscal went ahead with the prosecution. I wasn't too bothered; getting Wee Shug off the street was fine by me.'

'Was he living in Tollcross at that time?'

'That's always been his patch.'

Rebus paid for the second round of drinks. 'Was he the violent type?'

'Not that I ever saw. I mean, he had a temper when

63

roused, but who doesn't? That was the thing about the rape, there were no physical injuries.'

'What about corroboration?'

'We had a bundle of circumstantial evidence. Neighbours heard raised voices, a scream, the girl herself was in a terrible state, crying and all. Plus Wee Shug admitted having sex with her, said he knew it was illegal and all but, as he put it, "only by a few months". The girl said it wasn't consensual, and we just about put together a case.'

'Say, for the sake of argument, that it *was* consensual.'

'Yes?'

'Then he's just come out of a four-year stretch for something he didn't do.'

Davidson shrugged. 'You're looking for a motive behind the suicide?'

Rebus was thoughtful for a moment. 'Suicides interest me right now.'

'And we're always looking for motives, eh, John?'

Rebus drank his drink. 'What about guns? Did he ever have anything to do with firearms?'

'Nothing. But he's probably still got cronies out there who know where to get them.'

'It was a sawn-off.'

'I can believe it. You couldn't get a full-length shotgun in your mouth and be able to pull the trigger. Far easier with something shorter.'

'Messy though.'

'No doubt, but it would do the job. You don't want to go off half-cocked, do you? With a sawn-off, there's less margin for error.'

'No margin at all,' said Rebus.

It was only when they were leaving that he thought to ask a question.

'McAnally's victim, what was her name again?'

64

Davidson had to think about it. 'Mary something. Mary Finlay. 'No ...' He screwed shut his eyes. 'Mary Finch.'

Rebus stared at him. 'Maisie Finch?'

Davidson thought again. 'That's it, Maisie.'

'She lives next door to the McAnallys.'

'Did then, too. She'd known them for years.'

'Christ,' Rebus said quietly. 'I've just sent her down to the mortuary to help Tresa McAnally identify her husband.'

'What?'

'Do me a favour, will you? Lend me a car and a driver.'

'I'll do better than that, I'll drive you myself.'

But by the time they reached the mortuary, it was too late. The ID had been completed and everyone had gone home. Rebus stood on the Cowgate and looked longingly back towards the Grassmarket. Some of the pubs there would still be open, the Merchant's Bar for one. But he got back into the car instead and asked Davidson to take him home. He felt tired all of a sudden. God, he felt tired.

10

'He what?' Rebus said.

He was on the phone from St Leonard's to Dr Curt at the university's Pathology Department. They kept Curt and his colleagues busy, no mistake about that. On top of police work, Curt had a full teaching load in the Faculty of Medicine, and did crossover lectures to law students too.

But then Curt had an advantage over mere mortals: he never slept. You could call him out at any hour, and he was always alert. You could catch him in his office at eight in the morning.

It was actually eight-fifteen, and Rebus was nursing a large black decaf coffee from the early-opening deli on the Pleasance.

'Morning deafness, John?' Dr Curt said. 'I repeat, he was dying anyway.'

'Dying how?'

'Great big bloody tumours. Pancreas and large colon to start with. The man must have been in agony. I'm willing to bet the toxicology tests show the presence of powerful painkillers.'

'You mean he was out of his box?'

'He'd have to be to stand the pain.'

Rebus frowned. 'I don't get it.'

'Haven't you heard of voluntary euthanasia, self-inflicted in this case?'

'Yes, but with a sawn-off shotgun?'

'Well, that's not my department. I can give you effect, not cause.'

Rebus terminated the call and went to see his chief inspector.

Gill Templer had made more changes to Lauderdale's office. She'd brought in a few framed photographs of nieces and nephews, and a thriving yucca plant had appeared. There were also a couple of cards wishing her well in her new job.

'I hear you were at that suicide last night,' she said, motioning for him to sit.

He nodded distractedly. 'There's something not right about it.'

'Oh?'

So he set out what he knew. Gill Templer listened with her chin resting on both hands, a gesture he knew of old. He recognised the perfume she was wearing, too.

'Hmm,' she said when he'd finished, 'a lot of questions. But are they any of our concern?'

He shrugged. 'To be honest, I'm not sure. Give me a day or two, I might have an answer.'

'Those two lads on the bridge,' she said. 'Another suicide, another connection with the district council.'

'I know. It could just be coincidence.'

'I don't see how it could be anything else. OK, take a day or two, see what you come up with. But report back to me regularly – at least a couple of times a day.'

Rebus stood up. 'That's good,' he said. 'You're already managing to sound like a chief inspector.'

'John,' she said warningly, 'remember what I said.'

'Yes, ma'am. Will there be anything else?'

Gill Templer shook her head. She was already getting down to some paperwork.

Rebus left her office – it was hers now, no doubt about it – and walked straight into Siobhan Clarke.

'Any news on Paul Duggan?'

'He's coming in for a chat this afternoon.'

'Good,' said Rebus. 'Need me along?'

She shook her head. 'Brian and me have perfected our Jekyll and Hyde routine.'

'Which one of you plays Hyde?'

She ignored this. 'So what are you up to today?'

It was a good question. Rebus formed his answer. 'Chasing ghosts,' he said, making for his desk.

He phoned Tresa McAnally. She'd identified her husband's clothes, and had been able to identify his body, albeit with the face discreetly covered. Now all that was left for her were the funeral arrangements.

'Sorry to bother you again,' Rebus said, after introducing himself.

'What do you want?'

'Just wondered how you were coping.'

'Oh aye?' He should've known she wouldn't fall for that sort of patter.

'You knew your husband was ill, Mrs McAnally?'

'He told me he was.'

'Seriously ill though?'

'He never really said.'

'Well, what did he tell you was wrong with him?'

'Where do you want me to start? High blood pressure, kidney stones, ulcers, a heart murmur, emphysema ... see, Wee Shug was a bit of a hypochondriac.'

'But he *was* ill; he was on medication.'

'You know what doctors are like, they'll hand you a placebo and kiss you goodbye. I've read the stories, I know what goes on.' She paused. 'If you don't mind me asking, what's the point asking about his health now?'

'Well, I've reason to believe your husband was seriously ill. Terminally ill, Mrs McAnally.'

'I should've guessed,' she said finally, her tone chastened. 'He was different when he came out this time, quieter like. Was it the big C?'

'Yes.'

'Used to smoke rollies. I always told him, that's the way my own mother went.' Another pause as she dragged on her filter-tip. 'Is that why he did himself in?'

'What do you think?'

'Makes sense, eh? Poor wee bugger.'

Rebus cleared his throat. 'Mrs McAnally, have you any idea where he could have got the gun?'

'Not a clue.'

'Are you sure?'

'What's the difference where he got it? He only hurt himself.'

Thinking back to Councillor Gillespie and Miss Profitt, Rebus wondered about that. It seemed to him that Wee Shug McAnally had managed to hurt a lot of people … which brought him to thoughts of Maisie Finch.

'The funeral's next Tuesday, Inspector. You'd be welcome at the house.'

'Thanks, Mrs McAnally. I'll do my best.'

The sun was out, bathing the tired buildings in dazzling light. Edinburgh's architecture was best suited to winter, to sharp, cold light. You got the feeling of being a long way north of anywhere, some place reserved for only the hardiest and most foolhardy.

Rebus was glad to be out of the office. He knew he worked best on the street. Besides, the office was a battleground. He knew Flower would already be plotting against Gill Templer, marshalling his forces, waiting for her defences to slip. But she was tough – the way she was handling Rebus was proof of that. He knew she would keep him at arm's length and beyond. She was right, he did have

a bad reputation. She wouldn't want any of his failures to rub off on her. So what if they'd known one another, had been an item? She was right – it was a long time ago. Now they were colleagues; more than that, she was his acting superior. He hadn't known many women make chief inspector. Good luck to her.

He drove past the Infirmary, chiding himself for not stopping to visit Lauderdale, and headed for Tollcross. He didn't want Tresa McAnally this time though.

He wanted her neighbour.

He pressed the buzzer marked FINCH and waited, shuffling his feet. His tooth was acting up. He'd made the mistake of opening his mouth to take a deep breath, and the frozen air had made straight for the nerve. He pressed the buzzer again, hoping he wouldn't have to visit a dentist.

The intercom came to life.

'Who is it?' The voice was neutral.

'Miss Finch? My name's Inspector Rebus, we sort of met last night.'

'What do you want?'

'Can I come up?'

The door buzzed and Rebus pushed it open. At the top of the stairs, he all but tiptoed past Tresa McAnally's door. Maisie Finch's door was ajar. He closed it after him.

'Miss Finch?'

She emerged suddenly from the bathroom, wearing a short towelling-robe and brushing her hair. He could smell soap and feel the warmth from her body.

'I was in the bath,' she said.

'Sorry to trouble you.'

He followed her into the living room. It wasn't what he'd expected. Half the space was taken up with what looked like a hospital bed, with cast-iron frame, roller wheels, and a side-guard. Next to it was a liver-coloured commode. The

mantelpiece was like a chemist's display, two dozen assorted boxes and bottles standing in a row.

Maisie Finch was moving magazines from the sofa. She motioned for him to sit, and took the commode for herself, tucking one leg under the other.

'What's the problem, Inspector?'

Her face was too angular to be good-looking, and she had slightly protruberant eyes, yet she was undeniably ... the word that came to his mind was *charged*. He shifted on the sofa.

'Well, Miss Finch ...'

'I suppose it's about Tresa?'

'In a way, yes.' He looked at the bed again.

'It's my mum's,' she explained. 'She's house-bound, I have to look after her.' Rebus made show of looking around for the missing parent, and Maisie Finch laughed. 'She's in hospital.'

'I'm sorry.'

'Don't be. They take her every few months, just for a few days. It's to give me a break. This,' she said, opening her arms wide, 'is my winter holiday.'

Her movements had loosened her robe. She didn't seem to notice, and Rebus tried not to look. Men, he thought, are daft bastards.

'Want something to drink?' she asked. 'Or is it too early for you?'

'One person's early is someone else's late.'

She went into the kitchenette. Rebus walked over to the mantelpiece and examined the array of prescription drugs. He found a bottle of paracetamol and shook two into his hand.

'Heavy night?' she said, coming back with two bottles.

'Toothache,' he explained. He took the narrow bottle. It was chilled.

'San Miguel,' she told him. 'Spanish lager. Know what I

do?' She sat down again, legs apart, resting her elbows on her knees. 'I stick the heater on as high as it'll go, shut my eyes and imagine I'm in Spain, poolside at some posh hotel.' She closed her eyes to prove the point, and angled her head towards an imaginary Mediterranean sun.

Rebus washed the pills down with lager. 'I'm sorry to hear about your mum though,' he said.

She opened her eyes, not pleased to have her reverie broken. 'Everyone tells me what a saint I am.' She mimicked a much older woman: '"There's no' many like you, hen." Too right, there's not many as *daft* as me. You know how some people say life's passing them by? Well, in this case it's a fact. I sit on the commode between her bed and the window, and just stare out at the street for hours on end, listening to her breathing, waiting for it to stop.' She looked over at him. 'Have I shocked you?'

He shook his head. His own mother had been bed-ridden; he knew the feeling. But he hadn't come here for any of this.

'Sitting by the window all day,' he said, 'you must have seen Mr McAnally coming and going?'

'Yes, I saw him.'

'You don't like him, do you?'

'No, I don't.' She stood up abruptly.

'Mrs McAnally's all right though?'

She was moving towards the kitchenette, but stopped and turned on him. 'I'm not the saint; that woman's the saint! She's suffered, you wouldn't believe how she's suffered.'

'I think I would.'

She wasn't listening. 'Married to an animal like that.' She looked at him. 'You know what he did to me?' Rebus nodded, and she took a step back, recovering. 'You do?' she asked quietly. 'Is that why you're here?'

72

'I'm here because I'm curious, Miss Finch. I mean, you still live next door, you're friends with his wife.'

'What? You think mum and me were going to move out ... because of *him*?'

'Something like that.'

'She's been offered sheltered accommodation, but in Granton. We've always lived in Tollcross. We always will.'

'This last week, it must have been awkward.'

'I kept out of his way. You can bet he kept out of *mine*.' She was by the window now, staring down on to the street, her back resting against the wall. It was as if she didn't want to be seen. 'He deserved what he got.'

Rebus frowned. 'You mean, what he did to himself?'

She looked at him, blinked. 'That's what I said.' Then she smiled and put the bottle to her lips.

11

The Ballistics facility at Howdenhall Forensic Science Lab wasn't Rebus's idea of a good time. There were too many guns around for his liking. He read the report and looked up at the white-coated scientist who'd prepared it. The other thing Rebus didn't like about Howdenhall, all the forensic boffins looked about nineteen years old. They'd been in their smart new building a year, and still looked pleased with themselves. The new facility had been financed by selling property, including police homes. Rebus didn't want to know how many homes the lab had cost.

'Not much, is there?' he said.

The white coat, who liked to be called Dave, laughed. 'You CID,' he said, plunging his hands into his pockets, 'you always want more. Who fired it? Where did he get it?'

'We know who fired it, smart-arse. But your second question's a good one. Where *did* he get it?'

'I'm Ballistics, not Intelligence. It's a common enough make of shotgun, the identifiers have been filed off. We've tried the usual processes, and there's no chance of recovering them. The cartridges were common stock, too.'

'What about the barrel?'

'What about it?'

'When was it filed off?'

Dave nodded. 'The edge the file left is still shiny; say in the last couple of months.'

'Have you checked the register?'

'Of course.' Dave led Rebus to a computer terminal and

74

punched a couple of keys. 'There are over seventy thousand shotgun certificates on issue.'

Rebus blinked. 'Seventy *thousand*?'

'Compared to thirty-odd thousand for all other firearms combined. Nobody's really concerned about the amount of shotguns around.' He tapped another key. 'See? Ownership's highest in rural areas – Northern, Grampian, Dumfries and Galloway. It's not some brewhead from Gorgie that's buying these things, it's the establishment: farmers, landowners.'

'What about thefts?'

'They're on the computer, but I've checked. Nobody around Edinburgh has lost a shotgun recently.'

'Can I take a look anyway?'

'Sure.' Rebus sat down and Dave punched the keyboard again. The list of recently reported thefts was not large; nearly all of them were south of the border. 'Want a print-out?'

'Yes.' Not that a print-out would help him.

'What's the big deal anyway?' Dave asked. 'It's a simple suicide, isn't it?'

'Suicide's still an offence.'

'The only one we don't prosecute after the fact. Is there something you're not telling me?'

'No,' Rebus said quietly. 'But there may be things some people aren't telling *me*.' He took the print-out and folded it into his pocket. 'One other thing.'

'What?'

'The prints on the gun, were they the deceased's?'

Dave seemed amused by the question. 'His and his alone. What are you up to, Inspector?'

But John Rebus wasn't about to answer that.

'Thank you for coming in, Councillor.'

Rebus had just come into the interview room. He'd been

biding his time outside the door, letting Tom Gillespie get a bit nervous. An interview room could do that; it could destroy all your pre-planning. You walked in knowing what you were going to say, the line you were going to take with the police, but then the room started to work on you.

The thing was, it was just a room – crime prevention posters on the walls, a table, three chairs, four electrical sockets. There was a tin ashtray, commandeered from a local pub. The walls were creamy matt custard, institution yellow, and there was strip lighting on the ceiling. The lights burred continuously, an almost subliminal electric hum. Rebus wondered if it was that noise that got to people. He guessed there was a simpler truth: the interview room was in a police station, and if you were there, you were going to be interviewed by the police.

And when it came down to it, everyone had something to hide.

'Not at all,' Gillespie said, crossing one leg over the other to let Rebus know how relaxed he was. 'I hear the poor devil was an ex-prisoner.'

'He'd served just under four years for the rape of a minor.'

'Four years doesn't seem very long.'

'No, it doesn't.' They sat in silence for a moment, until Gillespie broke it.

'I had a friend once who committed suicide. He was still at university – this is going back a while. He was worried about exams, and his girlfriend had left him.' He paused. 'Left him for me. I should add.'

'Do you mind if I smoke?' Rebus asked.

'I thought smoking was forbidden in police stations.'

'If it bothers you, I won't light it.' He stuck the cigarette in the corner of his mouth and offered one to Gillespie. The councillor shook his head.

'I'd prefer it if you didn't light up.'

'Fair enough,' said Rebus, putting away cigarettes and lighter both. Well, he thought, this is interesting. The guy's been studying for *this* exam. Tells a personal story, one that doesn't paint him in the rosiest glow, and then asserts his authority. And all it was supposed to be was a few follow-up questions.

'How did he do it?' Rebus asked.

'Who?'

'Your friend.'

'Flung himself out of the halls of residence. Fifth floor. He was still alive, so they took him to hospital, checking for broken bones and internal bleeding. They were so busy, they didn't notice he'd taken an overdose before the jump.'

'Well,' Rebus said, 'both are fairly common roads out, aren't they? You leap or you sleep. Mr McAnally, on the other hand ...'

'You were at the Forth Road Bridge, weren't you? When those two kids jumped? I saw your name in the paper.'

'We're here to talk about McAnally, Councillor.'

'Well, guns are a popular mode of suicide too, aren't they?'

'Maybe among gun owners, but McAnally didn't own a gun and probably had never used one before.'

Gillespie uncrossed his legs and crossed them the other way. 'But given his background, he'd find it easy enough to take possession of a gun.'

'I agree,' said Rebus. 'All the same ...'

'What?'

'Why go to all the bother? I mean, even if you're determined to blow your head off, why walk from Tollcross to Warrender in the middle of a blizzard with this big heavy gun clutched beneath your jacket? And why walk into a school which would have been locked tight on every night of the month except one?' Rebus had risen to his feet. He rested his buttocks against the edge of the table and folded

his arms. 'Why walk into a classroom and make sure Councillor Tom Gillespie is present? Why do that? Why did he specifically want to top himself in front of *you*? No other witnesses, no one else invited. It doesn't make sense to me.'

'Well, the man was obviously unhinged ... maybe on drugs.'

'I've just seen the toxicology results. The police lab has all these smart machines –'

'At Howdenhall?' Rebus nodded. 'Yes, I know. I was there for the official opening.'

'Well, the results show that the deceased had had a couple of drinks, but no drugs, not one single painkiller.'

'What's your point, Inspector?'

Rebus turned around so that his hands were resting on the table. He was leaning over Gillespie, and Gillespie wasn't enjoying it.

'See, Councillor, Wee Shug McAnally was dying. He didn't have long to live at all. His insides were rotten, and he should have been doped to the eyeballs to stand the pain. Those drugs, though, they make your brain mushy, and Wee Shug didn't want that. He wanted to be *compos mentis* when he pulled the trigger.' Rebus stood up straight. 'Makes even less sense now, eh?' He popped the cigarette back into his mouth.

'Look, I don't see what any of this has to do with me.'

'Frankly neither do I. All I know is, it has *some*thing to do with you. Now what could that be?'

'There was a line of perspiration on Gillespie's top lip. He took off his glasses and pinched the bridge of his nose. Rebus walked to the far wall and lit his cigarette. He didn't think the councillor would object.

'Look,' Gillespie said quietly, 'I really don't see any connection between this man McAnally and me, none at all. I've never met him, never heard of him, and he didn't live

in my ward.' He shrugged. 'Maybe he held some sort of mad grudge, something linked to his time in prison.'

Rebus walked slowly back to the table and sat down opposite Gillespie. 'That's it?' he said. 'That's your explanation?'

'I don't *have* an explanation! I just ... give me a cigarette, please.'

Rebus lit the cigarette for him.

Gillespie studied the burning tip, then looked at Rebus. 'Why are you doing this?'

'I've already told you, Councillor, I've to prepare a report on a sudden, violent death, and there are inconsistencies.'

'You mean you don't know why he did it?'

'That's what I mean.'

'Well, I can't help you, I'm afraid.' Gillespie got to his feet, making ready to leave.

'Can't or won't?'

Gillespie glared at Rebus, then sat down again. 'What does that mean?'

'It means I think you're hiding something.'

'Such as?'

'That's what I have to find out ... before I can finish my report.'

'Are all policeman like you?'

'No. Some of them you wouldn't want to meet.'

'I meet quite a few actually. A colleague of mine – regional councillor rather than district, but the same party – is chair of Lothian and Borders Joint Police Board.' Gillespie drew on his cigarette and blew the smoke out in a thin stream. 'He's quite a good friend.'

'It's always nice to have friends.' Rebus said.

Gillespie got to his feet again. 'Look,' he began. He swung his arms, as if he was deciding to say something he'd rather not say. 'I promised ...' He sighed and sat down yet

again. 'This may mean something or nothing, Inspector.' Rebus busied himself tidying the end of his cigarette against the ashtray. 'It's Helena, Helena Profitt.'

'Your ward secretary?'

'She ... she told me she knew him.'

'McAnally?'

Gillespie nodded. 'When McAnally came into the room and saw her ... there was a moment when he just stared. I asked her about it afterwards, and she told me she'd known him a long time ago. She wouldn't say any more than that.'

12

'What's wrong with your mouth?'

'Huh.'

'You keep poking it with your finger.'

'Nothing's wrong with it.' But Rebus knew something was wrong; he was just hoping it would go away. There was pressure inside his gum and top lip, a dull, unpleasant sensation that was now spreading either side of his nose. It felt as if his whole face should be swollen, but it was just a little red beneath the nose – and that could have been the drink or the weather.

'Whose idea was this?' he said, folding his arms around himself. They were walking on Portobello beach, the only souls mad enough in this seizure-inducing wind.

'Mine,' said Mairie Henderson.

Rebus had turned up at her flat expecting a hot drink and a soft couch, but instead she'd dragged him out for what she euphemistically called her 'constitutional'.

'You'd have to have the constitution of an ox to survive this,' Rebus muttered to himself. The blasts of air against his ears meant he could barely hear what Mairie was saying, and every time he opened his mouth to yell something back, the malevolent air flooded in and attacked his tooth again. Mairie ran to a wall and hunkered down with her back against it. Her cheeks looked as if they'd been sand-blasted; which in a sense they had.

Rebus crouched beside her, thankful for the shelter. He liked to take an interest in Mairie, especially now she was a

freelance journalist. He worried about that lack of salary, but she seemed to be doing all right.

'So,' he asked, 'what exactly did you come up with?'

She smiled. 'You forget, I used to cover local government, regional *and* district councils. It was my first job on the paper. I didn't have to do much digging.' She leaned forward and drew a circle in the sand. 'Where do you want me to start?'

'Give me some background.'

'District council, not regional?'

'That's right.'

'Well, about the only glamorous angle attached to district councildom is the fact of a big budget, which means only the four major cities are worth the candle.'

'From a journalist's perspective?'

'It's the only perspective I can give.' She pushed the hair out of her eyes. 'Therefore, being a district councillor is not an attractive proposition. You've got long, boring working hours, requiring you to take time off from your daytime job, plus eating into your evening hours, since a lot of the meetings are evening affairs, as are surgeries if they're not on a Saturday.'

'OK, so I won't be standing for councillor, unless the money compensates.'

Mairie shook her head. 'It's not great for such a thankless task. Of course, you can claim expenses, plus if you chair a committee there's a bonus, but even so ... For all these reasons and others, you find that councillors tend to fall into one of several groups: retired, unemployed, self-employed, or with an affluent spouse.'

'The first two because they've got lots of time, the last two because they can make time?'

She nodded. 'Result? A lot of councils are not what you'd call dynamic. Edinburgh's more interesting than most.'

'So tell me about Edinburgh.' Rebus stared out towards Inchkeith Island.

'Well, we've sixty-two wards, Labour holding most of them.'

'No surprise.'

'But there isn't much of a gap between Labour and the Tories, only about seven seats. The Lib-Dems have a few, and the SNP a couple. As to what the council does, if you'd ever had to sit in on their meetings and then write them up as even vaguely interesting prose, you'd know.'

'Boring?'

'Most councillors could bore for Britain at the World *Ennui* Cup.'

'So that's how you pronounce that word.' This got him a smile. She didn't smile much these days, not since she'd led Rebus to a horror above the Crazy Hose Saloon. Rebus looked out to sea. It seemed all whitecaps as far as the horizon.

'There are all sorts of committees and sub-committees,' she went on, 'and the full district council meets once a month. But despite all that, what the council basically does is house people. Glasgow District Council is the biggest landlord in Britain – one hundred and seventy thousand houses. It's rumoured the district councils were only given the housing portfolio after local government reorganisation so they'd have something to do.'

'You've lost me.'

'The Tories wanted to keep housing out of regional council control.' She sighed at his puzzled look. 'It's all to do with politics and it's all intensely dull.'

'And the councillors are dull too?'

'Almost of necessity. Maybe "worthy" would be a better word.' She looked at him. 'We're focusing in nicely on Councillor Tom Gillespie. He chairs an industrial planning committee, looking at economic and property development.

83

The council has its own department – Economic Development and Estates – and mostly the committee would be checking to ensure that the department is working hard and not trying to fix anything.'

'Fix? You don't mean as in repair?'

'I don't. Land deals and building contracts can be worth millions. Even repairs to buildings can be worth hundreds of thousands. Suppose I handed you the contract to clean the windows of every council building in the city?'

'I'd have to buy a new chamois.'

'You could afford it. The only thing about Gillespie is that he's ambitious, but that's nothing new. Twenty years ago, just before the corporation became the district council, Malcolm Rifkind, George Foulkes, and Robin Cook were all councillors. That's another thing: the district council is about to disappear with effect from April 1996. There are elections coming up so we can install a sort of shadow authority, if anyone bothers to vote.'

'Any news of crooked deals, bent councillors?'

'Nothing. Tom Gillespie is a diligent, hard-working councillor with no bad press, no apparent skeletons in his closet, not even any rumours. He's not a tippler, not a gambler, and he doesn't cheat on his wife with the secretary –'

'What makes you say that?'

She shrugged. 'It's just one of those things people sometimes do.' She touched the back of his hand. 'Do you know something I don't?'

Rebus stood up. 'That'd be the day. Which is he, by the way: self-employed? Unemployed?'

'Wealthy spouse. His wife runs her own business.'

Rebus looked around. 'Is there a café open somewhere?'

'We could try the Fun Park.' She wiped her hands clean of sand. 'Am I in for an exclusive?'

Rebus rubbed his shoe over the circle she'd made in the sand, obliterating it.

'Well?' she persisted.

'Are you still singing in that country and western band?'

'Now there's a subtle change of subject. You were about to answer my question.'

'What question?'

'About the exclusive.'

'No I wasn't.' They came off the beach on to the promenade. 'Can you check a couple of other things for me?'

'What?'

'A company name: LABarum.' He spelt it for her. 'That's all I've got on it. Plus another name. Dalgety.'

'A company?'

'I don't know. I've checked, and there are companies called Dalgety, plus it's a place name *and* a surname.'

'So what do you want me to do?'

He shrugged. 'If you find out anything about LABarum, maybe Dalgety will tie into it.'

'I'll see what I can do. Oh, I forgot to say, I'm talking to your daughter later on.'

Rebus stopped. 'You *forgot* to say?'

'OK, I wasn't going to tell you. I'm interviewing her on the McAnally suicide.' Rebus started walking again, Mairie hurrying to catch him up. 'Any comment you'd like to make at this point, Inspector, strictly *on* the record?'

'No comment, Miss Henderson,' Rebus growled.

He'd decided the interview room might prove just *too* much for Helena Proffit, so made an appointment to see her at her work. She worked part-time in an office, on top of her post as Gillespie's ward secretary. But someone from her office phoned to say Miss Proffit had been taken ill with a migraine and had gone home. He tried her home

number, but got no answer. It could wait. Meantime he made another appointment, this time with the Governor of HM Prison Edinburgh. He told the governor's secretary that it concerned the suicide of an ex-inmate. The secretary booked him in for Tuesday afternoon.

'Sooner would be better,' he told her.

'Sooner isn't possible,' she replied.

That night, after the usual session with Doc and Salty, he drove out to the Forth Road Bridge, parked, and walked on to the bridge itself. For once there was no howling gale, hardly even a breeze. There was no moon, and the temperature was still a degree or two above freezing. The bridge had been reopened, some temporary repairs completed. Initial structural surveys had shown no real damage to the fabric, though if the car had snapped one of the thick metal support cables, it would have been different.

He stood there shivering after the warmth of the pub and his car. He was a few yards from where the boys had jumped. The area was cordoned off with metal barriers, anchored by sandbags. Two yellow metal lamps marked off the danger area. Someone had climbed over the barriers and laid a small wreath next to the broken rail, weighing it down with a rock so it wouldn't be blown away. He looked up at the nearer of the two vast supports, red lights blinking at its summit as a warning to aircraft. He didn't really feel very much, except a bit lonely and sorry for himself. The Forth was down there, as judgmental as Pilate. It was funny the things that could kill you: water, a ship's hull, steel pellets from a plastic case. It was funny that some people actually *chose* to die.

'I could never do it,' Rebus said out loud. 'I couldn't kill myself.'

Which didn't mean he hadn't thought of it. It was funny the things you thought about some nights. It was all so funny, he felt a lump forming in his throat. It's only the

drink, he thought. It's the drink makes me maudlin. It's only the drink.

13

Sometimes people who knew next to nothing about them called Edinburgh's drop-in centres drop-*out* centres. Rebus knew that the police weren't the most welcome guests, so he phoned ahead first.

He knew the person who ran the centre behind Waverley Station. Rebus had done him a favour once, bringing back a heroin addict who'd suffered sudden cold turkey on Nicolson Street. Some officers would have lifted the hapless wretch and taken him to the station for a knee in the groin and a long sweat. But Rebus had taken him where he wanted to go: the drop-in centre at Waverley. Turned out he was undergoing withdrawal, doing it all on his own.

'How is he?' Rebus asked Fraser Leitch, the centre's manager and guiding light.

Leitch was sitting in his mouldering office, surrounded by the usual mounds of paperwork. The shelves behind his desk were bowed under the weight of files, document boxes, magazines and books. Fraser Leitch scratched his grey-flecked beard.

'He was doing all right, last I heard. Retrained as a chippie and actually found a job. See, Inspector, sometimes the system works.'

'Or he's the exception that proves the rule.'

'The eternal pessimist.' Leitch got up and crouched in front of a tray on the floor. He checked there was water in the kettle and switched it on. 'I'll make a bet with you. I'll

bet you're here to talk about Willie Coyle and Dixie Taylor.'

'I'd have to be daft to cover a bet like that.'

Leitch smiled. 'You know Dixie was a user?' Rebus nodded. 'Well, as far as I know, with Willie's help he'd been clean for a couple of months.'

'His works were still under his bed.'

Leitch shrugged as he tipped coffee into two mugs. 'The temptation's always there. I'll make another bet with you, I'll bet you've never tried heroin yourself.'

'You'd be right.'

'Me neither, but the way I've heard it described ... Well, like I say, the temptation never goes away. You have to take it one day at a time.'

Rebus knew Fraser Leitch used to have a drink problem. What the man was saying was that once you had it, you had it for life, because even if you dried out, the cause of your problem was still there, never quite beyond reach.

'There's a joke I've heard,' Leitch said, as the kettle started to boil. 'Well, it's not much of a joke. Here it is: what kind of boat should Dixie have landed on?'

'I give up.'

'A sampan, because they're both close to junk. Like I say, bad joke.' He poured water and milk into the mugs, stirred them, and handed one to Rebus. 'Sorry, we don't stretch to pure Colombian.'

'Is that another joke?'

Leitch sat down again. 'I knew Dixie,' he said. 'I only met Willie a couple of times.'

'Willie wasn't a user?'

'He probably toked up, maybe dropped some E.'

'Pretty clean-living then? Were you surprised when you learned what they'd done?'

'Surprised? I don't know. How's your coffee?'

'Terrible.'

'Terrible or not, it's still twenty pence.' Leitch pointed to a box on the desk. Rebus found a one-pound coin and dropped it in.

'Keep the change.'

'Giving a quid qualifies you as a patron.' Leitch stuck his feet up on the edge of the desk, knees bent. He was wearing moccasins, their stitched seams coming undone. The bottoms of his denims were frayed too. He usually described himself as 'just another old hippy'.

'How's the centre doing?' Rebus asked.

'We're hanging on by the skin of our teeth.'

'You get district council funding?'

'Some.' Leitch frowned. 'Why do you ask?'

'What happens when the district council is replaced?'

'We pray the new authority keeps up our funding.'

Rebus nodded thoughtfully. 'I was asking if you were surprised about Willie and Dixie.'

Leitch thought for a moment. 'No,' he said, 'I don't suppose I was, except that it was a dafter stunt than I would have expected from them.'

'Because Willie was smarter than that?'

'He must have known they'd never get away with it. Dixie was a different proposition, crazy at times, a real heid-the-ba', but Willie could keep him under control.'

'Like Keitel and DeNiro in *Mean Streets*.'

'That's not a bad comparison. Dixie would do something daft, and Willie would slap him about the head. Dixie wouldn't have taken it from anyone else. You realise a lot of what I'm telling you is second-hand? Like I said, I only met Willie a couple of times.' He paused. 'You were there, weren't you?'

'I was there,' Rebus said quietly. He shifted in his chair. 'They just ... Willie put his arm around Dixie and then leaned back over the rail, and Dixie went with him. There

was no resistance. They didn't jump, they just slipped away.'

'Christ.' Leitch took his feet off the desk.

'Why would they do that?'

Leitch got up and walked around the desk. 'I think you know the answer to that, or at least you have an inkling. They couldn't go to jail.'

'I know,' Rebus said. Two people die rather than go to jail; another dies rather than be out. Rebus touched his mouth with a finger, feeling the pain, the pressure, almost enjoying it.

Leitch landed a hand on his shoulder. 'Have you seen a counsellor?'

'What?'

'Don't the police have counselling?'

'Why would I want counselling?'

Leitch squeezed Rebus's shoulder and withdrew his hand. 'It's up to you,' he said, going back to his chair. They sat in silence for a while.

'Ever come across a guy called Paul Duggan?' Rebus asked at last.

'Name rings a bell. I can't put a face to it. Maybe I've just heard him mentioned around the centre.'

'He loaned Willie and Dixie his car. He was their landlord.'

'Oh, right, yes. A couple of guys who sometimes come in are tenants of his.'

'Any idea where they live?'

'Abbey Hill, somewhere round there.'

'What about the name Dalgety – does it mean anything to you?' Leitch thought about it and shook his head. Rebus dug into his pocket and brought out the photo of Kirstie Kennedy. 'I know it's a long shot,' he said, 'but have you seen her around the centre?'

'This is the Lord Provost's daughter. A couple of

uniforms came asking about her just after she went missing.'

'The photo's a bit out of date, she'd look different now.'

'Then bring me a more recent photo. Don't tell me an out-of-date picture's the best her parents can do?'

Rebus thought about that as he left Fraser Leitch's office. The man had a point. Then again, how many photos did Rebus have of his own daughter? Precious few after age twelve. He was standing in the short dark hallway, half its walls taken up with noticeboards, the other half with marker-pen graffiti. Rebus studied the notices. One card was recent, its edges not yet dog-eared. It was printed, unlike its ballpoint neighbours. Altogether a very superior card.

ROOMS TO LET CHEAP.

There was a phone number and a name. The name was Paul. Rebus removed the card and put it in his pocket next to Kirstie Kennedy's photo.

He glanced into the two open rooms. In one, a couple of rows of plastic chairs were positioned in front of a TV. The TV was a twelve-inch black and white. One lad was in there, holding the indoor aerial above his head as he stared at the screen from a distance of about thirty inches. Another kid sat on one of the chairs, sleeping. In the other room, three more teenagers, two boys and a girl, were trying to play table tennis with one cracked ball, two rubberless bats, and a paperback book. Their net was a row of upended cigarette packets. They played quietly, without enthusiasm or hope.

On the steps outside, two more clients of the centre tried to bum first money and then cigarettes off him. He handed out a couple of ciggies, and even lit them.

'Shame about Dixie, eh?' he said.

'Fuck off, porker,' they said, moving back indoors.

* * *

Back at his flat, Rebus finally bled the central heating system, catching the water in empty coffee jars. One thing about the flat when he moved back in: plenty of empty coffee jars. He'd meant to ask the students why there were cupboards and boxes full of them.

He refilled the system, wondering what the pressure gauges on the front of the boiler should read. When he turned the system back on, there was a gushing, gurgling sound from the pipes, and the boiler shuddered as the gas jets burst into life.

He went through to the living room and stood with his hand on the radiator. It got warm, but stayed only warm, even with the thermostat all the way up. And there was a drip from the bleedcock. He twisted the key as hard as he could, but the drip remained. He tied a kitchen-cloth to it and let the cloth run down into one of the coffee jars. That would collect the drips, and stop them making a noise.

Yes, John Rebus had been here before.

He sat in his chair, lights out, and looked out of his window on to Arden Street, thinking of Maisie Finch, thinking of her mother and his own mother. There was frost on the roofs and bonnets of the parked cars. A group of students were laughing their way back to their digs. Rebus poured himself a whisky and told the students how lucky they were. Everybody out there was lucky. All the people sleeping rough, and bumming cigarettes, and plotting and scheming how to get ahead. Alister Flower, twisting and gnawing in his sleep; Gill Templer, still and unperturbed in hers; Frank Lauderdale, with an itch beneath his cast; Tresa McAnally, feet up in front of the TV; Kirstie Kennedy ... wherever she was. They were all of them lucky.

Edinburgh was a lucky fucking town.

Two

SHREDS

14

The following Tuesday, Rebus was at work uncharacteristically early.

But not so early as to be the first to arrive. Gill Templer was already there, her door ajar, fighting her way through paperwork. Rebus knocked and pushed the door open a little further.

'You're early,' she said, rubbing her eyes.

'What about you? Have you been here all night?'

'It feels like it. That coffee smells good.'

'Want me to fetch you one?'

'No, just give me half of yours.' She handed him a clean mug, and he poured half the contents of his beaker into it. Standing over the wastebasket, he was able to see what she'd been working on. She was trying to acquaint herself with every ongoing case, everything Frank Lauderdale had left behind.

'Tall order,' he said.

'You can help.'

'How's that, boss?'

'You're slow to type up your notes. The McBrane case and the Pettiford especially. I'd like to see them this morning.'

'Do you know how fast I type?'

'Just do it.'

'Would you settle for one out of two? I've a funeral on.'

'I want them both by lunchtime, Inspector.'

Rebus looked back at the open door. There was still no

one else around. 'You know,' he said quietly, 'I'm going to start taking this personally.'

She looked up from her work. 'What's that?'

'The way you've been treating me ever since you got here. Frankly, it stinks. At first I thought it was just for show, but I'm not so sure. I know you've got something to prove to everybody, but that doesn't –'

'Tread carefully, Inspector.'

Rebus stared at her. Finally she looked down at the work in front of her. 'Thanks for the coffee,' she said quietly. 'I still want those case-notes by lunchtime.'

So he went to his desk and worked on them. He didn't like typing up case-notes, the hard slog of always using the right words, of getting everything right. No police officer liked it when a report which had been painstakingly prepared was sent back by the Procurator-fiscal because of some tiny flaw in the surface of the whole. You were waiting for news that the precognition was being prepared, and instead the case came back to you with a note – 'unable to proceed as stands'.

The reporting officer – whose job was to liaise with the Crown – took most of the flak, and Rebus was RO on both the McBrane and Pettiford cases. It was his job to make a case that the Procurator-fiscal would accept. He supposed it was Gill Templer's job to make sure he did the work, but her attitude still rankled. As far as he could gather, she'd been a far from popular choice as Frank Lauderdale's replacement. If Lauderdale hadn't been universally respected, at least he'd been a *man*; and more than that, he'd been 'one of them'. Gill Templer had been brought in from Fife. And she was a woman. And she didn't even play golf.

The female officers seemed happy enough – the ill-feeling was among the males only. Siobhan Clarke, Rebus had noticed, had a new spring in her step, working under a

woman. Maybe she saw in Gill Templer a future that could be hers. But Gill would have to step carefully. Traps would be laid for her. She'd have to be careful who she trusted. Rebus had so far given her the benefit of the doubt, reckoning she was being hard on him because she couldn't afford to be soft.

So far it looked like a one-way street.

He took his finished notes to her office, only to discover she was in conference with Farmer Watson. He left them prominently on her desk instead, and went to the wash-room to change his tie, removing the blue one and replacing it with black. Brian Holmes came in as Rebus was checking himself in the mirror.

'Off to a party then?'

'In a manner of speaking, Brian. In a manner of speaking.'

Certainly, there was enough booze in the kitchenette to start a fair old hootenanny, but this was a wake rather than a celebration.

By the time Rebus got to Tresa McAnally's flat, the place was bursting at the seams with middle-aged men and women and their disgruntled offspring, plus a few older souls who had the honour of being given chairs to sit on. And in the middle of the living room, dressed top to toe in black but with red gloss fingernails, sat the widow. The curtains were closed, as were those of the neighbouring flats – a sign of solidarity. The Scots always rallied round for a send-off.

Rebus squeezed his way through the whispering throng, and held out his hand. 'Mrs McAnally,' he said.

She took his hand and exerted the minimum of pressure. 'Good of you to come.'

Then he was off again, backpedalling before she could turn to someone and say, 'This is the policeman who went

to the school, he saw Wee Shug flat out on the floor and missing half his head.' Normally at these occasions the men retreated to the kitchen and got stuck into the whisky. But here there was only the kitchenette, separated from the living area by nothing more than a breakfast-bar. So the men had crammed themselves into the kitchenette, for all the world like a rush-hour busful. They passed around clean glasses, and then the whisky. Tumblers of sweet and dry sherry were passed out to the ladies. Soft drinks for the younger mourners, though you didn't have to be *too* old to qualify for a nip of the harder stuff.

Rebus took a glassful and toasted the small man next to him. The man was in his seventies, and wore a wartime charcoal-and-chalkline suit. He had a pinched face and kept moving his lips, pursing and puckering them. When he spoke, it was in an undertone.

'Here's to you then, son.'

'*Slàinte.*' They drank for a moment, savouring the cheap whisky. Savouring was better than having to talk, one reason why so much whisky was consumed at funerals.

'The hearse gets here in ten minutes,' the man informed Rebus.

'Right.' A closed casket of course; Tresa McAnally had been denied a final peek at her husband's blasted remains.

'Here's the minister.'

There was nothing wrong with the old guy's eyesight, despite the thick smeary lenses in his glasses. Rebus watched the minister as he moved through the room towards Tresa McAnally. He wore black, with the white dog-collar, and as he moved the crush of mourners parted before him. Ministers didn't make friends, not easily; they were like cops that way. People were always afraid they'd say the wrong thing in front of them. They had a skill though, these men of the cloth: they could conduct a

100

conversation while remaining inaudible to all but the person they addressed.

The old man was unscrewing another whisky bottle, different brand. 'She's made the flat nice, hasn't she? I haven't been here for a couple of years.'

Rebus nodded, noticing that the huge TV set had been moved out to make more space. He guessed it was in the bedroom. He scanned the male mourners again, looking for old lags, known faces, looking for someone who could have procured a shotgun for Wee Shug.

'Oh aye,' the old man went on, 'it's lovely now. New carpets and wallpaper, really nice.'

And new TV, Rebus thought. New front door, and bedroom fittings that didn't exactly look superannuated. Money: where the hell had the money come from?

'New carpet in the hall, too,' the man was saying. He lowered his voice still further. 'I suppose she did it for Wee Shug. You know, to make his coming home a bit more welcome. I mean, after a jail cell you want something nice.'

Rebus looked at the man more closely. 'Served time yourself?'

'A long time ago, son. Back in the fifties. Saughton was a different place then, everything was different. And mind, I'm not saying it was worse.' Their drinks replenished, he screwed the top back on and passed the bottle to the next man along. Rebus wondered how many more old lags there were in the crush around him. Then he saw someone else coming into the room, and he stopped with his glass half an inch from his mouth.

She was dressed in black, a small woman with a pillbox hat and a short veil which covered her eyes but not her mouth. And behind her, much taller, a younger woman wearing a simple navy suit, low-cut and tight at the hips. It looked the sort of thing you would wear a blouse under, but

Maisie Finch wasn't wearing a blouse, or anything else beneath it that Rebus could see.

For now though, he was more interested in the woman with her. It was Helena Profitt. Rebus turned towards the draining-board, where a rubicund man, hot and jacketless and sporting bright red braces, was dispensing the drinks.

'Give us a couple of sherries,' Rebus murmured in the man's direction. The order was passed along and a few moments later Rebus had his sherries. He left his own whisky on the breakfast-bar and carried them into the living room.

Helena Profitt was having a muted conversation with Tresa McAnally, so Rebus tapped Maisie Finch on the shoulder. When she turned towards him, he handed her the glasses.

'Thanks.' She sniffed the contents before handing one glass on to Helena Profitt.

'Funny,' Rebus said, 'you never mentioned knowing Miss Profitt.'

She smiled, then took a sip of sherry and screwed up her face.

'Too sweet?'

'It's loupin'. Is there anything else?'

'Whisky, dark rum, soft drinks. Maybe some vodka.'

'A voddy would slip down.' She surveyed the scrum in the kitchenette and changed her mind, draining the glass.

'So,' Rebus said in an undertone, 'how *do* you know Helena Profitt?'

'Same way most folk in this room do.' She smiled again and turned to the widow. 'Tresa, hen, mind if I smoke?' The packet was already out of her pocket.

'Go ahead, Maisie.' A pause. 'It's what Wee Shug would have wanted. He liked a ciggie himself.'

Taking their signal from this, a lot of hands reached into

pockets and handbags. Packs were opened, handed round. Rebus took one from Maisie, and she lit it for him.

'Nice lighter,' he said.

'It was a present.' She looked at the slim onyx and gold lighter before returning it to her pocket.

'So,' Rebus said, 'Miss Profitt used to live in the tenement?'

'Floor below this.'

As more people arrived and had to offer their condolences, or else needed to say goodbye before leaving, Rebus and Maisie found themselves moved away from the widow and Miss Profitt. They ended up by the mantelpiece. Rebus picked up a bereavement card. It was signed simply, 'From all Shug's pals in Saughton. We shall remember him.'

'Touching,' Maisie Finch said.

'Either that or a bit sick.'

'How's that, Inspector?' He noted she said 'Inspector' quite loudly. The nearest mourners looked him up and down, and he knew word would now go around.

'Depends why he killed himself,' he said. 'Maybe it had something to do with Saughton.'

'Tresa tells me he had the big C.'

'That's only one possible reason.' He found her eyes. 'I can think of others.'

She looked away, almost casual. 'Such as?'

'Guilt, shame, embarrassment.'

She smiled sourly. 'Not in Shug McAnally's vocabulary.'

'Self-pity?'

'That'd be more like it.'

Rebus saw a pillbox hat and veil moving towards the door. 'I'll be back,' he said.

Helena Profitt was at the front door when he caught her.

'Miss Profitt?' She turned to him. 'I think we'd better talk.'

He led her into the McAnallys' bedroom.

103

'Can't it wait?' she asked, looking around her, not liking the surroundings.

Rebus shook his head. The TV was in here sure enough, giving them a narrow aisle to move about in. 'You've been avoiding me,' he said.

She sighed. 'Tom told me he'd told you.'

'You recognised Mr McAnally that night?'

'Of course I did.'

'Did he recognise you?'

She nodded. 'I'm certain he did.'

'Did he know beforehand that you were close to the councillor?'

Now she stared at him through her veil. 'What do you mean "close"? I'm his ward secretary, that's all.'

'That's all I meant.'

'How could he have known? No, I don't think he knew.' She suddenly saw what he was getting at. 'His suicide had nothing to do with *me*!'

'We have to check these things. Why didn't you say anything at the time?'

'I ...' She sat down on the edge of the bed, hands in her lap, then stood up again abruptly. Rebus watched the bedcover float, finding its level. It was a waterbed. Disconcerted, Helena Profitt patted her hat and tugged at her veil. It didn't make much of a hiding place.

'Is it to do with Maisie Finch?' Rebus asked.

She thought about it, then nodded solemnly before bursting into a fit of loud sobbing. Rebus touched her shoulder, but she spun away from him. A mourner opened the door and looked in. Rebus got the feeling there were others out there, all wanting to see the tears.

'She'll be all right,' he said, closing the door firmly. Helena Profitt had brought a hankie out of her sleeve and was blowing her nose. Rebus offered her his own handker-chief, and she used it to dab at her eyes. There was eye-

shadow on the white cotton when she handed it back. The door was pushed open again. The man with the red braces stood there.

'What's going on?'

'Nothing,' Rebus said.

The man glowered. 'We know who you are. Maybe you'd better leave.'

'What are you going to do – throw me out?'

The sweaty face creased in a sneer. 'You lot are all the same.'

'And so are you lot.' Rebus pushed the door hard until it closed. He turned back to Helena Profitt.

'What is it you're not saying?' he asked solicitously. 'It'll come out eventually, you know.'

'I moved out of this tenement four years ago,' she said. 'I've only been back a couple of times since. I should come more often. Maisie's mother misses my little visits ...'

Four years ago. 'After McAnally raped Maisie?' he guessed.

She breathed deeply a few times to calm herself. 'You know, we didn't do anything, none of us. We all heard a scream – I know *I* heard it – but nobody phoned for the police. Not until Maisie ran into Tresa's. It was Tresa herself who phoned, to say her own husband had just raped their next door neighbour's girl. We heard the scream, but we just went on minding our own business.' She wiped her nose again. 'Isn't that typical of this bloody city?'

Rebus remembered the words he'd used so recently: guilt, shame, embarrassment.

'You felt ashamed?' he offered.

'You bet I did. I couldn't stand to live here any longer.'

He nodded. 'Are you surprised Maisie stayed on, knowing McAnally would be back?'

She shook her head. 'Maisie's mum would never move.

Besides, Maisie and Tresa, they've always been close, especially so since the ...'

Rebus tried to imagine walking out of prison and into a situation like that. How much closer had Tresa and the younger woman grown in McAnally's absence?

'Tell me what happened that night.'

'What?' She tucked the hankie back into her sleeve.

'The night of the assault.'

'What's it to you?' Her cheeks were reddening with anger. 'It's none of your business. It's long past, long forgotten.'

'Forgotten, Miss Profitt?' Rebus shook his head. 'I don't think so, not by a long chalk.'

Then he turned from her and left the room.

He looked into the living room. Smoke hung in the air like winter fog. He saw Maisie, perched on the arm of the widow's fat armchair, one slim leg crossed over the other. She was holding Tresa McAnally's hand and giving it a pat, and Tresa, head bowed, was listening to whatever Maisie was telling her. Listening to it, and managing to smile. Rebus would have called Tresa McAnally 'feisty'; maybe even 'brassy'. But neither description fitted her just now. Maybe it was just the circumstances, the funeral, but he didn't think so.

'Car's here,' someone at the window said, meaning that the hearse was arriving. The minister got to his feet to say a few words, a tumbler of whisky in one hand, cheeks redder than they had been. Rebus pushed his way back into the hall, slipped out of the open door, and made his way down the tenement stairs. The man in the braces leaned over the guard-rail.

'I hope we meet again, pal, some place where there are no witnesses.'

The threat echoed down the stairwell. Rebus kept

walking. When he drove off, he left a space kerbside for the hearse.

15

Rebus wasn't the only one interested in Shug McAnally's suicide. He'd read the newspaper article, scanning it quickly first to see if he was mentioned. He wasn't, which was a relief. Mairie Henderson's was one of three names sharing the by-line. It was impossible to see where her contribution started and ended except, of course, that she'd interviewed Rebus's daughter Sammy; and though Sammy wasn't mentioned by name, the outfit she worked for was: Scottish Welfare for Ex-Prisoners, or SWEEP as it preferred to be known.

The police called it Sooty.

SWEEP, like the other care agencies mentioned in the piece, was concerned that Hugh McAnally's suicide only a week after his release from prison was evidence of a problem of readjustment and a lack of real concern 'within the system' – Sammy's words to be sure. Police, prison staff, and Social Services were marked out for criticism. The governor of HM Prison Edinburgh could do no more than explain to the journalists how inmates were prepared for release back into society. A 'spokesman for SWEEP' insisted that ex-prisoners – SWEEP never called them 'offenders' – suffered the same psychological problems as released kidnap victims or hostages. Rebus could hear the words in Sammy's mouth; he'd heard them from her before.

He'd been surprised to get a letter from his daughter a couple of months back, saying she'd got a job in Edinburgh

108

and was 'coming home'. He'd phoned her to check what this meant, and found it only meant she was returning to Edinburgh.

'Don't worry,' she told him, 'I don't expect you to put me up.'

The job she'd landed was with SWEEP. She'd been working for some time with inmates and ex-prisoners in London, ever since she'd visited a friend in jail and had seen the conditions and, as she put it, 'the loneliness'.

'This friend,' Rebus had unwisely said, 'what were they in for?'

After which their conversation had become stilted to say the least.

She didn't want to be met off the train, but he went to Waverley anyway. She didn't see him watching as she flung her army-style kitbag and scuffed red rucksack on to the platform. He wanted to walk forwards to greet her, maybe throw his arms around her, or more likely stand there in the hope that she'd throw her arms around *him*. But she hadn't wanted to be met, so he stood his ground, half hoping she'd see him anyway.

She didn't; she just looked around the concourse with a good deal of pleasure, swung the rucksack on to her back, and picked up her kitbag. She was thin, dressed in clingy black leggings, Doc Marten shoes, a baggy grey T-shirt and black waistcoat. Her hair was long these days, ponytailed with pieces of bright cotton threaded through it. She sported several earrings in either ear, and a nose-stud. She was twenty years old, a woman, and her own woman at that, striding with confidence from the platform. He followed her up the ramp out of the station. A bright winter day was waiting for her. He didn't suppose she'd worry about the cold.

Later, she'd come to Patience's flat for a meal. Rebus had suggested vegetarian to Patience, just to be on the safe side.

'I always cook vegetarian for the teens and twenties,' she'd replied.

'I might have guessed you would.'

After that visit, there had been others, Sammy and Patience growing closer as Patience and Rebus moved even further apart. Until one day Rebus had left, giving the students who rented his flat their marching orders and moving himself back in.

Two days later, his set of keys to Patience's flat had been handed over to Sammy, and she'd moved her stuff into the guest bedroom. Not a permanent arrangement, as both women said; just something they wanted to do for now.

Sammy was still there.

That first evening, the evening of the stuffed red peppers, Rebus and Sammy had argued about prison and ex-prisoners, right and wrong, society versus the individual. Sammy kept using the words 'the system'; Rebus niggled her by using the term 'con'. Although he agreed with at least some of her points – well thought out, persuasively argued – he found himself setting up in opposition to her. It was something he did, not just with her. Glancing across the table at Patience, he'd seen a weary smile. She'd told him before: he liked to antagonise just to get a response.

'Know why?' she'd said. 'Because conflict is more *fun* for you than consensus.'

'No it isn't,' he'd told her. 'I'm just the devil's advocate, that's all.'

So he'd ignored the weary smile and continued his joust with his daughter ...

He closed the paper, folded it, and tossed it into a wastepaper-bin. Gill Templer came into the office. He'd been waiting there for her for close to fifteen minutes. She didn't apologise.

'You forgot to tell me,' she said, 'that your daughter works for SWEEP.'

'It's not an issue.'

'You should have told me.'

He saw what she meant. 'You mean, before you gave an interview?'

'Some woman reporter, nice as ninepence until the end of the session, then: "and tell me, what is your feeling about one of your inspectors having a close relative so involved with SWEEP?"'

Mairie Henderson, thought Rebus. Probably not interested in the answer either, just trying to discomfit the interviewee, see if anything shook loose.

'What did you tell her?'

'I told her no comment. Then I went straight to Chief Superintendent Watson and asked him who the hell she'd meant.' She paused. 'It had to be you.'

'Is that my cue for a song?'

She slammed a hand down on her desk. 'It's your cue to get the hell out of my office!'

Rebus got the hell out.

Rebus's appointment with the governor of Saughton was in the late afternoon.

The guard-house phoned ahead, then let him through. He was met at the other side of the gate and taken to the governor's office. There was an ante-room where the secretary sat behind a computer. She was taking a phone call, but nodded for him to take a seat.

'You see,' she said into the receiver, 'control shift asterisk is supposed to clear that, but it's not doing it.' She listened, and tucked the receiver between cheek and shoulder so she could work on her keyboard with both hands. 'No, that's not working either. Hang on, that's got it. Thanks, bye.' She put the phone down and shook her

111

head in exasperation. 'Sometimes they're more trouble than they're worth,' she confided to Rebus. 'The governor will be back in a couple of minutes.'

'Thanks,' Rebus said. 'Typewriters are about as high-tech as I can manage.'

'They keep sending me on courses, but after half an hour I'm completely bamboozled.'

The door Rebus had come through opened suddenly, and the governor came in. Rebus stood up, they shook hands, and the governor led him into the inner sanctum.

'Sit down, Inspector.'

'I appreciate you seeing me, sir.'

The governor dismissed this with a wave of his hand. 'It's not often a suicide on the *outside* brings me into the equation, but I've had reporters hounding me on this one. McAnally's death seems to have stirred up a bit of debate. They must be hard up for news.' He sat back, resting his hands on his stomach. 'And now,' he said, 'I've got you.'

The governor was a handsome man in his late fifties. He peered at Rebus over metal-framed glasses. He was bulky rather than fat, and his silvering hair was thick and healthy. His suit looked expensive, his shirt laundered, and his unfussy blue tie had a sheen that Rebus took for silk. He saw himself as a 'man-manager', and was a public voice in the drive to reform Scotland's penal system: an end to slopping-out and cell-sharing; brighter, better equipped halls; a strong emphasis on vocational training, education and counselling. Not every sight-impaired Open University student knew that their braille text was probably transcribed by Saughton's Braille Unit.

It wasn't all sunny though: Saughton had its drug problems, its share of HIV-positive inmates. But at least it had a full-time medical staff to cope, or to begin to try to cope.

Rebus had never met the governor before, though he'd

seen him at functions, and come across him in the media. His name was Jim Flett or, more often, just 'Big Jim'.

'Well, you're right, sir,' Rebus said, 'I am here to talk to you about Hugh McAnally.'

'So I gather.' Flett tapped a manila file on his desk, the record of Prisoner 1117, C-Hall, HMP Edinburgh, McAnally, Hugh. Jim Flett opened the file. 'I've had a read of this, and I've been to talk to some of the warders and McAnally's fellow inmates.' He gave Rebus a grin. 'I *think* I'm prepared. By the way, something to drink?'

'I'm fine, thanks. This won't take long. Why was McAnally released so early?'

'Not *so* early. His good behaviour was taken into account, as was his illness.'

'You knew he was ill?'

'Inoperable cancer. Normally, the stage of sentence he was at, we'd be readying to transfer him to the TFF hostel.'

'What's that?'

'Training for Freedom. He'd have gone out unsupervised to a work placement. But Mr McAnally was a category C prisoner, and only category D's qualify for TFF. In any event, he was due parole.'

'What made him category C?'

Flett shrugged. 'A bust-up with a warder.'

'I thought you mentioned good behaviour?'

'The bust-up was a while back. The man was dying, inspector. We knew we weren't going to see him in here again.'

'Did he seem suicidal?'

'Not as far as I'm aware. I'm just glad he did away with himself on the *out*side: it makes him your problem rather than mine.'

'What about aggro? Was he subject to threats or violence?'

'How do you mean?'

'He was a convicted rapist, his victim legally a child at the time of the offence. I hear the stories, same as everyone else: if you're a sex offender and you're not put in a separate wing, you get beaten up, people pish in your tea, you're an outcast. Can't exactly be good for the spirit.'

'Spirit?' Flett gave a wry smile. 'Let's just say I'm not aware of any incidents of that nature. If any occurred, they'd be dealt with.'

'I don't suppose the victims lodge complaints that often.'

'You think you know so much about us, Inspector, maybe you should be sitting *this* side of the desk?'

'No, thanks.'

'Look, there's nothing in his time here that made anyone think he was about to stick a shotgun in his gub.'

Rebus thought for a moment. 'Did you know him?'

'No, I didn't. He'd only been here eleven months.'

'Where was he before?'

'Glenochil.'

'Any problems while he was there?'

'Not according to the files. Look, Inspector, I know what you're thinking, what you're trying to put together. But he didn't commit harry-carry because of anything that happened to him in here. His cellmate was as shocked as anyone when he heard what happened. McAnally had served two previous sentences; it's not as if incarceration was new or strange to him.'

Rebus thought again of Willie and Dixie, of what would have happened to them in prison.

'Surely,' Flett was saying, 'it's much more realistic to say that the illness wore him down and led him to kill himself.'

'With respect, sir, his previouses weren't for rape of a minor.'

Flett stared at Rebus, then glanced at his watch, letting him know the score.

'Just a couple of final questions, sir. How much money did he leave prison with?'

Flett had to check that in the file. 'There was eight pounds sixty among his effects when he came in.'

'And other than that?'

'Other than that, he was entitled to the same benefits as any other ex-prisoner. It seems an odd question to ask.'

'His flat shows signs of a recent overhaul; I'm wondering where the money came from.'

'Best ask his wife. Anything else?'

'Who was his contact on the outside?'

'You mean his supervising officer?' Flett looked this up too. 'Jennifer Benn at Social Services.' Rebus entered the name in his notebook. 'Well, if that's all, inspector ...?' The governor was on his feet. He walked around the desk and smiled towards Rebus, and Rebus suddenly knew the man was hiding something. He'd been edgy during the conversation, as though expecting some awkward question to arise. It hadn't, and his relief was evident in that smile, in his complete change of attitude.

Rebus tried to think what the question could be. Out in the secretary's office, while Big Jim was shaking his hand a final time, he was still thinking about it. I've let him off the hook, he thought. He reran the meeting in his head as he walked back to his car.

'Buggered if I know,' he announced to himself. But as he sat in the idling car, he knew he was going to have to find out.

That evening, he visited one of only two drop-in centres available to ex-cons in Edinburgh. It reminded him most of Fraser Leitch's establishment, except that here there was a colour TV rather than black and white.

Nobody could help him. Hugh McAnally hadn't been near the place, not as far as anyone knew. He wasn't about

to press the point or outstay his lukewarm welcome, but he took a quick look round before he left.

In a corner of the main room, a woman with a huge canvas bag slung over her shoulder was crouching down in conversation with a man who sat slumped in a chair. The man stared past her, not interested. Eventually the woman gave up, wrote something on a pad, closed it, and returned it to the canvas bag. The man leaned forward then and whispered something into her ear. She listened, her cheeks reddened, and she got to her feet, turning to walk away.

Rebus was right behind her. She brought herself up short to avoid a collision.

'You wouldn't be Jennifer Benn, would you?'

'That's me.'

'My lucky night.' Rebus looked past her, to where the seated man was rubbing his forehead, trying not to let Rebus see his face. 'Hiya, Pete.'

The man looked up and seemed to place Rebus. 'Evening, Mr Rebus.'

'How long have you been out?'

'Three weeks two days.'

'And you fancy another trip back already? Give the lady back her purse.'

The social worker stared in surprise as Pete slipped the bulging black leather purse out of his denim jacket. She snatched it back and checked the contents.

'Do you want to press charges?' Rebus asked. She shook her head. 'Fine, then let's have a little chat.'

By the time they reached the front door, Jennifer Benn had regained her composure.

'Where are we going?'

'Somewhere I'm a bit more welcome. There's a pub across the road.'

'I don't like pubs.'

'My car then?'

She turned to him. 'Can I see some ID?'

'I thought that scene back there would have been ID enough.' But she wasn't budging, so he dug out his warrant card, which she inspected slowly.

'All right,' she said, handing it back, 'we can talk here.'

'Here?' They were on the pavement. She wrapped a woollen scarf around her neck and pulled on sheepskin mitts. She was in her late-twenties and had frizzy blonde hair and outsized glasses. 'It's freezing here,' Rebus complained.

'Then best hurry up.'

He sighed. 'You were Shug McAnally's social worker?'

'That's right.'

'I'm investigating his suicide.'

She was shaking her head. 'I'm afraid I can't help. He never kept an appointment, we never met.'

'Did you report him?'

She nodded. 'But I didn't think anything would come of it. What punishment do you mete out to someone with terminal cancer?'

And with that she turned and walked quickly to her car. Rebus thought that she'd asked a very good question indeed.

16

Next morning, he found himself summoned to Chief Superintendent Watson's office.

Gill Templer was already there when he arrived. She was standing with her back to the filing cabinet, arms folded. There wasn't much room: three large cardboard boxes marked 'PanoTech' sat on the floor by the desk.

'My new computer,' the Farmer explained. 'Sit down, John.' The Farmer looked like a man with bad news: Rebus had been here before; same look, same tone of voice.

'I'd rather stand, sir.'

'Been up to anything we should know about, John?'

'No, sir.'

'Nothing at all?'

'Not that I know of, sir. Why?'

Watson glanced towards Gill Templer. 'I had a phone call yesterday evening from Allan Gunner.' Gunner: the deputy chief constable. 'He doesn't often call me at home.'

'Do I take it he had bad news?' Rebus decided to sit down after all.

'HM Inspectorate of Constabulary are thinking of investigating us.'

'Us?'

'B Division.'

'That's us all right.'

'It's no joking matter.'

Nor was it. HMIC was independent of the police service; it reported directly to the Secretary of State for Scotland.

HMIC's public remit encompassed examining police standards and indicating areas for improvement. It inspected all eight regional forces each year, but only four of these were full 'primary' inspections. They looked at rises in crime stats, falls in detection rates, and complaints from the public. No problem there: the recorded crime rate was steady when it wasn't falling, and recent clear-up rates were marginally improved. But HMIC could really screw up a station's working practices, just by being on the premises. There were long lists of questions to answer, an initial pre-inspection followed by the full inspection ... and, as everyone in the room knew, HMIC could sometimes stumble upon something better left unqueried. Or, as the Farmer put it,

'You know those buggers, John. If they want to find dirt on us, there's dirt to be found. We don't exactly work in an antiseptic environment.'

'That's because we don't deal with people who wash behind their ears every morning. What are you getting at, sir? So what if we've been picked out? It's the luck of the draw.'

'Ah,' Watson said, holding up a prodigious forefinger. 'I only said they were *thinking* of picking us out.'

'I don't get it.'

The Farmer shifted – so far as he was able – in his chair. He was not a small man; it was not a large chair. 'To be honest, neither do I, the DCC was being bloody cagey. I think the gist was, we're doing something naughty, and if we stop doing it, another division might find itself under scrutiny instead of us.'

'Did he actually say that?' Gill Templer asked.

The Farmer shrugged. 'I'm giving my interpretation, that's all. Now, after his phone call, I did some thinking. I asked myself: who would be getting up people's noses? Well, I know one copper who's like cocaine in that respect.'

119

'Nobody sniffs coke these days, sir.' Watson just sat there, unblinking. 'OK,' Rebus said, standing again. 'I went to see Big Jim Flett yesterday, probably a couple of hours before Gunner called you.'

'Why?' Gill Templer asked. She looked furious that he hadn't told her beforehand.

'McAnally.'

'The suicide?' The Farmer frowned as Rebus nodded.

'The thing is, sir, there's something ... I don't know, I just think there's something *there*. Why go all the way to Warrender School to blow your brains out in front of a councillor, a man who says he never even knew the deceased? And how come the widow's suddenly got money to spend? Those are two questions; I've got a wheen more.'

'Well,' the Farmer said, 'that might explain the second phone call. Also last night, and also at my home. It was from Derek Mantoni.'

'I don't know him.'

'*Councillor* Mantoni is chair of Lothian and Borders Joint Police Board.'

Rebus saw now: Gillespie had been complaining to his friend.

'He was asking about you, John.'

'Nice of him.'

'Apparently you've rubbed Councillor Gillespie up the wrong way. I should remind you that the councillor is a victim here, and one who's been through a terrible experience.' The Farmer sounded as if he was quoting Derek Mantoni.

'Inspector Rebus,' Gill Templer said, 'is there *any* reason to believe it wasn't a suicide?'

'No,' Rebus admitted. 'I'm sure it was suicide.'

'Then I don't see the problem.'

Rebus turned to her. 'Well, *I do*!' He jabbed his thumb into his chest to reinforce the point. 'And now everyone

120

suddenly wants it covered up!' She turned her head away from him.

'John,' the Farmer warned, 'that's out of order. I've been looking at the hours you've been putting in. You're due some time off ... a lot of time actually. It's a quiet time of year.'

Rebus held the Farmer's stare. 'You've got to back me up on this, sir.'

'I'm telling you to take some time off, that's all.'

'Who is it you're scared of: the DCC? Mantoni? HMIC?'

The Farmer ignored him. 'Take a week, ten days ... clear your head, Inspector.'

Rebus slammed both hands down on the desktop. A framed photo of the Farmer's family fell off and landed on a cardboard box. Gill Templer stooped to pick it up.

'You've got to back me up,' Rebus repeated. He knew Gill was a lost cause; he had eyes only for the Farmer, but the Farmer wasn't looking.

'I've given you an order, Inspector.'

Rebus gave one of the boxes a kick on his way out of the room.

When he thought it over later, Rebus didn't blame the Farmer. He was covering his arse; so was Gill, if it came down to it. Now Rebus was a free agent, or at least a loose one. He couldn't get anyone into trouble but himself, and that was fine with him. He'd cleared his desk, pushing everything into drawers and, when he ran out of space, the wastepaper-bin. He'd left St Leonard's without a word to anyone.

There were just the two problems — neither of them insignificant — and he pondered them as he sat in the back room of the Oxford Bar with a half of Caledonian Eighty and a double malt.

The first problem was, police routine gave his daily life

its only shape and substance; it gave him a schedule to work to, a reason to get up in the morning. He loathed his free time, dreaded Sundays off. He lived to work, and in a very real sense he worked to live, too: the much-maligned Protestant work-ethic. Subtract work from the equation, and the day became flabby, like releasing jelly from its mould. Besides, without work, what reason had he not to drink?

It worried him, because now there was nothing to stop him raising two fingers to the shade of Wee Shug McAnally, a man not exactly universally mourned, and get on with some serious bevvying instead. He could spend a seven-to-ten stretch in the Ox no problem, augmented by betting-shop gossip and nourished by pies and bridies. It would be wonderfully easy.

Then there was the second problem, not unconnected to the first.

For, now that he had so much time on his hands, what was to stop him booking a dentist's appointment?

The only thing to do was to keep working. Besides, there were some things he needed to do in a hurry, before word got around that he was on leave. The first of these involved another visit to C Division in Torphichen Place.

DI Davidson was again on duty, to Rebus's relief.

'I can smell it off you,' Davidson said, leading him to the CID room.

'What?'

'The drink. How can you torture me like that? There's another two hours before I finish my shift.'

Rebus saw that they were alone in the CID room. 'I need the casenotes on McAnally, the ones from the rape charge.'

'What for?'

Rebus shrugged. 'I just need to see them.'

Davidson went to a desk drawer and brought out a

bunch of keys. 'You know, John, there's enough to be getting on with in the here-and-now.' He went to a walk-in cupboard and opened it. 'I don't suppose there'll be a copy still here. Everything'll have been archived by now.'

There were reports packed tight along each shelf. On every spine, in fat felt-marker, was an officer's name, depending on whose copy the report was. The spines faced upwards, the base of each report facing out. On the base was the name of the accused. There was no McAnally.

So then they'd to traipse to another part of the building, locate another set of keys, and unlock a storeroom, inside which stood a dozen tall double-doored filing cupboards. Davidson stood in thought for a moment, then pointed at one.

'That's probably got the year we're after.' He unlocked the cabinet. There was a smell of musty paper, much stronger than in the cupboard they'd tried earlier, Davidson ran his finger along each row of spines. 'McAnally,' he said at last, pulling out two thick files of A4 paper and handing them to Rebus. Each was loose-bound, held together by two removable metal clips. The blue covers were faded at their edges. Davidson's surname was on the spine. Rebus read from one of the covers.

'"The Case Against Hugh McAnally, Born 12.1.44."' He flipped through both files, not surprised to see their bulk consisted of witness statements.

'Enjoy,' said Davidson, relocking the cabinet.

Rebus stopped off on his way home and bought a jar of coffee, rolls, bacon, and two four-packs of Export. He was preparing for a long haul.

The flat was fairly warm. He emptied the jar beneath the leaking radiator and replaced it, then turned the hi-fi on. He washed three aspirin down with a swig of beer, then checked his face in the bathroom mirror. The skin around

and below his nose was definitely inflamed. When he waggled one particular tooth it felt deadened, anaesthetised, while its neighbours jangled like they'd been wired to the mains. The blister on his palm had receded, and now sported only a thin strip of sticking-plaster. Beneath the plaster, the engine's serial number was still there.

I'm in great shape, he thought. I'm the perfect fucking specimen.

He took the beer through to the living room, sat down with the reports in his chair, and started to read.

He started with the Summary of Evidence, barely glanced down the List of Productions and List of Witnesses, skipped the Annual Leave of Officers, and got to work on the Statements and Tape Transcriptions. The witnesses comprised neighbours, the victim, the accused's wife, a couple of barmen, and the police doctor (Dr Curt, as it turned out), who had examined and taken samples from both victim and accused. Maisie Finch had been examined in hospital, where she spent the rest of the night under observation. It was noted that her mother – unaware of her daughter's presence – was in the same hospital at the time, just one floor up.

Hugh McAnally had been examined in the medical examination room at Torphichen. During the examination he kept protesting, 'I used a johnny, for fuck's sake, what's the problem?'

These words had endeared him to no one.

The story from the victim's point of view: Maisie had been alone in the flat, her mum being in hospital for a minor operation. At this time, her mother was already all but housebound, looking after her a full-time occupation for Maisie. (Nobody had asked her how it felt to be cooped up all day with an invalid; or how it felt when her mum had been taken into hospital ... Rebus remembered his own meeting with her – the bottles of strong lager, the 'holiday

124

mood'.) Maisie knew Mr McAnally very well, had known him for years. She regarded him not just as a neighbour but as a family friend.

McAnally told her he had come to ask after her mother. Though he smelled of alcohol, she'd let him into the flat and offered to make a cup of tea. He asked if she had anything stronger. She knew there was a bottle of whisky in the bottom of her mother's wardrobe. It had been there since her father's death. Maisie went to fetch it, and McAnally followed. He pushed her on to the bed so she was face down, and held her head down with one hand ...

Afterwards, he mumbled something. She thought it might have been an apology, but maybe not. He went out, leaving the door to the flat ajar. She could hear him tramping noisily down the stairwell. She ran to Mrs McAnally's door and thumped on it till she got an answer. Mrs McAnally herself called the police.

McAnally, by his own admission, left the tenement and headed for Lothian Road, drinking in a couple of pubs he frequented. This was backed up by the two barmen. Then he bought a fish supper, and was finishing it as he approached the main door of the tenement, where he was apprehended by two police officers who had been waiting in their car. He was taken to Torphichen Place police station and questioned, then charged.

McAnally's version was: he had indeed gone to Maisie Finch's flat to inquire about her mother, but also in the hope of having sex with Maisie. They'd had sex once before, while her mother was asleep in the other room. Both times, Maisie initiated proceedings. McAnally knew she was a 'good girl', but thought she got bored at home. He knew he was 'no spring chicken' nor yet 'Mr Universe', and her home life explained why Maisie wanted to have sex with him – 'I dare say I wasn't the only one.' Maisie herself

had never said anything, never explained, and McAnally wasn't really bothered, 'so long as I was getting my hole.'

After a minute or so's conversation in the living room, Maisie suggested going through to her mother's bedroom, her reasoning being that her mother had a double bed, while Maisie only had a single. (Asked to describe Maisie's bedroom, McAnally was able to, though this proved nothing, since as he later acknowledged, he'd been in there the previous month to change a faulty light-fitting.)

On the night in question, they progressed to the mother's bedroom, where – McAnally's version – intercourse took place, 'doggy style'. Asked why that particular position, McAnally said he thought maybe Maisie didn't like to look at his 'ugly old coupon'. (Rebus was glad *he* hadn't interviewed McAnally; he'd probably have taken a swing at him.) McAnally said he left the flat immediately afterwards, as Maisie didn't like him to hang about. One thing he said was that Maisie herself had provided the condom: 'I can't run around with johnnies in my pooch, Tresa'd be bound to find them.'

Yes, he was a choice article, Mr Hugh McAnally.

Rape cases could be difficult. Scottish law required corroboration, not just one person's word against another's. With allegations of rape, there was seldom absolute corroboration – rapists didn't work to an uninvited audience. But in this case there was the girl's cry, heard by some in the tenement (though not by all), and the fact that she made, as Davidson himself commented, a 'stonking good witness'. She would go into the witness box – not all rape victims would, for very good emotional reasons – and she would testify. She would 'put the old bastard behind bars'.

And she did.

Asked about the cry, McAnally at first said she was 'a screamer' – in other words, that she cried out at the point

of climax. Davidson had added a pencilled comment in the margin, perhaps meaning to erase it later: 'What young girl would climax with the likes of you?' McAnally then changed his mind and said there was no scream, no cry at all. Which was excellent news for the prosecution, who had witnesses ready to testify that they had heard a cry.

Which point, Rebus mused, though tiny in the wider scheme of the case, was almost certainly what had swung the jury. Mostly it was his word against hers; but there were witnesses to the scream, witnesses like Helena Profitt.

Miss Profitt had given a statement, but had not been called to give evidence at the trial. That was probably the Procurator-fiscal's decision. The Fiscal's office would have precognosced Miss Proffit, and would have made a note for future reference that she was timid, nervy, and unlikely to perform well in court. Crown counsel had picked the best neighbours to show to the jury. It was part of their particular skill.

Rebus reached down for another tin of beer, and found they were all empty. He went to the fridge and found a solitary can, a couple of months past its expiry. It was freezing to the touch, but had plenty of gas when he opened it. He was drinking these days with one side of his mouth only, avoiding the painful side with anything too hot or cold. He put the can down and fried up some bacon, cutting open two rolls. He ate the rolls at the kitchen table.

It has to be serious, he thought. The governor of Saughton, the deputy chief constable ... maybe even the Constabulary Inspectorate. They just didn't want him around. Why not? That was the question. It had to have something to do with McAnally. It looked to Rebus very much as though it had something to do with McAnally's time in Saughton.

He went back into the living room and got out McAnally's list of previous convictions. Small beer, he

thought, taking a drink. He'd been lucky though, landing more than his fair share of fines and tickings-off when a custodial sentence might have been more usual. He'd served a year one time, eighteen months another – both for housebreaking – and that was about it. Otherwise it was just fines and admonitions.

Rebus sat back, forgetting to swallow the beer in his mouth. He was thinking something, something he didn't want to think. There was only one good reason he could think of why Wee Shug had been so lucky, one good reason why a judge might be so lenient time and time again.

Someone had put in a word.

And who was it usually put in a word with the judge? Answer: policemen.

And why did they do it …?

Rebus swallowed the beer. 'He was a grass! Wee Shug McAnally was somebody's bloody snitch!'

Next morning, he woke up raring to go to work – then remembered he had no work to go to, no place he would be welcome. Just when he needed to ask some of his fellow officers a few very discreet questions.

He'd lain awake half the night, watching the amber streetlight on his bedroom ceiling, tumbling configurations in his mind. He couldn't get past the notion that McAnally had been somebody's eyes and ears on the street. All good policemen had them; anyone who wanted to get anywhere had them: grasses, stoolies, snitches, informers. They had a hundred titles and a hundred job descriptions.

It made sense; it explained those lenient sentences. But then McAnally had crossed the line – no judge was going to listen to too many pleas for leniency in a rape case. Four years off the street and a snitch lost his usefulness: there were new bandits around, people he didn't know and could

never get to know. Four years was a long time on the street; the world moved fast down there.

Something else had occurred to Rebus in bed, around three a.m. by the blue-lit numerals on his clock. It – whatever 'it' was, whatever it was people were scared of – had to do with McAnally, yes, but the councillor was involved too. Rebus had let the councillor slip from the equation. He'd been busy on fractions on one half of the board, while the councillor sat untroubled on the other. And the councillor, unlike McAnally, was still alive to answer questions. Rebus was only going to get so far following the trail of the dead. It was time to concentrate on the living.

It was time to get concerned.

17

Councillor Tom Gillespie lived in a huge, bay-windowed semi not five minutes walk from Rebus's flat. The house had been divided into two flats, one on the upper storey, one on the lower. Gillespie's was the ground-floor property. There was a trim lawn in front of the house, and a low stone wall topped with black glossy railings which ended in arrow-headed points. Rebus opened the gate and walked up to the front door. Clay-coloured road-salt crunched underfoot, spread up and down the path during the worst of the snow and ice. Now the ice had melted, apart from trimmings of sooty white in corners the sun never reached, and roads and paths throughout the city were blighted by salt, as treacherous underfoot as the ice it replaced.

Rebus could see movement behind the bay window as he rang the doorbell. It was an old-fashioned pull affair, the sprung bell chiming inside. Rebus heard an inner hallway door open, then a lock being pulled. The solid main door was opened by the councillor himself.

'Good morning, Mr Gillespie, mind if I have a word?'

'I'm up to my eyes in it, Inspector.'

From within, Rebus heard a motorised whine, then the sound of a woman sneezing. Gillespie's arm was across the doorway, blocking any attempt by Rebus to enter. It wasn't exactly Costa del Sol weather on the doorstep, but the councillor was sweating.

'I appreciate that, sir,' Rebus said, 'but this will only take a minute.'

'Did you speak to Helena Profitt?'

'I did, yes. And, by the way, thanks for setting the Joint Police Board on me.'

Gillespie wasn't about to apologise. 'I told you I had friends.'

There was a yip from within, like a Pekinese getting a deserved kick up the arse, and then a furious female voice.

'Tom! Tom!'

Gillespie pretended not to hear.

'I think you're wanted indoors,' Rebus remarked.

'Look, this really isn't the time for —'

'Tom, for Christ's sake!'

Gillespie snarled, turned on his heel and sprinted indoors. The front door was closing on Rebus with infinite slowness. He pushed it open and walked into the hall.

'Bloody thing's jammed again,' the woman was saying. 'Why the hell can't *you* do this?'

Then Gillespie, trying to keep his voice low. 'Just don't let him in! Go on then!'

A woman stumbled out of the front room like she'd been pushed from behind. She bumped into Rebus and some empty files clattered to the tile floor.

'Damnation,' she said. As the door closed behind her, Rebus could see that the bay-windowed room was some kind of office. He glimpsed a desk with a computer, chests of drawers with heaped documents slewed across their tops. He couldn't see whatever was making the noise, and he couldn't see Gillespie, but he heard a slap as the councillor either punched or kicked a piece of machinery.

He helped the woman retrieve the files. 'Nice colours,' he said.

'What?' She tucked some stray hairs back into place behind her ear. She was a tall, heavy-boned woman with a face full of strong features. Her thick dark hair was shoulder-length and parted to one side, a little lacking in

life. Her eyes were full of life though; her eyes were blazing. She looked harassed, but was dressed with thoughtful elegance in a pearl-coloured silk blouse and a long skirt of Black Watch tartan.

'The files,' Rebus explained. 'The ones I always seem to buy are blue or grey or green. These are ... well, they're more colourful.'

She looked at him like he was mad: they were only files.

'A stationer's on George Street,' she said.

Rebus nodded, trying not to look like he was memorising the letters on the front of the file he'd been studying. Not that the letters SDA/SE were difficult to remember.

'Something jammed?' Rebus asked.

She had been brought up a polite girl, taught manners at home and in school. She couldn't not answer a question so casually put, a harmless inquiry.

'The shredder,' she said.

Rebus nodded, confirming that he too had problems with his paper-shredder. 'You must be Mrs Gillespie?'

'That's right.'

'He's got you helping him, eh?'

She tried to laugh. 'Press-ganged.'

'I thought Councillor Gillespie had a secretary.'

Her smile vanished. She was thinking up some lie to tell him when the door opened and Gillespie emerged. This time, peering into the room, Rebus saw several cardboard boxes full of long thin strips of paper. Shredded documents.

Gillespie propelled his wife gently but firmly back into the office, closing the door after her. 'I don't recall inviting you in, Inspector.'

'Maybe you'll want to talk to your friend Councillor Mantoni again.'

Gillespie pulled out a handkerchief. 'Well, now you're

here, come into the kitchen.' He wiped the handkerchief across his forehead. 'I'm parched.'

He led Rebus down the long hall, past a sitting room and dining room. They took a left past the blocked-in staircase and passed through a shorter, darker passage into the kitchen. There was pine everywhere: pine units, pine tongue-and-groove covering every surface except the floor, which boasted boards freshly sanded and varnished. A conservatory had been added to the back, giving views on to the wide rear garden, mature rose bushes and laurel hedge; a small brick patio.

Gillespie busied himself with the kettle.

'I won't offer you a cup, Inspector. I know you'll be keen to be on your way.'

'I'm not that busy today actually, Mr Gillespie, but I won't stay for coffee.' Rebus paused. 'Thanks for the offer.'

Gillespie opened a cupboard and glowered at the mugs and glasses within. Reflected glare, thought Rebus.

'So what is it you want?' Gillespie reached for a mug.

'Dog shit,' said Rebus.

Gillespie fumbled the mug but retrieved it. 'What did you say?'

'Dog shit, Councillor: on the pavements, the grass … everywhere. It's a disgrace.'

'Are you trying to tell me you're not here in your official capacity?'

'Did I say I was? No, I'm here as a private individual, a constituent voicing a complaint to his elected representative.'

Gillespie opened a *cafetière* and poured ground coffee into it from a packet. By the time he finished he'd regained his composure.

'Well, Mr Rebus,' he said, 'people only usually complain in the summer. That's when the offending article is at its

softest and smelliest. I've never received a complaint in the winter.'

'Then I'm speaking for the silent majority.'

Gillespie managed a smile. 'What do you really want? If I had a mind, I could construe this visit as harassment.'

After what Rebus had seen, he didn't really want anything else, but he was enjoying himself, and what were holidays for if you didn't enjoy yourself?

'Just what I say,' he replied.

Gillespie poured boiling water over the coffee grounds. 'Well, I'm surprised at you.'

'Why?'

'Because I'd have expected you of all people to know that dogs fouling the byways are a matter for the police. It's down to the police to trace the owners and bring a prosecution.'

'And the council doesn't do anything?'

'On the contrary, we've a Dog Warden Section whose job is to educate owners to act responsibly. The wardens also help the police in cases of prosecution. The Warden Section is part of the EHD.'

'Environmental Health Department?'

'Precisely. I can give you their number if you like. It's the least I can do ... for a constituent.'

Rebus smiled and shook his head. He put his hands in his pockets and made as if to leave. But he stopped beside the councillor and lowered his voice.

'How scared are you?'

'What?'

'You look to me like you're shitting snowballs.'

The councillor started sweating again. He opened his mouth to say something, then changed his mind and concentrated on stirring the contents of the *cafetière*.

'All the shit that's about these days,' Rebus went on,

'you've got to watch you don't tread in it. You might end up on your arse, isn't that right, Councillor?'

'Just get out, will you?'

Rebus turned to leave. Gillespie put out a hand to stop him. 'Inspector, you're making a mistake.' Not a threat; a simple statement of fact.

'Talk to me.'

Gillespie thought about it, biting his bottom lip, then shook his head. Rebus stared at him, willing him to change his mind. But Gillespie was scared; it was in his eyes, in the sheen of his face.

The man was terrified.

'I'll let you out,' Gillespie said, leading Rebus back down the hall. He had the *cafetière* in one hand, two mugs in the other. Through the office door they could hear Mrs Gillespie cursing the machine again. She sounded like she was kicking it.

'Bit of a temper, your wife,' Rebus commented. He saw that Gillespie didn't have a free hand, so did the kindly thing and opened the office door for him.

'Has he gone yet?' Mrs Gillespie snarled.

'Just on my way, Mrs Gillespie,' Rebus told her, popping his head round the door, taking a good look round. 'Nice to have met you.'

Her face was flushed, anger turning quickly to embarrassment. 'I'm sorry,' she said.

'No need for that.'

And Rebus left them to it, whatever *it* was ...

18

It took Rebus half the afternoon to decide that he was doing the right thing.

More accurately, it took him ten minutes to make up his mind, and a couple of hours to drink himself into a state where he was confident enough to follow through.

He wasn't just drinking though, he was hunting; eyes and ears open for news of Rico Briggs.

Rico was just about the best and worst housebreaker on the east coast. It wasn't that he was cack-handed: he could be in and out of most homes in minutes flat, be the occupants asleep, slumped in front of the TV, or making merry at a party. Rico's problem was that he was conspicuous, and fences didn't like that. Rico had been a big Hearts fan, not missing a fixture in seasons 1977–80, except when he'd served a wee stretch in Peterhead. One night in Leith Walk, dizzy after a trouncing of the Hibees, Rico had marched into a tattoo parlour and demanded the works.

Next morning, Rico had looked at his face in his bathroom mirror and seen that both tender cheeks now boasted the Hearts badge, a maroon heart with a cross in the middle. It took him only a day or two to start loathing his once-loved team; which was ironic, considering he was now a public poster-site for the men of Gorgie.

Not surprisingly, the tattoos were unique, and as good as fingerprints as far as the police were concerned. Realising this, Rico had started sporting a balaclava when working,

which accentuated his other remarkable facial feature – a nose the dimensions of the Pyramid of Cheops. This, too, people tended to notice.

Rebus had tried talking Rico Briggs into retiring, and had been semi-successful. These days, Rico concentrated on passing his skills on to a series of apprentices; he'd even given Rebus a few clandestine lessons in lock-picking. They helped when the policeman mislaid his house-keys; and at other times too.

Rebus finally found Rico in a bar off Nicolson Street, a place whose sad-faced clients were usually in hiding after a haircut at the half-blind barber's next door. Surrounded by bad haircuts, it was surprising how Rico blended in.

'Hiya, Rico,' Rebus said, sliding on to the wooden stool next to him. 'How are you doing?'

Rico had the daily tabloid folded at the quick crossword, and was tapping it with a half-size betting-shop pen, the kind with a ten-minute lifetime guarantee.

'Eight letters,' Rico said in a voice like road-salt, 'M-something-R-something-O. "On a desert island".' He looked to Rebus.

'Marooned.'

'Thanks, in that case I'll have a double,' Rico chuckled. 'Not heard that one before, Mr Rebus?'

'Not since *Double Barrel* was at the top of the charts.'

Rebus ordered the drinks while Rico rubbed both cheeks, the idea being that if he rubbed them often enough he'd sand the tattoos away.

'So, Mr Rebus, is it a job?'

Rebus nodded, wary of saying too much: he might be surrounded by bad haircuts, but nobody's ears had been severed.

'Tell you later.'

They drank their drinks in silence. The whole bar was quiet. Further down the bar, a customer nodded to the

barman for a refill and the barman nodded back. A silent order, Rebus thought. Like monks. Which, given the tonsures, wasn't such a bad image.

They got out of the pub and walked towards the Pleasance. If they took a right, they'd come to St Leonard's, but they went left instead and headed to the Cowgate and Canongate. They talked as they walked, then entered a howff on the High Street to toast the mission.

At six o'clock, dark overhead except for an arc of moon looking like someone had pressed their thumbnail into the sky, Rebus and Rico sat in Rebus's parked car, engine running to keep the heater on. They were across the road from the Gillespie house, and Rebus was describing the layout. Rebus was more nervous than he would admit: if Rico were caught, if he talked, then Rebus could end up one of Big Jim Flett's clients. Rico asked a few questions, and Rebus supplied answers where he could.

'I'll go in through the conservatory,' Rico decided. 'You're sure about the alarm?'

'No alarm,' Rebus said.

People were hurrying along the pavement, faces down to avoid the icy wind which, Edinburgh fashion, was blowing horizontally just at head height. Rebus was having doubts about the whole enterprise, but could see no way round it. He thought of something else he'd wanted to ask Rico.

'Know anyone who's just come out of Saughton?'

'I don't mix with felons, Inspector.'

'Of course you don't, you've gone straight, we both know that.' Rebus's voice was quiet but insistent. 'Only, if you did know anyone, I'd like to talk to them. Nothing heavy or official, just a chat, a bit of info on Saughton itself.'

'There'd be a cash incentive?'

'There'd be a drink in it for both of you.'

'Well, wouldn't do any harm to ask around.'

'No harm at all,' Rebus agreed. He looked over to the Gillespie house. 'What time will you go in?'

'Two in the morning should do it. Best not stay here much longer though – we don't want to attract attention.'

Rico had a point: in Marchmont, you were always in somebody else's parking space. There were barely enough gaps for the residents, never mind visitors. Rebus put the gearstick into first.

'We'll get a bite to eat,' he said.

'Hiy, hold on.' Rico was pointing towards the house. The front door was standing open, and Mrs Gillespie suddenly appeared carrying two black binbags. Behind her, her husband carried two more. They opened their gate and deposited the bags on the pavement outside. Something wonderful dawned on Rebus. He looked up and down the street. Sure enough, a few bags were already out.

'Rubbish day the morn?' Rico suggested.

'Rico, it looks like I won't be needing you after all.'

In the end, Rico helped load the boot.

Rebus sat alone in his flat, having paid Rico off and dropped him back in the town centre. One of the binbags had contained nothing but empty tins, bags and boxes, and now it sat outside the main door of Rebus's tenement. But the other three sat open in the middle of Rebus's living room. He emptied the first bag on to the floor. Strands of white paper fell in a shivering heap. Rebus picked up one strand. It was the length of an A4 sheet and no more than two millimetres wide. He'd heard stories that shredded documents could be reconstructed. All it took was patience: colossal patience. He was sure there were clever ways of doing it – UV analysis or watermark-matching or batch sorting – but all he had were his eyes. He couldn't just march into Howdenhall and drop the stuff off. Too many

questions would be asked. He sat on the floor, picked up a few strands, and tried putting them together.

It took him about four minutes to realise the job was impossible.

He sat there smoking a cigarette, staring at the strands. They might tell him everything he needed to know. He finished the cigarette, poured himself a drink, and tried again. It took him a while to lose his temper. He dragged the kitchen table through and sat at it. Then he brought the anglepoise lamp through from his bedroom and plugged it in. The machine had jammed; there was a chance not all the strips had been separated completely.

He didn't find as many as two strips still joined at any one point.

He swore for a while and walked around the flat, emptied the coffee jar and set it back under the radiator, then put his coat on and went to buy cigarettes and whisky. The corner shop was closed when he reached it. His watch said eleven-fifteen; he couldn't believe it was so late.

He walked on to the nearest pub and waded through the smoky, shouting throng. The barmaid gave him change for the cigarette machine but couldn't sell him a carry-out: it was after last orders. She told him about a licensed chip shop he could try, but it was a car-run away, so he walked briskly back to the flat and sought out untried bottles. There was a quarter of Bacardi for emergency dispensation should he ever manage to drag a woman as far as his bedroom. The thought of neat Bacardi repelled him only slightly more than the thought of mixing it with anything.

Which means, he thought, I can't be an alcoholic.

He unscrewed the top from the Bacardi anyway and sniffed it, then screwed it back on. He'd have to be a lot more desperate ... say, come four in the morning. Then he remembered the freezer. He opened it up and chipped away at the ice until he'd broken through to two trays of ice

140

cubes, a single fish finger ... and a small bottle. It was Polish vodka; a neighbour had given it to him after a trip home to Lodz; a present for feeding the cat for a week.

Rebus found a glass, filled it, and belatedly toasted Solidarity before draining it. The stuff was as smooth as anything he'd ever tried. A third of a litre of eighty-four proof. He took glass and bottle into the living room and put *Exile on Main Street* on the hi-fi. It sounded as good as ever.

He got back into the game, then decided to leave the first bag and start on the second. He filled the first bag back up, then dumped bag two on to the floor.

And his doorbell rang.

It was a little after midnight.

The main door was sometimes left unlocked. No need for visitors, welcome or not, to announce their presence until they were outside the door of the flat.

At this time on a Thursday night?

Rebus looked at the mess on the floor, then went out into the hall and tiptoed to the front door, just as the bell rang again. He could hear two voices at least, little more than murmurs. Suddenly, fingers pushed open his letterbox. Rebus stood to the side of the door, back pressed to the wall.

'Maybe he leaves the lights on when he's out.'

'Aye, and maybe he's half-shot and sleeping it off.'

Rebus turned the snib silently and yanked open the door. Siobhan Clarke, who'd been peering through the letterbox, stood up, but Rebus's eyes were on Brian Holmes.

'Half-shot, is it, Brian? I'm glad you hold me in such high regard.'

Holmes just shrugged. 'It's what I'd do on holiday.'

Rebus filled the doorway, his arms folded. 'So what are you doing: canvassing, polling, or maybe you were just passing?'

141

'We were working,' Brian Holmes explained. 'We went to get something to eat afterwards, and when we ran out of interesting topics, the conversation came round to you.'

'What about me?'

'We wondered,' Siobhan Clarke said, 'what the hell's going on.'

Rebus smiled. 'You and me both.' He stood back from the doorway. 'You better come in. You're the first to arrive; I haven't even got the party snacks out.' He noticed a brown carrier bag on the landing behind Brian Holmes.

'We brought our own party with us.' When Holmes picked up the bag, Rebus heard cans and bottles collide.

'You're always welcome here, Brian,' Rebus said, leading them indoors.

They sat in the living room, staring at the pile of paper strips. Siobhan Clarke took a gulp of coffee.

'You *stole* these?'

Rebus shook his head. 'A public service; I saved the binmen a job.'

Holmes looked to Siobhan. 'We did say we were coming here to help.'

'Yes, but this lot …?' She flapped her arms. 'I doubt the "Blue Peter" appeal could sort this lot out. Talk about shreds of evidence.'

Rebus held up a pacifying hand. 'Look, this is my problem, not yours. I won't be disappointed if you scurry off home. In fact, it would be better for you if you did.'

'We know,' said Holmes.

Rebus looked at him. 'What do you mean?'

Siobhan Clarke explained. 'The Farmer spoke to us this afternoon. Basically, he warned us off. He said you were on leave, but he didn't think that would stop you sticking your nose in.' She looked up. 'His words, not mine.'

'We've been given new duties,' Brian Holmes added.

'Desk work, restructuring the filing system prior to full computerisation.'

'To keep you busy?'

'Yes.'

'And away from me?'

They both nodded.

'So naturally you come straight here?' Rebus got to his feet. 'You could be fucking up both your careers!'

'I'm not in CID to sort through a lot of old paperwork,' Siobhan Clarke retorted. Then she realised what she'd said, looked at the mound of shredded paper in front of her, and laughed.

They all did.

They hit lucky with the third bag.

'Look,' Siobhan Clarke said, 'it's not just white paper.'

Rebus took a strip from her: yellow card. 'Files,' he said. 'They shredded the folders as well!'

'Must be some machine,' Brian Holmes added.

'That's a bloody good point, Brian.'

The folders were a breakthrough. The problem with the paper was that there was so much of it. There wasn't nearly so much card, and what there was could be grouped by colour. The front of each file had a white printed label, and these were what Rebus wanted. He wanted the reconstructed labels.

But even knowing what they were looking for, it took time and effort. Rebus's eyes were stinging, and he kept rubbing them, which only blurred his vision.

'Get you two anything?' he kept saying. They would only shake their heads. Rebus demolished the cans on his own. He knew he'd had too much when he polished off a tin of Irn-Bru without realising it was non-alcoholic.

The streets grew quieter after the students had slouched home on the wings of blasphemy. Around two-thirty, the

central heating clocked off and Rebus turned on the gas fire. They each worked on a different colour of folder.

'I saw one of the folders when Mrs Gillespie dropped it,' Rebus said. 'It was marked SDA/SE. I presume the letters stand for Scottish Development Agency and Scottish Enterprise. Scottish Enterprise took over when the SDA was wound up. Councillor Gillespie, by the way, sits on an industrial planning committee.'

'So,' Holmes remarked, 'the SDA file could be completely innocent.'

'Certainly he had a genuine reason for having a file on the SDA. But why be in such a panic to shred it?'

Holmes conceded the point.

'I think I've got something,' Siobhan Clarke said. She'd all but completed a yellow file, the label intact save for a strip or two. 'Looks like the letters A C,' she said, 'then a name: Haldayne.'

Rebus fetched the phone book. There was no A C Haldayne in Edinburgh.

'Strange spelling,' Brian Holmes said. 'I've never come across Haldayne with a y.'

'Misspelt?' Siobhan Clarke said. 'The name of one of the councillor's constituents?'

Rebus shrugged. Half an hour later, it was Holmes's turn to complete a red file.

'"Gyle Park West",' he read out.

Rebus wasn't paying much attention; he was close to completing the last of the coloured folders, this one a lurid green.

'"Mensung",' he said, looking up. 'What the hell is Mensung?'

Siobhan Clarke yawned and rubbed at her eyes, then blinked a few times, looking around the room.

'You know,' she said, 'it's a good job this paper's lying everywhere. Without it, this place would look like a tip.'

* * *

It was six on Friday morning when Rebus's phone started ringing.

He fell off the chair, the duvet sliding with him. The phone was underneath one of the heaps of paper strips.

'Whoever you are,' he said, 'whatever you want ... you're dead.'

'It's Siobhan, sir. I've been thinking about A C Haldayne.'

'Me, too,' Rebus lied.

'I've been thinking about that funny spelling. American names are sometimes spelt differently, aren't they?'

'Is that why you woke me up?'

'Well, it would tie in with AC.'

'Would it?'

'Christ, you're slow, sir.'

'It's six in the morning, Clarke.'

'All I mean is AC could stand for American Consulate. Haldayne could be a surname, and AC the consulate.'

Rebus sat up and opened his eyes. 'That's not bad.'

'I tried phoning the consulate, but got an answering machine. It offered me a lot of options, mostly to do with visa applications, then put me through to the consulate proper, but all I got was another answering machine message telling me the opening hours.'

'Try again in the morning.'

'Yes, sir. Sorry for waking you.'

'That's all right. Listen, Siobhan ... thanks for helping me.'

'It's no problem, really.'

'Then you won't mind doing something else?' He could almost hear her smile.

'What?'

'That shredder. I'm wondering how long Gillespie's owned it.'

'You want me to check?'

'Yes.'

'Will do. Goodnight, sir.'

'Goodnight, Clarke.'

Rebus put down the receiver and decided to get up. Half a minute later, he was asleep on the living-room carpet.

19

On Sunday, Rebus was invited to Oxford Terrace for afternoon tea.

He was glad of the break, having spent much of the previous forty-eight hours trying to piece together some of the strands of A4 paper. He hadn't made any progress, but it had taken his mind off his swollen gum. By Saturday afternoon, he'd had enough and phoned a dentist, but of course by then all the dentists in Edinburgh were in the clubhouse, deciding over a second gin whether to bother with eighteen holes or, in this weather, just settle for nine.

On Sunday afternoon, dress smart but casual, he went to start his car and found it recalcitrant. Probably a loose connection. He looked under the bonnet, but was no mechanic. He was alone on the street, no one around to give him a jump-start, so he went back indoors and called for a cab, noticing too late that he had oil on his hands, a smudge of which had transferred itself to his trouser leg.

He was not in the best of moods as his driver took him north across the city.

Sammy answered the door. She was wearing thick black tights with a short jumble-sale dress falling over them. Under the dress she wore a white T-shirt.

'You're almost on time,' she said. 'We weren't expecting you so soon.'

'Did Patience teach you that one?'

He followed his daughter down the hall into the living room. Lucky the cat took one look at Rebus, seemed to

remember him, and stalked off into the conservatory. Rebus heard the catflap rattle shut. Now it was only two against one; the odds were improving in Rebus's favour.

He knew there were things fathers said to their daughters, little criticisms they were expected to make to show they cared. But Rebus knew what his little criticisms would sound like: they'd sound like criticisms. So he kept his counsel. Patience came out of the kitchen wiping her hands on a dish-towel.

'John.'

'Hello, Patience.' They kissed the way friends did, a peck on the cheek, a hand on the shoulder.

'Be about two minutes,' she said, turning back into the kitchen. He didn't think she'd really looked at him. 'Go into the conservatory.'

Sammy again led the way. The table had a clean white cloth on it, with some dishes already laid. Patience had brought her potted plants indoors for the winter, leaving not much room for anything or anyone else. The Sunday papers were heaped on the window-ledge. Rebus chose the chair nearest the garden door. Looking out of the conservatory window, he could see in through the kitchen window. Patience was busy at the sink, her face lacking emotion. She didn't look up.

'Liking it all right?' Rebus asked his daughter.

She nodded. 'It's great, and so's Patience.'

'How's the job?'

'Very stimulating; not easy, but stimulating.'

'What do you do exactly?'

'SWEEP's pretty small, we all muck in. I'm supposed to be developing communication skills in my clients.'

Rebus nodded. 'You mean so they can be a bit more polite next time they mug their granny?'

She glowered at him and he raised his hands. 'Just a joke,' he said.

'Maybe you need some communication skills yourself.'

'He's as blunt as a butt to the head,' Patience said, bringing in the teapot.

'Can I help?' Sammy offered.

'You sit there, I'll be back in a second.'

She was away far longer than a second; there was no conversation between times. Rebus watched Lucky the cat staring at him from the garden path. Patience returned with plates of cakes and biscuits. His mouth was imploring him: no hot drinks, no cakes or biscuits, no sugar, no crunching.

'I'll pour,' Sammy said. There was a clatter as Lucky came back in, seeking tidbits.

'Cake, John?' Patience said, offering him the pick from the plate. He took the smallest item he could find, a thin end-slice of madeira. Patience regarded his choice with suspicion: he'd always preferred ginger sponge, and she, who hated it, had bought one specially.

'Sammy,' Patience said, 'try the ginger.'

'It's a bit sweet for me,' Sammy replied. 'I'll just have a biscuit.'

'Fine.'

'This outfit of yours,' Rebus began.

'It's called SWEEP,' Sammy reminded him.

'Yes, SWEEP, who funds it?'

'We've charitable status. We get some donations, but spend more time than we ought to thinking up fund-raising schemes. The bulk of the money drips down from the Scottish Office.' She turned to Patience. 'We've this brilliant guy, he knows just how to word an application for funding, knows what grants are available ...'

Patience looked interested. 'Is he nice?'

Sammy blushed. 'He's great.'

'And he deals with the Scottish Office?' Rebus asked.

'Yes.' Sammy couldn't see where this was leading. She worked with people who were mistrustful of police officers

and other authority figures, mistrustful of their motives. Her colleagues were careful what they said in front of her. She'd been open with them from the start; she'd stated on the application form that her father was in Edinburgh CID. But there were some people who still didn't trust her entirely.

She knew one problem was the media. When the media learned who her father was, they sought her out for a quote – her background made it more interesting. They called it 'personalising the issues'. There were some people in SWEEP who felt resentful of the attention she got.

She didn't really blame them. It was the system.

'More cake, John?'

The catflap clacked again as Lucky went back outside.

'No, thanks, Patience,' Rebus said.

'I think maybe I'll try the madeira,' Sammy said. Which left an awful lot of ginger cake.

'You haven't touched your tea, John.'

'I'm waiting 'til it cools.' In the past, he'd always liked it scalding.

'Why are you so interested in SWEEP all of a sudden?' Sammy asked him.

'I'm not, but I might be interested in the Scottish Office.'

Sammy looked like she didn't believe him. She started to defend SWEEP, going on at length, her cheeks colouring with conviction. Rebus envied her that sense of conviction.

Then he said a couple of things, and an argument started. He couldn't help himself; he'd just had to take a contrary point of view. He tried drawing Patience into the debate, but she only shook her head slowly and sadly. Finally, when Sammy had collapsed into a sulk, Patience was ready with her summing-up.

'You see, Sammy, your father is the Old Testament type:

retribution rather than rehabilitation. Isn't that right, John?'

Rebus just shrugged, drank some lukewarm tea, and absent-mindedly chewed on a slice of buttered ginger cake.

'And he's the classic Calvinist, too,' Patience went on. 'Let the punishment fit the crime, and then some.'

'That's not Calvinism,' Rebus said. 'It's Gilbert and Sullivan.' He sat forwards in his chair. 'Besides, the problem is that sometimes the punishment *doesn't* fit the crime. Sometimes there's punishment and no crime at all. Other times there's crime but no punishment; and worst of all –' he paused – 'nearly all of the time there's *unfairness*.' He looked at Sammy, wondering what SWEEP would have done for Willie Coyle and Dixie Taylor, wondering if anything at all, anything worth a candle, would have been left of them after prison.

Eventually, they found other things to talk about. Sammy didn't contribute much; she just kept staring at her father, as if seeing him afresh. The sky outside conceded defeat and collapsed from slate-grey to late-afternoon black. While Patience and Sammy were clearing the table, Rebus stared at Lucky through the window, then went over to the catflap and locked it shut. The cat saw what he had done. It miaowed at him once, registering its protest. Rebus waved it cheerio.

They sat in the living room, and Patience handed over a few things he'd left behind after the move: his second-best razor, some clean handkerchiefs, a pair of shoelaces, a tape of *Electric Ladyland*. He stuffed everything into his jacket pockets.

'Thanks,' he said.

'You're welcome.'

Sammy saw him back to the door and waved him off.

That evening, back at the flat, Rebus sat listening to

Hendrix with a lined pad of paper in front of him. There were some words on it.

SDA/SE (Scottish Office?)

A C Haldayne (US Consulate?)

Mensung (?? – not in phonebook)

Gyle Park West (industrial estate)

He knew about Gyle Park West because he'd driven out there that morning. It was a low-rise sprawl of smallish industrial and commercial units, sited next to the imposing PanoTech electronics company. At the entrance to the estate there was a sign listing the various companies on the site, including Deltona. He remembered that Salty Dougary worked for Deltona, and that Deltona provided microchips for PanoTech, the PanoTech factory being more of an assembly line, constructing computers from components sourced elsewhere.

None of which seemed to tie Councillor Gillespie to Wee Shug McAnally. None of which was in itself suspicious. The councillor was on an industrial planning committee, which was excuse enough for owning files on the SDA and Scottish Enterprise and on Gyle Park West. But then why the panic, the hurry to destroy those files? *That* was what interested Rebus.

As he drove out of Gyle, an area of the city he didn't really know, he realised something else. Gyle itself had boomed in the eighties, gaining new homes, industries, even its own railway station. Before then, it had just been a place near the airport. The airport had been its big advantage in the eighties, making for good fast communications. These days Gyle had an identity, and a lot of that was down to the injection of cash into the place. But there was something else in Gyle's favour.

Its district councillor just happened to be the Lord Provost, Cameron McLeod Kennedy.

152

The telephone rang, bringing him out of his reverie. He snatched the receiver. 'Hello?'

'Hello yourself.' It was Mairie Henderson.

'I was beginning to think you'd forgotten me,' Rebus said.

'I've only finally managed to track down LABarum.' Rebus picked up his pen and moved the pad closer. 'The reason I had trouble was, it doesn't exist.'

'What?'

'Not yet at any rate. It's a PanoTech project. Do you know who they are?'

'The computer company?'

'That's right. LABarum is something they've been toying with. See, the problem with Silicon Glen, with the whole Scottish electronics industry, is that it's a manufacturer. It puts bits and pieces together, but that's about all. Everything's sourced elsewhere.'

'Not everything, there's Deltona.'

'A *very* small cog in the machine. What we need in Scotland is a software giant, a Microsoft, somebody researching, developing and producing software to go *into* the machines.'

'LABarum?'

'That's right. But my source tells me it's not up and running yet. There's a question of funding. The talent's there, but to keep it in Scotland is going to cost money, lots and lots of money.' She paused. 'My source was curious, how did you hear about it?'

'I saw a business plan.'

'You did? Where? At PanoTech?'

'No.' What could he tell her? In a sub-let council house in Stenhouse? Hiding behind a teenager's paperback collection?

'Where then? The City Chambers?'

Rebus started. 'Why do you ...?' Then he thought about

153

it. A plan to start up a computer software company, presumably in Gyle Park West … He looked at the writing on his pad. The district council would want to discuss it, they'd need to be aware of it. Tom Gillespie's committee would certainly know about it. And if it *was* to be sited in Gyle Park West, if it had anything to do with the district council at all, then the Lord Provost would know about it. Cameron McLeod Kennedy.

Rebus picked the business plan off the floor and looked at the initials on the front page. Mairie was telling him she'd drawn a blank with Dalgety, but he wasn't listening.

'CK,' he said quietly. Cameron Kennedy. 'Jesus, Mairie, those two kids did know Kirstie Kennedy after all!'

20

On Monday morning, Rebus went to the National Library on George IV Bridge. He passed through the security barrier and climbed the imposing staircase. At the main desk, he explained what he was looking for and was issued with a one-day reader's card. Then he found a spare computer console and sat down at it, reading the instructions for using the on-line system.

His search didn't take long. There was desperately little on the Scottish Development Agency; even less on Scottish Enterprise. He was sure that before its demise the SDA had been under the aegis of the Scottish Office, so tapped 'Scottish Office' into the computer. There were a lot of entries; he went through screen after screen of them: welfare, road-widening schemes, grants to the fishing industry, corporal punishment ... But nothing new on either the SDA or Scottish Enterprise.

Across the road in the Central Library he met with similar results. The Edinburgh Room directed him to the Scottish Library downstairs, and the Scottish Library's microfiches were every bit as unhelpful as the high-tech facilities across the way. Finally, Rebus approached one of the librarians. She sat at a desk, sorting newspaper cuttings into five distinct piles.

'Yes?' she whispered.

'I'm looking for information on the Scottish Development Agency.'

'Have you checked the fiches?'

'Yes.'

'Well, those are our holdings.' She thought for a moment. 'You might try the Scottish Office direct.'

Yes, he might at that. He walked down the High Street and across North Bridge, then made down the side of the St James Centre – noting that Anthony wasn't on his usual pitch – to where the Scottish Office had hidden itself in a concrete box called New St Andrew's House. He told the guard on the door what he wanted, and was pointed in the direction of the reception desk. The woman there was very pleasant, but couldn't help. She phoned up to the Library and Publications Room, who couldn't help either. Rebus found it hard to believe that there was no history of the SDA available.

'They say nobody'd be interested,' she explained, putting down the telephone.

'Well, *I'm* interested.'

'You could ask at the HMSO Bookshop.'

'On Lothian Road?'

'Yes.' She saw the look on his face. 'I've some other literature here you could take away with you.'

Desperate for something to show for his morning, Rebus picked out a few leaflets, one of which was an introduction to HM Inspectorate of Constabulary. Rebus wondered if it would mention anything about bribery.

'Thanks anyway,' he told the receptionist. There was a display in the reception area and he went over to look at it. New St Andrew's House was about to relocate to Leith. The move was costing millions. Rebus didn't feel any better for knowing where his taxes were headed. Sleet was coming down as he left the building.

Which gave him the excuse he needed to drop into the Café Royal. It was eleven-fifteen and he was the second customer of the day. He liked the place when it was empty. It was one of the few bars he knew which had less

atmosphere the busier it got. His feet were tingling from the walk. He'd left his car at home, only expecting to walk as far as George IV Bridge.

The sleet had stopped by the time he left the bar. He walked along George Street, in order to avoid the shoppers on Princes Street, then headed up Lothian Road. A Lothian Road wind was one of nature's wonders; people were walking into it at an angle close to forty-five degrees. The headwind could exhaust you in minutes. Rebus kept his eyes to the pavement and concentrated on putting one foot after the other, like he was getting the hang of false legs.

The new Convention Centre was up. There was a lot of recent building work around the city: the Festival Theatre, Convention Centre, court annexe, National Library annexe, not to mention the new Scottish Office HQ. He stopped in a doorway to catch his breath and to consider the scale of the building programme: new roads, new developments ... There was talk of building another road bridge across the Forth. But where was the money coming from? He walked on, deep in thought, and entered the HMSO shop. He'd been explaining his needs to the counter assistant for about thirty seconds when the man started to shake his head.

'I haven't finished yet,' Rebus snapped.

The man listened in silence, and when Rebus was finished he advised: 'You could try Scottish Enterprise direct.' He brought out the phonebook to find its address. The HQ was in Glasgow, but there was a branch in Edinburgh: LEEL, Lothian and Edinburgh Enterprise Limited, had offices in Haymarket Terrace, which wasn't that far to walk, not compared to the distance he'd come.

The smart new building which housed LEEL boasted two very bored-looking receptionists and no guard at all on the door. He explained that he wanted general background information.

'Agatha will bring down what we've got,' he was told

with a pleasant professional smile. 'If you'd like to take a seat …?'

He sat down and read the bumf spread across the table in front of him. He noticed that his calves were aching. This, he thought, is called exercise. Some people did it every day.

The lift opened and a young woman walked towards him. She too had a Stepford-wifely smile for the public as she handed over a lavish folder, inside which was a set of glossy documents.

'This is all we've got at the moment,' she said.

'Thank you, Agatha, this is fine.'

Since he was so close, he dropped into Torphichen for a coffee. Davidson wasn't around, but DC Robert Burns was, so Rebus chewed the cud with him, enjoying the feel of being back inside a cop shop. Then he asked Burns for a favour.

'I need a lift home, Rab,' he said. 'Medical reasons.'

Back in his flat, Rebus read through what little he had. He hadn't found anything on Gyle Park West or anyone or anything called Mensung. The sum total of his recent discoveries had nothing to do with Councillor Gillespie at all. But what he did know was that Kirstie Kennedy had known Willie and Dixie in some capacity: how else to explain a document belonging to the Lord Provost turning up in Willie's bedroom? What he didn't yet know was why it was there. He assumed Kirstie had taken it from her parents' house, but why? Had it meant something to her? And why had Willie hidden it?

His phone was ringing. It was Siobhan Clarke. 'Where've you been?' she asked.

'Walking.'

'*Walking*?'

'How are things at St Leonard's?'

'The chief super is keeping tabs on Brian and me, and he keeps piling the work on.'

'So you haven't been able to do anything?'

'On the contrary, I've some interesting news. Councillor Gillespie's document shredder wasn't bought, it was rented. There's a business supply company in Stockbridge, they hire out all sorts of office equipment. Which reminds me, when you get back there's a little surprise for you.'

'What?'

'The new PCs have arrived.'

'Good, we could do with a few more men on the beat.'

'Gosh,' her voice dripped irony, 'I've not heard that one today. Anyway, there's one on your desk, plugged in and ready to run.'

'When did Gillespie rent the shredder?'

'Wednesday. He told the shop assistant he'd been trying to find one for a few days, but they were too expensive to buy.'

'Thank God he's mean with money, or we might never know he'd shredded anything.'

'Want to hear the rest? I finally got through to the consulate and asked to speak to Haldayne.' She paused. 'They told me Mr Haldayne was out of the office. His first name's Richard. I got them to spell his surname for me: it has a "y" in the middle.'

'You're a genius.'

'Want to hear the rest?'

Rebus forgot all about his sore calves, his weary feet. 'Go ahead.'

'I ran a check on Mr Richard Haldayne. Have you ever had dealings with the diplomats in town?'

'No.'

'Well, I have. I handed out a few parking tickets when I was in uniform. My boss said I was wasting my time

ticketing a diplomatic plate. They never pay their fines, because we're not allowed to prosecute them.'

'So you looked in the computer?'

'Eighteen unpaid parking tickets dating back to 1985. That's under two a year, which counts as law-abiding for a diplomat.'

'It's still a lot of tickets. An officer might want a quiet word with Mr Haldayne about them.'

'Just don't get caught, sir.'

'Same goes for you, Clarke, and thanks.'

He put the phone down and tapped his fingers on the receiver. It was a start, definitely a start. He lifted the receiver again and dialled Sammy's work number. She wasn't there. The woman who told him this sounded upset.

'I'm her father,' Rebus said, 'is anything wrong?'

'She was in a terrible state. Someone had to take her home.'

'Why was she in a state?'

'Her landlady.' The woman sniffed.

'What about her landlady?'

'Well, *she's* upset, and she got Sammy all upset.'

Rebus stopped pretending to be calm. 'Upset about what?'

'I love cats,' the woman said.

'What?'

'Cats. It's her landlady's cat. It was torn to bits last night by somebody's dog.'

Rebus finally plucked up the courage to phone Patience's flat, and was relieved that Sammy herself answered.

'I heard,' he said. 'How's Patience?'

'She's gone out. She was ... it was horrible.'

Rebus swallowed. 'What happened?'

'Lucky was in the garden, and some dog must have come

160

over the wall. Lucky ran to the catflap to get in, but the catflap was locked ...' Her voice fell. 'And that was that.'

'Oh, dear,' said Rebus.

'The thing is, Dad, Patience blames *me*.'

'I'm sure that's not –'

'She says I must have locked the flap. She's hardly spoken a word to me since I got back.'

'The lock must have fallen by itself.'

'I don't know. But I know *I* didn't do it.'

'Look, Sammy, the reason I'm phoning –'

'Yes?'

Rebus stared at the notes in front of him. 'SWEEP's contact at the Scottish Office: can you give me his name ...?'

He had an appointment that afternoon with the Lord Provost.

Rebus hadn't been specific on the telephone; he'd just told the secretary that it was part of an 'investigation' – he'd been careful not to preface the word with 'official police'. The secretary had taken his home number and called him back. The Lord Provost could see him for five minutes at four o'clock.

'Five minutes should do it,' Rebus had said.

As he walked through the main door of the City Chambers, he looked down at the floor, aware that directly beneath it was Mary King's Close, Edinburgh's buried plague street. They'd covered the street up and built on it anew: that was the Edinburgh way, to bury and forget.

The Lord Provost came out of his office to meet him. He looked tired, his pale face deeply lined, his square jaw slack. He had dark hair streaked with silver, and thick black eyebrows. It was a strongly defined face, the kind that might have been found, a generation back, at the coal-face.

'Inspector.' They shook hands. The Lord Provost turned

to his secretary. 'My constitutional,' he said. 'I'll be five or ten minutes.' He turned back to Rebus. 'I like to get out of here for a few minutes in the afternoon, it clears my head. Do you mind?'

Rebus said he didn't.

No one on the street seemed to recognise Cameron Kennedy. He crossed the High Street and nodded towards St Giles' Cathedral. Rebus followed him into the huge old church. It was empty, save for a party of three tourists who huddled around their guidebook. Rebus and the Lord Provost walked the central aisle.

'How can I help you, Inspector?'

'Well, sir, it's about your daughter.'

The Lord Provost's face became more animated. 'Have you found her?'

'No, sir. But I know where she's been quite recently. You remember those two hoaxers?'

'Don't I just. You were in that terrible crash, weren't you?'

Rebus nodded. 'The thing is, it may not have been a hoax after all.'

'How do you mean?'

'Well, the girl you spoke to on the telephone ...'

'Ach, I don't think it was Kirstie.'

'It could have been. There's evidence she knew the two boys who died.'

The Lord Provost looked at him. 'Evidence?'

'Something we found in a bedroom.' Rebus brought out the business plan and handed it to the Lord Provost. 'This *is* yours, isn't it, sir?'

The Lord Provost studied it. 'Where did you say you found it?'

'It was hidden in the bedroom belonging to one of the boys. Do you know when and where you lost it?'

'No, I … It was a while back. I thought I'd taken it home with me …'

'Kirstie probably took it with her when she left.'

The Lord Provost nodded slowly.

'The question is, why? I mean, did it have any significance for her?'

'I don't see how it could.'

'Me neither, I was hoping you might help. Take a look at the last page, please.'

The Lord Provost turned to the last page and looked startled.

'Did you write that, sir?'

'No.' He was staring wide-eyed at the name.

'Is it Kirstie's writing?'

'I don't know.'

'Well, do you know what it means?'

The Lord Provost shook his head slowly and closed the report. 'Inspector, I … it seems to me maybe I'm making too much fuss over Kirstie. I'm sure she's managing fine.'

'What are you saying?'

'I'm saying I'm grateful to the police for trying to trace her, but maybe it's time to call a halt.'

Rebus narrowed his eyes. 'Why now?' He made to take the report back, but the Lord Provost was folding it into his pocket.

'Does there have to be a reason?'

'Is it something to do with that report?'

'You've read it?'

'Yes, sir.'

'It's just an initial report of a possible business venture.'

'In Gyle Park West?' The Lord Provost nodded. 'A new subsidiary of PanoTech?'

'You're well informed, Inspector.'

Rebus shrugged. 'I'm just curious why Kirstie would

take it, and why it was kept hidden, like it had some importance.'

Kennedy smiled. 'It's of no importance, Inspector. It's a projection, it's just something that might happen. God knows we could do with it.'

'Why's that, sir?'

'The jobs, of course.'

'Tell me, is the LABarum plan before any committee at present?'

The Lord Provost sat in a pew. Rebus sat one pew in front of him. 'I don't see what that could have to do with my daughter.'

Rebus shrugged. 'I'm just curious.'

'It will be discussed soon, yes.'

'By Councillor Gillespie's industry committee?'

'Initially, yes. Look, I really don't see what this has to do with Kirstie. I accept that she could have taken the document from my office at home. I'd say if it was anything, it was an act of pure rebellion – she took it because she *could*.'

'Is she a rebel then, sir?'

'Aren't all teenagers?'

'Not all teenagers are drug-users, sir.'

Rebus watched the colour come back to the Lord Provost's cheeks. 'What did you say?'

'That's why you didn't have a more recent photo to give us. Junkies aren't exactly photogenic.'

The Lord Provost shot to his feet. 'How dare you!' The tourists stopped consulting their guidebook.

'Then tell me I'm a liar,' Rebus said quietly. The Lord Provost opened his mouth, then closed it again. 'Tell me I'm a liar and I'll take back what I said.'

Cameron Kennedy's eyes were glistening in the half-light. He looked all around him, at the frayed standards hanging limply from the walls, at the altar and the windows

and the roof. Then he looked back to Rebus, shook his head, and walked away.

Rebus sat a few minutes by himself, hands clasped in his lap. He didn't exactly feel good about himself, but then that was nothing new.

21

The name of SWEEP's contact at the Scottish Office was Rory McAllister, and he agreed to meet Rebus for lunch the next day, suggesting an Italian restaurant at the top of Leith Walk.

When Rebus arrived at twelve-thirty, McAllister was already there. He'd just about completed the *Scotsman* crossword with an elegant chrome ballpoint pen. He stood up long enough to shake hands. Rebus noticed he was drinking mineral water.

'Stick to the businessman's lunch,' McAllister prompted, as a waiter handed Rebus an oversized menu. So Rebus stuck to the businessman's lunch.

Rory McAllister was in his late thirties with thinning, neatly cut hair and a face which still seemed to bear traces of both puppy-fat and acne. He peered at Rebus with eyes slightly narrowed, as if he might need spectacles but was too vain to wear them. His dark wool suit went well with a cream-coloured shirt and grey tie, knotted tightly at the throat.

Every inch the civil servant, Rebus thought. McAllister's voice was educated Edinburgh: nasal and lilting, not wanting to let go of the ends of syllables.

'So, Inspector,' he said, putting his newspaper out of sight under the table, 'your call was intriguing. What is it you want exactly?'

'I want you to tell me about the Scottish Office, Mr

McAllister. I also need to know about the SDA and Scottish Enterprise.'

'Well,' McAllister started to unwrap a bread-stick, 'let's order while I collect my thoughts, shall we?' He spoke to the waiter in a quiet, firm voice. Rebus knew the type: loud only in agreement, never in denial; when roused to anger, he'd bet McAllister's voice would drop to a whisper.

'The tomato soup's not bad,' Rebus was informed. 'Ditto the veal, but the *pollo* is very good, too. And as for the wine ...' Rebus shrugged assent with any suggestion McAllister might make. 'A half each of house white and red.' The civil servant snapped shut the wine list, another piece of business brought successfully to a close. He waved to two diners across the room. Their suits were like a uniform. The restaurant was filling quickly; half the diners looked like refugees from New St Andrew's House.

'So.' McAllister clapped his hands together and rubbed them. 'You want to know about the Scottish Office. Well, shall I start at the bottom or the top? You've met me, so that's the bottom taken care of.' He smiled to let Rebus know this was a joke. Sammy had said McAllister was a high-flier, clever and dedicated.

And helpful.

'So,' he went on, 'maybe I'll start at the top – the top, of course, being one of two men, depending on your situation. You can say that the Secretary of State for Scotland is the head of the Scottish Office, and as far as the public is concerned you'd be right. But politicians come and go, the Scottish Office remains.'

'You're saying the real head is the most senior civil servant?'

'Exactly, and that's the Permanent Under-Secretary, more usually known as the Permanent Secretary.'

'Why bother with two titles?'

McAllister laughed, a sound like a pig at the trough.

'Don't question; just accept.' A basket of bread rolls arrived, and he broke one into three. 'Now, the Scottish Office has responsibility for most functions of government in Scotland, excepting defence, foreign policy, and social security. We've a small outpost in Whitehall, but most of us are based here, either in St Andrew's House or New St Andrew's House.'

'St Andrew's House being ...?'

'It's on Regent Road. You know, it looks like the Reichstag.'

'Oh, the power station.'

McAllister conceded the image. 'That's where the Secretary of State and his advisors do their work. The rest of us are relegated to the neo-brutalism of New St Andrew's House – until Victoria Quay is ready.' Two bowls of thin-looking tomato soup arrived. 'The Secretary of State's retinue consists of the likes of the Lord Advocate and the Solicitor-General: they're both ministers of the Crown, of course.'

'Of course.'

'Plus a minister of State and three pusses.'

'Pusses?'

McAllister wiped the corners of his mouth with his napkin. 'Don't tell anyone I called them that: Parliamentary Under-Secretaries of State.'

'I thought you said there was only one?'

McAllister shook his head. 'Don't confuse Parliamentary with Permanent: the *Permanent* Under-Secretary is the only one who's a civil servant. He's the only one who is –'

'Permanent?'

McAllister nodded. He took some soup and chewed on his roll, preparing for another onslaught. The wine had arrived, and he poured a glass of white for himself. Rebus opted for red.

'Now,' McAllister said, 'we come to the departments.'

He counted them off on his fingers: 'SOID, SOED, SOEnD, SOHHD, SOAFD, and – shamefully prosaic – Central Services.'

Rebus smiled. 'Mr McAllister, I think you're purposely trying to bamboozle me.'

McAllister looked shocked. 'No, I assure you ...'

'Look, what I really want is a rundown on the SDA and Scottish Enterprise.'

'We'll get to them, don't worry.' The waiter came to take their bowls. 'Bit peppery today,' McAllister told him; not a complaint, a simple matter of interpretation.

The civil servant was halfway through his next dissertation before Rebus realised they'd moved on to the topics he was interested in.

'... so he was at SOHHD until the LECs came along. The SDA and HIDB became SE and HIE and the poor man, who'd been responsible for RDGs and RSA found himself –'

'Keep going, you might just drift back into English.'

McAllister produced another snorted laugh. 'Maybe I don't have enough dealings with the public. I'm used to people who understand the codes.'

'Well, I don't understand the codes, so humour me.'

McAllister took a deep breath. 'The SDA,' he began, 'was set up by Wilson in 1975, some say to appease the rising nationalism of that time. It had a budget of £200 million – which was not inconsiderable for the time – and took over from three old existing bodies, including the SIEC – the Scottish Industrial Estates Corporation. The SIEC brought with it twenty-five *million* square metres of factory space.'

'Sounds like a lot.'

'A hellish lot, a lot to keep occupied. The SDA got busy. It's been estimated there were as many as five thousand projects under its aegis at any one time. And remember, the

SDA didn't cover the whole of Scotland – there was the Highlands and Islands Development Board, too. In fact, HIDB was by far the elder of the two.' The pasta starters arrived. McAllister sprinkled parmesan cheese over his and got to work with his fork. 'Then someone had the bright idea of getting rid of the SDA.' He shook his head. 'Do you know the old saying, if it ain't broke, don't fix it? The SDA was in good fettle. It had been investigated by several bodies and committees and given a clean bill of health. It *did* get into trouble over the Glasgow Garden Festival, and over a deal with a building contractor called Quinlon, but by then the blueprint for Scottish Enterprise had already been set up.

'On the first of April – note the date – 1991, the SDA and HIDB became Scottish Enterprise and Highlands and Islands Enterprise. Basically, the changes were twofold: the new agencies took on the Scottish remit of the Training Agency and, more importantly, the central role of the SDA became more devolved.'

'How so?' Rebus wasn't touching the wine; he needed all his wits about him.

'Authority was devolved to a network of private-sector-led local enterprise companies, LECs for short.'

'Like Lothian and Edinburgh Enterprise Limited?'

'Yes, LEEL's one.'

'Is there any Scottish Office control?'

'Oh yes, Scottish Enterprise is sponsored by SOID.'

'The Scottish Office Industry Department?' McAllister gave a round of silent applause. 'Which leads us,' Rebus said, 'to funding.'

'Oh, I could talk all afternoon about funding, it's my specialty.'

'So what's Scottish Enterprise's annual budget?'

McAllister puffed out his cheeks. 'Around four hundred and fifty million.'

Rebus swallowed the last of his pasta. 'Forgive me, that sounds like a lot.'

'Well, the money has to be split: it covers Enterprise, environment, youth and adult training, plus admin costs.'

'Well, put like that I can see it represents excellent value for money.'

McAllister nearly choked with laughter. 'You sound just like a civil servant!'

'I was being ironic. Tell me, Mr McAllister, why did you agree to meet me?'

The question took McAllister by surprise. He took time forming his answer. 'I've never met a police officer before,' he said. 'I suppose I was curious. Besides, it's nice to meet someone who's actually *interested* in what we do, no matter what his motives. You know, only about one in three voters in this country even *knows* there's such a thing as the Scottish Office. One in three!' He sat back and opened his arms. 'And we've got a budget of millions!'

'Tell me,' Rebus said quietly, 'any word of any ... impropriety?'

'At Scottish Enterprise?'

Rebus nodded.

'No, none at all.'

'What about the SDA?'

One waiter removed their bowls, another set down the main course and accompanying vegetables. McAllister tucked in. He swallowed the first mouthful before answering Rebus's question.

'If there had been, Inspector, it would be dead and buried by now. When the SDA became Scottish Enterprise, the accounting procedures were changed: new set-up, new set of books. Like wiping the slate clean.'

'So what would have happened if any impropriety *had* been found?'

McAllister made a sweeping motion with his fork. 'Under the carpet with it.'

Rebus pondered this: wiping the slate clean, under the carpet … The district council was about to disappear, just as the SDA had done.

'You know, Mr McAllister, you don't seem very curious about *why* I want to know about the SDA and Scottish Enterprise.'

McAllister chewed on that. 'I suppose you'll tell me if and when you're ready. Until then, I don't see that it's any of my business. I'm not the curious sort, Inspector. In my line of work, that's seen as a strength.'

After a while Rebus asked: 'Who appoints the boards?'

'At SE and HIE, the Secretary of State.' McAllister poured the last of the wine into his glass. 'Not on his own, of course. He'd be advised by the Permanent Secretary. That, after all is the job of the Permanent Secretary: to advise. Though he implements too, of course.' McAllister glanced at his watch, then signalled for the waiter. 'I don't know about you,' he said to Rebus, 'but I think I might skip pud.' And he patted his ample stomach. When the waiter approached, McAllister ordered espresso.

'Is that what you're investigating, Inspector – impropriety at the SDA?'

Rebus smiled. 'I thought you weren't curious. Tell me, does the word Mensung mean anything to you?'

McAllister tried it out. He'd torn open a plastic toothpick, and was working on his mouth. The sight made Rebus's teeth jangle. 'I *do* seem to know it … can't think why or what it is. Want me to check?'

'I'd be grateful, sir. One other thing, any connection between the SDA or Scottish Enterprise and the US Consulate?'

Again, McAllister seemed surprised by the question. 'Well, yes,' he said at last, as his coffee arrived. 'I mean, we

172

do try to persuade American companies to locate here, so contacts at a consular level are helpful – vital, even. They were especially so in the eighties.'

'Why was that?'

'Microelectronics was booming. Silicon Glen. Locate in Scotland was working superbly. Did I mention LiS? It was part-SDA, part-Scottish office, with a remit to get foreign companies to locate here. Most of its successes were American, mostly in the early to mid-eighties. Rumour had it that its successes had less to do with canny persuasion and economic argument than with a kind of informal freemasonry.'

'How do you mean?'

'Well, a lot of top executives in American companies were and are Scottish, either born here or with Scottish roots. LiS would target those individuals and work on them, trying to get them not only to open a factory here, but to persuade other Scots in positions of influence. Look at IBM. Actually, this isn't an example of LiS at work; IBM has had a presence in Scotland for forty years. They started in Greenock, and they're still there – the plant's massive, about a mile and a half long. But what took them to Greenock in the first place? I'll tell you. It wasn't economics or a skilled workforce – it was *sentimentality*. The head of IBM at that time was in love with the west coast of Scotland; and that's all it was.' McAllister shrugged and blew on his coffee.

Rebus wanted to go back a stage or two. 'Is that how a lot of it works? Who you know?'

'Oh, definitely.'

'And bribes?'

'Not for me to say.'

Why not? thought Rebus. You've said every bloody thing but. It was two-thirty, the restaurant empty save for their table.

'I mean,' McAllister said, 'one man's bribe is another's "financial incentive". Look at Pergau Dam. There's always room to bend the rules without necessarily breaking them. Regional Selective Assistance, for example, was and is discretionary. Who's to say it doesn't make a difference if the person applying for it went to school with the person who'll make the final decision? It's the way the world turns, Inspector.' He tried to find some dregs of coffee in his cup, then unwrapped the amaretto biscuit.

Rebus paid their bill, and the waiter locked the door after them. McAllister's face was flushed, his cheeks a network of broken blood vessels. Now that he'd asked his questions, Rebus was keen to be elsewhere. There was something about McAllister he didn't like. He knew how easy it was to cover something up by talking about it at length. One confession could be made to disguise another. He'd had cleverer men than McAllister in the interview room, but not very many …

The two men shook hands.

'I appreciate you taking the time and trouble, sir,' Rebus said.

'Not at all, Inspector. I appreciate you paying for lunch. Besides, who knows? Maybe one day I might need a favour from you.' McAllister winked.

'You might at that,' Rebus said.

After all, it was the way the world turned, the civil servant was right about that. Rebus turned and headed off in any direction that wasn't McAllister's.

22

'All I've got,' Rebus admitted, 'are questions and loose ends, and none of it is getting me any closer to why McAnally killed himself or why the councillor's so scared. Added to that, the Lord Provost sees the word Dalgety scrawled on a sheet of paper and suddenly doesn't want us looking for his daughter any more.'

He was on the phone to St Leonard's, speaking with Brian Holmes. The drip from the radiator was getting worse. His mouth was getting worse. Behind him in the living room were the binbags full of paper. All the answers, he felt, were there, just beyond his abilities.

'So?' said Holmes.

'Thanks for the vote of confidence.'

'What do you want me to say?'

Rebus pushed at the skin around his nose, feeling the pressure increase on his poor tooth. 'The reason I phoned,' he said, 'is to ask what the state of play is with friend Duggan.'

Holmes rustled some papers. 'Now there I can help you. Paul Duggan is Edinburgh's answer to Rachman. He's been cheating the council for years. Lives with his parents, doesn't pay them a penny rent, but he's applied for and been allotted four council properties ... that's how many we've traced so far, there could be others. He doesn't mind hard-to-let flats, that's his secret.'

'How does he do it?'

'A series of pseudonyms, plus girls he drags along to

175

Housing Office interviews with a few bambinos in tow. The girls are friends of his, the kids aren't his.'

'But he becomes their father for the duration of the interview?'

'And gets himself priority listed. Once he's been allocated a place, all he does is let it out. I'm amazed he can find anyone for some of them. That place in Saughton was a palace compared to the others in his portfolio.'

Rebus dug into his back pocket and brought out the card he'd taken from the Waverley drop-in. Paul. Cheap rooms.

'Why do you think,' Rebus asked, 'Willie and Dixie had the pick of Duggan's properties? House that size, he could have squeezed a few more bodies in.'

'Right enough, the flat I checked in Granton had sleeping-bags in the living room, kitchen, and bathroom.'

Rebus studied the telephone number on the card. 'Maybe I'll have a wee word with our friendly slum landlord. Is the Farmer keeping you busy?'

'He keeps asking if I know what you're up to.'

'And what do you tell him?'

'I can keep my mouth shut. I just hope you know what you're doing, sir.'

'Well, Brian, there's a first time for everything.'

Rebus broke the connection and called the number on the card.

'Hello?' It was a woman's voice, polite, not young.

'Eh, is Paul there?'

'I'll just get him for you.'

'Thanks.'

She put the receiver next to the phone, and he could hear her calling for her son, who was probably in his bedroom counting shillings into a sock. Finally, the receiver was picked up.

'Aye?'

'Paul?'

'Who's this?'

'My name's John, I saw your notice at the drop-in centre.'

'Which one? I've got half a dozen notices up.'

'The one behind Waverley.'

'Oh aye, right.'

'I need a room.'

'Are you claiming social security?'

Rebus winged it. 'I'd be paying cash, if that's what you're worried about.'

'No, it's just that you've caught me at a bad time, John. Bit of pressure on me at the moment, if you know what I mean.'

'I know all about pressure.'

'So I'm not really opening any new transactions right this minute.' There was a pause. 'Did you say cash? Would you need a rentbook?'

'Cash, no rentbook.'

'Tell you what, John, can we maybe meet?'

Rebus's smile didn't translate to his voice. 'What's the address?'

'No address. Do you know Leith cop shop?'

Rebus stopped smiling. He'd been rumbled. But Duggan misinterpreted his silence.

'Not keen, eh? Been in trouble, have you?'

'A little bit.'

'We're only meeting outside. I can take you to a flat near there, down by the Shore. And that area's coming up in the world, by the way.'

Rebus almost admired the cheek. 'What time?'

'Five on the dot.'

'I'll be there,' said Rebus.

He phoned Brian Holmes back. 'Rachman's portfolio, anything down near the Shore?'

'Leith? No,' said Holmes, 'nearest one to Leith's the place in Granton. Why?'

'Just that you haven't tracked them all down yet, that's all.'

At five minutes to five, he was across the road from the police station. He stood two steps up from the pavement in the doorway of a disused building. Leith was taking a few faltering steps towards respectability. Trendy cafés and restaurants had opened in hastily refurbished premises, usually carved out of larger blocks of unrented space. There was a temporary feel to these new businesses; they always seemed to be 'under new management'. Leith's revival had begun down on the Shore and had all but stopped there, with warehouse conversions and a couple of upmarket bars. Now the revival had been given fresh momentum: the new Scottish Office HQ was under construction at Victoria Dock, and a sailors' home had been turned into a luxury hotel on Queen's Quay.

But Leith still retained its old, unique charm: it was still just about the only part of the city where you'd see prostitutes in daytime, freezing in short skirts and skimpy jackets. Rebus had passed some on his way down Bernard Street, readying themselves for the going-home trade: one quick leap for the homeward bound.

He stood in the doorway for quarter of an hour before Paul Duggan turned up. The young man was wearing an ankle-length black woollen coat, its collar turned up. On his feet were white trainers, so new they were almost luminous when caught in the headlamps of the passing traffic.

Duggan didn't pay any attention to Rebus as Rebus crossed the road; he was on the look-out for someone entirely different.

'Waiting for me?' Rebus asked.

It took Duggan a moment to place him. 'Christ, what do you want?'

'It was me that phoned. We didn't know you had another place on the Shore.'

'I don't know what you're talking about.'

'Come on, Paul, let's have a chat.'

'In there?'

Rebus looked towards the police station. 'No,' he said, 'not in there. This is just between us, understood?'

Rebus started walking, a hand on the sleeve of Duggan's coat.

'Where are we going?' Duggan asked.

'We're just walking, that's all. I've got a question for you. We know about four or five of your properties, and we know the Saughton let was the best of them by a fair old margin. So how come you only picked up two rents from it?'

Duggan stopped dead. 'Is this a trap? Are you miked up?'

Rebus laughed. 'For a tadpole like you? Behave, son, you're the council's problem, not mine.'

Rebus started walking again. Duggan caught him up. 'So what's the game?'

'I'm interested in Willie and Dixie, that's all. You told me you were their friend, so now I'm a wee bit interested in you, too.'

'That's why I gave them the house,' Duggan blurted out, thinking on his feet. 'They were my pals.'

'You *gave* them it? They didn't pay rent?'

'Oh ... oh aye, they paid rent. What I meant was –'

'Don't bother, son, don't compound one lie with another, you'll never keep track. My guess is they worked for you. What did they do?'

Duggan bit his lip. 'They collected the rents,' he said at last.

'And got free rent in return? That makes more sense. When I look at you, I see a skinny young kid, a sap. The kind of tenants you must deal with, you'd need back-up, isn't that right? Just in case someone decided not to pay.' Duggan nodded.

'They'd've been perfect for that,' Rebus continued. 'Willie had brains, he could reason with the non-payers, and if that didn't work, crazy Dixie could go to work. Is that about the score?'

'That's it.'

Rebus sniffed, and seemed to be thinking. 'Whose idea was the kidnap ruse?' he said casually.

'I've told you, I didn't know anything about that! They just asked for my car!'

'Must have been Willie's idea,' Rebus went on, as if Duggan hadn't spoken. 'Dixie didn't have the brains.' He turned to Duggan. 'Unless it was your idea, of course.'

Duggan made to protest, but thought better of it. They walked on in silence. 'OK,' he said at last. 'OK, between you and me, right?'

Rebus shrugged. 'Like I said, I'm not after you particularly, Paul, unless you lie to me. Lying to me is not advisable.'

'I knew what they were up to.'

'Of course you did. A tight-fisted wee bastard like you wouldn't lend someone the steam from his breath without there being a pay-off.' Rebus produced the photo of Kirstie Kennedy. 'You saw her with Willie and Dixie, didn't you?'

'No.'

'What about Dalgety?'

'Eh?' The name clearly meant nothing to Duggan.

'Come on,' Rebus said, 'I *know* you've seen her. You spend a lot of time in drop-in centres –'

'No, I don't.'

'You told me yourself your cards are up on half a dozen

noticeboards. How do they get there: by magic?' Rebus pushed the photo towards Duggan. 'You've seen her.'

'No.'

'You're lying. What are you afraid of, Paul?'

They were down on the Shore, and Duggan was just realising it. They walked close to the water's edge, across the street from the bars. Soon they'd be up to the dock entrance. Rebus stopped and tugged on Duggan's arm. 'Look at her!' he spat. Duggan averted his face. 'Look at her!'

Duggan glanced at the photo, then away again. His eyes were glinting in the streetlight.

'She knew Willie well enough to leave something in his bedroom. She *knew him* ... and I know damned well *you* knew her!'

Duggan blinked. 'What did she leave in his bedroom?' he asked quietly.

'Just tell me where she is.'

Duggan started to shake his head, and Rebus hauled him by the coat-sleeve to the water's edge. The street was empty save for a line of cars whose owners were all in the howffs.

'Fancy a dip, Paul? It can be invigorating at this time of year, if the sewage and the rats don't get you.'

'This coat cost a fortune!' Duggan squealed.

'You won't need it in jail, son. You'll be tucked up in bed with some big bad bastard keeping you warm.'

'All right, all right!'

Rebus released his grip. Duggan looked up and down the street.

'Run if you like, Paul. I'll find you.'

'Jesus, calm down, will you? OK, I've seen her. She hung around for a while with Willie and Dixie.'

'How long?'

'A week, maybe a bit longer.'

'Is she still around?'

'I haven't seen her. I only saw her a couple of times.'

'At the house in Saughton?'

'No, no, at a couple of drop-in centres.'

'But you don't know where she is, or what she's doing?' Duggan shook his head. 'Right, here's what we're going to do. You're going to find her for me.'

'What?'

'Somebody like you, lots of contacts … should be easy.'

'You don't know what you're asking.'

Rebus pointed to the water. 'There's your alternative.' He held out the photo. 'Take this, it might help.'

'It won't.'

'Why not?'

'That's not what she looks like. We had a laugh when we saw that picture in all the papers. I mean, I can believe she might have looked like that before she started using.'

'Drugs?'

'And plenty of them by the look of her.'

Rebus frowned. 'You think she's been on them long?'

'Long enough. Maybe a year or so.'

'A *year*?'

Duggan shrugged. 'Only a guess; I'm not into that scene.'

'I'll bet you don't mind them as tenants though, eh?'

Duggan straightened his shoulders. 'How about looking at it this way – I'm doing the council's work for it, putting roofs over the heads of people who'd be on the street otherwise.'

'Mr Social Conscience. They'll be giving you the keys to the city next. Get out of my sight, and take the photo, it's got my phone number on the back. If I don't hear from you in a day or two, we'll have another chat. Maybe at your place this time, with your mum and dad listening. How would you like that?'

Duggan didn't answer. He rearranged his coat, which had fallen down over one shoulder, then pocketed the photograph. Rebus watched him shuffle away, back towards the traffic.

So, now he knew for certain why the Lord Provost hadn't had a more recent photo of his daughter. He wondered why Duggan had been so curious about whatever Kirstie had left in Willie Coyle's bedroom. But Rebus was beginning to get an idea about that, too.

23

He drove to the Ox, where Doc and Salty stood in their allotted places. Room was made for Rebus, and Doc ordered him a pint.

'Oh what blessed company,' Rebus said, lifting the glass. He turned to Salty Dougary. 'I was out at Gyle Park West the other day.'

'In your professional capacity?'

'Sort of. What can you tell me about the place?'

'It's an industrial estate. I work there. What else is there to know?'

'The businesses there, would they have dealings with Scottish Enterprise?'

Salty nodded. 'LEEL,' he said. 'Our boss at Deltona is mad keen on "worker participation", which means once a week we have to sit in the canteen for twenty minutes listening to him rattle on about client satisfaction, inward investment, productivity and the like. He's always on about LEEL.'

'So Deltona has had money from LEEL?'

'John, *everyone* on that estate has had help of some kind: relocation incentives, start-up incentives, retraining incentives, you name it.' He raised his glass. 'God bless Scottish Enterprise.'

'Why the interest?' Dr Klasser asked. This was not their usual level of conversation.

'It could be peripheral to a case I'm working on.' Except

184

that there was no case and he wasn't supposed to be working.

'Well, keep your paws off Deltona,' Salty Dougary warned.

Rebus smiled. 'Ever heard of Mensung?' he asked.

'Don't they measure your intelligence?'

There was a snort from down the bar. 'They'd only need a six-inch ruler to measure yours, Salty.'

Salty laughed, so the speaker would know he wasn't amused. Rebus was still looking at him. 'To be honest,' Salty told him, 'it does ring a bell, way at the back of the old brainpan. I think it was a company.'

'On the estate?'

Dougary shrugged. The barman was taking a phone call. His eyes met Rebus's.

'For you, John.' He brought the telephone over. Rebus had another question for Salty.

'What about LABarum, ever heard of that?'

'What is this, "Mastermind"?'

Rebus took the receiver from the barman. 'Hello?'

'Is that you, John?'

Rebus recognised the voice – but it couldn't be, not calling him by his first name.

'Is that you, Flower?'

'Yes.'

DI Alister Flower – the Little Weed – calling Rebus 'John'. Something was wrong.

'What's up?'

'Just wondered if you could drop into the station for a chat.'

'A chat? Will you have the tea and biscuits ready?'

Flower laughed like he hadn't heard a better one all day. Rebus was more than curious.

'When?' he asked.

'Whenever you like.'

Rebus said he'd be there in half an hour.

The station was mid-evening quiet. To keep busy, most of the CID contingent had gone off to the scene of a car smash. The smash had taken place outside one of the neighbourhood's better Indian restaurants. So there was no one around the main office; no one but Alister Flower.

'John, how's the holiday?'

'I'm having a bit of trouble getting a tan.'

Rebus studied Alister Flower. There were a hundred reasons to dislike or even thoroughly loathe the man. The fact that he was a complete prick came pretty close to the top. Flower's eyes were always in movement, seeking out an angle or the main chance. The eyes were puffy, like the skin around them was constantly swollen. It could be genetic or to do with boozing, and it turned his eyes into slits. Rebus didn't like the fact that he couldn't always see those eyes.

Flower had friends around the station: spies, junior officers, who were a bit like him and would even like to *be* him. It scared Rebus. But there were no allies with him tonight. He sat on a desk, his feet on a chair. It wasn't his desk, wasn't his chair. Walking past his own desk, Rebus saw the new computer console. It didn't interest him at all.

'I was promised tea and biscuits,' he said.

'We can nip down the canteen after.'

'After what?'

'After I've shown you something. Come on.'

And he led Rebus down to the cells. There was a man in there, long-haired, unshaven, not happy.

'So who is he?'

'His name's Terry Shotts,' Flower explained. 'He's from Newcastle. We found him leaving a house in Prestonfield Avenue … with half the contents under his arm.'

'So?' Rebus closed the viewing-flap in the cell door.

'So we went to his digs. There was some other stuff there, including some that we could trace immediately from the register. His scam is, he thieves here and sells in Newcastle, and what he thieves there he lays off *here*.'

'It's a tremendous feat of detection, Flower. I want to thank you for sharing it with me.'

Rebus started back upstairs, Flower following. He handed Rebus a folded sheet of paper.

'This is a list of the stuff the Geordies found in his flat. They traced some of it to a couple of break-ins, but the lists didn't match. Looks like he'd already sold some of the stuff on. Including a shotgun.' Rebus began to see the point. 'Shotts has been up here three weeks. I think he sold it to Shug McAnally.'

'Have you asked Mr Shotts?'

'He's as good as admitted it.'

Rebus stopped. 'Maybe I should talk to him.'

Flower blocked his path. 'I don't think that would do any good.' Rebus wasn't in the mood for a fight, so kept on walking. 'I thought you'd be pleased. I mean, it ties up the loose ends, doesn't it?'

'It might tie up one of them, but it just unravels a couple more. Want to know what they are? Number one, why are you interested? Number two, why would you want me to be "pleased"?'

They were back in the CID room.

'Well,' Flower said, making for his desk, 'I just thought you'd want to know.'

'That's just so much keech, Flower. What are you up to?'

Flower reached into a drawer and showed Rebus a bottle of whisky. Rebus shook his head, but Flower poured himself a measure into a broken-handled mug.

'What are you so damned paranoid about, Rebus?'

'You, for a start.' Flower took a gulp of whisky, then lit a cigarette.

'It's a fair point,' he conceded, through a wreath of smoke. 'OK, I'll tell you straight. Someone *asked* me to talk to you. You know I wouldn't do it otherwise.'

'That's more like it.' Rebus sat on the edge of a desk. 'So who's the someone?'

'Just someone important.'

'The Farmer?'

Flower smiled and exhaled noisily. Someone higher than the Farmer then, a lot higher.

'And just what,' Rebus asked, 'does this anonymous patron want me to know?'

Flower examined the tip of his cigarette. 'That you're on your way out, the way you're going.'

'Out?'

'Of the force.' Flower paused. 'At the very least.'

'Why?'

'You don't need to know that.'

Which meant, thought Rebus, that it was because of something he *might* do rather than something already done.

'So what should I do?' he asked.

'Stop being so bloody nosy.'

'About what?'

'McAnally, for Christ's sake.'

'What does —'

'Look, I'm just the message-boy, OK?'

'If the cap fits …'

Flower's eyes narrowed still further. 'Look,' he said at last, 'you know if it was up to me, I'd leave you to squat on the pan and send your career down the lavvy like the night before's kebab. All I'm doing is a favour for someone who wants you to have a final warning. Hear me? A final warning.' He stood up and flicked his butt into a waste-bin.

'Pretty convenient,' Rebus said, 'the source of the

shotgun suddenly turning up ... Who is it, Flower? The DCC? Big Jim Flett? What have they got to hide?' Rebus was standing inches from Flower. 'What's it got to do with *you*?' He jabbed Flower's chest with his finger.

'Touch me again, you're dead.'

'Tell your friend, if he wants to threaten me, he should do it himself. Nobody's scared of the message-boy.'

Then he turned and walked away. He was worried though. If they were serious – whoever *they* were – when he was so far from solving the puzzle, how would they react if he got any closer? He stopped at the door.

'By the way,' he said, 'your fag-end just set fire to that bin.'

Flower turned and saw that the contents of the waste-bin were indeed smouldering. He reached for some liquid to douse the fire.

He'd forgotten that it was whisky, not coffee, in his mug.

Rebus's phone was ringing as he got home. It was Rico Briggs.

'I had a word with a friend,' he told Rebus. Rico never liked to say too much on the phone.

'And?'

'Be in the bus station at eleven.'

'Tonight?'

'Tonight.'

'Whereabouts in the bus station?'

'Just be there. You'll pay him his share and mine.'

The line went dead.

24

At ten to eleven, Rebus was in the St Andrew's Square bus station. A few early drunks had assembled for the last bus home. There was a pub in the bus station; it sounded busy. A man sprinted out of it, slipped in a patch of oil, and fell like a sniper's bullet had got him. He got back to his feet in time to see his bus pull away, and started swearing. There was a gash in the knee of his trousers.

Exhaust fumes lay in heavy strata just above ground level. Rebus tried not to breathe too deeply as he walked up and down the ranks. A few teenagers were asleep on the precarious benches. An old man, looking dazed, crossed the concourse dressed in a duffel coat, pyjamas and slippers. The slippers looked brand new, maybe a Christmas present.

'Where are you?' Rebus hissed, stamping his feet. He pushed his hands deeper into his pockets and walked the ranks again.

'Sit down,' a voice said.

Rebus looked down at the figure. He'd thought the man was asleep, arms folded, head tucked into the front of his jacket. He was sitting at the last rank. There was a bus there, but with its lights off.

Rebus sat down, and the man looked up at him. He had greasy brown hair which fell over one eye, and he could have done with a shave. There was a small scar, no more than a nick, below his right eye. The eyes were piercing

blue with long lashes. When he spoke, Rebus saw there was a tooth missing from the front of his mouth.

'Money.'

'You're Rico's friend?'

The man nodded. 'Money,' he repeated.

Rebus showed him two twenties, then handed them over. 'He said half for him.'

'He'll get half.' The voice was a lazy west coast drawl. 'You want to know about Saughton?'

'A man killed himself with a shotgun. He was fresh out of Saughton.'

'Which bit?'

'C Hall.'

The man shook his head. 'Can't help you then.'

A driver had come over to the bus, cashbox in hand. He opened the doors and went inside, closing them after him. Lights came on all the way up the bus.

'What do you mean?'

'Just what I say. I can't help.'

The engine started up, spewing fumes. A couple of people had joined the queue and were wondering whether to jump ahead of the two seated down-and-outs.

'Why not?'

'Never really knew anyone in C Hall.' The man stood up, Rebus rising with him. 'This is my bus.'

'Wait a minute.'

The man turned to him. The bus doors were opening, the people behind wanting to be in the warm. 'Ask Gerry Dip.'

'Gerry Dip?'

'He was in C Hall, came out a few weeks back.'

'Where can I find him?'

'Dipping fish, that's how he got the name.' The man climbed on to the platform. 'I hear he's working in a chip shop on Easter Road.'

* * *

Every chip shop in Scotland was at its busiest after the pubs had emptied. Even the bad ones, the ones with bony fish and rubber batter, had queues. Rebus took one look at the wares on display in the second chip shop he tried, and decided he would go without.

There was a queue almost out the door, but he walked to the front, ignoring the stares. A teenage girl was serving, mouth open in concentration.

'Salt and sauce?' she asked the customer.

'Is Gerry in?' Rebus asked.

She nodded further along the counter. There was a small man there dipping fish in a bucket of batter before tossing them into the fryer.

'Gerry?' Rebus asked. The man shook his head and pointed towards the back of the narrow shop, where a very tall, very skinny young man wearing a white cotton apron was playing the video machine.

It was one of those kick-and-chop games, the enemy bounding into view only long enough to be taken out again by the snarling cartoon hero.

'Gerry Dip?' Rebus said.

The player was in his mid-twenties, with cropped black hair and a nose-stud. His bare arms sported tattoos, and there were more on the backs of his hands. On his right wrist was a tattooed watch, the hands of which pointed to twelve. Rebus checked his own watch and saw that Gerry Dip's was dead-on.

Rebus saw that Dip was watching him in the screen's reflection. 'Not many people call me that,' he said.

'I'm a friend of a friend, someone you knew in Saughton. He said you could maybe help me. There'd be a drink in it.'

'How big a drink?'

Rebus had been to a cash machine. He laid a crisp twenty on the console. Maybe it affected Dip's concentration. A landmine tore the arms and legs off his man. The Game

Over message flashed, and a digitised voice said, 'Feed ...
Money ... Me ... Hungry.'

Gerry Dip palmed the note. 'Let's retire to my office.'

He led Rebus behind the counter and told the fish
batterer he'd swop places in five minutes. Then he pushed
open a door and led Rebus into a kitchen-cum-storeroom.
Sacks of potatoes waited to be peeled, and two large
freezers hummed.

'I hope you're not Environmental Health,' Gerry Dip
said, getting a glass of water from the sink and gulping it.
'Actually, I know what you are, it gets so you can smell it
after a while.'

Rebus let the remark go. 'A man was released from C
Hall a couple of weeks back. He stuck a gun into his –'

'Wee Shug.' Dip nodded. 'I knew him, played cards a
few times, talked about telly and the football.' Dip refilled
his glass. 'You're up from six in the morning till nine at
night, lights-out isn't till ten. You get to know people. Plus
I worked with him in the upholstery workshop. He said
he'd come down the chippie and see me – then I read about
him in the papers.'

'Did you know he was ill?'

'He saw the doctor a lot, never talked about it though. I
know he had some medicine: we wanted him to hand it
round so we could get a buzz. What was wrong with him?'

'Cancer.'

'That why he topped himself?'

'Could be.'

'Well, if you want to know about Wee Shug, you should
talk to his cell-mate. Now *there* was a fucking character.
Hoity-toity, stayed in his cell even when he didn't need to.'

Big Jim Flett had mentioned a cell-mate; Rebus saw
suddenly why Flett had been relieved at the end of their
interview.

'Gerry, what was Wee Shug in for?'

'Housebreaking.'

'You sure about that?'

'That's what I heard.'

'Not rape?'

'What?'

No, thought Rebus, because rapists are usually kept away from the other prisoners. But the governor had let it slip that Wee Shug shared a cell.

'He wasn't inside for rape,' Gerry Dip said.

'How can you be sure?'

'We'd've known.'

'He's not likely to have told you himself.'

'No, but the screws would have, *somebody* would have. It's one secret you can't have in the nick.'

'Unless,' Rebus said quietly, 'nobody wanted you to know.'

25

Rebus called CID from a phone box near St Leonard's and, without identifying himself, asked to speak to either DS Holmes or DC Clarke.

It was a morning of heavy haar, floating across the city in a wet cloud from the coast. The kind of morning where you could imagine yourself back in time, a horse and coach clopping out of the mist rather than cars with their headlights on full. Rebus's skin and clothes were damp to the touch.

'DC Clarke speaking.'

'It's me. I want you to look up a name on the computer.'

'Well, it's a bit chaotic here just now. There was a small fire last night, a waste-bin went up. It's a bit of a mystery, nobody was here at the time.'

'Dear me.'

'The chief super's ordered an investigation. Meantime, half the office is off limits.'

'But the computer system's OK?'

'The only damage is the bin and the desk next to it. It was Inspector Flower found the blaze.'

'Really?'

'He threw a coat over the bin to snuff it out. It was Holmes's coat.'

'The one Nell gave him for Christmas?'

'That's the one. What's the name you want checking?'

'Charters.' He spelt it for her. 'I don't have a first name, but he's serving time in Saughton. I'd like his record. I'm

195

in a callbox about a hundred yards away. There's a café across from the DIY store, I'll wait for you there.'

'I'll be as quick as I can.'

'The dough-rings are on me.'

But when Siobhan Clarke finally turned up at the café, she ordered a fried-egg sandwich instead, then handed Rebus a manila envelope.

'Did anyone see you at the computer?'

'I don't think so.'

'Watch your back. It's not just the Farmer – Flower's up to something, too.'

'What?'

'Fire-raising for a start.' Rebus opened the envelope and read through the contents. Clarke's food arrived and she bit into it, dripping yolk on to the plate.

'"Derwood Charters",' Rebus read aloud, '"age forty-six, divorced, ex-company director. Found guilty of fraud, serving three years of a six-year sentence at HMP Edinburgh. Home address in Cramond till the place had to be sold. Date of birth … name of solicitor … no wife or next of kin".' Rebus skipped through what little else there was. 'It's a bit bald, isn't it?'

'A bit.'

'Like somebody's been into the computer and shorn it. Which station dealt with him?' He looked through the notes again. 'Well, well: St Leonard's.'

'But before our time?'

Rebus nodded. 'I was still at Great London Road. But then so was Chief Inspector Lauderdale, yet his name's down here as part of the team.' He was thoughtful for a moment. 'Right, what I want you to do is –'

'Go back to the station and pull the case-notes out of the vault?'

'I know it's asking a lot.'

'Only my career.'

But he knew she'd do it anyway.

Rebus waited over an hour for Clarke to return. She carried a supermarket carrier-bag with her, and laid it on the floor next to him. He ordered her a mug of tea; his own stomach was swilling with the stuff.

'It wasn't where it should have been,' she told him. 'It had been put back out of order.'

'Like someone wanted to hide it?'

'But without being too obvious. There are so many reports in the vault, it's easy for one to disappear if it's filed in the wrong place.'

'Did anyone see you?'

'Brian came to see what I was up to. I got him to keep an eye out for anyone else. Meantime, the sooner you read the case-notes, the sooner I can put them back.'

The woman who ran the café brought Siobhan Clarke's tea, and saw Rebus lift a heavy folder out of the carrier-bag.

'Thinking of taking up residence?' she asked him.

'I'm doing you a favour,' he said, glancing at all the empty tables. 'Nobody comes into an empty café.'

'You did,' she replied.

Rebus just smiled and opened the case-notes, starting to read.

At lunchtime, Rebus made a dentist's appointment.

When he explained the problem, the receptionist asked him to hold the line. When she came back, she told him Dr Keene could squeeze him in at five.

The surgery was in a substantial semi-detached property on Inverleith Row, facing the entrance to the Botanic Gardens. Rebus was in a sweat as he sat in the waiting room. There was a woman in there with him, and he was relieved when she was called first. But that left only him. His ears seemed more receptive than usual. He could hear

197

the whine of a drill, the clatter of metal probes being dropped on to trays. When the woman patient came out, she walked to the reception desk to make another appointment. The dentist was with her. Then the dentist turned and, smiling, came to the waiting-room doorway.

'Mr Rebus? Through here, please.'

He wore a white coat and half-moon glasses, and Rebus judged him to be in his late fifties.

'Sit down, please,' Dr Keene said, washing his hands. 'Some swelling around the mouth?'

Rebus sat on the chair and swung his legs up on to it, his hands gripping the armrests. Dr Keene came over.

'Now, just lie back and try to relax.' Rebus could hear his own hoarse breathing. 'That's it.' The dentist used an electric foot-switch to set the chair back so it was nearly flat, and to raise it up. He angled the lamp over the chair and switched it on. 'We'll just take a look.' He swivelled a tray of dental tools towards him and sat down on a high chair by Rebus's side.

'Open wide.'

There was music playing. Radio Two, the airwaves' answer to a placebo. Rebus opened his eyes and stared at the ceiling. There was a blown-up photograph there, a huge black and white aerial shot of Edinburgh, from Trinity in the north to as far south as the Braid Hills. He started to map out the streets in his mind.

'Looks like a wee abscess,' the dentist was saying. He put down one tool and reached for another, tapping it against one of Rebus's teeth. 'Feel anything?' Rebus shook his head. The assistant had joined them. Dr Keene said a few things to her in a language the patient wasn't supposed to understand, then started packing Rebus's mouth with cotton.

'What I'm going to do is drill into the tooth from behind, to try to drain off the poison. That'll release the pressure.

198

The tooth is pretty well dead anyway, I'll do a root canal later. But for now the abscess needs to drain.'

Rebus could feel sweat on his forehead. A tube was being placed in his mouth, hoovering up what saliva there was.

'A little injection first. It'll take a minute or two to take.'

Rebus stared at the ceiling. There's Calton Hill, where Davey Soutar ended up. There's St Leonard's ... and Great London Road. Hyde's Club was just down there. Ooyah! There's Stenhouse, where Willie and Dixie lived. You could see Saughton Jail quite clearly. And Warrender School, where McAnally blew his head off. He had a sense of the way the streets interconnected, and with them the lives of the people who lived and died there. Willie and Dixie had known Kirstie Kennedy, whose father was Lord Provost. McAnally had sought out a councillor as witness to his act of self-destruction. The city might cover a fair old area, its population might be half a million, but you couldn't deny how it all twisted together, all the criss-crossed lines which gave the structure its solidity ...

'Now,' the dentist was saying, 'you might feel some discomfort at first ...'

Rebus raced up and down the streets. Marchmont, where he lived; Tollcross, Tresa McAnally's home; South Gyle, only just taking off when the photograph was taken. There was no sign of the newer building work around the town. He saw holes in the ground and areas of wasteland where now there were structures and roads. And Jesus Christ Almighty it was hurting!

'Ah,' Dr Keene said at last, 'there we are.' Rebus could feel something nasty trickling down his throat. The pressure beneath his nose was easing. Like bleeding a radiator, he thought. 'Drill into the poison,' the dentist was saying, almost to himself, 'and you relieve the pressure.'

Yes, Rebus thought, that was absolutely right.

The dentist gave the rest of his mouth a once-over. The

assistant had a card in her hand and was writing on it as Dr Keene recited a litany of decay.

'I won't do any of these fillings today,' he said to Rebus's relief.

Eventually he was allowed to rinse and spit, and the assistant removed the elasticated bib from around his neck. Rebus ran his tongue around his mouth. There was a gaping hole in the back of one of his front teeth.

'We've got to let that drain, give it a few days. Once it's drained, I can do the root canal. All right?' And he smiled at Rebus. 'Incidentally, when did you last have your teeth checked?'

'Eleven, twelve years ago.'

The dentist shook his head.

'I'll make up your appointments,' the assistant said, leaving the room. Dr Keene removed his latex gloves and went to wash his hands.

'Now that we all wear gloves,' he said, 'I don't really need to wash them. But I've done it for thirty years, hard to break the habit.'

'You wear the gloves because of HIV?'

'Yes. Well, goodbye then, Mr –'

'Inspector Rebus, actually.'

'Oh?'

'I wonder if I might have a word?' Rebus knew he was mumbling – the anaesthetic had frozen his mouth. But Dr Keene had no trouble understanding him.

'You mean officially?'

'Sort of. I believe you know a man called Derwood Charters?'

Dr Keene snorted and started rearranging his instruments.

'I'll take that as a yes,' Rebus said.

'Very much to my cost. Like you, he walked into my surgery one day requiring treatment. Then I bumped into

200

him socially. We met a few more times, and he put a proposition to me.'

'A financial proposition?'

'He needed investors for a start-up. The man had a proven track record, he'd helped finance the PanoTech start-up for one thing, and you'd hardly call *that* a failure. Mind, I didn't just take his word for anything; I had my accountant look at the figures. The projections seemed sound, professionally done.'

'What was the company?'

'Derry was very persuasive, he always stipulated the downside of any project. Somehow, the more he talked them down, the more attractive he made them sound. He came across like he wasn't trying to sell you anything. The scheme I invested in, the company was going to profit from the downturn in the economy. That was the downside: other people's misery was going to make his investors money. He was offering retraining and counselling for employees who suddenly found themselves "reorganised" out of a job. He explained that once the company was up and running – it was to be called Albavise – he'd be able to draw on European Community grants, Scottish Office funding, all that. What he needed was start-up capital.' Dr Keene paused. 'Know what? I believed him then and I believe him now: if he'd used the money to start the company, it would have succeeded.'

'But he didn't set up a company, did he?'

Dr Keene sighed. 'He used it to pay off debts, and to finance his lifestyle. He'd picked out ten investors, each handing over five thou. Fifty thousand pounds, Inspector, and he blew the lot inside three months.'

Yes, and then tried to do a runner. Only, one of his investors had an accountant who was sharper than most. Charters was arrested as he made to board the shuttle to London.

'Once they started investigating his affairs – the Inland Revenue, Fraud Squad, what have you – they found a lot of discrepancies, none of which Derry was willing to discuss. He kept his peace all through the trial.' He looked at Rebus. 'Has something happened?'

Rebus shrugged. 'Early days yet, sir.' The stock response, but Dr Keene accepted it.

'It wasn't the cash that hurt, you know,' he told Rebus. 'It was that sense of betrayal.'

'I can imagine.'

The Charters case-notes had made for fascinating reading. For example, Rebus now knew that Frank Lauderdale had been attached to the Fraud Squad at the time they'd been investigating Albavise and Derwood Charters' other business interests. Thinking back on it, Rebus did recall a period when Lauderdale had been away from Great London Road. But Lauderdale was the least interesting part of it. For the man who had been head of the Fraud Squad back then, Chief Superintendent Allan Gunner, was now deputy chief constable of Lothian and Borders Police.

And that wasn't all ...

'Dr Keene, do you know a man called Haldayne? Spelt with a y.'

'I don't think so.'

'He's American, works at the consulate.'

Dr Keene was shaking his head. 'No, I don't know him. Is it important?'

'He's another of the investors ripped off over Albavise. I thought you might have met, that's all.'

'We might have met in court, had any witnesses been called. But Charters changed his mind at the last minute and pled guilty.'

'Really? Any idea why?'

'None. My solicitor was amazed. The case against him

was by no means watertight and, as I say, he had a very good track record. It was possible he might have gone free, or at least got off with a heavy fine. But instead, he went to jail. I've often wondered why he did that.'

Rebus was wondering the same thing. 'Maybe,' he said, 'to protect someone or something that could have come to light at the trial.'

'But who or what?'

Rebus just smiled and winked. He collected his coat and put it on in the hallway. The assistant had already gone home. There was an appointment card on her desk. Dr Keene picked it up and handed it to Rebus.

'See you in a few days.'

Rebus looked at the card. There was a long column of appointments listed on its back. Six of them. Dates and times.

'Dr Keene,' he said, 'exactly how many fillings do I need?'

'Fifteen,' the dentist said matter-of-factly. Then he saw Rebus to the door.

26

That night, Rebus went to see Tresa McAnally.

The tenement door wasn't locked, so he climbed the stairs to her flat. He could hear music inside, good-time music, and the sounds of hands clapping in time. Rebus pressed the bell and waited, then pressed it again. The music was turned down. A voice came from behind the door. 'Who is it?'

'Inspector Rebus.'

'Wait a minute, will you?' She was a long time opening the door; even then she kept the chain on. 'What do you want?'

Behind her, the door to the living room was closed. There was a case of mixed spirits on the hall carpet. Tresa McAnally was dressed casually – baggy T-shirt, tight black slacks, looped gold earrings – and she was sweating from recent exertion.

'Can I come in?' Rebus asked.

'No, you can't. What is it?'

'It's about Wee Shug.'

'He's dead, end of story.' She made to close the door. Rebus pushed his hand against it.

'Where did the money come from, Tresa?'

'What money?'

'The money you spent on the flat.'

'You've no right to –'

'Maybe not, but I'll keep coming back till you tell me.'

'Then you'll be coming back till doomsday.'

Rebus smiled. 'That may be closer than you think.' He lifted his hand from the door, but she didn't shut it.

'What do you mean?'

'Who's in there with you?'

'Nobody.'

'Nobody?'

Not even Tresa McAnally was brass-necked enough to repeat the lie. She pushed the door closed.

Rebus stood for a moment, listening, then walked along to Maisie Finch's flat. He rang her bell, but she couldn't very well answer, not when she was busy hiding behind Tresa McAnally's living-room door.

Next morning, Rebus called the US Consulate.

'You're not another recording, are you?' Rebus asked.

'No, I'm not.'

'Good, can you put me through to Mr Haldayne, please?'

'Your name?'

'Detective Inspector John Rebus.'

'Hold the line, Inspector.'

He didn't have to hold long.

'Inspector? What can I do for you?' An American accent, smooth, urbane. Rebus wasn't exactly sure what 'Ivy League' meant, but Haldayne's voice brought to mind the image.

'Well, sir, for one thing you can start paying your parking tickets.'

A confident chuckle. 'Goodness, is that what this is all about? Well, certainly, if you insist. I wouldn't want to make a diplomatic incident out of it.'

'But you could, is that what you mean? The tickets aren't the main reason I'm ringing. I'd like to talk to you about Derwood Charters.'

'Jesus, what has he done this time?' A pause. 'Don't tell me I'm getting back my money?'

'Could we discuss it in person?'

'Yeah, I guess. You want to come here?' The US Consulate, where Haldayne would be at his most consular.

'The North British,' Rebus suggested, 'for morning coffee.'

'It's not called the North British any more, is it?'

'You've got a lot to learn about Scotland, Mr Haldayne. Ten-thirty?'

'That's fine, Inspector. I look forward to meeting you.'

Rebus's next call was to St Leonard's. He asked for Siobhan Clarke. 'How's life?'

'Ms Templer had me in her office first thing, wanting to know if you'd been in touch. She was asking a lot of questions.'

'Let her ask. As far as you know, I'm in Lanzarote.'

'Right.'

'Listen, Haldayne's parking tickets, what were the exact locations?'

'I think I jotted them down.' He could hear her searching her notebook.

'How goes the blaze inquiry?'

'A non-starter. It's down to an Act of God. They didn't find a cigarette or a match in the bin.'

'Of course not, Flower tidied up before he reported the fire.'

'Here we are: Princes Street, James Craig Walk, and Royal Circus. Those are all I've got, and no dates. The last two were multiples.'

Rebus thanked her and hung up. He found his *A–Z* and looked up James Craig Walk. It was hard by New St Andrew's House. So Haldayne *did* have dealings with the Scottish Office. Princes Street could just mean he was shopping. Rebus wasn't sure what or who Royal Circus represented. He remembered the councillor's files: SDA/ SE; A C Haldayne; Gyle Park West; Mensung.

He still didn't know anything about Mensung. He was hoping Haldayne could help.

Rebus sat in the lounge of the Balmoral Forte Grand – formerly the North British – and told staff he was waiting for a guest but he'd order anyway: coffee for two – decaffeinated – and cakes or biscuits or something.

'Fruit scones, sir?'

'Fine, whatever.'

'Thank you, sir.'

Rebus was glad he was wearing one of his better suits. They'd made a good job of the hotel. Last time he'd had morning coffee here, it had been with Gill Templer, way back when they'd been 'an item'. The walls had had cracks in them, and the whole place had seemed faded and slightly seedy.

Rebus knew the American as soon as he walked in. He was tall and exceptionally well groomed and wearing a cream-coloured Burberry raincoat. Haldayne had fair hair, so fine and thin you could see pink scalp beneath it. He was around forty, and wore glasses with tortoiseshell circular frames. His face was thin, his forehead bulbous and shiny.

'Inspector Rebus?' He shook Rebus's hand, and Rebus motioned for him to sit.

'Cold enough for you over here?' Rebus asked.

'I was brought up in Illinois.' Haldayne slipped his coat off. 'We got winters you wouldn't believe.' He shivered at the memory and chuckled again; it was becoming an annoying habit.

Rebus had an annoying habit too: he kept poking the tip of his tongue into the hole in his tooth and trying to suck the poison out. He was getting to like that little bore-hole.

'Do you know a Dr Keene?' he asked the American.

Haldayne made a sceptical mouth. 'Care to give me a clue?'

'He's a dentist, and another of Derry Charters' victims.'

Haldayne sat back in his comfortable chair. 'Took me for five biggies. That still hurts; I'm a diplomat, not a millionaire.'

'What do you do at the consulate?'

'I have an industry remit. In some countries that would be a two-way process, but there aren't too many Scottish companies thinking of setting up plants in the US, so I tend to look after American companies who're thinking of setting up here. It's not as busy as it was.' He looked left and right. 'Waiting staff are slow.'

'I've already ordered. I hope you don't mind.' Haldayne shrugged. 'How did you come to know Derry Charters?'

'I was introduced to him at a party. Can't recall now who did the introducing ...'

'Can you remember whose party?'

'Oh, it was some Scottish Office thing, that's why I was there.'

'And Mr Charters?'

'Well, he was a businessman. How much do you know about him before his bust?'

'Practically nothing,' Rebus lied, wondering what tack Haldayne might take.

'He ran a few companies, and ran them profitably. But he was always looking to expand. I think he just got bored, simple as that. He liked to set things up, get projects running, but after that he lost interest and started looking for something new. He was good at what he did, though; that's why I wasn't overcautious when he asked me to be a backer.'

'Did you know him well?'

'Not really. When he was talking deals he was fine, but he wasn't a social animal. I got the feeling normal polite conversation bored the hell out of him. He was a genuine product of the eighties, one of Lady Thatcher's bulls.'

The tray arrived, with *cafetière* and a plate of fruit scones with butter, jam and clotted cream.

'Hey, this looks great, thank you,' Haldayne said to the waiter. He immediately took over, putting the cups out, serving the coffee. While he was pouring, Rebus asked a question.

'Ever heard of something or someone called Mensung?'

'Run it by me again.'

'Mensung.'

Haldayne shook his head, and handed Rebus a cup and saucer. He hadn't spilled a drop, hadn't even paused while pouring.

'If you help American companies, Mr Haldayne, does that mean you have dealings with Scottish Enterprise?'

'All the time.'

'And Locate in Scotland?'

'I've had dealings with them all, Inspector. Thing is, you're just beginning to establish a working relationship, then the government changes everything: changes the name, the rules, the players. SDA becomes Scottish Enterprise, HIDB becomes HIE, and I've got to start again from scratch, building up contacts, letting people know who I am.'

'It's a tough life.'

'But somebody's got to do it, right?' Haldayne spread cream on to half a scone. 'I love these pastries,' he confided, before taking a huge bite.

'You've been here a while?' Rebus asked.

'Nine years, on and off. They did send me back to the States for a couple of years in the middle, but I wangled my way back over again. I love Scotland – my ancestors came from here.'

'I heard a rumour once,' Rebus said, 'about a kind of Scottish mafia at the top of some US businesses, persuading people to locate in Scotland.'

Haldayne wiped cream from his mouth with a napkin. 'It happens,' he said. 'What can I say? It's not illegal.'

'What *would* be illegal, Mr Haldayne?'

'Bribes, money changing hands.'

'Companies can set up here very cheaply, can't they?'

'Some areas, some types of plant, sure. A lot of grant money swilling around, some from the European Community, some from British Government coffers.'

'There was the DeLorean scandal,' Rebus said.

'But the guy did have a sensational car.'

'And he took the British taxpayer for millions.'

'You'd still have paid those taxes, Inspector. If DeLorean hadn't taken them, some other guy would.' Haldayne shrugged again. His expressions, whether vocal or physical, were always slightly exaggerated, slightly more than you'd get from a Scot.

'So the Scottish mafia story is true?'

'I'd guess so. I'm being as open with you as I can.'

'I appreciate it, sir.'

'Hey, you're the one holding those parking tickets at my head.' Another chuckle. 'What kind of coffee is this?'

'Decaf.'

'It's not bad actually, but I do miss that caffeine rush. Waiter!' A teenager trotted over. 'Can I have a double espresso? Thank you.' Haldayne turned back to Rebus. 'So what's the story here, Inspector? We don't seem to be talking about Derry Charters any more.'

'Just part of an ongoing inquiry, sir. I'm not at liberty to –'

'Well, that's hardly fair, is it? Hardly *British*?'

'You're not in Britain now, Mr Haldayne.'

'But I've told you mine, now you should tell me yours.'

Rebus saw that Haldayne was having a good deal of fun at his expense. Suddenly he didn't know how much of Haldayne's story to believe. Lies usually came gift-wrapped

in a thin tissue of truth. Rebus knew he would have to examine the wrappings later.

'Come on, Inspector,' Haldayne persisted. 'You're checking up on Derry, this much I know. But he's still serving time, right? So what has he done – set up some paper company from his cell?'

'Paper company?'

'You know, one that exists only on paper.' Haldayne came to an abrupt stop and reached into his pocket for a handkerchief.

He's stalling, thought Rebus. Why is he stalling? The espresso arrived, and Haldayne took a couple of appreciative mouthfuls, regaining his composure.

'I came here in good faith, Inspector,' he said at last. 'I didn't need to speak to a man who's not here in his official capacity.' Haldayne saw the look on Rebus's face, and smiled. 'I wanted to check that you were who you said you were. We US diplomats can't be too careful these days. Your chief inspector told me you're on official leave.'

Rebus took a bite from his scone, saying nothing.

'For a man on leave, Inspector, you sure as hell look busy to me.' Haldayne finished his cup of sludge. 'I'd like to say it's been a pleasure, but in fact it has been deeply frustrating.' He started to push his arms back into the sleeves of his coat. 'I don't expect to be troubled by you again, Inspector. I sent a cheque off today to cover those parking fines. As far as I'm concerned, there's no other reason for you to contact me.'

'Who do you know who lives in Royal Circus?'

Haldayne was disconcerted by the question. 'In the New Town?'

'That's the only Royal Circus I know.'

Haldayne made show of thinking about it. 'Not a soul,' he said brightly. 'My superior might move in those kinds of circles, but not me.'

'What kinds of circles?'

But Haldayne wasn't about to answer that. He got to his feet and made a little formal bow from the waist. 'I hope you don't mind picking up the tab, Inspector.' Then he turned and walked away.

Rebus let him go. He had plenty to think about, and plenty of coffee still to drink.

27

Rebus had two options: he could go home and wait for the Farmer or Gill to catch him; or he could go to St Leonard's and get it done with. He chose the latter route.

He'd been in the building less than three minutes before the Farmer spotted him.

'My office – *now*.'

Rebus noticed that the Farmer's computer was up and running. It had taken over his desk. The photo of his family had been moved to the top of the filing-cabinet.

'Getting to grips with it all right, sir?' Rebus asked. But the Farmer was not to be deflected.

'What the hell are you playing at? I ordered you to take a holiday!'

'And I'm enjoying every minute, sir.'

'Making a nuisance of yourself at a foreign consulate, that's your idea of fun?'

'I couldn't afford to go abroad.'

'The way you're going, maybe you can't afford not to.'

'It was just a bit of unfinished business, sir.'

'What sort of unfinished business?'

'It's not really a police matter, sir.'

The Farmer glowered at him. 'I hope to God that's the truth, Inspector.'

'Cross my heart and hope to die, sir.'

'You're one step from an official reprimand, two steps from suspension.'

And three steps from heaven, Rebus thought. He told the Farmer he understood.

In the main office, he checked for messages. There were half a dozen, stuck on to the screen of his new PanoTech computer. Around him he could hear the soft clack-clack of muffled keyboards. He stared at his own console as if it was an unfriendly visitor. His reflection stared back at him.

Three of the messages were from Rory McAllister at the Scottish Office. Rebus picked up the telephone.

'McAllister speaking.'

'Mr McAllister, it's John Rebus.'

'Inspector, thanks for getting back to me.' McAllister sounded relieved, but also edgy, not like himself.

'What's wrong?'

'Can we meet?'

'Sure, but give me some idea –'

'Calton Cemetery at one o'clock.' The phone went dead.

During the day, Calton Cemetery was more or less deserted. In summer, you'd get visitors looking for David Hume's grave. The more knowledgeable or curious might seek out the resting places of the publisher Constable and David Allan the painter. There was a statue of Abraham Lincoln, too, if it hadn't been sledgehammered by vandals.

At one o'clock on a crisp winter's day, nobody was interested in headstones. Such, at least, was Rebus's first impression as he walked through the cemetery gate. But then he saw that a gentleman was perusing the monuments, using a black rolled umbrella as a walking-cane. What hair he had mixed black with silver, and was slicked back from the forehead. His face and ears were red, maybe just from the cold, and he wore a black woollen overcoat, belted at the waist.

He saw Rebus, and gestured for him to join him. Rebus climbed the stone steps towards him.

'Haven't been here in years,' the man said. His voice had been Scots once, before the inflexions and elisions had been milked out of it. 'I take it you're Rebus?'

Rebus studied the man. 'That's right.'

'McAllister's not coming. I'm a colleague of his.'

Close up, the man's face was pockmarked and he had one slightly lazy eye. With his free hand, he played with the cashmere scarf tucked inside the collar of his coat.

'What's your name?' Rebus asked. The man seemed both surprised and amused by the question's bluntness.

'My name's Hunter.' Something about the way he said this, and his whole bearing, told Rebus he wasn't so much McAllister's colleague as his superior.

'Well, Mr Hunter, what can I do for you?'

'I'm interested in your line of inquiry, Inspector.'

'And what line is that, sir?'

'You were asking certain questions of McAllister.' A bus roared past, and Hunter raised his voice. 'The line of those questions intrigues me.'

'Why?'

'Why? Because the Scottish Office likes to take an interest.'

'In what exactly?'

The bus gone, Hunter lowered his voice again. 'I'll be succinct. I'd prefer it, Inspector, if you would discontinue your present line of inquiry. I don't believe it germane.'

'You'd *prefer* it?'

'There may be a conflict of interests.' Hunter lifted the walnut handle of his umbrella until it rested under his chin. 'Of course, I'm a civil servant and you are a policeman: it's not for me to interfere with your business.'

'Good of you, I'm sure.'

'But we are both, are we not, servants of the State?' Hunter swung the umbrella at some leaves on the ground. 'All I can say to you at this point, Inspector, is that your

215

inquiries may well interfere with longstanding investigations *we* are pursuing.'

'I didn't know investigation was part of the Scottish Office's remit, Mr Hunter. Unless you're talking about an internal inquiry?'

'You are a clever man, Inspector, and I appeal to your intellect.'

'To be honest, sir, you don't appeal to me at all.'

Hunter's face darkened slightly. 'Let's not cross swords on this.' He swung at more leaves.

'Cooperation?'

Hunter considered this. 'Not yet. I'm afraid. The affair is confidential. But later, definitely. *Full* cooperation. What do you say?' He held out his hand. 'A gentleman's agreement.'

Rebus, knowing himself no gentleman, took the hand, just to put Hunter's mind at rest. The older man didn't look relieved, just quietly pleased that negotiations had been bloodless and – in his eyes – successful. He turned to leave.

'I'll call you when I've something I can say,' he told Rebus.

'Mr Hunter? Why did you get McAllister to phone me? Why not just call yourself?'

Hunter smiled with half his mouth. 'What's life without a little intrigue, Inspector?' He negotiated the steps carefully, with a slight limp. Too proud to carry a cane, he used a brolly instead. Rebus waited half a minute, then walked quickly to the gate and peered along the street to the right. Hunter was walking along Waterloo Place as if he owned it. Rebus kept well behind him as he followed.

It was a short walk, only as far as the Reichstag: St Andrew's House. Which, Rebus recalled, was where the most senior Scottish Office bureaucrats did their business. He recalled, too, that it was built on the site of the old

Calton Gaol. Rebus walked past the sooty building and crossed the road. He stood outside the old Royal High School, putative HQ for any Scottish Assembly that might come along. It was mothballed, and a lone protestor had taken up residence outside, his banners arguing for devolution and a Scottish Parliament.

Rebus stared at St Andrew's House for a couple of minutes, then walked back along Waterloo Place to where he'd illegally parked his car. It had received a ticket, but he could square that later. Over the years, he'd collected more tickets than Haldayne, a wheen more. Do as I say, he thought, not as I do. There had been other 'fringe benefits' along the way, too: cafés and restaurants where he ate for free, bars where his money was no good, a baker who'd slip him a dozen rolls. He wouldn't call himself corrupt, but there were some out there who'd say he'd been bribed, or greased for a future bribe. There were those who'd say he'd been bought.

Do as I say, not as I do. And with that he tore up the parking ticket.

Back at his flat, Rebus got out all the information he had on the Scottish Office. He didn't find the name Hunter anywhere. The documents were shy about naming names where civil servants were involved, though happy to trumpet the names of the incumbent Secretary of State, Minister of State, and Parliamentary Under-Secretaries, all of whom were either MPs or held seats in the House of Lords. As McAllister had explained, these were the temporary boys, the figureheads. When it came to the *permanent* force – the senior civil servants – Rebus found only silence and anonymity: modesty, he wondered, or discretion? Or maybe something else entirely.

He called Mairie Henderson at her home.

'Got a story for me?' she asked. 'I could do with one.'

'What do you know about the Scottish Office?'

'I know a bit.'

'Senior management?'

'There may have been changes since I last looked. Phone the paper, talk to – who'd be best? Home Affairs or Parliament? – yes, Roddy McGurk, talk to him, say I gave you his name.'

'Thanks, Mairie.'

'And I'm serious about the story. Inspector ...'

Rebus called the newspaper office and asked for Roddy McGurk. He was put through immediately.

'Mr McGurk, I'm a friend of Mairie Henderson's. She said maybe you could help me clarify something.'

'Fire away.' The voice was West Highland.

'It's an identity, actually. A man called Hunter, Scottish Office, late-fifties, uses an umbrella when really he should have a stick ...'

McGurk was laughing. 'Let me stop you there. You're describing Sir Iain Hunter.'

'And who's he when he's at home?'

McGurk laughed again. 'He *is* the Scottish Office. He's the Permanent Under-Secretary, usually known as –'

'The Permanent Secretary,' Rebus said, feeling queasy in his gut.

'Policy initiator for the whole country. You might call him "Mr Scotland".'

'Not a very public figure though?'

'He doesn't need to be. In the words of the old song, he's got the power.'

Rebus thanked McGurk and put the receiver down. He was trembling slightly. Mr Scotland ... he's got the power. He wondered what he'd got himself into.

Then the telephone rang.

'I forgot to say ...' Mairie Henderson began.

'Yes?'

'Remember you asked if there was any dirt on Councillor Gillespie?'

'Go on.'

'Well, there wasn't in my day, but I got talking yesterday to someone at BBC Scotland. You know I'm doing some radio stuff down at Queen Street? Anyway, it's not really Gillespie, it's about his wife.'

'What about her?'

'Word is, she's involved with someone else.'

'Having an affair, you mean?'

'Yes.'

Rebus remembered his visit to the councillor's home. There had seemed little love lost, but at the time he'd blamed other things.

'Who's her partner in crime?'

'That I don't know.'

'So how does your source at the Beeb know?'

'He didn't say, it's just some rumour he picked up when last in the City Chambers. The way it was told to him, he thinks maybe it's another councillor.'

'Well, let me know if you hear anything more. Bye, Mairie.'

Rebus put the phone down and tried to put his thoughts into some semblance of order. He stared at the bags of shredded paper, but they didn't help. He ended up repeating a question to himself.

What have I got myself into?

28

Chief Inspector Frank Lauderdale was in an open ward of the Royal Infirmary, but his bed was in a corner by a window, with a view over the Meadows. He'd drawn the curtain between his own bed and his neighbour's, affording some privacy. There was a vase of flowers on his bedside cabinet. They looked ready to expire in the hospital's infernal heat.

'You can almost see my flat from here,' Rebus said, looking out of the window.

'That's been a constant source of comfort to me,' Lauderdale said. 'It's taken you long enough to visit.'

'I don't like hospitals, Frank.'

'Neither do I. You think I'm in here for the good of my health?'

They shared a smile, and Rebus examined the patient. 'You look like shite, Frank.'

Lauderdale's face looked like an infant had tried shaving it with a safety razor. There were dozens of nicks and scars where the windscreen had cut him. His eyes were bruised and swollen, and there were black ugly stitches on his nose. With all the plaster and bandages he sported, he looked like the joke patient from a comedy sketch.

'How are the legs?' Rebus asked.

'Itchy.'

'That's supposed to be a good sign.'

'Oh, I'll walk again ... so they say.' Lauderdale smiled nervously. 'Maybe I'll have a limp or two.'

'Two would be better,' said Rebus. 'They'd balance you up.'

'Want to sign my stookie?'

Rebus looked at the plastercasts on Launderdale's legs. They'd been signed by several visitors. 'Which one?'

'Take your pick.'

Rebus took a ballpoint pen from his pocket. It wasn't easy to write on the coarse surface, but he did his best.

'What does it say?' Lauderdale asked, craning his neck.

'"Clunk-click every trip."'

Lauderdale lay back again. 'What's happened about those two?'

He meant Willie and Dixie. 'Search me,' said Rebus. 'I'm on holiday.'

'So I'd heard.'

'Oh?'

'Your new boss told me. Frankly, I have my doubts: if I know you, while you're still in this city, you'll always be working. How is she shaping up?'

He meant Gill Templer. Rebus nodded. 'She's doing fine.' He wasn't sure this was what Frank Lauderdale wanted to hear. He pulled a chair over to the bed and sat down. 'I've got a problem actually, Frank.'

'Of course you have, that's why you're here.'

'It's not the Lord Provost's daughter ...'

'You haven't found her yet?'

'I'm getting closer. She *did* know those two in the car.'

'I'd not heard that.'

Rebus shifted in the chair. 'I haven't exactly gone public with it.'

Lauderdale shook his head. 'Christ, John ...'

'Like I say, *she's* not my immediate problem. My problem is a small-time loser called Wee Shug McAnally.'

'The one who gave himself a sawn-off haircut?'

'Yes.' Rebus ran his tongue over the hole in his tooth.

'See, he shared a cell in Saughton with a fraudster called Derwood Charters. Wee Shug was moved from another jail, and just happened to end up in that cell.' Rebus was staring hard at Lauderdale. 'It also just happened that none of the other cons knew what McAnally was in for. It was rape, by the way. Of a minor. Now, Frank, what does all that tell you?' Lauderdale said nothing. 'What it tells *me*,' Rebus went on, 'is that there was collusion at the top to stop the other cons getting to know.'

'Give me some water, will you?'

Rebus poured some for Lauderdale. 'Why would anyone do that?' Lauderdale asked, taking the beaker.

'There could be a multitude of reasons. Let me try one on you: say McAnally was in there as a plant.'

Lauderdale took his time drinking the water. 'A plant?' he said at last.

'Either to spy on Charters, or else to gain his trust. Now,' Rebus pulled his chair closer, not that Lauderdale was going anywhere, 'the reason Charters is inside is for fraud, and he was put inside by the Fraud Unit. Leading the investigation was Chief Superintendent Allan Gunner, now deputy chief constable. It so happens the DCC was the one who fixed me up with this lovely holiday. He threatened the Farmer with an HMIC inspection if I wasn't reined in.'

'He should have known better.' Lauderdale paused. 'But HMIC is an independent body, how could the DCC have control over their decisions?'

It was, Rebus conceded, a good point. The people who ran HMIC were civil servants rather than police officers.

'Well, anyway,' he said thoughtfully, 'it *was* Gunner who applied the pressure, I'm sure it was.'

'Other officers might have taken the hint, John.'

'Not me. Now, on that initial investigation of Charters were at least two officers of my acquaintance: yourself and

Alister Flower. And Flower's been warning me off, too. Which makes for a nice little circle, don't you think, Frank?'

'Why come to me?'

'Maybe because you're the only person I can try. Maybe because, despite myself, I almost trust you. I mean, you're a schemer, a chancer, and you'd like the Farmer's office. But at heart you're a copper.' Rebus paused. 'Same as me. So come on, Frank, tell me about McAnally.'

'I can't.' Lauderdale saw the look on Rebus's face. 'I can't, because there's nothing to tell. You're right, I did work on the Albavise inquiry, but that's as far as it goes. I know this, though: if you're crossing not only Flower but the likes of the DCC and Big Jim Flett, then you'd better watch out.'

'I think it goes further than that even,' Rebus confided. 'The Scottish Office, maybe even MPs or ministers.'

'Christ, John,' Lauderdale whispered.

Rebus stood up. 'So maybe as you're packing your bags to go home, they'll be wheeling me in to take your place.'

'Don't joke about it.'

'Who said I was joking?'

'And don't tell me any more. The less I know the better.'

'For you or for me?'

Lauderdale sat up as best he could. 'Let it go,' he advised. 'For once in your dunder-headed life, just walk away.'

Rebus put the chair back where he'd found it. 'I can't do that, Frank.' He pushed his tongue into the hole again. The poison hadn't all drained yet.

'Take care of yourself,' he told Lauderdale.

'That should probably be my line.'

Rebus was halfway down the ward when he heard Lauderdale calling for him. He walked back to the bed.

Lauderdale had propped himself up and was staring out of the window.

'Flower,' he said, not turning to look at Rebus.

'What about him, Frank?'

'McAnally was Flower's eyes and ears.'

'His snitch?'

Lauderdale nodded, eyes still on the window.

'I appreciate this,' said Rebus, turning away again.

'I hope you do, John,' Frank Lauderdale said quietly.

There was an envelope lying on the hall carpet. The post had already been; this had been delivered by hand: no stamp, just his name in blue ink. There was an embossed official crest on the sealed flap – the lion and the unicorn holding a shield between them. Rebus knew it was the Scottish Office crest. He flexed the envelope in his hands. It was thin and light, yet fairly solid. Leaving it on the arm of the chair, he went to the kitchen and added tap-water to a glass of whisky. He found a knife in the drawer, and took both glass and knife back through to the chair. He took a mouthful of whisky before slitting open the envelope.

It was a white card, an invitation, elaborate black embossed script with a gold border.

Sir Iain Hunter

requests the pleasure of your company

Saturday 4 March

Ruthie Estate

Twelve Noon Perthshire

Rebus's name had been added in blue ink at the top of the card. There was no RSVP, just an address, and no telephone number. Rebus turned the card over and saw that it bore a printed map showing the location of the estate,

about halfway between Perth and Auchterarder. Saturday was only two days off.

Rebus carried the invitation to his mantelpiece and leaned it against the otherwise bare wall. The only estate he'd ever been to before was the housing kind. He didn't suppose Ruthie Estate would be very like those at all.

Rebus was still wondering if he'd go or not when he set out for his evening session at the Ox.

Dr Klasser wasn't there. He'd telephoned to say he'd be very late, if he made it at all. The barman placed Rebus's pint in front of him, just as Salty Dougary walked in.

'It's bitter out there,' Dougary said.

'But it's called eighty-shilling in here. Go on, Jon, pour the man his poison.'

Dougary eased himself on to the barstool next to Rebus. 'I've got something for you.'

'What?'

'Remember you asked me about Mensung?'

Yes, Rebus remembered. He'd asked Rory McAllister too, only McAllister had been warned off; Rebus doubted he'd ever hear from him again.

'What about it?'

'I've remembered what it was,' Dougary said matter-of-factly. His drink had appeared, and he ordered some crisps.

'So what is it?' Rebus asked.

'Salt and vinegar, Jon,' Dougary told the barman. The volume on the TV was being turned up for some sports report. Dougary turned to Rebus. 'It was a company.' He took a mouthful of beer. 'And a packet of ready salted,' he told the barman.

'Did you say a company?'

'Eh?' Dougary's attention was already turning towards the TV. Rebus hauled him off the stool and out of the door,

into the chill, dark street. Traffic rumbled past on Castle Street.

'It's freezing out here!' Dougary protested.

'Just tell me.' Dougary looked longingly towards the pub door. 'Tell me here,' Rebus persisted.

'Remember when I worked for that semiconductor company?'

'It was called Mensung?'

'It wasn't called any such thing. But it had this policy of trying to retrain workers it turfed out.'

'So?'

'So I was a turfee, and there was this agency, outplacement sort of thing. The agency ran seminars, or was supposed to. It was supposed to have all these fancy retraining schemes and programmes, half of which never materialised. *That* bunch of cowboys was called Mensung.'

'Is it still around?'

Dougary shrugged. 'I've been laid off twice since, and never come across it again.'

'Where was it based?'

'By the Playhouse, top of Leith Walk.'

'Do you still have any information on it, anything in writing?'

Dougary stared at him. 'I'd have to check with my secretary.' The irony was so heavy, you could hear it fall.

Rebus smiled. 'Stupid question, Donny. Sorry.'

'Can I go back in now?'

'Sure.'

'Is anything wrong?'

'How do you mean?'

'You called me Donny instead of Salty.'

'It's your name, isn't it?'

'I suppose it is,' said Dougary, pushing open the door.

29

One of the reasons Rebus drank was to put him to sleep.

He had trouble sleeping when sober. He'd stare into the darkness, willing it to form shapes so that he might better understand it. He'd try to make sense of life – his early disastrous Army years; his failed marriage; his failings as father, friend, lover – and end up in tears. And if he did eventually stumble into sober sleep, there would be troubled dreams, dreams about ageing and dying, decay and blight. The dark took on shapes in his dreams, but he daren't look at them. He'd run blindly instead, sometimes bumping into them, feeling the darkness mould itself around him.

Drunk, his sleep was dreamless, or seemed that way on waking. He might be drenched in sweat, but he wouldn't be shaking. So he always tried to have a few drinks last thing at night, usually in his chair – and since he was already comfortable, what was the point of getting up and going through to the bedroom?

He was in the chair, dead to the world, when the buzzer sounded. He sat up and switched on the lamp, then blinked his eyes open to check his watch. It was one-thirty. He staggered into the hall like he was learning to walk, and unhooked the intercom.

'Hello?'

'It's Patience.'

'Patience?' Without thinking, he buzzed her up, then went back into the living room to put on his trousers.

When he got back to the door, she had almost reached his landing. She walked slowly, with purpose. Her head was bowed, eyes on the steps, not looking at him. Her hair was unbrushed.

'What's happened?'

She stood directly in front of him, and he could see how angry she was. She was so angry, she was preternaturally calm.

'I was lying in bed,' she said quietly, 'and I don't know what happened ... I suddenly saw it.'

'What?'

'You know Lucky's dead?'

'Yes, I'm sorry.'

She nodded to herself. 'Well, thanks for being there for me, I appreciate that. I was thinking, that's pretty cold-hearted, even for him. Sammy told me she'd told you. I wondered why you hadn't been in touch, and then I remembered. Stupid of me to forget. You were there on Sunday. You were sitting right next to the conservatory door.' Her voice grew even quieter. 'You locked Lucky out.'

'Patience, I –'

'*Didn't you?*'

'Look, it's late, why don't –'

'*Didn't you?*'

'Christ, I don't know ... all right, yes, if it makes you feel any better.' He rubbed a hand over his face. 'Yes, the racket he was making was driving me mental, so I locked the flap and then forgot. I'm sorry.'

She had opened the shoulder bag and was lifting out a smaller plastic bag. 'This is for you.' And as he put out a hand to take the bag, she slapped him hard on the left cheek. Then she turned and started downstairs.

'Patience!'

She didn't even pause. She just kept on going. He held up the bag, then opened it and looked inside.

It was just some bits and pieces, that was all.

Bits and pieces of Lucky the cat.

In the morning, he took the bag out to the back garden.

The garden was actually a shared drying-green, with a flower border tended by Mrs Cochrane on the floor below Rebus. Just inside the back door of the tenement was a padlocked walk-in cupboard. It was communal storage space, only Rebus didn't have anything he wanted communally stored. But he unlocked the door and lifted out the spade which had belonged to dear departed Mr Cochrane.

He sat the plastic bag down next to the flower border, looked around and up at the windows to see nobody was watching, then raised the shovel.

When it hit soil, he felt the collision all the way from his wrists to his spine. He tried again, and chipped away a sliver of frozen earth. He stooped to pick up his prize. It was like toffee, frozen toffee.

'Jesus,' he said, trying again. He could see his breath in the air. In the tenement across the back, someone making breakfast had come to their kitchen window. It wasn't daylight yet, but Rebus knew they could see him clearly enough.

It was all the exposure he needed to convince him he should give up.

Instead, he drove to the Cowgate, parked the car, and carried the bag with him into the City Mortuary.

'Inspector,' one of the staff said. 'What can we do for you today?'

Rebus handed over the bag, said thank you, and left.

He'd arranged to meet Holmes and Clarke in a trendy café near the university, but the place hadn't opened for the

day, so they walked along to Nicolson Street and found a clean, well-lit coffee shop.

He asked them how things were at St Leonard's. They reckoned they were still under close scrutiny, but they could cope.

'Good,' he said, 'because I've got something else I want you to do for me. I want to know about a company. It probably no longer exists, but it was around in '86–'87.'

'A limited company?'

'No idea.'

'Directors?'

Rebus just shrugged. 'About all I can tell you is that it was called Mensung.'

Clarke and Holmes looked at one another. 'The councillor's file?' they said as one.

'It was a retraining company, not a very good one apparently. It had premises at the top of Leith Walk, next to the Playhouse. I want you to check Companies House, any registers you can find, any lists of retraining companies in Scotland.' He nodded to the waitress that they were ready to order. 'Now don't stint yourselves,' he told them. 'Believe me, you're going to earn this meal.'

He checked Leith Walk himself.

Next to the Playhouse was a pub, and then a newsagent's, but between them was a door, not quite shut. There were a couple of business plaques on the wall outside, and spaces where other plaques had been removed. Rebus pushed open the door, noting that it was none too steady on its hinges, and entered an unlit hallway smelling worse than many a bar's convenience. The stone steps up were deeply worn, the walls decorated with graffiti.

On the first floor, he was met by two solid doors, one with a card pinned to it saying Combined Knitwear, the other with a much older-looking nameplate: J Joseph

Simpson Associates. Rebus climbed to the second floor, but the doors here were anonymous and heavily padlocked. He went back down to the first floor and knocked on the door of Simpson Associates, then pushed the door open.

He was in a hallway, much like his own flat's. Rooms led off, and there was a Reception sign pointing into one of them. The door was already open, so Rebus walked in. Seated behind desk and typewriter, an elderly man was on the telephone. Rebus was not totally surprised to see a male secretary, but he'd never come across such a superannuated one. Paperwork slewed across desk, chairs, and the carpet.

The man looked startled by Rebus's entry, and slammed the phone down.

'Sorry to interrupt,' Rebus said.

'Quite all right, quite all right.' The man made show of gathering up some of the sheets of paper. 'Now, what can I do for you, sir?'

The man reminded Rebus of Charles Laughton. He was rotund, with several chins, and had puffy, worried eyes with blotched shiny skin. He wore a suit which had been in fashion forty years before, including waistcoat and watch-chain. It struck Rebus for a moment that he would pass for Sir Iain Hunter's bloated and seedy elder brother.

Rebus showed his ID. 'Inspector Rebus, sir. I'm interested in a company that used to have its offices here.'

'Here?'

'In this building. About eight years ago, were you here then?'

'Most certainly.'

'The company was called Mensung.'

'Curious name.' The man repeated it silently a few times. 'No,' he said, 'I can't say I've heard of it.'

'Are you sure?'

'Completely sure.'

'Maybe if I could have a word with your employer?'

231

The man smiled. 'I *am* my employer. Joe Simpson at your service.'

'I'm sorry, Mr Simpson.'

'You thought I was the secretary?' Simpson looked amused. 'Well, I suppose I am at that. My last secretary left after only two days. Hopeless, these girls the agency sends. It's all hours with them, don't ever try to get them to stay a minute later than five o'clock.' He shook his head.

'You don't know who your secretary was eight years ago, Mr Simpson?'

Joe Simpson wagged a finger. 'You think her memory might be better than my own, but you'd be wrong. Besides, I've no idea. There. have been so many women at this desk.' He shook his head again.

'So, Mr Simpson, eight years ago, what companies were there in this building?'

'Well, there was mine, of course, and then there was Capital Yarns.'

'Now Combined Knitwear?'

'The woman who ran Capital Yarns left in 1989. The place was empty the best part of a year, then a computer showroom opened – that lasted all of three months. The place was empty again until Mrs Burnett arrived. She's Combined Knitwear.'

'What about upstairs?'

'Oh, years back those were offices. Now they're just stockrooms, have been for a decade or more.'

Rebus was at a dead end, as surely as if he'd stayed on the floor above. He tried Simpson with the name Mensung again, spelt it for him, wrote it down, and all the old man did was twitch his head and say definitely and positively 'no'. So Rebus thanked him and went back out on to the landing, resting against the banister. These small tenement businesses, there were a lot of them in Edinburgh. Small, shifting and anonymous, he didn't see how they ever made

money. It struck him that he didn't even know what J Joseph Simpson Associates did. But he was willing to bet there were no associates, perhaps never had been.

He was about to leave when the door of Combined Knitwear opened and two women stepped out. They glanced towards him before continuing their conversation. One of the women wore a coat and carried two bulging plastic bags, which didn't seem heavy. Wool, Rebus surmised. The other woman wore a knitted two–piece, red and black check, and a string of pearls. A pair of glasses hung by a string around her neck. She was petite, trim, probably Rebus's age.

'Well, thanks again,' she said to the departing customer. Then to Rebus: 'Can I help?'

'Mrs Burnett?'

'Yes.' She sounded uneasy.

'Inspector Rebus.' Again he showed his ID.

'Is it a break-in? Those stockrooms could have steel doors, they'd still find a way in.'

'No, it's not a break-in.'

'Oh.' She looked at him. 'Look, I'm about to put the kettle on, do you fancy a cup?'

Rebus accepted her offer with pleasure.

Combined Knitwear's premises were laid out like Joe Simpson's: four rooms leading off a narrow hallway. One room served as an office. Mrs Burnett was in there at the sink, filling a kettle. Rebus looked into the other rooms. Wool. Lots and lots of wool. Deep shelves had been installed to display the stuff. There were boxes of knitting patterns, a Perspex case filled with pairs of needles. The walls and doors were decorated with blown-up photos from the fronts of various knitting patterns. Smiling, untroubled men. Women who looked like models from fifteen or twenty years ago. From a series of dowel-rods on one wall hung skeins of thick white wool. Rebus liked the smell of

the place. It reminded him of his mother, and all his aunties and their friends. His mother used to tell him off for using her knitting needles as drumsticks.

He turned and saw that Mrs Burnett was standing in the doorway.

'You looked very peaceful there for a minute,' she said.

'I felt it.'

'Tea's about ready.'

'Do you happen to know what Mr Simpson next door does?'

She laughed lightly. 'I've been wondering that for years.'

'Years?'

'Did he tell you I was a newcomer? He doesn't remember me, but I used to work here when it was Capital Yarns. It wasn't my business, I was staff. But when I decided to set up for myself, and saw that this place was available – well, I couldn't help myself.' She sighed. 'Sentiment, Inspector. Nostalgia – never be swayed by it. Not too many customers are willing to make the trek from Princes Street. I'd be better off somewhere more central.'

Rebus recalled the story of how IBM had come to set up in Greenock: nostalgia again, but on a grand scale.

He followed Mrs Burnett through to the office. 'So were you working here eight years ago? Around 1986 or '87?'

She poured water into two mugs. 'Oh yes.'

'Was there an outfit here at that time called Mensung?'

'*Mensonge*?'

He spelt it for her.

'No,' she said, 'by that time there was just Mr Simpson and Capital Yarns. You're sure it was this address?' Rebus nodded, watching her dip the tea-bags. 'Milk and sugar?'

'Just milk, please.' She handed him the cup. 'Thanks. Why did you use that pronunciation just now?'

'*Mensonge*?'

'Yes. It sounds French.'

'It is French. It means lie.'

'What?'

'As in falsehood, fib, untruth. Is there something wrong with the tea, Inspector?'

'No, nothing at all, Mrs Burnett. The tea's fine. Just fine.'

To make absolutely sure, Rebus asked in the newsagent's. The owner, who had run the place eighteen years, shook his head. Then Rebus had a word with the letting agency, who confirmed that there was no record of any company called Mensung ever renting office-space at the address.

'Can you tell me who owns the property?' Rebus asked. 'Just out of interest.'

The woman wasn't sure she could. Rebus stressed again that his inquiries were part of a police investigation, and she gave in.

'The owner's name,' she said, 'is a Mr J Simpson. As an individual, Mr Simpson rents space to Simpson Associates, Combined Knitwear, and a Mr Albert Costello.'

'Costello?'

'The newsagent next door,' the letting agent said.

'Nothing so far,' Brian Holmes said over a lunchtime drink. 'No record the company ever existed.'

Rebus chewed on his last piece of bridie. 'I'm beginning to think it didn't. Where's Siobhan, by the way?'

'At the gym.'

'What's a gym?'

Brian Holmes smiled at that. He'd put on weight this past year or so, and now sported a dough-ring stomach and the beginnings of beer jowls. Perks of the job, some people said.

'I thought you worked out some lunchtimes?' he said.

'Haven't done it for ages.'

But Rebus went swimming that afternoon, managing twenty thoughtful lengths, after which he had to sit in his cubicle for a while. That was the problem with exercise: it wasn't any fun. None of the fit and active people he saw around him seemed any happier than anyone else. No point exercising to elongate your life, when you weren't getting any more out of life than any other poor sod. He made up for the swimming by arriving early at the Ox, waiting to have a word with Salty Dougary, but Dougary didn't come, and Rebus decided to break the rules.

He'd visit Dougary at his home.

Dougary was divorced and rented the top floor of a sizeable house not a conversion-kick away from Murrayfield Stadium. He couldn't have looked more surprised to see Rebus if he'd found him servicing his ex-wife on the doorstep.

'What are you doing here?'

'I need a word, Salty.'

'I didn't feel like a drink tonight. Our boss is driving us like slaves, a big order with the deadline approaching, and Mathieson screaming down the telephone.'

'Mathieson?'

'Head honcho at PanoTech. You should see the way our boss –'

'Salty? Sorry to bring it up, but it's freezing out here.'

Dougary stepped aside to let Rebus in. 'I'll warn you,' he said, 'the place is a midden.'

Certainly, Rebus thought, it was no advert for the bachelor life.

'Have you run out of binbags or something?'

'I never seem to get time to clean up. Want a beer?'

'Thanks.' Rebus lifted pizza boxes, crisp bags and a couple of empty cans off the sofa and sat down. Salty came back with a couple of cans and handed one over.

'So what's the emergency?'

Rebus sipped froth from the top of the can. 'You said Mensung was at the top of Leith Walk.' Dougary nodded. 'Next to a newsagent's?' Another nod. 'Well, I took a look this morning, and nobody's heard of them.'

'So?'

'So, are you sure that's where they were?'

'That was the address on their letter-heading.'

'You're sure you wouldn't have any of their letters lying around?' Rebus scanned the room. His meaning was clear: you seem to hang on to everything else.

'Everything got chucked when Fiona and me split up. I mean *everything*. Letters, photos, I even lost my birth certificate. See, John, I never actually went to see Mensung at that address. The courses I did, they were held at a place on Corstorphine Road.'

'Do you remember the number?'

Dougary nodded. 'One-six-five Corstorphine Road. See, it's the date Fiona and me got married, sixteen-five, that's how I remember.' His face turned wistful. 'Two chips soldered together on the motherboard of life.'

Rebus tried to remember when he and Rhona had married. He thought it was probably June or July, but that was as much as he could recall.

First thing next morning, he drove along Corstorphine Road looking for number 165. Rebus didn't exactly know what a paper-chase was, but this was beginning to feel like one. The American, Haldayne, had mentioned paper companies, and Rebus felt he was chasing one now, something no more substantial than the sum of its letter-heading. His visit to Corstorphine Road seemed to confirm it.

The present occupants of the office suite told him that back in '86 and '87 the premises had been under a short let, sometimes for only days at a time. But there were no

records of the actual occupants at that time. The suites had changed ownership several times since.

'Thanks for your help,' Rebus said.

Dead end, he thought. Dead company. He'd have to get Councillor Gillespie to talk to him, there was no other course left open. It was either that, or drop it altogether. That, after all, was what everyone wanted, but then he'd never been a crowd pleaser. He'd never played to the gallery.

He'd talk to Councillor Tom Gillespie. But after the weekend. And meantime, he had some fast shopping to do. New clothes. For some reason, he wanted new clothes to wear to Sir Iain's.

Three

ZUGZWANG

30

Two low-built stone pillars marked the start of the long, snaking driveway. Rebus turned off the main road on to the gravel track and stopped the car. There were no signs, nothing at all to tell him this was the right turning. He looked at the map on the back of his invitation and decided it was. The very anonymity of the track seemed to fit with Sir Iain Hunter. Either side of Rebus were open fields, but these soon gave way to dense woodland. Dry-stane dykes overgrown with moss separated the driveway from the trees.

Finally, after half a mile, he emerged from the shade into a bright expanse of tended lawn with greenhouses and a walled vegetable garden off. And directly in front of him stood a grey stone house in the Scots baronial style, boasting two turrets – probably ornamental – which started at the level of the first floor and tapered to slate-covered points above the roof-line. There were three cars – a Rover 800, Jaguar, and Maserati – parked on the clean pink gravel. Rebus stopped beside them and got out, trying not to be impressed. In the distance, a stream bisected the trim lawn, with a narrow humpbacked bridge across it. It reminded him of nothing so much as one of the fairways at St Andrews.

'It's a lovely view, isn't it?' The voice was Sir Iain's. He was walking towards Rebus, leaning lightly on a carved walking-stick. At home, it would appear the brolly wasn't necessary.

'Just thinking I should have brought my three iron.'

'Ah, you play golf?'

'Only with a three iron.'

Hunter laughed and placed a hand on Rebus's shoulder. 'Find the place all right?'

'No trouble.'

'Good.' Hunter was steering Rebus towards the house. 'I thought we'd have a drink first, then do a spot of shooting and just have a light lunch.'

'Shooting?'

'I take it you've handled a gun, Inspector?'

'I've handled a lot of things.'

'I did wonder if we might try for pheasant or winter hare, but decided on clay pigeon.'

'Well, it tastes nicer, doesn't it?'

Sir Iain Hunter shook his head, amused. 'There's no telling what you'll say next, Inspector.'

They entered a capacious hall with white marble floor and paintings on the walls: modern art, which surprised Rebus. A lot of the stuff looked ill at ease in a setting of wood panelling and fluted columns. A staircase with a wrought-iron balustrade climbed up the middle of the hall and peeled off to left and right.

'In here,' Hunter said. 'Let me take your coat.'

Rebus slipped off his new raincoat and shrugged himself back into his sports jacket. He patted his tie flat and walked into the morning room.

A servant was dispensing drinks from a series of decanters on a trolley. So, Rebus thought, I was important enough to be met by the boss rather than the flunky. He stood there, not really looking at anyone, biding his time until Sir Iain came back into the room.

'Hello, John,' someone said, walking towards him, hand held out. The man held a heavy crystal tumbler in his other

hand, and looked slightly embarrassed. It wasn't until Rebus had taken the man's hand that he recognised him.

It was Allan Gunner, the deputy chief constable.

'Do you know everyone?' Gunner said, leading Rebus to the drinks trolley. Rebus's first thought, after he'd recovered from the surprise, was: at least Gunner had the grace to look embarrassed. His second thought was: I've walked into this, fair and square.

The servant was waiting for Rebus's order. He was a little stooped from a lifetime's obsequiousness, and had a trying-to-please smile on his thin lips. He wore a tight little jacket of blue nylon, all its buttons done up. It probably helped with the stoop.

'I'll take a malt,' Rebus said.

'West Highland or Strathspey, sir?'

'Strathspey, and no water.'

Another guest laughed. 'Sir Iain won't allow water of any form near his whiskies.' He held his cigar and glass in one hand so he could extend the other towards Rebus.

'Colin Macrae,' he said.

'Sir Colin,' Gunner added, 'is Scottish Office Minister for Agriculture and the Environment.'

'John Rebus,' Rebus told the man.

Which left only two guests, both male, both involved in a muted discussion by the french windows. But Gunner was applying discreet pressure to Rebus's arm, manoeuvring him away from the drinks trolley, where Sir Colin was ordering a top-up. They ended up beside a massive stone fireplace.

Gunner spoke in a fierce whisper. 'I don't know what you're doing here –'

'Me neither.'

'But while we're in company, we'd better show a united front, especially in front of these characters.'

'Agreed.'

'So first-name terms, no formalities.'

'Fair enough, sir.'

'The name's Allan.'

'Allan.'

'Ah,' Hunter said, entering the room and pointing at them with his stick, 'the same old story, everyone's got a drink but the host.'

The servant poured without being asked. A telephone sounded in the hall, and he went to answer it, head bowed as he left the room.

'Cheers,' said Sir Iain. He motioned for Rebus to join him. 'Met everyone?'

The couple from the window were coming back to replenish their glasses. Rebus nodded towards them.

'Robbie,' Sir Iain said, 'come and meet Detective Inspector John Rebus. John, this is Robbie Mathieson.'

Mathieson shook Rebus's hand. He was tall, well built, and had thick black hair and a black beard. The glasses he wore sported blue tints.

'Pleased to meet you.' His accent was slightly American.

'PanoTech?' Rebus guessed.

Mathieson nodded, a bit put out by the recognition, and Sir Iain looked interested that Rebus should know Mathieson. Sir Iain turned to Allan Gunner.

'Chief Constable, is it a wonder the crime rate is falling and the detection rate rising when you can boast men of this calibre?' He looked back to Rebus. 'It's almost uncanny.'

A game was being played, and Rebus didn't know what it was. But he knew that his knowing who Mathieson was was part of it.

Gunner was correcting Sir Iain. 'It's *Deputy* Chief Constable.'

'A slip of the tongue,' Hunter said, with a wink to the general assembly. 'Perhaps I was merely looking into the

future. That's what we civil servants are good at, you know. Dugald, your glass needs a top-up.'

Dugald held out his hand for a refill. Nobody had introduced him because nobody needed to. He was quiet, thoughtful, or maybe he just didn't waste words. Hardly surprising, when everything he said might be taken down and passed to the media, who might use it in evidence against him. He couldn't afford to trust those he did not know.

Certainly, he didn't know Rebus, but Rebus knew him. He was Dugald Niven, the Right Honourable Dugald Niven.

He was Secretary of State for Scotland.

'Let's take our drinks through to the gun room,' Sir Iain said, 'and get everyone kitted out.'

Rebus poured and drank another half glass before following everyone out of the room.

It was barely above zero outside – 'bracing' and 'fresh' according to Sir Iain – and they were going to have a picnic. The provisions would be waiting for them at the clay-pigeon site. To get to the site itself necessitated a walk through the woods. In the gun room, they'd been fitted with green sportsmen's jackets, sleeveless and thickly padded with cartridge-belt attached. They were handed a shotgun each, broken open for safety's sake.

Rebus stayed to the rear of the party, and Gunner slowed down to join him.

'So what *are* you doing here?' Gunner asked.

'I thought you'd know.'

'*Me?*'

'You've had me taken off an investigation.'

'I've done no such thing.'

'OK then, you *requested* I be taken off.'

Gunner tucked his shotgun more firmly under his arm. 'What's that got to do with you being here?'

'I wish I knew. If you're asking me to make an inspired guess . . . ?'

'Go on.'

'Well, I've been brought here so you can work on me.'

'What?'

'You're going to warn me off again, and I'll be so impressed by the surroundings and the company, I'll fall to my knees and plead forgiveness.'

Gunner gave him a blazing look. 'That's ridiculous.'

'In that case, what are *you* doing here?'

'I'm in the dark. First time I've been invited. Maybe Sir Iain wants to get to know me. He's a canny diplomat, as well as being a manipulator.' Gunner paused. 'The chief constable will be retiring soon.'

'Bit young for that, isn't he?'

'His wife's ill, she needs looking after.'

'So you'll be promoted?'

'I assume so.'

'Always supposing you're given a clean bill of health.'

'What?'

'By HMIC, for example. That kind of threat works both ways, Allan.'

Gunner narrowed his eyes. 'What do you mean?'

'Shug McAnally kills himself. I try to find out why. Turns out he's recently been sharing a cell with a man called Charters. This despite the fact McAnally's in for a sex attack. Only, none of the other inmates knows that.'

'I still don't see what you're getting at.'

'Yes you do. McAnally was Alister Flower's grass. Flower worked under you on the case against Charters. McAnally was put in Charters' cell to see what he could glean. Now, Flower hasn't got the weight to set up something like that; it'd need someone more senior to have

a word with Big Jim Flett — someone like yourself, sir.'
Gunner kept his eyes on the ground and said nothing. 'And
now,' Rebus went on, 'I've got the likes of Hunter warning
me off, too.'

Gunner looked up at the knot of men ahead. They were
picking their way over fallen branches and through stunted
undergrowth between mature trees.

'I want us to talk,' he said.

'Fine.'

'But not here.'

Sir Iain had stopped and was gesturing. 'Come on,
slowcoaches! I've got one good leg and I'm still beating
you.' He waited for them to join him.

'How much land have you got here, Sir Iain?' Gunner
asked, suddenly the well-mannered guest.

'A hundred and seventy acres, but don't worry, we're not
walking all of it.'

Soon they broke out of the woods into a rutted field of
stubble. By the side of the field was a track just wide
enough for the vehicle that sat there, a venerable Land
Rover the same olive green as their jackets. The servant was
at the back of the vehicle, unpacking a large wicker hamper.
There was another man halfway across the field, standing
beside some apparatus Rebus took to be the clay-pigeon
release.

Rebus ended up standing next to the Secretary of State.
The man didn't seem inclined to speak. Rebus wondered
what he'd been discussing with Robbie Mathieson in the
morning room. Rebus turned to Mathieson.

'A friend of mine works for one of your suppliers.'

'Oh?' Mathieson didn't sound particularly interested.

'Deltona,' Rebus said.

Mathieson's beard moved in what might have been a
smile. 'Then I hope he didn't have plans this weekend. I've
been promised that plant will work all weekend. I'm due a

big order from them by midweek. I wouldn't want to have to find a new supplier.'

'How's the work on LABarum progressing?'

Mathieson stared at him, then fed cartridges into the shotgun's double chamber. 'It's going pretty well,' he said. 'Can I ask how you know about it?'

Rebus shrugged. 'Word gets around.'

'Does it?' Mathieson snapped shut the gun.

'Actually, I came across a copy of your business plan in a council house in Stenhouse.'

'What was it doing there?' Mathieson seemed calm enough.

'I haven't the faintest idea,' Rebus told him. 'Someone had scrawled the word "Dalgety" on it.' Mathieson flinched and dropped a cartridge.

'Pull!' Sir Iain called. A clay disc sprang into the air. There was an explosion, then another, and the disc shattered. Sir Iain broke open his gun.

'Damned good shot,' commented Sir Colin Macrae.

'You know, it's unusual. Sir Iain's Saturdays are normally corporate affairs, but today we've got *two* policemen.' Mathieson looked like he wanted Rebus to tell him something, but Rebus didn't know what.

'Pull!' More gunshots filled the air.

'Not bad, Dugald, not bad!'

'Tell me,' Rebus asked Mathieson, 'do you know a man called Derwood Charters?'

'I don't think so.'

'I've heard he helped finance PanoTech in the early days.'

Mathieson laughed. 'You're misinformed.'

'Come on, Allan, you're next!'

When Robbie Mathieson's turn came, he missed the target with both barrels.

'Not like you, Robbie,' Sir Iain laughed, glancing

towards Rebus. He looked uncommonly pleased. Rebus felt he was being used; he still didn't know why or how.

When his own turn came to shoot, he missed with both barrels. Sir Iain insisted he try again straight away.

'You're a tyro,' he said, 'you need the practice. I'm sure we all missed a few in the beginning.'

This time, Rebus chipped a bit off the disc with his second shot.

'See?' said Sir Iain. 'Now you're getting the hang of it!'

Maybe he was at that.

Ears still ringing, Rebus joined the others at the Land Rover. There were flasks of Scotch broth, sandwiches in silver foil, hip-flasks of whisky and larger flasks of tea. Rebus's sandwich was brown bread and smoked salmon. The salmon was sliced thick, and had been sprinkled with lemon juice and pepper. He took a small nip of whisky when the hip-flask came round, then drank two mugs of strong tea. With all the games he felt were going on, he wanted to clear his head. He wasn't sure if he was a player, a counter, or the dic. He'd been shown one thing, though – the game was dangerous, at stake his professional career, which was everything he lived for. Practically every man present had it within his power to push Rebus off the playing-board and off the force. He started to get angry: angry with himself for coming; angry with Sir Iain Hunter – so smug, so manipulative – for bringing him here. Rebus knew now that he hadn't just been brought here so he could be warned off. He swallowed the anger down and held it in his gut. It was hotter than tea, stronger than whisky.

They were almost back at the house when Sir Iain gripped Rebus's elbow and led him towards the greenhouses.

'We'll catch you up!' he called to the others. Then, to Rebus, still holding him by the elbow: 'Have a nice chat

with Robbie Mathieson?' Rebus shrugged off Sir Iain's hand. 'And with Allan Gunner too, I noticed.'

'Why am I here?'

'I admire your directness. You're here because I want to know if you've decided.'

'Decided what?'

'To stop your investigation.'

'Are you willing to tell me why you're so interested?'

Sir Iain's gaze hardened. 'I'm willing to tell you one thing, *if* you're willing to listen.'

They were standing in front of one of the long greenhouses. Looking through the misted windows, Rebus could see trestle tables and empty flower-pots and seed-trays, but there was nothing growing in there, nothing at all.

'I'm listening,' he said.

'Then I'll tell you that Scottish jobs are at risk.'

'At risk from what?'

'From *you*, Inspector, if you continue stumbling blindly around. Let it take its course, that's what I'm saying.'

Rebus turned to him. 'Let what take its course? You're not telling me anything, how am I supposed to know what to do and what not to do?'

'You know what to do,' Hunter said calmly: 'stop your little private investigation. If it goes any further, hundreds of jobs could disappear. Do you hear me? *Hundreds*. You wouldn't want that on your conscience, I'm sure.'

'I don't believe you,' Rebus said.

Hunter looked at him with something near pity. 'Yes, you do, Inspector.'

He did, too. It was in Hunter's voice, in the way his frame shivered when he spoke. He believed what he was saying, believed it with a passion. *Hundreds of jobs*.

Sir Iain started to walk towards the house. Rebus followed, making sure he never caught up.

* * *

As agreed, Rebus and Gunner left the house separately but met up at a hotel in Auchterarder.

'I don't usually drink,' Gunner confided, washing down two aspirin with an orange juice. They sat in a corner of the quiet lounge bar. For a Saturday, the main street was quiet. The shoppers would all be in Perth, keeping warm in department stores and superstores. The TV was showing *Rio Bravo*, John Wayne doing his John Wayne walk.

'I don't usually shoot,' Rebus said.

'So now we've both seen how the other half lives.' Gunner put down his glass and took a deep breath. 'Let's get down to business. Whatever you think, Inspector, I wasn't there to "scare you off". I got my invite in the mail, same as you did. I've been thinking, and my conclusion is that Sir Iain wanted to play us off against one another. Or perhaps he thought that my presence would serve to unnerve you.'

Rebus nodded agreement. 'One other option,' he added. 'We were both there to scare someone else. Mathieson didn't like it that policemen were present.'

'What are they so worried about?'

'Hunter told me it has to do with jobs.'

'Jobs? What kind of jobs?'

Rebus shook his head. How far could he trust Gunner? The man was the first person who'd tried to take him out of the game. 'Are you going to own up about McAnally?'

Gunner examined his fingernails. 'You're right in just about every detail. I had McAnally moved to Saughton and into Charters' cell. Then he went and got cancer, and wasn't getting any information out of Charters, so I arranged for his early release.'

'And he went straight to Councillor Gillespie and blew his head off in front of him.'

'I don't know why he did that.'

'Why was McAnally in Charters' cell?'

'To see if he could talk himself into Charters' confidence. I wanted to see what Charters was hiding. I knew he was hiding something, but couldn't think what to do about it until Flower suggested McAnally.'

'And what is Charters hiding exactly?'

'Money, what else? I don't mean he's hiding it literally, though perhaps he is. But back in the mid-eighties he was coining it, and we weren't sure where the cash was coming from. He had about half a dozen companies – legit, as far as the Fraud Unit could tell – but they made more money than they should have.'

'I thought that's what Thatcherism was all about. Was one of his companies called Mensung?'

'Yes.'

'And were all his companies involved in retraining?'

'That sort of thing. Their paperwork was so convoluted – positively labyrinthine – that even our specialists couldn't find a clear path through it. They were all agreed on one thing. Derry Charters had a genius for muddying the water. You could track a company of his for months and not get to the bottom of its financial status.'

'I've heard he helped finance PanoTech at one time.'

'Who told you that?'

'Is it true?'

'I don't think so. Did one of Charters' investors tell you?' Rebus nodded. 'Probably a story he spun them. He could be very persuasive.'

'But all this was eight, nine years ago.'

'Yes, and since then he's cleaned up his act, or had done until he burnt people's fingers with Albavise.'

'So why are you still chasing him over a piece of ancient history?'

'A couple of reasons. One, I spent a lot of my time and effort in the Fraud Unit chasing him, without getting a result. It represents probably the only blot on my record.

Two, our best guess when we investigated him was that he was fiddling millions.' He had Rebus's full attention. 'Millions,' he repeated. 'And for me, that makes him worth the chase.'

'Where did he fiddle these millions from?'

But Gunner just shrugged. Rebus was thoughtful for a moment. The bar was filling, and the TV had been switched over to show the football scores. Not that many games were being played: the pitches were dangerously hard.

'I've read the case against him on Albavise. Any chance that I can see the other paperwork?'

Gunner studied him. 'There's a hell of a lot, and it's in no particular order. You think you can spot something our financial gurus couldn't?'

Rebus shrugged. 'Just for my peace of mind. I'd like to talk to Charters, too.'

'What?'

'His cellmate's committed suicide. It looks strange if nobody's been near to ask him about McAnally's state of mind prior to release. I mean, who'd know better than him?'

Gunner nodded. 'Fair point.'

'Speaking of McAnally, how much did you pay him?'

'What?'

'He was working for you, feeding you information, I'm assuming he was paid.'

'He didn't give us anything of relevance. We gave him a few pounds here and there, nothing more.' Rebus was seeing Tresa McAnally's flat in his mind: new door, new décor, new TV. 'Does it matter?'

'It did to Wee Shug,' Rebus said quietly. Someone had given him the money, money he'd passed on to Tresa, almost like life insurance. Who did Wee Shug know with money apart from his cellmate?

Gunner finished his drink. 'I wonder what Sir Iain will be up to tonight.'

'The way he was tucking into the hooch, sleeping it off, I'd imagine. Does he drive to Edinburgh and back every day?'

'He only uses Ruthie at weekends. When he's at work, he has a flat in the New Town.'

'Whereabouts exactly?'

'Royal Circus, I think.'

Royal Circus, thought Rebus, where Haldayne collected some of his parking tickets. Life was just full of coincidences, if you happened to believe, as Rebus himself did not, in coincidence.

31

Early Sunday morning, a sleepy-eyed detective sergeant from Lothian & Borders Police Headquarters turned up at Rebus's flat.

'You'd better give me a hand,' he said.

Rebus followed him down to where a patrol car idled kerbside. He peered in through the passenger side window.

'Maybe we'd better hire a winch.'

It took them four trips to transfer the boxes from the car to Rebus's living-room. Rebus put the binbags behind the sofa to make room on the floor.

'Sign here,' the DS said. He had a typed chitty: RECEIPT OF ALL CASE-NOTES (8 BOXES) CONCERNING DERWOOD CHARTERS. Rebus signed.

'Date and time, too,' said the DS.

'You'll be wanting a tip next,' Rebus muttered.

'If you're offering.'

'Well, here's one for you: when lifting, bend your knees, not your back.'

He phoned Siobhan Clarke.

'Why me?' she said.

'Because Brian Holmes has a home life.'

'That could be construed as discrimination. When do you want me there?'

'Say an hour.'

He tidied the living room a bit, depositing the bin bags in the hall and setting the file boxes in a row on the floor.

Then he collected up all the dirty mugs, glasses and dishes and took them through to the kitchen. He emptied the coffee-jar and put it back under the radiator, and opened the living-room window an inch to air the place. The sun was out, showing that the windows hadn't been cleaned since the autumn. Rebus decided enough was enough.

'She's coming here to work,' he told himself, 'not for a candlelit supper.'

They got two breaks, both late in the afternoon.

The first was a client's name: Quinlon.

'I've come across that name before,' Rebus said. It took him a while to place it. 'The civil servant, Rory McAllister, he mentioned someone called Quinlon; a building contractor. There'd been some shady business between the SDA and him – it was one of the things held against the SDA when they were deciding its fate.' Rebus flipped back a page in the notes. 'And Charters' client happened to be a building contractor.'

'So?'

'So, somehow the media got to hear about the SDA and Quinlon, and that story helped sink the SDA. Who was going to gain by the SDA's demise?'

'Charters?'

'Yes, because the financial slate was going to be wiped clean, and there'd be no possibility of a future investigation into where the SDA millions had gone.'

'You think Charters grassed on his client?'

'I wouldn't put anything past him.'

The second break came soon after.

It was clear from the case-notes that the Fraud Unit had been focusing on Charters. When his 'associates' were mentioned, they were dismissed as fronts or moneymen. Nobody thought the directors had anything to do with whatever swindles Charters was perpetrating.

Which was why they weren't mentioned often, and in the case of Mensung, not at all. But then Rebus picked up the photocopy of a letter sent by Charters to the SDA. The Mensung logo was at the top, together with the non-existent Leith Walk address – referred to as 'Mensung House'. At the foot of the letter was the company's registration number.

'You couldn't find Mensung in Companies House, right?'

'Right,' said Clarke. 'I had their archivist take a good look.'

'Well, either they were registered, or this is a phony number.'

'The records could have been mislaid.'

'Now wouldn't *that* be a coincidence.' The final line of the sheet was blurred. Rebus peered at the row of names, the names of Mensung's directors.

Because he knew what he was looking for, he could pick out the name Charters quite easily; the others were more difficult. It took real effort to decipher J Joseph Simpson's name.

'Figures,' Rebus said. He wanted another word with Simpson anyway, but this explained why he'd lied about Mensung's address: the company had been dodgy, under investigation, and Simpson had been a director. It wasn't the kind of thing you wanted to publicise when you were still in business.

As for the third and last name . . .

'Can you make that out?' Rebus asked, passing the sheet to Siobhan Clarke.

'Starts with an M,' she suggested. 'Murchieson?'

'Murchieson?'

'I don't know, maybe Matthews, something like that.'

Rebus took the sheet back from her. Matthews . . .

Murchieson . . . 'Mathieson,' he said, staring at the slewed writing. 'Could it be Mathieson?'

She shrugged. 'As in . . .?'

'I met a man yesterday called Robbie Mathieson. He runs PanoTech.'

'Silicon Glen's homegrown success story?'

Rebus nodded. 'We've all just been supplied with PanoTech computers, haven't we?'

'Everybody from the chief constable down.'

Which meant that Allan Gunner would have one, too. 'Who do you suppose would decide something like that?'

'Like what?'

'Like which manufacturer was going to supply us?'

'It would be the director of Corporate Services, wouldn't it?'

'But the DCC would have a say.'

'Probably. Is it relevant?'

Rebus wondered. PanoTech put the computers together in Gyle Park West, and Gyle Part West was one of Councillor Gillespie's files. Mensung was another. There was the story that Derry Charters had something to do with the early financing of PanoTech. And PanoTech's boss just happened to be at Sir Iain Hunter's, looking worried about something. And Allan Gunner was there too . . .

Wheels within wheels, he thought. Scotland was a machine, a big machine if you looked at it from the outside. But from the inside, it assumed a new form – small, intimate, not that many moving parts, and all of them interconnected quite intricately. Rebus knew he was still outside the machine, but he knew now that one reason why he'd been invited to the shooting party was that Sir Iain Hunter was inviting him *in*. They could make him part of the machine, a chip on the motherboard. All it took was friends in the right places.

After that, anything could happen.

* * *

They worked solidly till five-thirty.

'I hope I'm being treated to dinner,' Clarke said, stretching her spine.

'Who's taking you?'

'You are,' she said.

Rebus shook his head. 'I've other plans tonight, sorry.'

'Well, thanks a lot. I give up my precious Sunday to help you, and then you boot me out.' She narrowed her eyes. 'Got a date?'

She was attempting a peculiarly Scottish tactic: being serious while pretending levity.

'I'm working,' Rebus said.

'Working?'

'I've got to talk to someone.'

'Anyone I know?'

Rebus shook his head. 'But don't think I don't appreciate your help.' He saw her to the door

When the bell rang two minutes later, he thought she must have forgotten something. But it wasn't Siobhan Clarke standing on his doorstep. It was Gill Templer.

'Mind if I come in?' she said, walking past him.

'I was just on my way out.'

'This won't take long. I tried phoning, but it was engaged all afternoon.'

'I had it off the hook,' Rebus said, following her into the living room. She looked at the boxes of documents.

'I see you're really taking your furlough seriously.'

'Come on, Gill, it was foisted on me. You were there, remember.'

'I remember. The chief super had been getting incredible flak; in his shoes, I'd have done the same thing.'

'This isn't sounding like a social call.'

'That's because it isn't one. The Lord Provost is your latest victim. He called the chief super and said you'd been rude to him.'

259

'Did he mention specifics?'

'No.'

'I didn't think he would.'

'The Farmer will probably call you in the morning himself. I'd imagine it'll be an official reprimand, maybe even a suspension.' She turned to him, her eyes blazing. 'How could you do this to me?'

'What?'

'I'm your immediate superior! I'm in the post barely a week, and already you've caused the most unholy ructions. How do you think that makes me look?'

'It's got nothing to do with you.'

'Yes it bloody well has! It's got *everything* to do with me. You're one of my officers. How am I supposed to work, to get a feel for the job, when all the chief super does is fret about what grenade you're going to chuck next?'

Rebus nodded his understanding. 'That's what this is about. You're pissed off because the Farmer's not paying you enough attention. You want to create a good impression, and you're not making any impression at all.'

'Now you're just twisting my words.'

'Am I?' He grabbed her by the arms. 'Look me in the face and tell me that. Tell me I'm not right.'

She shrugged free of his grip. 'John,' she said, more calmly. 'I came here to warn you. Tomorrow morning could spell the end of your career.'

'You think I care about that?' He tried to sound casual.

She took a step towards him. 'Yes,' she said quietly, 'I think you do.' Her green eyes seemed to bore into him. 'I think, beneath it all, you're scared.'

'Scared?' He smiled. 'Of course I'm scared. I wouldn't mind if it was some big hard bastard who had me cornered in an alley, or if some kind of contract was out on me. But this is worse, this scares me to death.'

'Then drop it. Say you're sorry to a few people, and come back to work.'

He smiled again. 'It would be that easy, wouldn't it? You'd do it.'

'Yes, I would.'

'Well, I'll think about it.'

She tried to measure his sincerity, but it was like measuring haar.

32

Big Jim Flett was nowhere to be seen.

'Even the Big Man has to take a few hours off here and there,' his deputy said, leading Rebus down one of the corridors inside Saughton Jail.

'I'm sure,' Rebus said, even though he was sure the governor was avoiding him. He had lied to Rebus, and now Rebus knew it.

'Derry doesn't get many visitors,' the deputy said. He was a brisk, nervous man, ruddy-faced and jacketless with his shirt-sleeves rolled up.

'You know him then?'

'We've had conversations.'

'I was told he didn't mix.'

'That's true, but I've always found him pleasant enough.'

'He hasn't tried to sell you anything, has he?'

The deputy laughed. 'No, not yet. He'd make a damned good salesman though.'

'What's he like?'

'Quiet for the most part, never gives us any trouble.' They were nearing a metal door, beside which stood a warden. The warden unlocked the door and swung it open.

'You're sure you don't want me to stay?' the deputy asked Rebus. Rebus shook his head, but with a gracious smile. 'Well, Munro here will take Derry back to his cell when you're finished.'

'Thanks again,' Rebus said.

The door closed after him, the key rattling in its lock. Rebus was alone with Derwood Charters.

Charters was pacing the floor, arms folded, head bowed as if he was pondering some problem.

'Do you play chess?' Charters asked, without looking up.

'No.'

'Pity.'

Rebus looked around the room. There was a table, its legs bolted to the floor, and two chairs beside it. On one wall, a blackboard provided the room's only hint of decoration.

'Mind if I sit?' Rebus said.

'Make yourself comfortable.' Charters smiled at his little joke. He continued to pace the floor, and Rebus studied him. Charters was in his mid-forties, tall and broad-shouldered. He was immaculately groomed, his hair parted just so, his face shiny and clean-shaven. His fingernails looked manicured.

'Do you know what *zugzwang* means?'

'Sounds German,' Rebus said.

For the first time, Charters looked at him. 'Of course it's German. It's a chess position. It's when you've to play, only any move you make will spell disaster. Yet you've got to make a move. There was a chess puzzle in today's paper, and I'm damned if I can solve it.'

'The solution's easy,' Rebus said.

Charters stopped pacing. 'What?'

'Take up golf instead.'

Charters considered this, then smiled. He came and sat down opposite Rebus, folding his hands on the table. 'May I see some identification?'

Rebus took out his warrant card. Charters examined it against the light, as though it might represent a particularly brilliant forgery.

'On a Sunday night,' he said, handing it back.

263

'Pardon?'

'I don't get many visitors, let alone on a Sunday night. And a police officer at that.'

'I'm here to ask you a few questions about Wee Shug McAnally.'

'Ah yes, Hugh.' McAnally probably hadn't been called 'Hugh' by anyone apart from the minister at his christening and the judge who pronounced sentence on him. Charters seemed to read Rebus's mind. 'I respect a person's name, Inspector. It's all we bring into this world, and it's all we take out of it. My own name is sometimes abbreviated to Derry. In here, that has earned me the nickname "the apprentice boy".'

Charters' voice – quiet, atonal – had a mesmeric quality, and once his eyes had fixed on Rebus's, they never left them.

'You know he committed suicide, Mr Charters?'

'Very unfortunate.'

'Suicides have to be investigated.'

'I didn't know that.'

'Whether you know it or not, it happens to be the case. Tell me, did McAnally talk to you much?'

'All the time. To be frank, it annoyed me. Even when I was trying to read, he'd be blethering on about nothing of consequence, just filling the cell with noise. As though there wasn't enough noise in here already. At the start, I thought he'd been allotted my cell as some subtle form of punishment. You know, psychological torture.'

'So what did he talk about? I'm assuming these were fairly one-sided affairs?'

'They were soliloquys. As to the substance … he talked about his background, his wife – interminably about his wife; I feel I know her as well as her gynaecologist must. He spoke of his affairs with other women, which I didn't believe for one second. And every time he finished a story,

he'd ask me, *plead* with me, to tell him something about myself.' Charters paused. 'What do you make of that, Inspector? I mean, Hugh was obsessed with himself, and yet every now and then he'd suddenly stop and ask me something. Don't you think that's strange?'

Rebus ignored the question. 'What was he in for?'

'You see? You've avoided answering! That's what I had to do twenty times a day.'

'Are you going to answer?'

'He told me it was for housebreaking.'

'And I believe you're inside for fraud, is that correct?'

'Interesting,' Charters mused, patting his fingers against his mouth. 'Why would you ask me what Hugh was inside for?'

'I just wondered,' Rebus improvised, 'if the two of you ever talked about it. I'm trying to build up a picture of him.'

'To hazard a guess as to why he killed himself?'

'Yes.'

'Well, obviously he killed himself because he was dying of cancer.'

'Did he tell you that?'

Charters smiled again. 'I'm only guessing.'

'Well, you're probably right, that's probably why he did kill himself. What it doesn't explain is the manner.'

'You mean, why would he pick on a city councillor to witness his last rites?' Rebus nodded. 'Have you tried asking the councillor?'

'Yes.'

'And what did he say?' Charters was trying to sound casually curious. Rebus stared at him.

'Do you know the councillor?' he asked.

'Never met him.'

'That's not what I asked.'

265

Charters sat back and folded his arms. 'Now you're learning subtlety, Inspector. Our contest can only improve.'

'It's not a game of chess, Mr Charters.'

Charters looked penitent. 'Of course not, I'm sorry.'

'Do you know the councillor?' Rebus repeated.

'I read newspapers, Inspector, I keep up with events. So to a certain extent, yes, I *know* Councillor Gillespie.'

'And does he know you?'

'Why should he?'

It was Rebus's turn to smile. Charters had used the word 'subtlety'. Rebus was learning that he must needs be oblique.

'You ran a company called Mensung, didn't you?'

'A long time ago, yes.' Rebus noticed that though he was outwardly well groomed, Charters' teeth were the colour of dead fish. 'I like these tangents, Inspector. Your mind moves in mysterious ways. Difficult to *zugzwang* someone who plays so erratically. Why are you interested in a company I wound up seven years ago?'

'I told a friend of mine I was coming to speak to you. He said he attended some retraining seminars held by Mensung on Corstorphine Road.'

The response seemed to satisfy Charters. 'Which company did he work for?'

'He didn't say. He still works in electronics, for one of PanoTech's subcontractors.'

'Then maybe the seminars did him some good.'

Rebus nodded. 'I heard a story that you helped finance PanoTech when the company was in its infancy.'

Charters raised an eyebrow. 'Stories tend to become confused over time.'

'You'd nothing to do with it then?' Charters shook his head. 'By the way, why did Mensung go bust?'

'It didn't "go bust" – I wound it up. I was bored with it, and couldn't find anyone to buy me out.' He shrugged. 'I'm

easily bored.' He got up and started pacing the room again. 'You know, Inspector, you told me you were here to ask a few questions about Hugh. We've strayed a long way from that particular topic, wouldn't you say?'

Rebus stood up.

'Going so soon?'

'You're enjoying yourself too much, *Derry*. This isn't supposed to be fun. A man's dead.'

Charters stopped pacing. 'A man who was dying anyway. A man who chose his own route out. Luckier than most of us, I'd wager. If the doctors told me I had only a few agonising months to live, I think I'd go find myself a gun, too. But the world would look so unfair to my eyes – all those people so alive and vibrant around me, all those ill people being cured in hospitals – maybe I'd want a witness to the injustice of it all, someone representing authority in my eyes and the eyes of those around me. Maybe I'd want him to *see* my agony, to share in my horror. It would have to be an easy target though ... and a councillor is such an easy target – accessible, public, approachable. I'd be making a point to the world. I would *refuse* to die in silence!'

The silence after Charters had finished was resonant. He had worked himself up to a pitch, and now calmed only slowly. There had been anger in his voice, and fervour, and conviction. His eyes were on Rebus's. *He'd make a damned good salesman.*

'I don't buy it,' Rebus said, going to the door.

'Inspector.' Rebus paused. 'You called me "Derry" – that was a cheap shot. Apart from that, you did pretty well.' He paced the floor again. 'Hugh didn't really talk about his wife that often. There was another woman ... he described her so accurately, I could probably paint her for you even now. Her name was Maisie. He talked about her all the time. I think he loved her more than anyone in the world. Perhaps you should talk to her.'

267

'I already have, Mr Charters.'

Rebus left the cell feeling that Charters had given a name to his own feelings about the investigation, Willie and Dixie, and life in general.

The word was *zugzwang*.

It was four a.m. when his phone rang. He came awake, but left it to ring. Four a.m., news just had to be bad. The caller persisted, and at last Rebus picked up the receiver.

'Mr Rebus?'

A young voice, insolent, a bit drunk. Loud music and voices in the background: a party.

'Yes?'

'It's Paul. Paul Duggan.'

'Paul, nice of you to call.'

'Is it late? I don't have my watch on.'

'It sounds like a great party, Paul. Give me the address and I'll drop by with a few uniforms.'

'Don't be like that Mr Rebus. I bring glad tidings. I've found her.'

'Kirstie Kennedy?'

'Aye.'

'Is she all right?'

'Not bad for a junkie.'

'Can I speak to her?'

'Listen, she's adamant she's not going home. She says her stepmum's a lunatic.'

'I'd like to see her. There's no question of her having to go home.'

'I don't know.' Duggan sounded doubtful.

'Paul, don't hang up! Listen, would she talk to me if I paid her?'

'Look, I'll have a word with her. No promises, but I'll have a word, see what she says.'

'Just do me a favour. Phone in daylight next time.'

'If you're lucky, I might even phone when I'm sober.'

33

It was eight a.m. when his phone next rang.

'Yes?' he croaked, trying to find some saliva in his mouth.

'John?' It was the Farmer's voice.

Here it comes, thought Rebus. 'Morning, sir. What's it to be – reprimand, suspension, or dismissal?'

'Damn you, John. I had a hell of a weekend because of you.'

'I'm sorry, sir. I never meant to get you into trouble.'

'That's your problem, Inspector – you're selfish, no other word for it. I think you know damned well that these obsessions of yours end up damaging everyone around you, friend, foe and civilians alike.'

'Yes, sir.'

'But it doesn't bother you, does it?' Rebus didn't answer. The Farmer had obviously been preparing his speech for a while. 'As long as your own personal morality is satisfied, that's all that counts. Sod everybody else, isn't that right?'

'It feels that way sometimes, sir,' Rebus said quietly.

'Well, maybe you should consider that morality of yours, because it's no code *I'd* want to live with.'

'You don't have to live with it, sir. I do.'

'Well, you lead a charmed existence, that's all I can say.'

Rebus frowned. 'How do you mean?'

'I've discussed things with the DCC. He said he'd apologise to the Lord Provost on your behalf. He also said

he thought HMIC would be investigating F Troop instead of us.'

F Troop: meaning F Division, Livingston. 'What are you saying, sir?'

'I'm saying I want you back here. The holiday's over. Report to my office this morning.'

'I've a dentist's appointment.'

'Well, this afternoon then.'

'Yes, sir.'

'Look, John, have you and the DCC had any contact?'

'I've been on holiday, sir.'

'Yes, but all the same?'

'Well, maybe I did bump into him by the pool ...'

It was another grim day. No snow or ice, but a freezing wind and gusts of rain, the sky oppressively weighted with cloud. It was like the city was in a box, and someone had pushed the lid on too tightly.

Rebus's second visit to Dr Keene wasn't so traumatic. You could get used to anything. The tooth had drained nicely, and Keene did the root canal while Rebus concentrated on the photograph on the ceiling. He plotted Paul Duggan's property portfolio. Maybe Duggan had a point: nobody was suggesting he was overcharging his 'tenants' – he was making a profit out of each house and flat, but nothing outrageous. And meantime, he was putting roofs over heads. Rebus knew there might needs be a trade-off: if he wanted to see Kirstie, Duggan might want Rebus to put in a good word come trial time. Always supposing it came to trial. The district council was about to be replaced with another body. Who knew what would be written off?

Suddenly, something clicked in Rebus's brain. He saw something he should have seen before. He was so busy thinking that he didn't hear Dr Keene say that, while Rebus was there, he might as well start on the fillings ...

* * *

There were no cheers, no banners or bunting as Rebus walked back into St Leonard's and poured himself a cup of coffee.

'A word to the wise,' Siobhan Clarke said.

'What?'

'You're pouring coffee down your tie.'

It was true: with his mouth still numb, he was dribbling. He went to the toilets and pulled out a clump of paper towels, soaked them in water and dabbed at his tie.

'Here he is,' said Flower, pushing open the door, 'the proverbial bad penny.'

'Don't be so hard on yourself,' Rebus retorted. Flower came to the sink and checked his hair in the mirror. 'I see you managed to start a fire, then take credit for putting it out.'

Flower chuckled. 'Word gets around, eh?'

'Speaking of words that get around, I had a chat with someone about your snitch.'

'Which one?'

'Shug McAnally. We could all have been spared some grief if you'd told me at the start he was working for you.'

'It's not the sort of thing you can publicise. I mean,' Flower looked around, 'planting a snitch in somebody's cell.'

'You don't mind telling me now though. Has the DCC had a word?'

'He said you'd been asking.' Flower looked unnaturally pleased with himself. Rebus could guess why.

'You think you're quids-in with the DCC, don't you?'

'Well, if it ever came out about McAnally, the DCC could get into trouble.' Flower winked. 'He needs to keep me sweet.'

'What you mean is, you've got him either way. If the plan succeeded, it'd be because of you. If it went badly, it would need covering up – which would take your help.

271

Gunner would still owe you. That's why you've been blocking me: you didn't want me getting to the DCC – he's your little investment.'

Flower chuckled again, and tucked a stray hair back behind his ear. There was a sound of flushing from one of the two cubicles. Flower's head jerked around, his mouth open, as the cubicle door opened and the Farmer came out.

This came as no surprise to Rebus: he'd seen the Farmer enter the toilets just before him.

'Morning, sir,' he said.

Flower didn't say anything. The Farmer pointed at him. 'My office, Inspector Flower, *now*!' Then he opened the door and was gone. Flower turned on Rebus.

'You knew! You bloody well knew!'

Rebus tossed the ball of sodden paper into the bin. One-nil.

Someone was at the front desk asking for him, that was the message. But when Rebus got there, there was nobody about. Then he saw a figure outside, motioning to him. It was Paul Duggan. He was wearing his long black coat again, but it had a small tear in the sleeve, and a white smudge on one shoulder.

'Nothing personal like,' he said when Rebus joined him outside, 'but I hate police stations.'

'There's a café across –'

Duggan was shaking his head. 'She's waiting for us.'

'Kirstie?' Duggan nodded. 'Where?'

'Have you got a car?'

They went to Rebus's car.

Duggan directed him down the Pleasance and right on Holyrood Road. This was a dispiriting part of town; all empty sites and disused warehouses. The Younger Universe was under construction, and was going to make everything all right again, if you believed the publicity.

272

Rebus hoped it would succeed; he liked the symbolism: the USA had Disneyland, and Scotland gets a theme park built by a brewery. The theme park would be a neighbour to Holyrood Palace, the monarch's Edinburgh residence. This, too, Rebus liked.

'Where are we going?'

'Just park by the palace gates.'

It was easy to park this time of year; in warmer seasons, the place was a log-jam of tourist coaches. A kid was at the locked gates, peering through them at the palace beyond.

'Toot your horn,' Duggan ordered. Rebus did so, to no effect.

'She's on another planet.' Duggan wound down his window. 'Hiy, Kirstie!'

Slowly the 'kid' turned, and Rebus saw a face older than the frame which supported it. Nobody had said Kirstie Kennedy would be so scrawny, so tiny. But as she walked towards the car her face was set like cement. Lipstick, eyeshadow and panstick provided her with a mask. She wore tight black jeans, accentuating her matchstick legs, and a long shapeless black jumper whose arms stretched down past her hands. Her hair was greasy, shoulderlength, tied back with a band. A spiky fringe, dyed blood-red, fell into her eyes. She was chewing gum. She pulled open the back door and climbed in.

'Hello, Kirstie,' Rebus said. 'Where do you want to go?'

'I want ice cream.'

Rebus thought of Luca's, but it was too far. 'Tollcross?' he suggested.

Tollcross would do her.

They sat in the ice-cream parlour and she ordered the biggest concoction on the menu, plus a giant Coke. The place was quiet: an old couple, smoking and drinking frothy

coffee; a harassed mother hissing at her two children who were arguing over bowls of garish ice cream.

Rebus had ordered coffee, Duggan orange juice and some apple pie with cream. Rebus remembered that he used to bring Sammy in here when she was a kid. He looked at the Lord Provost's daughter and tried to remember she was seventeen.

'Paul says you want a word.' Her voice was polite in a way no attitude could hide. Rebus knew that her street diction, her low-class language, had been only recently learned.

'How long have you been on the Bob Hope, Kirstie?'

'You mean the Merry?'

Duggan looked at Rebus. 'Merry Mac, crack,' he explained.

'Long enough,' Kirstie answered.

'Long enough to be tired of it?'

'Long enough to know you never get tired of it.' Her ice cream arrived: three different flavours with chocolate sauce, nuts, tinned peaches and wafers. The sight of it made Rebus's teeth crackle.

'Your dad's been worried,' he said.

'So what?'

'And your mum.'

Her sudden convulsion almost sent a mouthful of ice cream on to the table. 'My mum died when I was five. What you mean is, "that woman who lives with my dad".'

'OK.'

'Have you met her?'

'No.'

'She's off her trolley, praise the Lord.'

'So you don't get on with her. Is that why you ran away?'

'Does there have to be a reason?'

Rebus shrugged. 'Only, most teenagers I know who run away, they go a bit further.'

'You mean London? I didn't like it. My pals are all up here.'

'You mean pals like Willie and Dixie?'

She put the spoon back on her plate and started on the Coke. 'I liked Willie. Dixie was a nutter, you never knew what he'd do next, but Willie was all right.'

'You heard what they did?'

She nodded.

'You left that wreath for them on the bridge, didn't you?'

Another nod. She dipped her finger into the chocolate sauce. She was trying not to care, but there was still a core of sentiment buried in her brain, a precious nugget of guilt.

'Was it your idea, Kirstie?' She looked up at him. 'It was, wasn't it?'

She got to her feet. 'I have to go to the toilet.'

Rebus snatched her wrist. 'Why did you do it, Kirstie? Just for the money? Why did you take the LABarum plans from your father's office?'

She shook free of his grip. 'Let me go!' She stumbled away from the table and ran to the toilets. Rebus sat back and started to light a cigarette.

'No smoking,' the waitress told him.

'Can I get a beer?'

'We're not licensed.'

Rebus nicked his cigarette and put it back in the packet. He looked across the table at Paul Duggan.

'You like her, don't you?' Rebus said.

Duggan said nothing. He was making circles in the cream with his spoon.

'Remember I told you she'd left something in Willie's bedroom? It was some papers stolen from her father. Do you have any idea why she took them?'

Duggan shook his head slowly but determinedly. 'She's ... go easy on her, OK?'

'Or what?'

'Or she'll run.' Duggan paused. 'Again.'

Eventually the toilet door opened and she walked back to the table, arms hanging in a lazy slouch. Rebus looked into her eyes and saw pupils shrunk to pinheads.

'That was stupid.'

'So what?' she said, starting back into her ice cream. After two mouthfuls, she pushed the plate away.

'The kidnap,' Rebus said, 'the ransom demand – it was all your idea, wasn't it?'

'Yes.'

'To get back at your stepmother?'

'My dad.'

'To get back at your dad?'

She nodded. 'And everything he represents, the old bastard.' She was much more together now, more confident. She didn't care what she told him.

'You know you committed an offence?' Rebus asked.

'I'd deny it in court. I'd deny it everywhere. Where's the proof that it wasn't just two wee boys with a daft scheme in their heads?'

'There's corroboration.' Rebus glanced towards Duggan.

'You think Paul would grass on me?' She leaned into Duggan's shoulder and stroked his face. 'He wouldn't do that.'

'Not even if I offered him a deal on his slum landlord scam?'

Kirstie shook her head. 'Paul wouldn't hurt me. His mum likes me too much.'

'Well, maybe I don't need Paul. Maybe all I need is that LABarum document. It links you to Willie.' He paused. 'Did you write "Dalgety" on the last page?' She nodded. 'Why?'

'It's something I heard my dad say on the phone … when I was listening in. Dalgety sounded important, someone he was worried about.'

'Dalgety's a person then?'

'Yes.'

'Kirstie, *why* did you steal the LABarum plan?'

Her face creased in a sneer. 'It's my dad, don't you see? If you look closely enough at it, if you read all the small print and between the lines, all you'll find there is my dad's face, smiling smugly back at you.'

'Why is he smug?'

'Because it's going to make him a hero. And it's all crooked. I heard him on the phone, they were talking about how to cover it all up. The whole fucking thing is just a lot of ... a lot of ... it's all just so much *shit*!'

'I can't have language like that,' the waitress warned. 'There are children in here.'

'Well, fuck them!' Kirstie screeched, jumping to her feet. 'Because they're all fucked anyway, just like everybody else!'

'I'll have to ask you to leave.'

Rebus and Duggan were on their feet too.

'Come on, Kirstie.'

'That girl's on drugs or something, I know it!'

Rebus threw money down on the table. Kirstie Kennedy's legs had buckled, and Duggan was holding her upright.

'Let's get her into the car,' Rebus said, knowing he should take her straight to St Leonard's, angry with himself because he knew that's the last thing he was going to do.

Instead, Duggan gave him directions back to where she was staying. It was a flat in Leith, in the maze of narrow roads behind Great Junction Street.

'One of yours, is it?' Rebus asked Duggan. But Duggan was busy stroking Kirstie's forehead, even though she was asleep.

They walked her up the stairs, one on either side, arms around her back, her arms over their shoulders. Rebus

could feel the swell of a small breast, and the thin rib-cage beneath.

'You did say you wanted to see her,' Duggan was saying, exculpating himself.

'And I'll want to see her again.' He knew there was more she could tell him, more he needed to hear from her.

He was trying to figure out who or what was responsible for the deaths of Willie and Dixie. This weightless creature he carried? The lads themselves? The police for giving chase? The Lord Provost for agreeing to it all? Maybe even the stepmother for driving Kirstie away? Except that it hadn't just been the stepmother, it had been some realisation about the Lord Provost himself ...

Maybe it was the system, that same system Sammy so passionately attacked. A system that had failed Willie and Dixie as surely as it nurtured people like Sir Iain Hunter and Robbie Mathieson. In nature, there had to be balance; as some rose, others fell or were pushed or made the leap for themselves.

Or maybe ... just maybe it had been Rebus himself, for crawling from the wreckage still with the need to confront them ... standing there in front of them, forcing *them* to choose. My obsession, he thought. My private morality. Maybe the Farmer was right ...

'Will you stay with her?' he asked Duggan when they reached the top of the stairs.

Duggan nodded. Rebus knew she'd be all right. She had someone who'd look after her.

'What about you?' Duggan asked. 'What are you going to do?'

But Rebus had released his hold on the body and was heading back downstairs.

He went into a dive he knew near the foot of Leith Walk. It

had a burgundy linoleum floor and matching coloured walls, and was like staring into somebody's throat.

'Whisky,' Rebus said. 'A double.'

And when the whisky came, he drank it down in two gulps.

'Know something?' he said to the closest drinker. 'A couple of days ago, I was eating wild smoked salmon and shooting clay-pigeons.'

'Better that than the other way round, son,' the elderly drinker said, adjusting the cap on his head.

That night, Mrs Cochrane came upstairs to tell him there was a small dark patch on her living-room ceiling. Rebus had forgotten to empty the coffee-jar. Water had soaked the bare floorboard beneath.

'Wait till it's dried out,' he said by way of apology, 'and I'll touch up the paintwork.'

He'd been asleep in his chair, but now felt wide awake. It was half past eleven, too late to do anything. Then the telephone rang, and he picked it up.

'I'm not interested,' he said.

'You'll be interested in this.'

Rebus recognised the voice of DC Robert Burns. 'Don't tell me West End needs my help?'

'We're not that desperate. I just thought I'd do you a favour. Looks like we've got a murder.'

Rebus's grip tightened on the receiver. 'Anyone I know?'

'Identification near the body suggests the name's Thomas Gillespie.'

'*Councillor* Gillespie?'

'I haven't told you the best part yet. He was found in a lane connecting Dundee Street to Dalry Road.'

Rebus tried to fix the geography. 'Next to the cemetery?'

'Yes. The lane's called Coffin Walk.'

* * *

Coffin Walk climbed quite steeply from Dalry Road. It had the busy Western Approach Road on one side, Dalry Cemetery on the other. It was a narrow alley, well lit but long.

'If someone stopped you halfway,' Burns told Rebus, leading him down the lane, 'there'd be no escape.'

'But you'd see an attacker, wouldn't you? There's no place to hide.'

Burns nodded at the cemetery wall. 'You could stand behind there, listen for someone coming, then jump over when they got close. It's the perfect site for an ambush.'

'You think that's what this was?'

Burns shrugged. They were close to the body now. Police officers with torches were in the cemetery, looking for footprints and the murder weapon. The lane had been sealed off at both ends, and though there was a knot of policemen near the body, the only person actually next to it was the pathologist, Professor Gates. Gates was telling the photographer what to do, and DI Davidson was talking to the undertaker. Even in mufti – padded jacket and jeans rather than the black suit – an undertaker was recognisable.

'So what happened?' Rebus asked Burns.

'Somebody came out of the Diggers, walked up Angle Park Terrace, looked down here, and saw the body. They thought it was a tramp sleeping rough. Well, there's a night shelter on Gorgie Road, so the guy came down here to say so.'

'Like a good citizen.'

'He saw the blood, knew fine well what had happened, and called us.'

Rebus pointed to a wallet, which lay a couple of feet from the body. 'That was lying there?'

'Yep, driver's licence, blood donor card ...'

'But no cash or credit cards?'

'Cleaned out.'

'And nobody saw the attack?'

'My guess is, he hoofed it back over the wall.'

Professor Gates had finished his initial examination. 'We can wrap this one up,' he said.

But Rebus wanted a look first. Tom Gillespie lay in a protective foetal position. He hadn't been dead when he dropped. He'd curled himself around the pain in his gut.

'Stab wound,' Professor Gates said. 'The shock probably killed him.'

'Has his widow been notified?'

'Are you volunteering, John?' Davidson said.

'This isn't my patch, remember.'

'No, but you knew the deceased. Anything you want to tell us?'

Rebus shook his head. 'I will ask a question though: what was he doing here? He lives in Marchmont, chances are he'd never even heard of Coffin Walk. God knows I hadn't. So why was he here, where was he headed?'

'Maybe the Diggers.'

The Diggers was actually the Athletic Arms pub, but got its nickname from the gravediggers who'd used it in the past.

'Not much of a shortcut, is it?'

'Not much,' Davidson agreed. 'Lots of questions, John.'

'I know the way your mind works, Davidson. You think it's a simple mugging gone wrong – assailant: unknown; motive: robbery.'

'So let's hear your theory.'

Rebus smiled. His head was full of theories. Maybe too many for his own good. 'Give me a cigarette,' he said.

'Not at the locus, John,' Davidson warned. Rebus looked at the body again. It was being bagged. A trip to the mortuary first, and then the funeral parlour, your last journeys in the world as predictable as your first.

'I asked if you had a theory,' Davidson said.

'OK, OK.' Rebus put his hands up in surrender. 'Take me back to your nice warm police station, give me a cigarette, and I'll tell you a story. Just don't blame me if it doesn't make sense.'

He would tell Davidson what he knew, which wasn't half as much as he suspected.

Which itself wasn't half as much as he feared.

34

Next morning, when DI Davidson went to the widow's house, Rebus went with him.

The curtains were closed, reminding Rebus of the day of McAnally's funeral, inside Tresa's flat. The door was answered not by Mrs Gillespie but by Helena Profitt, dressed in circumspect black – skirt, tights and shoes – and a plain white blouse.

'I came as soon as I heard,' she said, leading them inside. She looked surprised to see Rebus. We must, he thought, stop meeting like this.

'Two policemen to see you, Audrey,' Miss Profitt said, opening the living-room door.

It was a big light room, with prominence given to the floor-to-ceiling bookcases which lined two walls. The TV didn't look much used, and though there was a video machine, Rebus couldn't see more than half a dozen tapes. At one end of the room was a huge desk covered in paperwork, and a small table supporting a telephone and fax machine. The room, it seemed to him, was little more than an extension of the office at the front of the house, making Rebus wonder about Gillespie's family life or, more pertinently, the lack of it.

His widow sat on the sofa, legs tucked beneath her. She'd started to rise, but Davidson had waved her back down. She looked as if she hadn't slept. There was an empty mug on the floor, and next to it a tiny brown bottle

of tablets. Despite the central heating, Audrey Gillespie was trembling.

'Shall I make some tea?' Helena Profitt asked.

'Not for us, thanks,' Davidson said.

'Well, I'll leave you to it. Shall I pop back later, Audrey?'

'Only if it's not too much trouble.'

'Of course not.' Her eyes were red-rimmed from crying. Rebus saw through her act, saw she was as broken up as anyone. He followed her out of the room.

'Could you wait in the kitchen? I'd like a quick word.'

She nodded hesitantly. Rebus went back into the living room and sat down next to Davidson.

'Remember me, Mrs Gillespie?' Davidson was saying. 'We met last night.'

Davidson was good, better than a lot of coppers. It was a skill, handling other people's grief, gauging what to say and how to say it, knowing how much they could take.

Audrey Gillespie nodded, then looked at Rebus. 'And I know you, too, don't I?'

'I came to talk to your husband once.' Rebus strived for the same tone Davidson had used.

'Has the doctor seen you, Mrs Gillespie?' Davidson asked.

'He gave me pills to help me sleep. Ridiculous to think I could sleep.'

'But you're all right?'

'I'm ...' She sought the words expected of her. 'I'm coping, thank you.'

'Do you feel up to answering a few more questions?'

She nodded, and Davidson relaxed a little. He brought out his notebook and consulted it.

'Now,' he said, 'you said last night that your husband had gone out to visit a constituent – that was what he told you?'

'Yes.'

'But he didn't say where he was meeting this constituent?'

'No.'

'Or the constituent's name?'

'No.'

'Or what they were going to discuss?'

She shrugged, remembering. 'We ate dinner at eight as usual – I'd done chicken casserole, Tom's favourite. He had two helpings. After that, I thought he'd either work in his office – he *always* has work to do – or else read the paper. Instead, he said he had to go out.'

'You're surprised he ended up in Dalry?'

'Very. We don't know anyone in that part of town. Why would he lie to me?'

'Well,' Rebus put in, 'he *was* hiding things from you, wasn't he?'

'What do you mean?'

Davidson gave Rebus a warning look, and Rebus softened his voice a little.

'I mean, the day I came here you were busy shredding documents – sackfuls of them – in a shredder your husband hired specially.'

'Yes, I remember. Tom said he was running out of space in the office. They were ancient history. As you can see, it's pretty cramped with all the paperwork.' She waved a hand around the room.

'Mrs Gillespie,' Rebus persisted, 'your husband headed the Industrial Planning Committee – did the documents have anything to do with that?'

'I've no idea.'

'If they were ancient history, why bother to shred them, why not just chuck them out?'

Audrey Gillespie got up and walked to the fireplace. Davidson gave Rebus an angry look.

'Tom said they could fall into the wrong hands.

Journalists, people like that. He said it was to do with confidentiality.'

'Did you look at the files at all?'

'I … I don't remember.' She was frantic now, her wet eyes everywhere but on the two policemen.

'You weren't curious?'

'Look, I don't see what any of this has to do with *anything*.'

Rebus walked over to her and took her hands in his. 'It might have everything to do with your husband's murder, Mrs Gillespie.'

'Now, John,' Davidson complained, 'we don't know …'

But Audrey Gillespie looked into Rebus's eyes, and saw something there she could trust. She blinked away the tears. 'He was very secretive,' she said quietly, forcing herself to be calm. 'I mean, about whatever it was he'd been working on. He'd been at it for months – for the best part of a year, actually. I used to curse the hours he put in. He told me it would be worth it, he said we should always focus on the long view. By that he meant he would one day be an MP, it was what he lived for.'

'You've no inkling what this project of his was?'

She shook her head. 'It was something he'd discovered while serving on the committee, and I know it was to do with accounting. I could work that much out from the kinds of things he was reading – balance sheets, profit-and-loss accounts … I trained as an accountant, something Tom sometimes forgot. I run a string of shops now, but I still handle the books. I could have helped him, but he always had to do everything for himself.' She paused. 'You know, the only reason he really needed me was my money. I'm sorry if that sounds heartless.'

'Not at all,' Davidson said.

'Were these company accounts, Mrs Gillespie?' Rebus persisted.

'I think they must have been, the numbers involved: hundreds of millions of pounds.'

'*Hundreds* of millions?'

So it wasn't just Mensung, or even Charters' empire. It was much bigger. Rebus thought of PanoTech, and then recalled that someone else had used the phrase 'hundreds of millions' ... Rory McAllister, or someone like him.

'Mrs Gillespie, could these figures have been to do with the SDA?'

'I don't know!' She slumped back on to the sofa.

'OK, John,' Davidson said, 'you've had your say.'

But Davidson might as well not have been there.

'You see, Mrs Gillespie,' Rebus said, sitting down beside her, 'the thing is, someone tried to scare your husband, and it worked. They paid a man called McAnally to put the fear of God into him. I don't know if they knew how far McAnally would go. McAnally confronted your husband, and I think gave him a message, a warning of some kind. Then McAnally killed himself, just to force the warning home. He was dying anyway, and he'd been paid handsomely. Your husband got scared, rightly so, and rented that shredder so he could destroy everything he'd been working on, all the evidence.'

'Evidence of what?' she asked.

'Of something very big. Now, McAnally slipped up, he died *too* spectacularly, and that got me curious. I don't think I've discovered even half what your husband knew, but that's not the point. The point is, these people suspect either that your husband was helping me – maybe he'd given me his notes – or that he would talk to me eventually. Either way, they decided he was beyond scaring. They had to go a bit further.'

'What you're saying is that, if you'd left well alone, Tom might still be alive.'

Rebus bowed his head. 'I accept what you're saying, but

I didn't kill your husband.' He paused. 'I'd like to find out who did.'

'What can I do to help?'

Rebus glanced towards Davidson. 'You can start by telling us anything you think might help. And you could go through your husband's papers; there might be some clue there.'

She thought for a moment. 'Will I be in danger, too?'

Rebus laid a hand on hers. 'Not at all, Mrs Gillespie. Look, is there no one Tom might have confided in?'

She started to shake her head. 'No, wait ... there *is* someone.' Then she got up and left the room. Davidson was staring grimly at Rebus.

'See,' Rebus told him, 'you're great with the hearts and flowers, but weakness is there to be exploited.'

Davidson didn't say a word.

Audrey Gillespie carried a desk diary into the room. 'This is last year's,' she said, sitting down next to Rebus. 'Tom began all this cloak-and-dagger stuff back in May, but it only really took off in October and November.' She flipped to the pages for those months. Each day had its fill of meetings and engagements.

'See?' Mrs Gillespie said, pointing to a page. 'These meetings here. Two this week –' she flipped a couple of pages – 'two the next –' two more pages – 'then three more.'

The meetings were just a series of times, plus the same two letters – CK. 'Cameron Kennedy,' Rebus said.

'Yes.'

'Who?' Davidson asked. He'd come over to the sofa to look at the diary.

'The Lord Provost,' Mrs Gillespie explained. 'They kept meeting for lunch. I remember because Tom had to have his suits dry cleaned; he had to look his smartest for the Lord Provost.'

'He didn't tell you why they were meeting so often?' Rebus had taken the diary from her and was flipping through it. There were no meetings with 'CK' until October, after which they took place once a week at least.

'Tom hinted there might be a good job in it come reorganisation. He's in the same political party as the Lord Provost.'

'This is interesting,' Rebus said, sitting back, the better to peruse the diary.

Davidson had some questions to ask – the usual ones – so Rebus excused himself. He found Helena Profitt seated at the kitchen table, tugging at a lace handkerchief.

'Terrible thing,' she said.

'Yes,' said Rebus, sitting down opposite her. He thought of Charters' 'subtlety', and the way Davidson had confronted the widow, and still he couldn't find an easy way to ask what he wanted to ask. 'Miss Profitt, this may not be the time ...' She looked at him. 'But I was wondering if you knew ... that is, if you had any suspicion that Mrs Gillespie and her husband ...?'

'You mean,' she said softly, 'what was their marriage like?'

'Yes.'

Her face turned stony. 'That's despicable.'

'This is a *murder* inquiry, Miss Profitt. I'm sorry if I've disturbed your sensibilities, but questions must be asked. The sooner I ask them, the sooner we may catch the killer.'

She thought that over. 'You're right. I suppose. But it's still despicable.'

'Was Mrs Gillespie having an affair?'

Helena Profitt didn't say anything. She rose from the table and buttoned her coat.

'All right,' Rebus said, 'what about the Lord Provost? Did Councillor Gillespie tell you why they kept meeting?'

'Tom told me he had to brief him.'

'What about?'

'He didn't say. Something to do with the Industry Committee, I expect. Is that all, Inspector?'

Rebus nodded, and Helena Profitt walked out of the kitchen. He heard the front door open and close. I handled that beautifully, he thought.

He got back to the living room just as Davidson was closing his notebook and thanking Audrey Gillespie for her time.

'Not at all,' the widow replied, polite to the last.

Rebus and Davidson sat in the car outside, talking things over. They were pulling away when Rebus saw another car cruising the street, seeking a parking space. It was a sporty Toyota the colour of ashes.

'Stop for a second,' Rebus said. He adjusted the rearview mirror so he could watch the Toyota manoeuvre into a space. Its door opened and Rory McAllister got out, looking anxious. He locked the car, tidied his hair, and side-stepped puddles on his way to Audrey Gillespie's front door.

Rebus took Davidson to Arden Street and up the two flights to his flat.

'Got something for you,' he said, pointing to the binbags in the hall.

Davidson stared in amazement. 'The shredded documents?' Rebus nodded. 'I won't ask how you came by them.'

'Mrs Gillespie isn't going to kick up a fuss, especially if they help us find the killer.'

'I'm thinking what a defence lawyer could do with them.'

'I can think up a story between now and then.'

'So what am I supposed to do with them?'

'You're heading a murder investigation, Davidson. The identities of whoever planned Gillespie's murder are in

there. So take them back to Torphichen Place and get a team working on reassembling the pages.'

'I can't see my boss going for it; we're short-handed as it is. Can't you take them to St Leonard's?'

Rebus shook his head. 'Know why? I don't know who I can trust, and the last thing I want is for these bags to be conveniently mislaid. So: you tell no one what all this paper is, and you tell no one where you got it. When you've put together the jigsaw, I'll bet you'll have names *and* motives. Come on, I'll help you load your car.'

'Generous to a fault,' said Davidson, picking up one of the bags.

They drove to the mortuary to talk with Professor Gates, but he was eating lunch in the university Staff Club, so they climbed up from the Cowgate to Chambers Street.

Rebus had been in the Staff Club before, and knew that if you looked like you belonged, you could breeze in. But the porter came out to stop them, so maybe they didn't look the academic type. Rebus showed his ID, and that made everything all right again.

Gates was dining alone, a newspaper folded on the table beside his plate. A half-bottle of wine and a bottle of water stood in front of him.

'What brings you here?' he said as they sat down. 'You're not eating?'

'No, thanks,' Davidson said.

'A drink maybe,' Rebus prompted.

'I can recommend the water,' Gates said, protecting his wine.

They decided on beer, which the waitress would bring from the bar.

'What can I do for you?' the pathologist asked, dissecting a last floury potato.

'Just wondered if you'd anything for us.'

'On last night's stabbing? Give me a chance, will you? Have you located the murder weapon?'

'No,' Davidson admitted. 'We didn't find any footprints either. The ground in the cemetery was frozen.'

'Well, it was a long-bladed knife, serrated by the look of the skin around the wound. And that's about as much as I can say for now. The victim had tried to protect himself, there were defence nicks on the hands. Plus he'd been eating something greasy. There was grease on his fingers.'

Rebus looked at Davidson. 'Did you find any wrappings near the body?'

'Nothing fresh. What's your point?'

'Gillespie ate a big meal at eight – chicken casserole, two helpings. Do you think he ate it with his fingers?'

'Probably not.'

'So how come less than three hours later he decides to visit a chip shop?' Rebus turned to the pathologist. 'When you look at stomach contents, I'm willing to bet you won't find anything but chicken casserole.'

'I did think,' the pathologist said, 'that it was odd. I mean, most people would wipe their fingers afterwards. But this grease or lard, it was quite solid.'

Which told Rebus everything he needed to know.

35

It was still lunchtime when Rebus walked into the chip shop on Easter Road, and two men in jackets and ties queued behind a teenager in a thin parka with the stuffing bursting from its seams: Rebus waited at the back of the queue, and smiled and waved towards the server, who didn't return the greeting.

Finally it was Rebus's turn. 'Hello, Gerry.' Gerry Dip wiped the work surface where some sauce had spilt. 'Remember me?'

'What do you want?'

Rebus leaned over the counter. 'I want to know where you were last night between the hours of nine p.m. and eleven, and it better be the alibi to end them all.'

'What for?' Gerry Dip said.

Rebus just smiled. 'Come on, let's go for a ride.'

'I can't. I'm here on my own.'

'Then switch everything off and we'll lock the door after us, maybe put up a sign saying "Other fish to fry".'

Gerry Dip bent down as if reaching for a switch, and then flicked something across the counter at Rebus. It was a battered fish, straight out of the fat. Rebus ducked and it flew over his head, fat spattering him. Gerry Dip was on the move, shouldering open the door to the kitchen. Rebus ran around the counter and followed. In the kitchen, Dip had hauled a sack of potatoes on to its side and was already halfway out the back door. Rebus stumbled over the potatoes, dived and just missed Dip's ankles. He clambered

to his feet and ran outside, finding himself in an alley. To his left was a dead end. To his right, Gerry Dip, running for it, the white apron flapping around his knees.

'Stop him!' Rebus yelled.

Davidson didn't need telling twice. He was waiting at the mouth of the alley, hands in pockets like a casual onlooker. But as Dip ran past, he flung out an arm and caught him in the throat. Dip flew back like he was attached by elastic to the ground. His hands went to his throat and he started gagging.

'You could have crushed his windpipe,' Rebus said, but not in a nasty sort of way.

At four p.m., with Gerry Dip still maintaining his vow of silence in the interview room, Rebus went for a drive.

Gerry was an old hand: he knew how to play the game called Helping Police With Their Inquiries. He'd keep quiet, with or without a solicitor. All he'd said so far was that this was harassment, and that he wanted to talk to someone from SWEEP. It would take more than Rebus's gut feeling to convict him of murder. There must needs be evidence. Rebus had explained to Davidson the complex series of connections which had brought Gerry Dip to mind. Now it was up to Davidson to convince his superiors that there was due cause for the granting of a search warrant for Gerry Dip's digs and the chip shop itself. The chip shop's owner had already explained that Gerry hadn't had a shift the previous night. Rebus saw it all clearly. A meeting arranged, Gillespie turning up, Gerry Dip surprising him, Gillespie trying to defend himself from the attack, grabbing at Dip's greasy shirt or jacket ...

One thing nagged: Gerry Dip alone couldn't have lured Gillespie into the trap. There must have been someone else, someone he trusted, someone he wanted to meet ...

* * *

The Right Honourable Cameron McLeod Kennedy, JP, had a detached bungalow in what would have tried calling itself Corstorphine had South Gyle not taken off. The houses were descendants of the boxy bungalows on Queensferry Road. There weren't many cars parked roadside; most of the bungalows boasted a garage, or at the very least a car-port. Rebus parked outside the Lord Provost's home. The door was open before he had reached the garden gate. The Lord Provost stood in the doorway, his wife a little behind him.

'You were so mysterious on the phone,' Kennedy said, shaking Rebus's hand. 'Is there any news?'

'The Lord will do as He sees fit,' his wife burst out, the voice booming from her heavy frame. The Lord Provost ushered her back indoors and led Rebus to the front sitting room.

'I've seen her,' Rebus said.

'Where is she?' Mrs Kennedy snapped. Rebus studied her. She had wide unblinking eyes and small pudgy hands which she'd rolled into fists. Her hair had been coaxed into an untidy bun, and her cheeks blazed. Rebus guessed at West Highland stock; it wasn't a wild stab in the dark to say she'd had a religious upbringing. For zeal, some of the Wee Frees could beat any Muslim Fundamentalists.

'She's safe, Mrs Kennedy.'

'I know that! I've prayed for her, of course she's safe. I've been praying for her soul.'

'Beth, please ...'

'I've prayed harder than I've ever prayed in my life.'

Rebus looked around the room. The furniture had been positioned with exact precision on the carpet, and the ornaments looked like the distances between them had been calibrated by a professional. Net curtains covered the two small windows. There were photos of young children, but

none of anyone aged twelve or over. Hard to imagine a teenager passing her evenings here.

'Inspector,' Cameron Kennedy said, 'I haven't asked you if you'd like something to drink.'

Rebus guessed that alcohol would not be on the list. 'No, thanks.'

'We've ginger cordial left from New Year,' Mrs Kennedy barked.

'Thanks, but no. The thing is, sir, I'm not here primarily about your daughter. I'd like to talk to you about Tom Gillespie.'

'Terrible business,' the Lord Provost said.

'May the good Lord take his soul unto Him in heaven,' his wife added.

'I wonder,' Rebus said pointedly, 'if we might have a word in private.'

Kennedy looked to his wife, who didn't look like moving. Finally, with a sniff, she turned and left. Rebus heard a radio come on through the wall.

'A terrible business,' the Lord Provost repeated, sitting down and gesturing for Rebus to do the same.

'But it didn't come altogether as a surprise, did it?'

The Lord Provost looked up. 'Of course it did!'

'You knew the councillor was playing with fire.'

'Did I?'

'There'd already been that one attempt to scare him off,' Rebus smiled. 'I know what Gillespie was on to, and I know he approached you with the information, and made frequent progress reports thereafter.'

'That's not true.'

'Your little lunchtime meetings, we've records of them. He knew you'd be interested. For one thing, you're the Lord Provost. For another, his findings related directly to Gyle Park West, which is in *your* ward. I don't know what Gillespie's idea was. If I were being charitable, I'd say he

was working in the public interest and would eventually have gone public with his findings. But really, I think he was trying to pressure you into helping further his career. It could be that his findings would never have come to light, but somebody couldn't be sure of that. Somebody tried scaring him, then decided to murder him instead.'

The Lord Provost sprang to his feet. 'You surely don't think *I* killed him?'

'I'm pretty sure I could convince my colleagues that you're a prime suspect. You'd have to explain the secret meetings and everything else.'

The Lord Provost's eyes narrowed, his eyebrows meeting in the middle. 'What is it you want?'

'I want you to tell me all about it.'

'You say you already know.'

'But I've yet to hear anyone say the words.'

The Lord Provost considered, then shook his head.

'Does that mean,' Rebus said, 'that your ward is more important than your own reputation?'

'I can't say anything.'

'Because PanoTech's involved?'

Kennedy's face contracted as if he'd been punched. 'It's got nothing to do with PanoTech. That company is one of the largest employers in Lothian. We *need* it, Inspector.'

'If it has nothing to do with PanoTech, does it still have to do with Robbie Mathieson?'

'I can't say anything.'

'Who's Dalgety? Why does he scare you so much? Kirstie told me she heard you talking about him with someone. And when you saw she'd written his name on the LABarum plan, you suddenly didn't want her found.'

'I've told you, I'm saying *nothing*!'

'In that case,' Rebus said, 'I won't trouble you any further.' He stood up. 'I'm sure you've got plenty to keep

you busy, such as writing your speech of resignation.' He walked to the door.

'Inspector ...' Rebus turned. 'About Kirstie ... *is* she all right?'

Rebus walked back into the room. 'Would you like to see her?' The Lord Provost seemed in two minds. Weakness was there to be exploited. 'I could bring her here, but it would have to be a trade.'

'You don't "trade" with an innocent life!'

'Not so innocent, sir. I could think up half a dozen charges against your daughter, and between you and me I'd be failing in my duty if I didn't apprehend her and put her in a cell.'

The Lord Provost turned away and walked to the window. 'You know, Inspector, I'm no virgin, believe me. You want dirty tricks, underhand tactics, there's a lot you can learn from politics, even at district level ... *especially* at district level.' Kennedy paused. 'You say you can bring her here?'

'I think so.'

'Then do it.'

'And we'll have a little chat, you and me? You'll tell me what I want to know?'

The Lord Provost turned to face him. 'I'll tell you,' he said, his face ashen.

They shook hands on it, and the Lord Provost saw him to the door. Somewhere behind them in the bungalow, Mrs Kennedy was singing a hymn.

So all Rebus had to do now was persuade Kirstie Kennedy that east or west, home was still the best.

Rebus went to her flat first, but there was no one home. He tried a couple of the drop-in centres, including the one behind Waverley – no joy – then started on the burger bars on Princes Street before driving back to Leith and visiting

298

three pubs where pushers and users were known to meet. Nothing. He took a breather in a bar where he was less likely to get himself stabbed, then went to have a word with the few chilled prostitutes plying their trade near the Inner Harbour. One of them thought she recognised the description, but she could have been lying: it was warmer in his car than outside.

Then Rebus remembered something Kirstie had said, about how Paul's mum liked her. So he drove to Paul's parents' address. Duggan was embarrassed to see him, but his mother, a tiny, kindly woman, invited Rebus in.

'No night to be yacking on the doorstep.'

It was a tidy little flat just off Abbeyhill. Duggan gave Rebus a warning look as he led him, at his mother's insistence, into the living room. Duggan's dad was there, smoking a pipe and reading the paper. He stood up to shake Rebus's hand. He was small, like his wife. So here was the arch criminal, Paul Duggan, in his lair.

'Paul's not in any trouble, I hope,' the father asked, teeth grinning around the stem of his pipe.

'Not at all, Mr Duggan, I'm just looking for a friend of Paul's.'

'Well, Paul will help if he can, won't you, Paul?'

'Aye, sure,' Paul Duggan mumbled.

'It's Kirstie,' Rebus said.

'Kirstie?' Mr Duggan said. 'That name's familiar.'

'Maybe Paul's brought her back here once or twice, Mr Duggan.'

'Well, Inspector, he does sometimes bring a girlfriend back – but not for hanky-panky, mind you.' He winked. 'We keep an eye on him.'

The two men shared a laugh. Paul Duggan was shrinking almost visibly, bowed over on the sofa, hands between his legs. The years were peeling off him like paper from a damp wall.

'I haven't seen her,' he told Rebus.

'Since when?'

'Since the time we took her home.'

'Any idea where she could be?'

Mr Duggan removed the pipe from his mouth. 'I'm sure Paul would tell you if he could, Inspector.'

'Have you tried the flat?' Paul asked. Rebus nodded.

'She's not in your bedroom, is she, Paul?'

Duggan twitched, and his father sat forward in the chair. 'Now, Inspector,' he said, trying for another grin. Trying too hard.

'Where's your wife, Mr Duggan?'

Rebus got up and walked into the hall. Mrs Duggan was about to sneak Kirstie Kennedy out the front door.

'Bring her through here instead, Mrs Duggan,' Rebus said.

So they all sat in the living room, and the Duggans explained everything.

'See, we know who Kirstie is', Mrs Duggan said, 'and she's told us why she ran away, and I can't say I blame her.' The Lord Provost's daughter sat next to her on the sofa, staring into the fire, and Mrs Duggan ran her hand through Kirstie's hair. 'Kirstie's got a problem with drugs, she accepts that and so do we. We thought if she was going to fight it, she better move in here for a wee while, get right away from all the ... from the people who live that sort of life.'

'Is that right, Kirstie? Are you kicking it?'

She nodded, suppressing a shiver. Mrs Duggan put an arm around her. 'Sweats and shivers,' she said. 'Mr Leitch told us to expect them.' She turned to Rebus. 'He works at the Waverley drop-in.' Rebus nodded. 'He told us all about cold turkey.' She turned her attention back to the girl. 'Cold turkey, Kirstie, like on Boxing Day, eh?'

Kirstie snuggled deeper into Mrs Duggan's side, like she

was a child again and Mrs Duggan her mother ... Yes, thought Rebus, the mother she's been denied. And here was a willing substitute.

'See,' Mr Duggan said, 'we're afraid you've come to take her away. She doesn't want to go home.'

'She doesn't *have* to go home, Mr Duggan. The drugs apart, she's done nothing wrong.' Paul and Kirstie looked at him, and saw he wasn't going to mention the hoax kidnap. 'But the thing is,' Rebus said, his eyes holding Kirstie's, 'I need a favour. I've seen your stepmother, and I don't blame you for not wanting to see her ... But what about your father? Would it hurt you to talk to him for five minutes, just to let him see you're all right?'

There was a long silence. Mrs Duggan whispered something in Kirstie's ear.

'I don't suppose so,' Kirstie said at last. 'Just now? Tonight?'

Rebus shook his head. 'Tomorrow will be fine.'

'I might be worse tomorrow.'

'I'll take that chance. Just one other thing: last time we met, you were telling me why you took that document from your dad's office.'

She nodded. 'I heard him talking on the telephone. He was talking about covering something up, some scandal. I heard him mention LABarum. He'd always told me I had to follow his example, but he turned out to be just like all the others – a liar, a cheat, a coward.' She was bursting into tears. 'He let me down again. So I grabbed that ... whatever it was. I saw it was about LABarum.' She took a deep breath. 'Maybe I just wanted him to know *I* knew. It's all rotten, all of it.'

Mrs Duggan was still trying to quiet her as Rebus left the flat.

Back home, Rebus got the feeling the phone had just

301

stopped ringing. Two minutes later, with the Stones softly on the hi-fi, it rang again. He'd been sitting with the whisky bottle in his lap, wondering if he could resist, wondering why he bothered.

'Yes?'

'It's Davidson.'

'Still at the station?'

'That I am. Gerry's still not talking.'

'Have you offered him a deal?'

'Not yet. We're holding him on a charge of assault, naming you as the injured party.'

'I'll never get the grease off that jacket. What about the search warrant?'

'We got it. I'm just waiting for Burns to get back. Hold on, here he comes.' Davidson put his hand over the mouthpiece. Rebus unscrewed the bottle with his free hand, but couldn't find a glass. Davidson came back on the line. 'It's a result. Two credit cards, Access and Visa, in the name of Thomas Gillespie, hidden under the mattress.'

'So now will you go for a deal?'

'I'll talk to his solicitor.'

'We don't just want Dip, remember. We want whoever ordered the hit.'

'Sure, John.' There wasn't what Rebus would call fervour in Davidson's voice. 'Now the bad news.'

'Listen, I'm serious – we want the paymaster!'

'And *I'm* serious about it being bad news.'

Rebus quietened. 'OK, what is it?'

'You told me to check if Charters had had any visitors since you saw him Sunday night. Well, he had one the next morning, and then again today. She's a regular apparently.'

'Yes?'

'Her name's Samantha Rebus. Now, John, it may be nothing at all. I mean, she's visited other prisoners too, and we know she works for SWEEP. It could just be that she –'

But John Rebus was already on his way.

'I don't see what the big deal is,' Sammy said.

'What?'

'I don't see what's the big deal.'

He'd been so steamed up, he'd rung Patience's doorbell twice before remembering the unpleasantness surrounding his last visit. But Sammy opened the door.

'Grab your coat,' he hissed, 'tell Patience it's a friend and you're going out.'

They'd gone to a hotel just around the corner from the flat. The bar was almost deserted, just the barmaid and one regular at the corner of the bar, the hatch open so there was no barrier between them. Rebus and Sammy took their drinks to the furthest corner.

'The big deal is,' he said, 'you smuggled something out of jail for him.'

'Just a letter.'

She calmly sipped her tequila and orange. Fathers and daughters, Rebus thought. He pictured the Lord Provost and Kirstie. You knew they had to make choices, and nobody in life made the right choices all the time. Daughters never grew up; in their fathers' eyes, all they did was become women.

'I've done it before,' Sammy was saying. 'You know the warders read all the mail before it goes out? They censor it and leer over it and ... and I think it's revolting.' She paused. 'They can get very sniffy about gay love letters.'

'Charters told you he was gay?'

'He hinted at it: "a very special friend", he said.'

Rebus shook his head. 'Gerry Dip's special, all right. He's absolutely choice. Did you take the note to his flat?'

'The only address Derwood had was the chip shop.'

'And did you read the note?'

'Of course not.'

'A sealed envelope?' She nodded. 'Quite a fat envelope?'
She thought about it. 'Yes,' she said.

'That's because it was full of money.'

'What have I done?' Her face was reddening, her voice rising. 'Broken some lousy prison rule, that's all.'

'I wish it were,' Rebus said quietly.

She quietened. 'What then?'

He couldn't tell her. He couldn't do *that* to her ... But it would all come out eventually, wouldn't it?

'Sammy,' he said, 'I think Charters paid Gerry Dip to kill a man. That envelope you delivered contained instructions and payment.'

Her face lost all its lovely colour. '*What?*' The way she said it turned Rebus's gut liquid. She tried picking up her drink, but spilt it, then retched into her cupped hands. Rebus got a handerkerchief out of his pocket and handed it over.

'You're trying to scare me,' she said, 'that's all. You don't like my job and you're trying to scare me off!'

'Sammy, please ...'

She got to her feet, spilling the rest of her drink over his trousers. He followed her to the door, watched by barmaid and customer, and called after her. But she was running: down the steps on to the pavement, and then along to the corner and around it, back into Oxford Terrace.

'Sammy!'

He watched her run, watched her until she'd disappeared.

'Shite!'

A drunk, walking past, wished him a belated happy new year. Rebus told the man where he could stick it.

36

As arranged, Rebus drove to South Gyle next morning. He parked his car around the corner from the Lord Provost's house, then went and rang the doorbell. The Lord Provost himself opened the door, and looked to left and right as if expecting her to be there.

'We'll have to go for a little drive,' Rebus informed him.

Then a figure came storming along the passage behind Cameron Kennedy and brushed him aside.

'Where is she?' Mrs Kennedy's voice trembled with emotion, her nostrils flaring. 'Where's the lost lamb?' She turned to her husband. 'You said he'd bring her!'

The Lord Provost looked at Rebus, who said nothing. 'I have to go with Inspector Rebus, Beth.'

'I'll fetch my coat,' Mrs Kennedy said.

'No, Beth.' The Lord Provost laid a hand on her arm. 'Best I go alone.'

An argument started. Rebus turned and walked back towards the gate. The Lord Provost came after him.

'Don't you want a coat?' Rebus asked.

'I'll be fine.'

His wife was calling to them from the door. '"Thy will be blyther in heiven owre ae sinner at repents nor owre ninetie-nine saunts at need nae repentance."'

'She's learned the New Testament in Scots,' the Lord Provost explained. 'She knows it backwards.' It didn't sound like a boast.

Kirstie was sitting in the back seat of Rebus's car. Beside

her was Paul Duggan. She'd had a bath, and her hair had been washed and rearranged. She was wearing clothes Mrs Duggan had bought for her — styles parents thought teenagers liked. You'd take her for a normal, sulky, shoulder-bechipped teenager, nothing more — if it wasn't for the vomiting fits and the muscle spasms, the bolts of lightning through her bones.

Kennedy gasped when he saw her.

'I said I'd bring her,' Rebus told him. 'Now get in.'

The Lord Provost's face was like chiselled stone as they drove towards the Forth Bridges, the same route Rebus had taken that night with Lauderdale. He told himself he'd chosen the meeting place because it was nearby, open and private. But he thought maybe he had a deeper motive.

They came off the A90 and went three-quarters round the roundabout, then headed towards the Moat House Hotel, whose huge, desolate car park overlooked the Forth. At this time of day, this time of year, the car park was deserted save for a Ford Capri which looked as if it had been abandoned after a joyride. Rebus stopped the car and turned off the ignition.

'This is where we get out,' he told Paul Duggan.

Duggan squeezed Kirstie's hand. 'Will you be all right?' he asked her.

'I'll be fine,' she said coolly, watching her father in the rearview mirror, just as he was watching her.

So Rebus and Duggan got out.

Rebus walked across the tarmac and stood at the furthest edge. You got a great view of both bridges, and of the Fife coast beyond. You also took a beating from the wind, which blew from all directions. Rebus rode with it, swaying a little from the ankles. With his head tucked into his overcoat, he managed to light a cigarette at the sixth attempt. The smell of butane caused momentary nausea.

Paul Duggan was a little way off, resting one arm on a

306

dull metal pay-view telescope. Rebus left him alone and just stared at the scenery. The clouds crawled past, looking as if they'd been hurt in too many bar room brawls. Beneath them, Fife was a slab of grey-green pavement.

Paul Duggan had finally arrived beside him. 'Thinking about Willie and Dixie?' he suggested. Rebus glanced at him but said nothing.

'I'm not just a pretty face, Inspector.'

'I was thinking that they got me into this. Their suicide. They got me thinking about things … asking myself questions. When McAnally killed himself, I was interested enough to want to know why.' He smiled. 'You don't know what I'm talking about.'

Duggan just shrugged. 'I'm listening though.' There was silence between them for a while. Duggan scuffed his toes against the kerb. 'See this trouble I'm in, with the police and council and that …?'

'You think I can help?'

'I don't know.'

It was strange that Kirstie should have run away from one smothering household only to end up in another, but Rebus thought he knew the reason why. After the deaths of Willie and Dixie, she'd disintegrated. To her, they had represented 'real life', a life well away from her father and his political conspiracies. Willie and Dixie had been the other side of the coin, a side she'd come to like, maybe even admire. And she'd killed them, after which she'd spiralled downwards until she realised she needed shelter and comfort, or she too might die. Paul Duggan had been there for her, and so had his parents.

'You know,' Rebus said, thinking aloud, 'I think I know why she scrawled "Dalgety" on that document. If her father had paid the ransom – maybe even if he hadn't – she was planning to send the LABarum plan back to him. It was a warning, a message that she knew something, and

that he should leave her alone if he didn't want her to reveal it to the world.'

'Never mind Kirstie for the moment, what about me?'

'Everybody's got to pay, Paul,' Rebus said, not looking at him. 'That's the way it works.'

'Aye, right,' Duggan said dismissively. 'And if I was some rich bastard that had been to Fettes, I'd have to pay too, is that right? I'd be treated the same as an Oxgangs drop-out? Come *on*, Inspector, Kirstie's told me the way it works, the whole system.'

He turned and shuffled away.

He had a point, one Rebus would happily concede, only he had other things to think about right now. The wind had finished his cigarette in double-quick time, so he lit another. Duggan was over at the abandoned car, peering in. He tried a door, opened it, and got in. Shelter accomplished. Some people said the weather made the Scots: long drear periods punctuated by short bursts of enlightenment and cheer. There was almost certainly something to the theory. It was hard to believe this winter would end, yet he knew that it would: knew, but almost didn't believe. A matter of faith, as the old priest would say, or maybe the reverse of faith. Rebus hadn't been to church in a while, and missed his conversations with Father Leary. But he didn't miss the church, or even the Church. Leary would have no problem with suicide, in either concept or practice: it was a great sin, full stop. Assisted suicide, too, was a sin, every bit as heinous.

But when Rebus's mother had been ill that last time, she'd begged his father for release. And one day, young John had walked in and had seen his father on the edge of her bed. She was asleep, her chest making awful, liquid sounds, and his father sat there with a pillow in his hands ... looking at that pillow, then up at his son, asking to be told what to do.

Rebus knew if he hadn't walked in, his father might have done it, might have put her out of her misery.

Instead of which, she lingered for weeks.

He turned away from the Forth and found his vision blurred. He angled his head upwards, swallowing back the tears, and walked over to the abandoned car. Inside, Paul Duggan was crying.

'They were my friends, too,' he bawled. 'And her stupid plan killed them! And yet I can't hate her for it ... can't even get angry with her.'

Rebus put a hand on Duggan's shoulder.

'Nobody killed them,' he said quietly. 'They chose for themselves.'

The two of them sat there for a while, out of the wind, in shelter that wasn't theirs.

Afterwards, Rebus drove them back into town. The teenagers in the back were both pink-eyed from crying; the two men in the front were not. He didn't feel proud of the fact. He drove past the turn-off to Kennedy's estate, and the Lord Provost still said nothing. Eventually, Rebus pulled the car on to the kerb outside Duggan's Abbeyhill home.

'Where are we?' Kennedy asked.

'Kirstie's staying with some nice people,' Rebus explained.

The Lord Provost turned to his daughter. 'You're not coming home?'

'Not yet,' she said, as if each word was costing her something.

'You said you'd bring her back.'

'I didn't say she'd stay,' Rebus said. 'Kirstie's got to decide if and when.'

She was already getting out of the car, as was Duggan.

On the pavement, she doubled over and dry-heaved, spitting up foamy saliva.

'Something's wrong with her,' Kennedy said. He made to open his door, but Rebus pulled the car abruptly off the kerb and into traffic.

'You know what's wrong with her,' he said. 'Now she's coming off, and I think she'll be all right.'

'You infer,' Kennedy said coldly, 'that she wouldn't be "all right" at home.'

'What do you think?' Rebus said, and he left it at that.

'Where are we going?'

'One good thing about Edinburgh, Lord Provost – there's always a quiet spot nearby. You and me are going to have a talk. At least, *you'll* be talking, I'll be listening.'

He directed them around the base of Salisbury Crags and up to a car park near the summit of Arthur's Seat. There were a few cars already there, parents and children out braving the gale. They would probably call it 'blowing away the cobwebs'.

But Rebus and the Lord Provost stayed in the car, and the Lord Provost did the talking – that had been their bargain, after all. And afterwards, with the silence between them like an extra seat, Rebus drove the Lord Provost home.

There was a man at the top of the hill. He was mending a wall.

Rebus followed the line of the dry-stane dyke, climbing slowly. He was between Edinburgh and Carlops, in the foothills of the Pentland range. There was no escape from the wind and the cold up here, but Rebus was sweating as he neared the top. The man saw him coming, but didn't stop working. He had three piles of stones close to him, varying in sizes and shapes. He would pick one up, feel it, study it, then either put it back in the pile or else add it to

the wall. And with a fresh stone placed in the wall, a new challenge presented itself, and he had to study his mounds of stones all over again. Rebus stopped to catch his breath, and watched the man. It was the most painstaking work imaginable, and at the end of it the wall would be held together by nothing more than the artful arrangement of its constituent parts.

'It must be a dying craft,' Rebus said, having gained the summit.

'Why do you say that?' The man seemed amused.

Rebus shrugged. 'Electric fences, barbed wire; not many farmers depend on dry-stane dykes.' He paused. 'Or dry-stane dykers, come to that.'

The man turned to look at him. He was ruddy-cheeked with a thick red beard and fair hair turning grey at the temples. He wore a baggy Aran sweater and green combat jacket, cord trousers and black boots. He wasn't wearing gloves, and kept blowing on his hands.

'I need to keep them bare,' he explained. 'I feel the stones better that way.'

'Is your name Dalgety?'

'Aidan Dalgety, at your service.'

'Mr Dalgety, I'm Detective Inspector Rebus.'

'Is that right?'

'You don't sound surprised.'

'In a job like this, you don't get many visitors. That's one of the things I like about it. But since I started this wall, it's been like a main thoroughfare rather than a deserted hillside.'

'I know Councillor Gillespie visited you.'

'Several times.'

'He's dead.'

'I know.'

'And that's why you're not surprised to see a detective?' Dalgety smiled to himself and judged another stone,

311

turning it in his hand, weighing it in his palm, feeling for its centre of gravity. He placed it on the wall, then thought better of it and moved it to another spot. The process took a couple of minutes.

Rebus looked back the way he'd come, following the wall down to the by-road where he'd parked his car. 'Tell me, how many stones go into a wall like this?'

'Tens of thousands,' Dalgety said. 'You could spend years counting them. Men took years building them.'

'It's a far cry from computers.'

'Do you think so? Maybe it is. But then again, maybe there's *some* connection.'

'I understand you were Robbie Mathieson's partner, back in the early days of PanoTech.'

'It wasn't called PanoTech in my day. The name belongs to Robbie.'

'But the early designs ... the early work was yours?'

'Maybe it was.' Dalgety tossed a stone from one pile to another.

'That's what I hear. He ran the company, but you designed the circuits. Your ideas made the company work.' Dalgety didn't say anything. 'And then he bought you out.'

'And then he bought me out,' Dalgety echoed.

'Is that the way it happened?'

'It happened just the way I told it to the councillor. I had a ... I'd been working too hard for too long. I had a breakdown. And when I came out of it, the company wasn't mine any longer. Robbie had kissed me goodbye. And all the designs were his, too. The whole company was his. Dalmat, we were called – Dalgety and Mathieson. That was the first thing he changed.' Dalgety was weighing another stone.

'How did he find the money to buy you out? I take it you were bought out?'

'Oh yes, it was all above board. He had some money

invested somewhere: it paid a handsome profit and he used it to buy my share.' He paused. 'That's what the lawyers told me afterwards. I didn't remember any of it – discussions, signing the papers, none of it.'

'You must have been bitter.'

Dalgety laughted. 'I had another breakdown. They put me in a private nursing home. That took care of a lot of the pay-off money. When I came out, I didn't want anything to do with the industry, or any industry like it. End of story.'

'PanoTech's grown since.'

'Robbie Mathieson is good at what he does. Do you know about him?' Rebus shook his head. 'His family moved to the States when Robbie was eighteen. He joined one of the big boys, IBM or Hewlett Packard, someone like that. The company had operations in Europe, and Robbie was posted here. He liked Scotland. I was working on my own at the time, designing stuff, messing about with ideas, most of them impractical. We met, got to like one another, and he told me he was resigning and starting up his own computer business right here. He persuaded me along with him. We had a couple of good years ...' Dalgety seemed to have forgotten about the stone he was holding. The wind was hurting Rebus's ears, but he didn't let it show.

'I'm not telling you the whole truth,' Aidan Dalgety said at last. 'I was an alcoholic; or, at least, I was on the verge of becoming one. I think that's why Robbie wanted rid of me. Seemed to me afterwards that he must have been planning it for a while. I signed away the rights to a couple of components which went on to make PanoTech a lot of money.' He took a deep breath. 'But that was then and this is now.'

'This money Mathieson used to buy you out, where did it come from again?'

'There was a man called Derwood Charters. He got to know Robbie early on. I think he wanted to become

313

company secretary, something like that. He had a lot of money-making schemes. Or should I say scams. Robbie told me about a couple of them. Charters would set up paper companies and then screw grants from all over the place – local authority, SDA, European Community. He had a genius for that sort of thing. I think he must have wangled development money for PanoTech somewhere down the line – the company grew so fast so quickly.'

'And you've never said anything about any of this?'

'Why should I? Good luck to them.'

'But Mathieson practically robbed you!'

'And now he keeps a lot of people in employment. I'm not such a high price to pay for an outcome like that.'

Rebus sat down on the cold earth, his back against the wall, and ran his hands over his head.

'You know,' Dalgety said. 'I still take an interest in the industry. I don't mean to, but I do. Thirty-five per cent of all the PCs manufactured in Europe are manufactured here, twenty-four per cent of all semi-conductors. Two million computers a year come out of IBM's Greenock plant – that includes their *world* supply of screens and every IBM computer sold in Europe.' He was laughing. 'Fifty thousand people in the industry, and it's growing. The Japanese come here because productivity's so high – can you believe that?' He stopped laughing abruptly. 'But the root system's shallow, Inspector. We're big in hardware, but we need software, too, and we need to start sourcing – we source only fifteen per cent of all our components. We're an assembly line. Maybe PanoTech can change that.' He shrugged. 'Good luck to them.'

'So why did you talk to Gillespie?'

'Maybe to get it off my chest.' He examined the stone in his hand a final time, then threw it far into the distance. 'Maybe because nothing I say can make any difference. No investigation of PanoTech is going to get very far.'

314

'The councillor found that out.' Aidan Dalgety looked at him, but said nothing. 'You're not scared?'

'No,' Dalgety used both hands to lift a larger rock on to the wall. 'I'm not scared at all. This wall will be here after I'm gone, whether I live to be a hundred or drop dead tomorrow.' He patted the wall with his hands. 'I know what lasts.'

Rebus got to his feet. 'Well, thanks for talking to me.'

'No problem. I get bored sometimes just talking to the wall.' He was laughing again as Rebus headed downhill. 'You know that old saying about walls having ears ...?'

It was a day for open spaces. In the late afternoon, Rebus walked in the Botanic Gardens with Sir Iain Hunter.

'I like this place,' Sir Iain said, striding gamely with his rolled umbrella across the grass towards Inverleith House. 'Of course, it's lost something since they moved the Gallery of Modern Art. What do you think?'

'I think you're stalling.'

Sir Iain smiled. 'I've conducted meetings here before, Inspector. It's my open-air office. I choose the Botanics for some meetings precisely because they *are* so open. No chance of being overheard.' He stopped, looking around. The city centre was a panorama before them. 'Marvellous view,' he said.

'Nobody's listening in on us, if that's what you're worried about.'

'Well, the thought had crossed my mind. Nowhere is safe in this age of electronic eavesdropping.'

'I don't need to bug conversations,' Rebus said. 'I've got Gillespie's files.'

'Poor Councillor Gillespie.'

'Yes, poor Councillor Gillespie, lured to an alley and then stabbed in the guts by an ex-con hired by Derwood Charters, just as Charters paid McAnally to put a scare into

315

Gillespie. I don't suppose he knew how far Wee Shug would go, what he'd do ... He went too far.'

'And brought you scurrying to the scene, Inspector. Yes, perhaps that was a mistake. Well, I'm going to trust you. I'm going to assume you're not recording this little tête-à-tête.' Sir Iain tucked his cashmere scarf a little tighter around his neck. 'Now, why did you want to meet?'

'Because you're at the centre of it all.'

'Can you prove that?'

'Like I say, I've got –'

'Yes, yes, you've got Gillespie's files, but what do *they* prove?'

'You should know. The Lord Provost told you everything Gillespie told him. They prove that Charters' various companies existed only as shells for the most part. The front company was legit, but the others ... well, if anyone decided to check, Charters would rent short-term office space, pay someone to take in mail addressed to Mensung House ... that sort of thing. And I'm assuming he had someone at the Scottish Office tipping him off about any forthcoming investigations – he couldn't have run his scams so well for so long without help. How am I doing so far?'

Sir Iain was admiring the view. 'Wild inaccuracies compounded by conjecture.'

'Charters had sleeping partners. See, once the fake companies were running, he could apply for grants and other incentives, but to get the companies going in the first place required cash, working capital, and that's where the sleeping partners came in. He could guarantee a huge return on investment, provided the grant money came through. He was a wizard at playing the system, running rings around it. He made quick money for a lot of people, including Robbie Mathieson. I'm sure Mathieson wouldn't want anyone to know that the early money for PanoTech

316

came from ripping off SDA and European Community schemes.

'Then there's Haldayne at the US Consulate. He'd met Charters socially, and was keen to make money. As an aside, I'd guess that once he was involved, you were able to pressure Haldayne into helping persuade American companies to move here. Same goes for Robbie Mathieson – he had US connections in the computer industry.'

'That's slanderous,' Sir Iain remarked, his smile unimpeachable.

'Well, Haldayne's been to your Royal Circus *pied-à-terre* plenty of times – we've got the parking tickets. You must have had *something* to talk about. Charters couldn't have got away with it, not to the same extent, without a network of friends and people he bribed. Civil servants predominantly. I've been asking around, Sir Iain. Eight years ago, you weren't nearly so high up the pecking order. But then you started a string of successes bringing new business into Scotland, and you started your ascent. And Ruthie Estate must have cost a bit. I wonder, did you buy that in the past eight years?

'The whole thing worked brilliantly for a long time. Companies came and went, and sometimes their registration documents disappeared with them. Then the SDA became Scottish Enterprise, accounting procedures changed, and nobody was going to be looking back at old projects financed by a dead organisation. But Charters couldn't stop, and one time he got sloppy, and was caught early on. He pled guilty, protecting his friends and making sure nothing would come out at a trial, and then Gillespie caught a glimpse of something, and it got him wondering. He started digging, and word got back to Charters.' Rebus paused. 'You told me once that you liked a bit of intrigue: how am I doing?'

Sir Iain just shrugged, looking bemused.

'Well,' said Rebus, 'I'm just getting to the best bit. Now, who passed the word back to Charters? Because whoever did is partly to blame for Gillespie's eventual murder. Gillespie had told his story to the Lord Provost – only natural that he'd tell somebody – but he never guessed the Lord Provost would go straight to Mathieson and tell *him*. But what else was he going to do? Mathieson is the biggest employer in his ward; the Lord Provost thought he'd warn him what was coming.'

'You think Mathieson told Charters?'

'Possibly. It could have been any of you.'

'*Us?*'

'You're in it up to your cashmere scarf.'

'Careful what you say, Inspector. Be *very* careful.'

'Why? So I don't get a knife in the guts?'

Hunter's cheeks coloured. 'That was ...' He swallowed back the rest.

'Charters' doing?' Rebus guessed. 'Well, someone had to tell Charters in the first place, and they did so knowing *he'd* do something about it, something they were scared to do themselves.'

Sir Iain's eyes were watering, but it was from the breeze, not contrition.

'What are you going to do, Inspector?'

'I'm going to nail as many of you as I can.'

Finally Hunter turned to him. 'Do you recall what I said to you that day on my estate? Jobs are at risk, *lives* are at risk.' He sounded grotesquely sincere.

'It's all just policy to you, isn't it?' Rebus said. 'No right and wrong, legal and illegal, no fair and corrupt, just politics.'

'Listen to yourself, man,' Sir Iain Hunter spat. 'Who are you, some Old Testament prophet? What gives you the right to hold the scales?' He dug the tip of his umbrella into

the ground, and waited for his breathing to ease. 'If you'd look into your heart, you'd see we're not on opposite sides.'

'But we are,' Rebus said determinedly.

'If this ever became public, there'd be more than a scandal – there'd be a crisis. Trust would be lost, overseas investors and corporations would turn away from Scotland. Don't tell me you want that.'

Rebus thought of Aidan Dalgety, busying himself with an endless wall – his only answer to frustration and anger. 'None of it's worth a single human life,' he said quietly.

'I think it is,' Hunter said. 'I really do think it is.'

Rebus turned to walk away.

'Inspector? I'd like you to talk with some people.'

It was the invitation Rebus had been waiting for. 'When?'

'Tonight if at all possible. I'll phone you with the details.'

'I'll be at St Leonard's till six,' Rebus said, leaving the old man to his view.

But Rebus couldn't face the police station, so went home instead.

And found, slowly but with growing confidence, that his flat had been broken into in his absence. It was a clean, meticulous job. There were no signs of forced entry, nothing had been taken, almost nothing looked out of place. But his books had been moved. He had them in what looked like unplanned towers, but were actually the order in which he'd bought them and intended to read them. One of the towers had been knocked over and put back up again out of order. His drawers had been closed, too, though he always left them open. And his record collection had been rifled – as if he could hide sacks of shredded paper inside album sleeves ...

He sat down with a glass of whisky and tried not to think

any thoughts. If he thought, he might not act. He might drop out, like Dalgety, and let them get on with it. He loathed Sir Iain Hunter for the way he used people. But then Paul Duggan used people too, if it came down to it. Kirstie, too, had used and abused her friends. Everybody used someone. The difference was, Sir Iain and his kind had everything – heart, soul, silver and gold – only nobody knew it, never even gave it a thought.

What was more, probably nobody cared.

His phone rang at seven.

'I did try St Leonard's,' Sir Iain said. 'They told me you'd not been back this afternoon.'

'Don't worry, your friends had left before I got back.'

'I beg your pardon?'

'Nothing, forget it. But hear this: Gillespie's files are in a safe place, and I mean *safe*.'

'You're not making much sense, Inspector.'

'Is that for the benefit of anyone listening in?'

'I only called to remind you of our meeting. Nine tonight, would that suit?'

'Let me just check my social calendar.'

'You know Gyle Park West?'

'I know it.'

'The PanoTech factory. You'll be expected at nine.'

37

PanoTech had won awards for the design of its Gyle Park West factory, with its automated shopfloor delivery system (a series of robot fork-lifts on a network of rails), and its bulbous shape with optimised interior light. The reception area was chrome and grey metal with a black rubberised floor.

There was a security guard on the desk, but Rebus was expected. As he walked through the automatic doors, an automatic voice telling him he was entering a 'Positively No Smoking Zone', he saw Sir Iain Hunter standing by a display case. There was a sheet over the case, but Sir Iain had lifted it, the better to inspect the model beneath.

'The new LABarum building,' he explained. 'They'll start construction in the spring.' He turned to Rebus. 'New jobs, Inspector.'

'And another feather in your cap. What'll it be this time – *Lord* Hunter of Ruthie?'

Sir Iain's smile evaporated. 'They're waiting for us in the boardroom.'

They took a bright elevator to the third and top floor, and emerged into a compact hallway with three doors off. Sir Iain pressed four numbers on a wall console, and pushed open one of the doors. Inside, three men were waiting, standing by the window. A light airplane was taking off from Turnhouse, so close you could almost see the exhausted executives inside.

Rebus looked at Haldayne first, then at J Joseph

Simpson, and finally at Robbie Mathieson. 'The gang's all here,' he commented.

'That's a cheap shot.' Mathieson came forward to take Rebus's hand. He was wearing an expensive suit, but showed he'd put aside the day's cares by having shed his tie and undone the top button of his shirt.

'Good of you to come,' he told Rebus, with what some people would have taken for sincerity.

'Good of you to ask me,' Rebus said, playing the game.

Mathieson waved a hand around the room. It had cream walls, some blown-up photos of computer chips, and a dozen framed awards for export, industry and achievement. There was a large oval table placed centrally, black like the floor. 'I have this place swept for bugs once a week, Inspector. Industrial espionage is a constant threat. Unfortunately, this meeting was arranged at short notice ...'

'So?'

'So I don't have any of the relevant devices to hand. How can I be sure *you're* not bugged?'

'What do you want me to do?'

Mathieson tried to look embarrassed. It was just an act. 'I'd like you to remove your clothes.'

'Nobody said it was going to be that sort of party.'

Mathieson smiled, but angled his head, expecting compliance.

'Anyone want to join me?' Rebus said, removing his jacket.

Sir Iain Hunter laughed.

Rebus studied the four men as he stripped. Simpson looked the most ill at ease; probably because he was the least of the group. Haldayne had seated himself at the table and was toying with a fat chrome pen, as if already bored with proceedings. Mathieson stood by the window, averting

his eyes from the disrobing. But Sir Iain stood fast and watched.

Rebus got down to underpants and socks.

'Thank you,' Mathieson said. 'Please get dressed again, and I apologise for putting you through that.' He was using his business voice, deep and confident, the American burr touched with Scots inflexions. 'Let's all sit down.'

Simpson hadn't even reached his chair before he started blurting out that he didn't know what he was doing here, it was all such a long time ago ...

'You're here, Joe,' Mathieson reminded him firmly, 'because you broke the law of the land. We all did.'

Then he turned to Rebus.

'Inspector, a long time ago, almost in another age, we all profited from enterprises set up and run by Derwood Charters. Now, the question in court would be: did we know at the time that those profits were being made by fraudulent means?' He shrugged. 'That's a question for the lawyers, and you know how lawyers can be, especially with questions of corporate law. They might take years and several million pounds to come to their conclusions. A lot of time, a lot of money ...' He opened his palms wide, a showman with his spiel. 'And for what? The fact of the matter is, some of those profits – illicitly gained – went to build this very factory, bringing jobs to hundreds, with spin-off benefits creating and sustaining hundreds, maybe thousands more. Including, as you told me yourself, a friend of yours. Now, in *law*, none of this would count for anything – quite rightly so. The law is a stern mistress, that's what they say.' A little smile. 'But the law, I would argue, isn't everything. There are considerations of a moral, ethical and economic order.' He raised a finger to stress the point, then touched it to his lips. 'Moral law, Inspector, is something else again. If bad money is used to good purpose, can it really be called bad money? If a child stole

some apples, then went on to be a life-saving surgeon, would any court convict him of the original theft?'

Mathieson had prepared his lines well. Rebus tried not to listen, but his ears were working too well. Mathieson seemed to sense a change in him, and got up to walk around the table.

'Now, Inspector, if you want to drag up ancient history, you must do so, but the consequences will rest on *your* conscience. They sure as hell won't be on mine.'

Rebus wondered if it was possible that Mathieson had compiled a dossier on him, had people watch him, talk to acquaintances. No, those methods would not have told the essential truths, they wouldn't have revealed the man to whom Mathieson was appealing so subtly and cleverly. It had to be more than that. It had to be instinct.

'A murder has been committed,' Rebus said.

Mathieson had been expecting this argument. 'Not with the knowledge of anyone in this room,' he said.

'You're saying it was Charters alone?'

Mathieson nodded, stroking his beard. Rebus wondered if he'd grown it in memory of Aidan Dalgety. 'Derwood has most to lose,' he was explaining. 'He's been in prison all these years, and if you make public what you know, he'll stay there.'

'But Gillespie was set up by someone he knew. He wouldn't have been in that alley otherwise.'

'Why not?'

'Because he was scared.'

'Then who was it?' Mathieson asked.

'I would guess Sir Iain,' Rebus said. Four pairs of eyes fixed the Permanent Secretary. 'Maybe Charters himself will tell us. As you say, he's got most to lose. He might be all too willing to bargain down any extension to his sentence.'

'This is preposterous,' Hunter said, thumping the floor with his cane.

'Is it?' Rebus said. 'You like guns, Sir Iain. You've got a whole room full of shotguns. What if I checked them against the records? Would they all be there, or would one be missing – the one you passed on to Shug McAnally?' Rebus turned to Mathieson. 'I want him. I want him tonight. The rest of you, maybe later.'

'Hold on,' Haldayne interrupted, 'what evidence do you have? We've told you we don't know any –'

'Save your defence, Mr Haldayne. I know Sir Iain's been controlling you all these years.'

Mathieson was shaking his head slowly. 'It would be very unfortunate indeed if *any* of this leaked out. If you arrest Sir Iain, you'll precipitate a media circus as well as political questions. Why can't you just charge Charters?'

'Because then you'd all be getting away with it.'

Mathieson looked frustrated. 'Inspector, understand one thing: I don't care about Sir Iain, I don't care about anyone here tonight – including myself, if it comes down to it.' His voice was rising the way it must have at other boardroom meetings, propelling him towards victory. 'What I care about – more deeply than you would ever understand or believe – is PanoTech.' Now the voice fell away. 'LABarum will be a major expansion, Inspector. A new factory, new R and D unit, meaning more suppliers, contractors, a huge injection of hard cash and confidence into the local economy. But more than that, LABarum will be Europe's Microsoft – Scotland will be producing its own software to install in the computers it manufactures.'

'No wonder everyone wants you kept sweet.'

'And you're going to put all that in jeopardy over something that happened eight years ago and hurt no one at the time; no one but the taxpayer, who wouldn't have known anyway how his or her money was being spent. A

few million was a drop in the ocean, hardly even a ripple. Do you have any idea the scale of fraud being perpetrated in mainland Europe? A non-existent training scheme for airline pilots in Naples netted *seventeen* million pounds. Farm products and animals are shipped to and fro across borders, netting a subsidy every time. The EC has paid a *billion* pounds to have vineyards destroyed, yet there are more vines every year. The Greeks lop a branch off a vine and stick it in the ground so they'll be paid for *two*. I repeat, a few million hurt no one.'

'It hurt Aidan Dalgety.'

'Aidan hurt himself. You didn't know him then. He was becoming so erratic, he could have dragged the company down with him.'

'It's hurt other people since.' Rebus thought of Kirstie, finding out her father was no icon. He thought of her plan, a plan they all thought they could get away with because her father wasn't going to get his daughter back – they'd been bartering for the LABarum document, and for Kirstie's knowledge of the whole affair ... And Willie and Dixie had died.

'I accept,' Mathieson was saying, 'that a man died. Derwood's gone crazy, that's what it comes down to.'

'There's one other consideration,' said Sir Iain, who'd had time to recover. 'As Mr Haldayne will acknowledge, two more US companies have seen the benefits of locating their European operations in Lothian. If my name, or Mr Haldayne's, were to be bandied about ...' Hunter gave a modest shrug.

'Well,' Rebus said, 'this is turning into a harder sell than a Costa del Sol time-share.' He turned to Simpson. 'What about you, Joe?'

Simpson nearly slid from his chair. 'What about me?'

'Do you have any properties to bargain with in this little

game of moral "Monopoly", or have you just picked up the Go-To-Jail card?'

'I can't go to jail! All I did was provide an accommodation address. It's not illegal!'

'Then why are you here?' Rebus looked to Mathieson, whose lips twitched.

'An offering,' he said.

'Hear that, Joe?'

Simpson had heard. He rose trembling to his feet.

'You could always testify against them,' Rebus told him.

'With what?' Haldayne said.

'Mr Haldayne has a point, Inspector.' Mathieson was sitting down again, in his big chief executive chair at the end of the table. Tables without corners were supposed to make everyone equal, but Mathieson's chair was a leather throne. He looked and sounded completely unruffled by events thus far, while Rebus felt as if his head would explode.

Hundreds of jobs, spin-offs; happy, smiling faces. People like Salty Dougary, pride restored, given another chance. Did Rebus have the gall to think he could pronounce sentence on the future of people like that? People who wouldn't care who got away with what, so long as *they* had a pay-cheque at the end of the month?

Gillespie had died, but Rebus knew these men hadn't killed him, not directly. At the same time he hated them, hated their confidence and their indifference, hated their certainty that what they did was 'for the good'. *They* knew the way the world worked; *they* knew who – or, rather, *what* – was in charge. It wasn't the police or the politicians, it wasn't anyone stupid enough to place themselves in the front line. It was secret, quiet men who got on with their work the world over, bribing where necessary, breaking the rules, but quietly, in the name of 'progress', in the name of the 'system'.

Shug McAnally was dead, but no one was grieving: Tresa was spending his money, and having a good time with Maisie Finch. Audrey Gillespie, too, might start enjoying life for the first time in years, maybe with her lover. A man had died – cruelly and in terror – but he was all there was on Rebus's side of the balance sheet. And on the other was everything else.

'Well, Inspector?' Mathieson could see something in Rebus's eyes – a red light that had changed to amber. He rose from the throne. 'Let's have a drink.'

Rebus hadn't noticed that the far wall was a series of recessed cupboards, their doors flush and handleless. Mathieson pushed the edge of one door and it opened automatically.

'I hope malt whisky's all right for everyone,' Mathieson said, as lightly as if they'd just finished a few rubbers of bridge.

'You don't have a drop of gin?' Joe Simpson squawked.

'You're right, Joe, I don't.'

'Then I'll take whisky.'

'Yes, Joe, you will.'

'Inspector,' Haldayne said in reasoned tones, 'we're in your hands. It's your decision now.'

'Let the man have a drink first,' Mathieson chided.

Sir Iain was staring levelly at Rebus, his mouth a moral pout. There was a line from a song stuck in Rebus's head, just when he least needed it: '*you can't always get what you want, but if you try some time, you'll find you get what you need*'.

I need a drink, he thought. And Robbie Mathieson – caring, smiling – brought him one.

'You're all right anyway,' Rebus told Haldayne. 'You'll have diplomatic immunity, the Get-Out-Of-Jail-Free Card.'

Haldayne snorted his porcine laugh. 'I'm also the only

one here who lost five grand to Derwood Charters over Albavise.'

'And you should have stayed out of it,' Sir Iain snarled.

'Hey,' Haldayne said, light glinting from his glasses, 'it worked in the past, didn't it?'

'You know, Inspector,' Mathieson said, rising above all this, 'any other policeman, any other public official, I might have been tempted to try offering a financial incentive.'

They all shut up to listen. Rebus sipped from his crystal tumbler.

'But with you,' Mathieson went on, 'I think that might have the opposite effect from the one intended.'

'And how much cash would I be worth to you, Mr Mathieson?'

'To me, nothing. But if it were a question of saving PanoTech ... Well, it wouldn't be a matter of actual cash, of course. Cash is messy, and you wouldn't want any problems with the Inland Revenue.'

'Perish the thought.'

'But a new house with its own grounds, a trust fund for a daughter, shares in a company which is going to do extraordinarily well in the next few years ... And then there are less tangible rewards – but no less valuable for that: friends in the right places, help when needed, a word in the right ear come promotion time ...' Mathieson's voice died away as he handed out the final drink – a very mean whisky for Joe Simpson – and took one for himself. He stood behind his throne, a plane droning in the night sky behind him.

'A little bit of bribery, eh?' Rebus commented.

Sir Iain Hunter sat forward. He looked like he was losing patience fast. He tapped his stick on the floor as he spoke. 'Is it wrong,' he said, 'to bribe rich foreign companies to come to a depressed region? I'd say, Inspector, that morally speaking, anyone who did that would be in the right.'

'Blackmail's blackmail,' Rebus said.

'I disagree.'

'And tell me, is nobody lining their own pockets?'

Sir Iain savoured his whisky. 'There must needs be incentives,' he said drily.

Rebus laughed. He felt a little looser after the drink. 'Exactly. And all this love of country and duty to the workers stuff is just so much shite. Tell me, why did you bring the DCC and me together that day?'

Sir Iain twisted in his chair. 'I saw how dangerous Charters had become. I wanted him stopped, but my position would not allow me to ... I felt it best to point you in the right direction rather than leading you there.'

Rebus laughed again. 'You old fraud. We were there to put the wind up Mathieson, to stop him even *thinking* about talking.' He turned to Mathieson. 'You were sweating like a pig in the killing pen.' Then back to Sir Iain. 'You used us the same way Charters used McAnally. *And* you've blackmailed Haldayne into helping bring firms here. What is it, is corruption part of the job description?'

Hunter said nothing. He was too angry to speak.

'Answer me this. Charters had a client called Quinlon, a building contractor who'd made money illicitly through a deal with someone in the SDA. Charters shopped Quinlon to the authorities so they'd think more seriously about closing down the SDA. Now, you all knew Charters back then, didn't you? You all knew that if the SDA disappeared, all accounts would be closed and the various frauds would remain undiscovered. So did you know about Quinlon?' He looked at Sir Iain. 'Did Charters maybe come to you with the story, and leave *you* to see that the right people heard about it?'

'This is sheer paranoia,' Sir Iain said. 'I refuse to discuss it.'

'OK, let's try this – Charters made a couple of million

through his paper companies. Enough to make a stint in jail worth while. That's why he pled guilty. And when he gets out, the money's waiting for him. You all know that, and you're not going to do a thing about it. You know he's a murderer, too, but you've kept quiet about that as well.'

'Inspector,' Haldayne said, 'we're not leeches.'

'I know that — leeches are medicinal. You know something?' He was talking to all of them now. 'Tom Gillespie said something to me. He told me I was making a mistake. At the time, I took it as a threat, but it wasn't – it was the literal truth. I thought because he had something to hide it must be something illicit. I was wrong about him all down the line; all he was was scared. He was terrified. Those last days of his life, all he felt was fear.' And dear God, Rebus knew what that felt like.

'Nobody's mourning him!' Sir Iain snapped.

Rebus turned to him. 'Now how do you know that?'

'What?'

'He's got a widow: you don't think she's in mourning?' Sir Iain studied the handle of his cane. 'I forgot,' he said.

'No, you didn't,' Rebus said quietly.

'So, what's it to be, Inspector?' Mathieson himself was beginning to look impatient. He knew he had won the argument, but might still lose the fight. He had his glass half raised, ready for a toast if Rebus gave the right answer, the answer everybody wanted. 'Just remember, if you want it, there's a place for you.'

Rebus was still staring at Sir Iain Hunter. He finished his whisky in one go and put the glass down. With his hands on the table, he pushed himself upright out of the chair.

'Here's my answer, Mr Mathieson,' he said.

He walked out without saying another word.

38

Because he hadn't decided.

His pride wouldn't let him kowtow to people like Hunter and Mathieson – they were men, not gods. And he hated people putting one over on him, which was exactly what would be happening if he gave in. But ... but ... He kept seeing those hundreds of faceless workers, driving to work in their new cars, or signing on in a sweltering dole office. One man's life against thousands ... It wasn't fair, it shouldn't be down to him to decide.

Well, what was stopping him taking it elsewhere? He drove into town along Corstorphine Road, past the office suite used by Mensung, and decided to drop into Torphichen Place. Davidson probably wouldn't be there at this hour, but he could find out what was happening with Gillespie's files.

The duty desk officer let him through the door. Rebus walked along the silent hall and up the stairs. The only person in the CID room was Rab Burns.

'Hiya, John, what brings you here? The urbane conversation? The ersatz coffee?'

'Bags of rubbish, to be precise.'

'Eh?'

So Rebus explained, and Burns shook his head. 'I don't know anything about them.'

'Maybe they were locked away at close of play.'

'They'd be in the cupboard. Hold on, I'll fetch the key.'

But there was nothing in the cupboard. 'You don't suppose they could have been thrown out by mistake?'

A shiver went across Rebus's shoulders. 'Mind if I use your phone?' He punched in Davidson's number and waited until the detective answered. 'It's me, where are the files?'

'John, I was going to call you.'

'Where are the files?'

'Orders, John.'

'What?'

'They were requisitioned. I was going to tell you in the morning.'

'Who was it?'

Davidson was a long time answering. 'The DCC's office.'

Rebus slammed down the receiver. Allan bloody Gunner! 'Any idea of the DCC's home number, Rab?'

'Oh aye, we're close friends like.'

Rebus's look shut him up. They found the number on the Emergency roster. Rebus rang and waited and waited. A woman picked up the receiver. There was laughter in the background. A party, maybe a dinner party.

'Mr Gunner, please.'

'Who shall I say?'

'Walt Disney.'

'Pardon?'

Rebus was shaking with anger. 'Just get him.'

A full minute later, Gunner lifted the receiver. 'Who is this?'

'It's Rebus. What the fuck are you playing at?'

'How dare you speak to me like that!' The words were hissed, Gunner not wanting his guests in the other room to hear.

'All right then. With respect, sir, what the fuck are you playing at?'

'What do you mean?'

'The Gillespie files, where are they?'

'In the incinerator.'

And Gunner cut the connection. Rebus tried again, but the line was busy – the receiver had been left off the hook. Rebus grabbed the Emergency roster from Burns and looked down it for Gunner's address.

'You can borrow my computer if you like,' Burns said.

'What for?'

'To write your letter of resignation.'

'Rab,' Rebus said to him, 'you stole that line from me.'

Rebus gave the bell a good long ring. Gunner didn't look surprised as he unlocked the door.

'Come into the study,' he said angrily.

As Rebus followed him, he heard the sounds of the dinner party. Instead of following Gunner into the study, he walked to a closed door and opened it.

'Evening,' he said. 'Sorry to drag the host away, we'll only be a minute.'

Then he smiled at the guests, closed the door again, and went into the study. Around the table had been seated the Lord Provost and his wife, the chief constable and his wife, and Gunner's wife. There were two other place settings, one for Gunner himself.

'Sir Iain couldn't make it then?' Rebus guessed.

Gunner closed the study door. 'He'll be joining us for coffee.'

'Cosy.'

'Look, Rebus –'

'I had a little think on the way here, and something occurred to me. Here it is. McAnally wasn't in Charters' cell to get to the bottom of anything; he was there so you could be sure Charters *was* keeping his mouth shut. And you got proof of that, because Charters paid McAnally to

334

scare off the councillor. It was a cover-up from the beginning, whether Flower knew that's how you were playing it or not. You wanted the whole thing kept hidden, and now that you've burnt those papers, that's the way it'll stay.'

'That's up to you.'

Rebus shook his head. 'No, I'm worthless. It's up to people like *you*, and you're not going to do a damned thing. You're going to remain Hunter's puppet, all the way to chief constable.'

The doorbell rang again, and Gunner walked out, returning with Sir Iain Hunter.

'Well, Inspector,' Hunter said, removing his topcoat, 'you do seem to pop up everywhere.' He slipped a hand into his pocket and pulled out a cassette. 'It's all there,' he said, handing it to Gunner.

Rebus felt the floor move beneath him. 'You were bugged?' he said.

Hunter smiled. 'Thank God he didn't make us *all* strip.'

Rebus nodded. 'I begin to get it.'

'Sir Iain,' Gunner said, 'has been gathering evidence of an embarrassing scandal.'

'A scandal,' Rebus added, 'that will conveniently lack one important name. I should've known the Scottish Office was involved from the start. I can't see a prison governor, especially one like Big Jim Flett, covering up McAnally's record on the say-so of the police alone. But the DCC backed up by the Permanent Secretary ... well, that would be a different story. After all, the Scottish Office pulls the purse-strings.' His eyes fixed on Hunter. 'And a lot of other strings besides.'

'Inspector Rebus,' Hunter said coolly, 'it is a fact of life that you simply *can't* have the Permanent Secretary mixed up in anything unsavoury. For the good of the country, he must be protected.'

'Even if he's in it up to his eyeballs?'

'Even then.'

'This stinks,' Rebus said. 'What's the tape? An insurance policy?'

'I'm preparing a file,' Gunner said. 'Unofficially, and to be kept under lock and key.'

'And if anything should happen to leak out in future ...?'

'The file will show,' said Hunter, 'that Charters and others acted unlawfully.'

'To the extent of murder?' Hunter nodded. 'What about Mathieson? Will he be implicated?' Rebus smiled. 'Sorry, daft question. Of course he will. You'd sell everything to the court to save your own neck, you –'

'Hypocrite?' Hunter suggested. 'Hypocrisy is acceptable if it is for the public good.'

'You know,' Gunner added, 'I could have you booted off the force.'

'I'd fight you all the way.'

Gunner smiled. 'I know you would.'

Hunter touched Gunner's arm. 'We've kept your guests waiting long enough, Allan.'

Gunner's eyes were still on Rebus. 'Under normal circumstances, you'd be welcome to join us.'

'I wouldn't join you if you were coming apart at the seams.'

'The stories I hear,' Gunner said, 'it's *you* that's been coming apart at the seams.'

'Bear something in mind, Inspector,' Hunter said, examining his cane. '*You* were at that meeting, too. You're on the tape, listening to men confess their part in illegal acts. I didn't hear you caution them, I didn't hear you do anything much. If questions should ever be asked, they'll be asked of you along with everyone else.'

'I'll see you to the door,' the chief constable-in-waiting told Rebus.

39

John Rebus did what he had to do – went on a forty-eight-hour bender.

It wasn't difficult in Edinburgh. Even in winter, without the benefit of extended summer opening hours, if you paced things right you could drink round the clock. It was all down to permutations of late-licence restaurants, casinos, and early-opening bars. You could always drink at home, of course, but that wasn't what a bender was about. You could hardly do your bender justice when the only person around to listen to your stories was your own sour self.

Rebus didn't worry about missing work. He'd been on benders before, after losing cases he'd tried desperately to win. Always he did it with the blessing of his superiors, who might even chip in towards expenses. He thought maybe he'd phoned the Farmer from some pub along the way, and maybe the Farmer had said something about Allan Gunner having okayed things. Hard to tell though, hard to remember.

Still harder to forget.

He'd grab an hour's sleep, then be awake a couple of minutes at most before the knot was in his guts, reminding him of things he'd far rather forget.

Towards the close of the first day, he was in a bar on Lothian Road, and noticed Maisie and Tresa there, having a good time to themselves. They were at a table, and Rebus was at the bar. Pairs of men kept accosting them – to no

avail. Then Maisie saw Rebus and got up, weaving towards him.

'I see the period of mourning's over,' Rebus said.

She smiled. 'Ach, Wee Shug was all right.'

'Why don't you tell me about it?'

Her eyes were only half open, heavy-lidded. 'See,' she began, 'it wasn't him I wanted, it was Tresa.' She lit a cigarette for herself, using the onyx and gold lighter. 'He came to see me the day he topped himself, told me what he was going to do. He gave me this lighter. Maybe he was looking for sympathy, or someone to talk him out of it. Daft bastard: he was doing just what I wanted. I wanted Tresa. I love her, really I do.'

Rebus remembered something she'd told him before, about Wee Shug: 'He deserved what he got.' He realised now that she hadn't meant it vindictively; she'd meant he deserved whatever he was paid. She'd stuck him in prison, and he'd still come back to her, telling his story ...

'Was it rape?' Rebus asked.

She shrugged. 'Not really.'

He sucked on his cigarette. 'Did you scream?'

Now she laughed. 'The neighbours thought I did. They *wanted* to have heard it, otherwise there'd be no guilt. We Scots need a bit of guilt, don't we? It gets us through the day.'

Then she planted a kiss on his cheek, and stood back to gaze at him, before making her way back to where Tresa McAnally sat waiting for her.

She was right about the guilt, he thought. But there was more to it – the neighbours hadn't done anything at the time, and that was typically Edinburgh. People would rather not know, even if there was nothing there – they didn't want to be told that their body (or their country) was rotten with cancer, but nor did they want to be told that it wasn't. And in the end they just sat there, *zugzwanged*,

338

while the likes of Charters and Sir Iain Hunter got on with another game entirely.

In the middle of the second day, in the same rancid clothes as the day before, wreathed in a fug of nicotine and whisky, and in possession of a hangover he was trying to drink away, he met Kirstie Kennedy. Maybe it was halfway down Leith Walk, or at the top of Easter Road. She was shorter than him, and wanted to whisper in his ear. She didn't need to stand on tiptoe to do it – he stooped under the weight of his skull and shoulders.

'You should get straight,' she told him. 'Killing yourself's no answer.'

He recalled her words later, when more or less seated on a bench in what purported to be a bar on Dalry Road. It had the dimensions and atmosphere of a bonded warehouse. He had just been speaking to the old thin man, the one who liked American history. Rebus had started to give him a history lesson which didn't have much to do with Hopalong Cassidy, and the man shuffled off to another part of the bar, where Tartan Shoelaces stood protectively close to his erring wife Morag. Rebus had stood them all a couple of drinks when he'd come in.

Some young turks were playing pool, and Rebus tried to concentrate on their game, but found himself yawning noisily.

'Not keeping you up, are we, pal?' one of the players snarled.

'Cut it out,' the barmaid called to them. 'He's polis.'

'He's guttered, that's what he is. Plain mortal.'

And then Kirstie's words came back to him. *You should get straight. Killing yourself's no answer.* Well, it depended what the question was. Get straight ... straight, as in even. Someone sat down next to him. He tried turning his head to look at them.

'Found you at last.'

'Sammy?'

'I got a phone call from somebody called Kirstie. She said she was worried.'

'I'm fine. Nothing wrong with me.'

'You're a mess. What's happened?'

'The *system*, that's what's happened. You were right, Sammy. And I knew you were right, all the time I was saying you were wrong.'

She smiled at him. 'Well, you were right, too. I shouldn't have smuggled that note out for Derwood Charters.'

'Don't worry about it. Gerry Dip isn't talking. We'll pin him for the credit cards if nothing else. There'll be no mention of Charters at the trial. You won't be involved.'

'But I *am* involved.'

Rebus shook his head. 'Just keep your mouth quiet, that's what everyone else is doing. Nothing's going to happen.'

'Is that what this is about?'

Rebus straightened his back. He didn't like Sammy seeing him like this; that thought had only just struck him.

'Look,' he said, 'whether you can put this behind you or not is down to you and your conscience. That's what I'm saying.' He got to his feet. 'I'm going to clean up.'

He made it to the toilets. He didn't want the pool players coming in for a 'Dalry Discussion', so wedged the door shut with paper towels while he stuck his head under the cold tap. He dried himself off, then was copiously sick into the bowl. Unjamming the door, he walked back into the bar.

'Feeling better?' Sammy asked him.

'Ninety-five per cent to go,' Rebus told her, taking her hand in his.

Who could he go to?

The Lord Advocate? Hardly: he was probably on pheasant-shooting terms with Hunter. He was the *Establishment*, and the Establishment would be protected at all costs. The chief constable? But he was retiring, and wouldn't want anything to tarnish his last few months in office. The media perhaps, Mairie Henderson? It was the story of the year, except there was no proof. It would be the word of an embittered policeman against ... well, *everybody*.

He'd spent time steeping in the bath at home, then showering. Sammy had made him drink a couple of litres of orange juice, and about a packet of 'Resolve'.

'I can't forget what I did,' she told him quietly.

'Maybe you got my guilt complex along with my genes,' he told her.

After Sammy had gone back to Patience's, Rebus had called Gill Templer. He needed advice, he told her. They arranged to meet at her health club. She had a sauna and massage booked; they could talk in the bar after that.

There was a view from the bar's first-floor window down on to a quiet New Town street. All around Rebus sat healthy people, tanned and smiling with good teeth and trim confidence. He knew he fitted in like a paedophile in a classroom. He had trashed his bender clothes, just trashed them, and was wearing the gear he'd bought for the trip to Sir Iain's.

Gill came in and nodded towards him, then went to the bar and bought herself something non-alcoholic. Her skin glowed as she came over to his table. 'You look rough,' she said.

'You should have seen me earlier. You could have sanded doors with me.'

She picked a sliver of orange out of her glass and sucked on it. 'So what's the big mystery?'

He told her the whole story. She started to look

341

uncomfortable halfway through, the look changing by degrees to simple bemusement.

'I'll take another orange juice, if you're buying,' she said when he'd finished.

She needed time to think, so Rebus didn't hurry the barman. But when he came back to the table, she still didn't have anything to say.

'See, Gill, what I need is the nod on a search warrant, so I can go into Gunner's house and seize the file and the tape. We could get one from a JP – there are enough councillors left to choose from.'

Her face darkened. 'Why me?' she said.

'Why not?'

'How good do you think *I'd* come out of this? Do you think anyone would forget that I was the one who'd helped you?'

'For Christ's sake, Gill.'

Her voice softened. She stared into her drink. 'Sorry I'm letting you down, John.'

'They could crucify me if they wanted to.'

She stared at him. 'They don't want to. You don't know, do you? You really don't know.'

'Know what?'

'You're going to be promoted to chief inspector. There's an opening in Galashiels. It came down to the chief super from the DCC.' She smiled. 'You're trying to arrange a search warrant for his house, and he's busy giving you a hike up. How's *that* going to look in court?'

'It's true,' Chief Superintendent Watson confirmed.

Rebus was in the Farmer's office, but not sitting. He couldn't sit, couldn't even stand at ease.

'I don't want it, I won't accept it. That's allowed, isn't it?'

The Farmer made a pained face. 'If you refuse, it's a

snub no one will forget. You might never get a second chance.'

'I don't mind snubbing Allan Gunner.'

'John, Gunner didn't recommend you for promotion, I did.'

'What?'

'Several months back.'

'You did?'

'Yes.'

'Well, it's a damned coincidence Gunner's held off making a decision until now. Whose idea was Galashiels?'

'It happens to be an opening.'

'It happens to be in the middle of nowhere. I can see they'd need a chief inspector down there, what with the farming vendettas and the Saturday night punch-up.'

'For once in your life, John, go easy on yourself, do yourself a favour. Stop beating yourself up like you're the Salvation Army drum. Just ...' The Farmer shrugged.

'Drums don't beat themselves,' Rebus said. He was staring at the Farmer's computer, not listening any more. And then he started to smile, and looked at the Farmer. 'OK,' he said, 'tell Gunner I'll take it.'

'Good.'

But the Farmer wasn't as pleased as he'd expected he'd be. There was something going on, some motive he couldn't fathom. It was so bloody typical of Rebus to make him feel like a win was a draw, a draw a defeat.

'And, John,' he said, standing up, stretching out his hand, 'congratulations.'

Rebus stared at the hand but didn't take it. 'I didn't say I was accepting the promotion, sir, I just said to *tell* Gunner I was.'

And with that he left the Farmer's office.

Flower was on night-shift again.

Rebus didn't know why or how Flower got so many night-shifts. Maybe because at night he was more likely to see a spot of trouble. Rebus looked like trouble as he strode towards his adversary's desk, dragging a chair over and sitting astride it.

'Done any good fire-raising lately?'

Flower just sneered.

'Some good it did you,' Rebus went on.

'What?'

'I don't mean setting the bin on fire. I mean letting the DCC use your man McAnally like that. Whose idea was it to put him in Charters' cell?'

'What's it to you?'

'Humour me.' Rebus offered Flower a cigarette. Flower took it warily, and even then laid it to one side.

'All right,' he said, 'it was the DCC's.'

'That's what I figured. And you went along with it. I mean, who wouldn't? It meant the DCC owed you a favour – very handy that. But it didn't work out.'

'You've lost me.'

'I mean, the DCC had a hidden agenda. He wanted to use your man to make sure Charters *wasn't* talking, because some people on the outside were getting sweaty. Charters was protecting certain people, people like the head of PanoTech, and the Permanent Secretary at the Scottish Office. But a local councillor had started sniffing. Eventually, he would have talked to Charters – maybe he already had. That worried people, they needed to know how safe they were. As it turned out, Charters knew about the councillor and paid McAnally to give him a fright.'

'Shite.'

'Is it? Well, no matter.' Rebus sucked on his cigarette. He'd got Flower thinking, but that process might take weeks. 'Tell me,' he said, 'your friend the DCC, he didn't

even get you Lauderdale's job. Didn't that make you think?'

'It was too soon. It would have looked suspicious.'

Rebus laughed, further discomfiting Flower. 'Is that what he told you?'

'Never you mind.'

'Well, bonny lad, I've got news for you – the DCC's just offered *me* promotion to chief inspector.'

'Away to hell.'

Rebus just shrugged. Flower picked up the cigarette he'd been given and lit it. Then he called the Farmer at home. They had a bruising conversation during which Flower brought up everything from his years in the force (three more than Rebus) to his charitable works. When he finally put the phone down, he was shaking.

'Know who you should phone now?' Rebus suggested. 'Your pal Allan Gunner. Ask him why me instead of you. Know what he'll say? Well, he might not say it, but it's the truth. He's promoting me because I'm dangerous to him. I'm too dangerous for the usual demotion, so instead he's offering a bribe. And you're being left behind because he can afford to ignore you. That's a simple fact.'

'Why are you telling me this?' Flower hissed.

'Believe me, it's not just for the thrill of seeing you squirm.'

'Why then?'

Rebus leaned forward. 'How,' he asked confidentially, 'would you like my promotion?' Flower just sneered. It hurt Rebus to say what he was saying, but he tried not to let that show. He would sacrifice this and much more for a single, risky shot at his quarry. Above all, though, he wouldn't tell Flower about the move to Galashiels that went along with it ... 'I mean it,' he said.

Flower saw with deep amazement that he did. 'What do I have to do?'

40

Winter mornings could sap you of good intentions and foolhardy schemes. Rebus and Flower wanted to be in their separate beds, tucked beneath a nice heavy woman, but instead were sitting in Rebus's car, across the street from Allan Gunner's house. It was still dark. A milk van passed, and a bread van, and a few bleak souls on their way to catch the first bus of the day.

'So this is morning,' Flower said.

'Not a pretty sight, is it?'

'You think this will work?'

'Have faith.' Rebus looked towards the house. 'He's up.'

Flower peered out through the windscreen. A light had come on upstairs in the Gunner household.

'We'll give him five minutes,' said Rebus.

But only two minutes later, the downstairs lights came on.

'Could be the wife,' Flower suggested, 'cooking a hearty breakfast for her deserving husband.'

'Have you ever heard the phrase "New Man"?'

'It's a shop, isn't it? What do you reckon, a couple more minutes? Let him get his feet under the breakfast table?'

'My legs are blocks of ice,' Rebus said, opening the car door. 'Let's do it now.'

They rang the doorbell, and heard Gunner's voice calling, 'I'll get it!' Then the door opened, revealing the deputy chief constable in shirt but not yet necktie or

cufflinks, a mug of coffee in his hand. He took a step back into the hall.

'What the hell are you doing here?'

'Canvassing for the Natural Law Party,' Rebus said, stepping into the centrally heated house.

Gunner ran upstairs to have a word with his wife, and Rebus and Flower walked uninvited into the kitchen. Smoke was pouring from the electric grill. Flower lifted the grill-pan out and blew on the cremated bread. 'New Man, eh?'

Rebus switched the kettle back on and lifted two mugs from the draining-board. He was unscrewing the lid from the coffee-jar when Gunner returned. Gunner snatched the jar from him.

'Christ, you've got some gall.' He switched the kettle off. 'Why are you here?' He checked his watch, saw he hadn't put it on yet, and glanced instead at the wall-clock. 'Half a minute, then you're on your way.'

'We want the file you've compiled,' Rebus said, 'and the tape Sir Iain made. I think that'll do for now.'

Gunner looked to Flower. 'He's roped you in, eh? You must be mad. I could have you both up before the chief constable.'

'We'd like nothing better,' Flower said. He threw the remains of the toast into the bin. 'You lied to me.'

'If we don't get the file and the tape,' Rebus said, 'we take it further anyway. We're going to kick up such a stink, you'll think your drains have backed up. It'll be everywhere, believe me. There won't be enough clothes-pegs to go round.'

'You *are* mad. I'm not going to give you anything.'

'We'll start with the chief constable and the newspapers.'

Gunner folded his arms. 'Be my guests. You've just dug yourselves a very deep hole.'

'Holes have their uses,' Rebus said, 'when the bullets start to fly.'

'Get out!' Gunner snarled.

They got out.

'Think we were too obliging?' Flower muttered as they walked back down the path. 'We could have been harder on him.'

'It went fine. It's down to him now. Is he watching?'

Flower glanced back. 'Bedroom window.'

'Right.'

They walked to Rebus's car, got in and drove off.

A hundred yards along the road, Rebus stopped long enough to let Flower out. Flower's own car was parked there, and he got into it quickly. Rebus checked in his rearview, but Gunner hadn't come out of the house to check their departure, not on a morning like this. He drove on, went around the block, and ended up on the other side of Gunner's house.

They daren't trust to police frequencies, so had borrowed a couple of on-line cellular phones from a dealer who'd owed Rebus a favour. Rebus's phone rang, and he picked it up.

'Any sign of him?' Flower said.

'Not yet.'

'Maybe he's on the mark-two toast.'

'I don't think he'll have much of an appetite.'

It was five minutes more before Rebus heard a door bang shut. Then Gunner's gate opened. His Rover 800 was directly outside, and he unlocked it, got in, and started the engine.

'Bingo,' said Rebus.

'Has he anything with him?'

'A briefcase.'

'Well, here's hoping.'

Rebus had parked away from the street-lighting, and was

careful not to start his engine until Gunner was already on the move. Smoke billowed from his exhaust, hanging in the sub-zero air. Gunner's back windscreen was frosted over, and he hadn't taken time to scrape it.

'Fall in behind me,' Rebus told Flower, just before passing his stationary car.

Soon they joined a slow-moving stream of commuter traffic heading into town. The Rover's rear de-mister had taken care of the frost. When they came to a section of dual carriageway, Flower overtook Rebus.

'Where's he headed?'

'Not to work,' Rebus said. 'Not this way.'

They'd discussed routes he might take, places he might go. Princes Street hadn't figured in their calculations. There was light in the sky now, a deep bruise hanging over the Castle and the Old Town. Rebus's heater wasn't working properly – it only did that in the summer – and he curled his toes inside his shoes.

'He's signalling,' Flower said. 'Turning left on to Waverley Bridge. Maybe he's got a train to catch.'

Rebus thought he knew. 'No, but he's headed for the station.'

A long line of black taxis crept up from the subterranean concourse of Waverley Station, waiting their turn to take the commuters to business appointments and power breakfasts. They headed past the taxis, down the steep slope until they were underground. Gunner drove past the pick-up/drop-off point, and looked for a moment as if he was going to head up the exit ramp and back on to Waverley Bridge. But he took a left instead, and found a parking bay towards the back of the station.

'Find yourself a space,' Rebus told Flower, 'and follow on foot.'

'What if he sees me?'

'Get on to the platform, walk down it.'

'What if he goes on to the platform?'

'He hasn't come here for the trains. Hey, and take your phone with you.'

Rebus parked and headed round the other side of the concourse, anti-clockwise to Gunner's clockwise. He managed a light jog, as if he was fighting a tight schedule. He walked down a platform towards the rear of the station, the telephone up to his face, as much for camouflage as anything.

'Oh, yes,' Flower said. And then Rebus was in position. In the distance, he could see Flower, and halfway between them Allan Gunner. He was where Rebus had guessed he'd be – at the Left Luggage counter. Rebus stood half-hidden by a billboard advertising industrial space to let. The irony wasn't lost on him as he watched Gunner hand over the briefcase and accept a ticket. When Gunner headed back the way he'd come, Rebus came from around the advertising hoarding and walked briskly towards Left Luggage, just in time to see the employee place the case on a rack right at the front.

'Well?' Flower said.

'Let him go.'

'Is it there?'

'Sweet as a nut, Flower. Sweet as a nut.'

Rico Briggs took some persuading.

Between them, in their many and various ways, Rebus and Flower were expert at the art of persuasion. Well, hadn't they panicked – persuaded – Gunner into getting rid of the evidence? If he'd had time to think, if it hadn't been early morning, he might have thought of a better hiding place. Left Luggage was a stop-gap – he just didn't want the stuff in his house. Rebus had read him just right, and in fact a Left Luggage office wasn't bad, not as a stop-gap.

Rebus and Flower took turns keeping the office under

surveillance. Surveillance was easy in a railway station: there were so many people just hanging around. They didn't want Gunner coming back and lifting the case without them knowing, though Rebus's guess was that it would stay there overnight. Gunner would work the day like any other, then go home and think about it, maybe make a few telephone calls – calls he wouldn't want to make from his own office. With the briefcase and its contents out of the way, he'd feel more confident. He'd want to use that time to think things through.

So the briefcase would be there overnight.

Rebus called Rico and got him to come down to the station. They met in the bar. Rebus had already consumed too much coffee and junk food, and the smell of stale alcohol in the bar almost did for him. The bar smelt the way bars always did at the start of a new day's business – of the previous day, of accumulation; too much smoke and spilt beer.

'Pint of lager,' Rico told the barman. The barman tried not to stare too hard at his customer's tattooed cheeks. Rico gave them a brisk rub while his drink was poured. When he saw there was a gaming machine in the bar, he walked over to it and fed in some coins. Rebus paid for the drink and carried it over to Rico. He had his cellphone in his free hand. I look like a businessman on the way down, he thought.

Maybe he was, at that.

Rebus explained the situation to Rico while Rico played the machine. When Rico ran out of coins, Rebus gave him more. Then his cellphone beeped.

'What does he say?' Flower asked.

'So far, he says no.'

'Let me talk to him.'

So Rebus relieved Flower. He let twenty minutes pass, then phoned the bar.

'Well?'

'He's just about cleaned me out of money,' Flower reported. And in the end it was the gaming machine that was the real persuader. It persuaded Rico to borrow money from Flower – real money – and suddenly Rico owed the policeman twenty pounds.

For the promise of more money, and a clean slate on his debt, Rico said he'd meet them at one in the morning.

Which was only thirteen hours away ...

Rebus and Flower spent the rest of the day watching Left Luggage, reading newspapers and magazines purchased from the station stall, eating overpriced sandwiches, drinking weak coffee, and generally learning a lot about the life of a mainline railway station.

The security cameras bothered Rebus, so he paid a visit to ScotRail's security office and spoke to the staff, on the pretext of alerting them to a gang of pickpockets just up from Newcastle. It was warm in the security chief's office, and the man was ex-CID, friendly. They traded stories, Rebus asked for a tour. Which was how he saw everything would be all right. The camera trained on Left Luggage was hazy, distant: they'd see anyone going in, but they wouldn't get a good description. This was very much to Rico's advantage.

Besides, no one watched after midnight. The camera would record, but that was all.

The station was locked overnight, but still open at one o'clock. There were weird night trains to deal with, freight-haulers, a sleeper bound for London. Rebus thought he'd probably caught something, he kept shivering at his core. He didn't think it could just be nerves.

True to his word, but ten minutes late, Rico turned up.

'I brought some balaclavas,' he said.

'We won't need them.' Rebus explained about the cameras. They'd taken their cars into Cockburn Street, parked them there. They had a quick discussion as they walked down Platform One towards Left Luggage. Rico had checked the office out earlier, and now carried the tools he needed, tiny picklocks which reminded Rebus of dental instruments. Instinctively, his tongue sought the hole, but there was no hole there, Dr Keene had seen to that.

It took Rico a very long minute, but at last they were in.

With the shutters down, the place was in utter darkness, but Rebus had a couple of torches and handed one to Flower.

'Keep listening at the door, Rico,' he ordered. Then they went to work.

There wasn't much luggage to choose from, and the briefcase was just where Rebus knew it would be. Locked, but that didn't matter. He lifted it up and walked to the door.

'Here, Rico, see what you can do with this.'

He stood with his torch pointed at the case, while Rico brought out his picklocks. Flower, meantime, was moving luggage around, switching tags.

'What the hell are you doing?' Rebus hissed.

'Maximising confusion.'

'Well stop it. Put everything back. We don't want anyone knowing we've been in here.'

Rico made a clucking sound with his tongue. They switched the torches off and stood very still in the darkness, listening. Slow footsteps, coming nearer. A whistled pop tune. Rico rested his weight against the door. Someone tried the door, pushing it a couple of times. Then the shutters jumped a quarter-inch and fell back, then jumped again. If someone shone a torch through the crack, they'd see Flower standing not three feet from them like the last

dummy in the shop window. The shutters clattered down again. The footsteps moved away.

Rebus started breathing again.

'I'm glad I thought to wear my brown underwear,' Rico whispered. Rebus shone the light back down on to the briefcase, and Rico tried the locks. They flipped open against his fingers.

Rebus lifted the lid of the case. Inside was a single fat document file and an audio cassette. Rebus lifted both out and instructed Rico to lock the case again.

'Is that it?' Flower said.

It took Rebus half a paragraph to be sure, then he smiled and nodded. He placed the evidence in a carrier-bag, put the case back on its shelf, and wiped it clean with the sleeve of his jacket. Rico was looking around at the other bags and cases.

'No way,' Rebus said, coming to wipe the door where Rico had held it shut. 'And don't even *think* of coming back here on your own, understand?'

They relocked the door behind them, and walked up the slope just before the gates were closed for the night.

41

Rebus couldn't sleep.

He sat in his chair smoking a cigarette, reading the file the DCC had prepared – maybe 'crafted' was a better word. He'd done a good job of making it look so thorough while leaving so much out. He played part of the tape, using headphones so he could turn the volume up. Sir Iain was right about one thing – any lawyer listening to the tape would think that the police officer present hadn't done very much. Rebus found that his hand was shaking. He hadn't had a drink all day, and didn't especially want one now. He was just a bit scared, that was all. He wasn't sure he had enough, even now ... especially now.

Then he thought of something, something he'd almost persuaded himself to forget, and reached for the phone-book, finding the page, running his finger down the names, then along to a particular address. A flat on Dublin Street.

It was past three o'clock when Rebus got there, the streets dead, not even any taxis rippling over the setts. Rebus pressed the buzzer and waited, then pressed it again. Then a third time, keeping his finger on it this time.

The intercom crackled into life. 'What? What?'

'Mr McAllister?' Rebus inquired, as if it was the middle of the day.

'Yes?'

'It's Inspector Rebus. If you're alone, I'd like to come up for a word.'

* * *

Rory McAllister was half dressed and less than half awake. He was on his own.

Rebus walked around the spacious living room, admiring the ornaments and books, while McAllister made them both a cup of coffee.

Then they sat down opposite one another. McAllister rubbed at his eyes and yawned.

'So what is it, Inspector?'

Rebus put his mug down on the polished wooden floor. 'Well, it's just this, sir. That day we met for lunch, you were ... well, how can I put it? It struck me afterwards that you were *too* enthusiastic, too willing to talk. Then I saw you going to see Audrey Gillespie and ... well, I started thinking.'

McAllister tried to hide behind his steaming mug. 'About what?'

'You don't deny you went to see Mrs Gillespie?'

'Not at all. I know her, of course. I met her husband several times, professionally and socially. Mrs Gillespie accompanied her husband on those social occasions.'

Rebus nodded. 'And the other occasions – there's interaction between the district council and the Scottish Office?'

'Of course, and both Councillor Gillespie and myself worked on an industry remit.'

'Mmm,' Rebus said. 'And did the councillor know you were seeing his wife behind his back?'

'Now hang on –'

'Let me finish. You see, Mr McAllister, all this stuff Tom Gillespie found out, is it possible he could have gleaned so much unaided? Someone had to be passing him the information, perhaps anonymously.'

'You've lost me.'

'Never mind, you'll catch up. I think *you* found out about Mensung and PanoTech and Charters' other scams.

356

Sir Iain trusted you, had you pegged as a possible successor. Maybe he had you go into Mensung to make sure there was nothing that could come to light.' Rebus stood up. 'Now, here's where it gets interesting. Because you either passed the information on so you could scupper Sir Iain – in other words, for the public good. Or you did it to keep Gillespie busy and out of the way while you enjoyed a fling with his wife – which might be called the private good. Either way, I think you did it.'

'And you were generous enough to drag me out of bed in the middle of the night to let me know your suspicions?' McAllister sat back in his chair, hands pressed to his chin as if in prayer.

'I came here,' Rebus said, 'because if you did it only to smooth your affair with Audrey Gillespie, then I'm sunk. Whereas, if you really *did* want to get at Sir Iain, then we could be of use to one another.'

McAllister looked up and frowned. 'How?'

So Rebus sat down again and told him.

It was Sir Iain he wanted. He'd cancelled out all the other numbers in the equation, except Charters and Sir Iain. And Sir Iain was one possible route to Derry Charters. Rebus wanted him. He wanted him because people like Sir Iain Hunter were always in the right, even when they were wrong. Sir Iain lived and worked by the same ground rules a lot of villains swore by. He was selfish without appearing to be, full of arguments and self-justifications. He espoused the public good, but lined his pockets with the public's money. He wasn't so very different from the likes of Paul Duggan. If Rebus tried hard enough, he found he could blame Sir Iain for the fates of Willie Coyle and Dixie Taylor. Kirstie had run away from home because her father had been shown the city's corrupt heart, and wasn't going

to do anything about it. But the heart was artificial, and Sir Iain Hunter was working the bellows.

When Rebus climbed the stairs to his flat, he found someone huddled in his doorway. It was Sammy. His hand on her shoulder woke her up, and she sprang to her feet.

'What's happened?' he asked.

'I've been phoning you all day. I was worried about you.' There were dried tearstains down both her cheeks. 'I thought I'd wait for you here.'

He let her in. She looked around the living room and saw the duvet on the chair. 'Is this where you sleep?'

'Some nights,' Rebus said, lighting the fire.

'You can't get much rest there.'

'It's all right. Do you want anything to drink?' She shook her head.

'Are you all right?' she asked.

He puffed out his cheeks, then exhaled. 'I think so, just about.' He sank into his chair. 'I'm a bit scared, that's all. I'm going to do something tomorrow; it may not turn out the way I want.'

'One reason I wanted to see you,' she began. 'I can't get it out of my mind, that note ... and what happened. I thought maybe if you could tell me the story, it would help.'

Rebus smiled. 'It's not exactly a bedtime story.'

His daughter had curled up in front of the fire, and held a cushion against her chest. 'Tell me anyway,' she said.

So Rebus told her, leaving nothing out – it was no less than she deserved. And afterwards, she fell asleep still clutching the cushion. Rebus placed the duvet over her, turned the fire down low, and sat down in his chair again, tears falling so softly that he knew he wouldn't wake her.

He was wearing his best suit.

Flower had phoned first thing to say he wasn't going. He

didn't explain, didn't need to. Rebus didn't need any more from him. Flower was thinking tactically: if it all went wrong — as it well might — Flower would be in the foxhole. He still had Rebus's promise: chief inspector. *If* it all worked out.

Sammy had helped him with his grooming. He hadn't had much sleep, but he didn't look too bad considering, and the suit definitely helped.

'Patience chose it for me,' he told his daughter.

'She has good taste,' Sammy agreed.

He phoned first, stressing secrecy and urgency. There were problems, but finally he was given fifteen minutes in the mid-morning. Fifteen precious minutes. He had a bit of time to kill, so paced the flat, emptied the jar and put it back under the radiator, found his dental appointment card and tore it up.

Sammy gave him a good luck kiss as he left the flat.

'We're not so very different,' she told him.

'Like father and daughter,' he said, returning the kiss.

He parked at the front of St Andrew's House, and a guard came out and told him he couldn't do that. Rebus showed his warrant card, but the guard was adamant, and directed him to the visitors' parking.

'Tell me,' Rebus said, 'if I was Sir Iain Hunter, would I still have to move the car?'

'No,' said the guard, 'that would be different.'

And Rebus smiled, feeling a little of the tension leaving him. The man was right: that *would* be different.

He walked up the steps to the building. Close up, it didn't look so much like a power station or the Reichstag. He was signed in at the desk and given a visitor's pass. Security had to check the contents of his bag — just some papers and a cassette. Someone came down to escort him upstairs, where he was passed on to someone else who took him to a secretary's office. On the way, in a short narrow

corridor, his escort nearly bumped into Sir Iain Hunter. She apologised, but Sir Iain wasn't paying her any attention. Rebus winked at him and smiled as he passed. He didn't look back, but he could feel the eyes boring into him, right between the shoulder-blades.

This, he thought, is for Willie and Dixie, and for Tom Gillespie. And for everyone who doesn't know the way the system works, the way it makes room for lying and cheating and stealing.

But he knew, above all, that he was doing it for himself.

There was no secretary in the secretary's office, just Rory McAllister, looking very ill-at-ease but there, as he'd promised. Rebus found another wink to spare. Then the secretary came in and ushered them into an ante-chamber. She knocked on the door in front of them and opened it.

He'd joked with the security man about the contents of his bag – 'I'd hardly be carrying a bomb in a Spar carrier-bag' – but now he walked into the room with the booby-trap tucked under his arm.

'Good of you to find time to see us, sir.'

He meant it, too. Dugald Niven, Secretary of State for Scotland, had a busy schedule. Rebus was sure it would go ahead as usual, no matter what.

READING
GROUP
NOTES

LET IT BLEED

© Rankin

ABOUT IAN RANKIN

Ian Rankin, OBE, writes a huge proportion of all the crime novels sold in the UK and has won numerous prizes, including in 2005 the Crime Writers' Association Diamond Dagger. His work is available in over 30 languages, home sales of his books exceed one million copies a year, and several of the novels based around the character of Detective Inspector Rebus – his name meaning 'enigmatic puzzle' – have been successfully transferred to television.

Introduction to DI John Rebus

The first novels to feature Rebus, a flawed
but resolutely humane detective, were not an
overnight sensation, and success took time
to arrive. But the wait became a period that
allowed Ian Rankin to come of age as a writer,
and to develop Rebus into a thoroughly
believable, flesh-and-blood character straddling
both industrial and post-industrial Scotland;
a gritty yet perceptive man coping with his
own demons. As Rebus struggled to keep
his relationship with daughter Sammy alive
following his divorce, and to cope with the
imprisonment of brother Michael, while all the
time trying to strike a blow for morality against
a fearsome array of sinners (some justified and
some not), readers began to respond in their
droves. Fans admired Ian Rankin's re-creation
of a picture-postcard Edinburgh with a vicious
tooth-and-claw underbelly just a heartbeat away,
his believable but at the same time complex
plots and, best of all, Rebus as a conflicted man
trying always to solve the unsolvable, and to do
the right thing.

As the series progressed, Ian Rankin refused
to shy away from contentious issues such as
corruption in high places, paedophilia and illegal

immigration, combining his unique seal of tight plotting with a bleak realism, leavened with brooding humour.

In Rebus the reader is presented with a rich and constantly evolving portrait of a complex and troubled man, irrevocably tinged with the sense of being an outsider and, potentially, unable to escape being a 'justified sinner' himself. Rebus's life is intricately related to his Scottish environs too, enriched by Ian Rankin's attentive depiction of locations, and careful regard to Rebus's favourite music, watering holes and books, as well as his often fraught relationships with colleagues and family. And so, alongside Rebus, the reader is taken on an often painful, sometimes hellish journey to the depths of human nature, always rooted in the minutiae of a very recognisable Scottish life.

The Oxford Bar – Rebus and many of the characters who appear in the novels are regulars of the Ox – as is Ian Rankin himself. The pub is now synonymous with the Rebus novels to the extent that one of the regular medical examiners called in to assist with investigations is named after the pub's owner, John Gates.

Edinburgh plays an important role throughout the Rebus
novels; a character itself, as brooding and as volatile as
Rebus. The Edinburgh depicted in the novels is far short of

the beautiful city that tourists in their thousands flood to
visit. Hidden behind the historic buildings and elegant
façades is the world that Rebus inhabits.

For general discussion regarding the Rebus series

How does Ian Rankin reveal himself as an author interested in using fiction to 'tell the truths the real world can't'?

There are similarities between the lives of the author and his protagonist – for instance, both Ian Rankin and Rebus were born in Fife, lost their mothers at an early age, have children with physical problems – so is it useful therefore to think of John Rebus and Ian Rankin as each other's alter egos?

Could it be said that Rebus is trying to make sense in a general way of the world around him, or is he seeking answers to the 'big questions'? And is it relevant therefore that he is a believer in God and comes from a Scottish Presbyterian background? Would Rebus see confession in both the religious and the criminal sense as similar in any way?

How does Ian Rankin explore notions of Edinburgh as a character in its own right? In what way does he contrast the glossy public and seedy private faces of the city with the public and private faces of those Rebus meets?

How does Ian Rankin use musical sources – the Elvis references in *The Black Book*, for instance, or the Rolling Stones allusions in *Let It Bleed* – as a means of character development through the series? What does Rebus's own taste in music and books say about him as a person?

What do you think about Rebus as a character? If you have read several or more novels from the series, discuss how his character is developed.

If Rebus has a problem with notions of 'pecking order' and the idea of authority generally, what does it say about him that he chose careers in hierarchical institutions such as the Army and then the police?

How does Rebus relate to women: as lovers, flirtations, family members and colleagues?

Do the flashes of gallows humour as often shown by the pathologists but sometimes also in Rebus's own comments increase or dissipate narrative tension? Does Rebus use black comedy for the same reasons the pathologists do?

Do Rebus's personal vulnerabilities make him understanding of the frailties of others?

How does the characterisation of Rebus compare to other long-standing popular detectives from British authors such as Holmes, Poirot, Morse or Dalgleish? And are there more similarities or differences between them?

LET IT BLEED

Two teenagers in a Cortina lead the police a merry dance one snowy night, but Rebus is shocked when they fall or, more probably, leap to their deaths from the Forth Road Bridge right before his eyes. And immediately he knows that this is going to make looking into the disappearance of the Lord Provost's daughter, 17-year-old Kirstie Kennedy, impossible to keep quiet. Has she been kidnapped, or is Rebus right in thinking it's all a hoax?

Rebus discovers he has a new boss and that she is former lover Gill Templer, but any thoughts of how this might pan out are pushed aside by the grisly suicide of an unknown constituent in front of Councillor Tom Gillespie, who had previously been most preoccupied with the thought of the upcoming council elections only seven weeks away. Rebus finds shady business ventures and evidence of backhanders, but soon he's ordered to cool his heels elsewhere, or else his blundering about may end up costing much-needed Scottish jobs. Meanwhile, a rash action from daughter Sammy means she becomes implicated in the investigation.

Rebus's response to this personal *zugzwang*? To rub shoulders with those in high places and stomp on their toes, while trying to ensure that his jousting with DI Flower goes his way. But when Rebus unravels a web of corruption that reaches to the highest level, he finds

himself faced with a moral dilemma to which he just doesn't feel equal.

Casting a cynical eye on Scottish Enterprise – or should this be Scottish enterprise, Rebus jokes – Ian Rankin offers his most revealing and intimate portrait yet of Rebus, allowing the reader a further insight into what makes him tick.

Discussion points for *Let It Bleed*

'*Rebus looked out of the window. It had started snowing. "Weather like this," he said, "there's never much trouble in Edinburgh, trust me."'* To what extent should the reader trust Rebus?

The silent actions of the two youths who died suggest to Rebus '*something fatalistic; something agreed between them*'. What does Rebus feel in response? Could it be said that he's so interested in these and other suicides generally because, aside from the very different motivations of murderers from suicides, he plays with his own well-being through the precarious way he looks after himself? Has he ever contemplated suicide himself?

Referring to the Rolling Stones, Rebus thinks, '*What a shambles the band were, yet sometimes they could get it so right that it hurt*.' Could the same be said of Rebus's police work?

Daughter Sammy is now back from London and living with Patience Aitken. How does this make Rebus behave? And how does Sammy's involvement with SWEEP further affect her relationship with her father?

Rebus is ordered to take some time off. How does Ian Rankin detail his response? What happens to Rebus's 'Protestant work ethic'?

What lesson does Rebus learn at the hands of Rico Briggs?

Why don't Wee Shug's actions in the surgery make sense to Rebus?

How lucky is Lucky?

Rebus feels that this case draws on connections and coincidences. Could the same be said for Ian Rankin's intricate plotting in *Let It Bleed*?

'That's your problem, Inspector – you're selfish, no other word for it. I think you know damned well that these obsessions of yours end up damaging everyone around you, friend, foe and civilians alike.' Do these words from the Farmer strike a chord with Rebus, or does he brush them aside?

Ian Rankin says that in some ways *Let It Bleed* is a return to the Scotland of his second novel, *Hide & Seek*. Would you agree?

Does *Let It Bleed*, as Ian Rankin claims, 'celebrate our national relationship with alcohol'? If so, what is the reader supposed to make of Rebus's signs of alcoholism? Why does *he* believe he drinks? And what does Rebus actually feel about his excessive drinking?

Is much of what Rebus discovers really a crime, or could it be considered instead just a sharp way of doing business?

The US edition has a different ending that ties up some of the loose ends, although this alternative dénouement isn't offered here. What are the loose ends left hanging? And do they worry the reader?